Vincent McInerney: After service in the Merchant Marine [Maritime POW Second India-Pakistan War] Vincent became a BBC editor for ten years. His own broadcast radio includes original plays: adaptations: dramatisations: drama-documentaries: poems: short stories. He was one of the three writers brought in to set up Radio 4's *Complete Sherlock Holmes*. All leading to his widely used and admired textbook *Writing for Radio*: MUP, 2001. ['Simply the best thing of its kind' – Andrew Taylor].

He has taught creative writing for over forty years; working in and around high-security prisons for six years – during which time he compiled and edited an inmate-driven anthology *Insiders Out;* and wrote and co-produced the stage play, *Four Murders and a Drugs Bust* [Landor Theatre, London] using first-hand inmate accounts ['Affecting and compelling' – *The Stage*].

He was a consultant for Screen East, and Director of the Great Yarmouth Film Festival. He wrote and produced the film short *Booked* [Richard Connaught – *Clockwork Orange*]. Full-length screenplays include the *Rector of Stiffkey* for Projectile Productions.

In a continuing focus on maritime history he edited the ten volumes of the critically-acclaimed 'Seafarers' Voices' series. ['... so important they should be compulsory reading' – S.W. Maritime review]. His maritime stage drama *Dead Reckoning* was produced by the Soho Poly ['Stands comparison with some of Conrad's best work'- David Hudson].

Forthcoming: *Collected Sea Stories.* A musical *Scrooge. Maggie's Harvest: A Novoflick. The Importance of Being Oscar – A Literary Journey.*

FAKES

A NovoFlick

Vincent McInerney

Matador
Unit E2 Airfield Business Park,
Harrison Road, Market Harborough,
Leicestershire. LE16 7UL
Tel: 0116 2792299
Email: books@troubador.co.uk
Web: www.troubador.co.uk/matador
Twitter: @matadorbooks

ISBN 978 1803130 637

British Library Cataloguing in Publication Data.
A catalogue record for this book is available from the British Library.

Printed and bound in Great Britain by 4edge Limited
Typeset in 11pt Minon Pro by Troubador Publishing Ltd, Leicester, UK

Matador is an imprint of Troubador Publishing Ltd

A NOTE ON CHRONOLOGY

Regarding *plot* chronology: FAKES maintains a tight linear line between February and April 1982. Regarding *historical* chronology: The period from the early '70s to the early '80s is manipulated in an attempt to depict the rich array of social / cultural changes occurring at that time.

Events around the taking to sea of the *Ocean Seaspray* and the ship's physical characteristics have also been modified to facilitate dramatic structure / momentum within the larger whole.

Acknowledgements

I would like to thank: Marilyn Ayres for very helpful comments regarding an early draft of this work. Martin Ayres for conversations regarding picture-framing in Chelsea in the late '60s / early '70s. Gill Hiley, for perceptive points raised in an intermediate draft. Jennie Spain for a telling analysis of a late draft.

I would also like to thank all the team at Matador/ Troubador for their efficiency and promptness in turning the manuscript into a book.

Finally, my literary advisor, John Corner, Leeds University, for his unswerving commitment to this work. The strong editorial grasp he applied to each successive draft together with the acute diligence and profound professionalism he brings to all his projects.

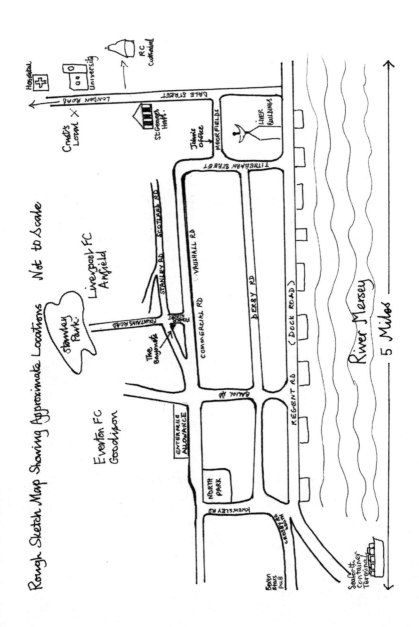

Rough Sketch Map Showing Approximate Locations   Not to Scale

*'Even the people with no money eat cakes all the time
and go everywhere in taxis.'*

Margaret Rosalie 'Susie' Convey,
early visit to Liverpool, late '60s

FAKES: A NovoFlick : is loosely based on the first of Vincent McInerney's Radio 4 Inspector Crust Trilogy: – *O'Rourke's First Case.*

Front Cover: *The Penitent Magdalen Bearing the Arma Christi*. Oil on canvas. 29 x 21 inches. Italian baroque. Unsigned. Collection of the author. Photographed by Liam Prior under stewardship Vincent John McInerney.

Back Cover: Container ship at Seaforth Terminal, Liverpool. Photograph by the author. Early 70's.

Map: Initial concept and drawing by author. Redrawn/ modified/clarified by Elizabeth McInerney.

SEQUENCE ONE

PROLOGUE

LATE '70s INTERIOR / DAY –
ART SHOP, CHELSEA, LONDON.

After a few minutes' conversation, Ronnie Raite came from behind the counter and walked the length of the long, narrow, wood-panelled shop, to the street door. The shop had once been a Chelsea 'gentlemen's tobacconist'. Raite put the snip on the door. Turned the shop sign to 'CLOSED'.

Raite was mid forties, slightly below average height, stocky build. His face was a pale oval into which was set a small straight nose. His eyes were almond-shaped with one slightly unfocussed. Their colour a washed-out blue. Black broken lines threaded his cheeks like the digestive tracts of uncleaned prawns. Sparse cold-red hair – each strand looking individually coiffured. Spatula hands of an Egon Schiele *Russian Prisoner of War* study.

Back at the counter, the Buyer studied the card in front of him.

Ronald R. Raite
Bespoke Framing and Gilding
Art Photography and Film
Paintings Bought and Sold
Discretion Absolute and Assured

Raite resumed his position once more behind the counter. "That sort of thing," he said abruptly. "A baroque Magdalen… Fairly rare."

"No hurry." The Buyer, neat and nondescript, had a soft American accent. Grey crew-cut hair. Light fawn raincoat. Grey suit. Subdued silk tie against a white shirt. Black leather shoes. Tanned face. Expressionless eyes.

"But definitely for a *private* collection?" asked Raite.

"That's it," agreed the Buyer.

"Baroque *Virgins*? Fairly available. But the 'fallen woman' herself; the *Magdalen*?" Raite paused. "Auctions…?"

The Buyer shrugged. "Fees. Commissions. Bills of sale…"

Raite stroked the mahogany counter. "This *would* be cash?"

The Buyer nodded.

"Which could mean… well… difficulties with *provenance*. Cash acquisitions often requiring a fair amount of… well… good faith?"

"So maybe something already known?" suggested the Buyer. "A signature? Date?"

"That's really asking something," said Raite. "While the price…?" He gestured upwards.

The Buyer considered Raite's monogrammed shirt with its grubby collar. The Olympic-medal-sized gold watch strapped to Raite's wrist. "Used dollars," he said. "But delivery in America."

Raite rubbed the counter again. "And definitely not for public show?"

"Never."

Obsessives. Hidden collections. Big money. No questions.

"Naturally," said Raite, "I'd have to pay up front. So if you'd already found one…?"

The Buyer smiled.

There was a clattering on the other side of the heavy door behind Raite, as if someone had fallen/stumbled down a set of stairs. Raite was turning as the door burst open.

The Buyer knew Los Angeles well. Las Vegas better. Casinos as well as art. Felt he'd seen the best of American female beauty. Blonde. Blue-eyed. Corn-fed. Pneumatically supple. Perfectly proportioned. But above that was another class of woman altogether, whose attractions – though overpoweringly physical – transcended the physical. In his life, the Buyer felt he'd seen two of this type. Now – in spite of the soiled, gaping nightdress / heavily ringed, bruised eyes / spool of drool – here was number three. Death Valley on legs.

The Buyer maintained a blank face as Raite quickly half-pushed, half-carried, the woman back inside and closed the door firmly.

"My wife, Liz…" explained Raite. "Not too well. London's *existential angst*."

3

The Buyer nodded.

"I'll get on it," said Raite. "But, as I say, it could be a slow process."

The Buyer made a slight hand gesture to signify he understood.

"How do I get in touch?" asked Raite.

The Buyer pointed to a notepad on the counter. Raite took up a pen and offered it to the Buyer. The Buyer wrote down a telephone number, ripped the sheet from the pad and showed the number to Raite. Handed Raite the pen. Raite wrote down the number on the next sheet on the pad. Tore off the sheet.

The Buyer pocketed the pad and his own sheet. "Public call box," he told Raite. Adjusting his raincoat, he turned to head back down the shop. At the door he unsnipped the lock and flipped over the sign to 'OPEN'.

Left without looking back.

SEQUENCE TWO

FRIDAY, 5th FEB, 1982. 14.30
EXTERIOR / FLOUR STREET, LIVERPOOL.
INTERIOR / O'ROURKE HOUSE

Frank O'Rourke, sixty-six, retired docker, made his way slowly down Flour Street between its two rows of terraced houses. Thursday afternoon. State pension day.

Flour Street ran down off Stanley Road. Stanley Road was the continuation of Scotland Road northwards out from Liverpool city centre. Passing into Bootle then becoming a succession of roads leading to Seaforth and its new shipping container terminal – then Waterloo – then finally Crosby – where civilisation was understood to begin.

Mr O'Rourke was about five foot six. Slightly built. Small brown eyes. A narrow face. Thinning silver hair. A pronounced limp; a drunken fellow docker having dropped a case of broached whisky down a ship's hold onto Mr O'Rourke's ankle – then accusing Mr O'Rourke of not being able to hold his liquor. Liverpool humour. There had been a few hundred quid 'compo'. That had soon gone. The limp had stayed.

Mr O'Rourke glanced at his watch. Took his house key from the pocket of his mac. Glanced up and down the street. A scattering of cheap cars parked on its tarmacked surface. He opened the front door and listened. Nothing. Walked down the hallway. Put on a brave face. Opened the kitchen door that was to the right of the bottom of the stairs.

John – his son – was sitting at the Formica-topped table, seemingly deep in a book. John was still wearing his anorak. Lying next to the book was an opened, official-looking, buff envelope that had arrived for John with the midday post.

"Back already?" Mr O'Rourke picked up the metal teapot from the table. Went to the sink. Switched on the geyser.

John grunted.

Mr O'Rourke pointed the teapot at the envelope. "Came for you dinner time."

John grunted.

5

Mr O'Rourke began to heat the teapot, swinging it casually beneath the hot water. "Cars they've got now…"

"Cars?" muttered John.

"One time, only cars you'd ever see down here'd be funeral or weddings. Horsepower was what was pulled the Co-op milkman's cart seven in the morning…"

"Then they invented electricity," said John.

"How'd it go? The interview?"

"Some young fella. More pens in his top pocket than a mad professor." John turned a page.

Mr O'Rourke dropped two teabags into the metal pot. "Thought you might be in with a chance this time…"

John looked up. "Dad! I'm a thirty-eight-year-old redundant maintenance fitter from a bedding factory that was obsolete day it was built!"

The thing about being a parent, thought Mr O'Rourke, *is you suffer twice. Once for the child and once for yourself.* "Maybe there's a job drawing Liverpool street maps. You've walked them enough."

"Apart from the fact I'm white, I was your token black!"

Mr O'Rourke brought the pot to the table and sat down facing his son. "What're you reading? Another detective yarn?"

No answer.

Mr O'Rourke said, "Called in The Bayonets after collecting my pension. Pint with Curly. Said I'd nip down; see if you were back. You want to go up for last orders?"

John poured the tea into two mugs. "Curly! Twenty-six. 'Casual labour' all his life. Never a sniff of anything steady."

"Never sniff of a pint we don't make it before three.

Come on. Get that tea down you. I won't suggest you put your coat on as you haven't taken it off."

John stood and leaned forward, fists pressed on the table. "Twelve years I was in that bedding factory. Took the redundancy. Now I'm expected to sit around all day eating thick-sliced toast and watching the idiot box! I won't do it!"

Mr O'Rourke nodded sympathetically. "What will you do?"

John held up the book he was reading. 'BRICK BRADSTREET – SUPERSLEUTH' across the top of the front cover. Under this, in murderer's red, the title: *Some Dames Do!* The cover illustration featured a man with enormous shoulders, a chiselled face, bright blue eyes and a square jaw. A trench coat and a black fedora hat. His left arm supporting a woman collapsed under the weight of her hair and breasts. His right hand [gripped in the jaws of an attack dog the size of a lion] holding a gun with a barrel like a bazooka. The colours as bright as human ingenuity could manufacture.

Mr O'Rourke made a slight gesture of incomprehension.

John picked up the buff envelope. "'Enterprise Allowance Scheme'"

Mr O'Rourke shrugged.

"Government thing," John told him. "You put in an idea for a small business and if they like it you get forty quid a week for a year… Few conditions, naturally."

"Naturally," said Mr O'Rourke. "Thinking of applying?"

"Already have done. Few weeks ago, now…"

Mr O'Rourke's face showed a sense of betrayal. He took a sip of tea. "Surprised you didn't mention it. Something that important."

"Didn't want to put either of us through the worry."

"OK," said Mr O'Rourke. "So what have you gone for?"

John waved his paperback in the air.

"Bookbinding? Much call for that now?"

"Private eye, Dad! Private eye! Just like Brick!"

"Holmes! I should have known!!"

"And had the interview! And this!" John held up the envelope. "Says I've got it! Back next Tuesday; sign the final forms. That new job centre on Balliol Road. Want to hear about it?"

Mr O'Rourke examined his son's face carefully. Was John serious? Forty quid a week? *Fucking politicians! Imagine even the biggest goballoon in Westminster putting his hand in his own pocket to fund something like this. But as long as they can use Joe Public's money...* He glanced at his watch. "Before you start. What about Curly waiting up in The Bayonets?"

"Curly?" said John. "Curly's going nowhere. Been stalled at the lights for years."

SEQUENCE THREE

SATURDAY, 6ᵗʰ FEB, 1982. 06.00
EXT / CAR PARK, EUSTON ROAD, LONDON.
INT/ CAR PARK

A highly polished off-white Porsche, its blinker flashing, personal number plate DAV 1D, waited to make a right turn into a multi-storey car park on Euston Road. Bitterly cold. Icy rain. From inside the car, Raite watched early workers scurrying across the facility's entrance. He revved the engine, relishing their anxious sideways glances. As if a switch had been thrown in his head, he suddenly yelled, "Baa!... Baa!!"

Once he'd heard Liz was being released he'd known he'd have to move fast. Out after only three months?! Plus psychodick Bogger waiting to meet her with open flies. Plus the owner of the backstreet garage in which he'd been keeping the Porsche about to roll over on him to the police. Plus every copper in London looking for the drugs money in the large dark blue canvas holdall now behind his seat. His photo under every airline desk.

Then he'd read an article about serious teething troubles at Liverpool's new container ship terminal. Liverpool to New York. People wandering on and off the dock. Stowaways. Containers being stolen with the aid of falsified paperwork. Security issues rife. He'd given it a lot of thought. A new start in America? Small studios in California specialising in 'art movies'. The Buyer waiting for his baroque Magdalen.

He'd made the calls. Old contacts from the picture-dealing world. Got a result. Then rang the container terminal at Liverpool and enquired about moving two containers of 'antiques' to New York. 'Yes', he'd been told. At the moment they'd accept containers – 'tins' – 'boxes' – up to a week before sailing. And there was a sailing scheduled for the 12th March...

Raite had asked if he would be able to get into the containers once they were on the dock – perhaps add some items. Remove some if he found buyers, etc.?... He was told that in the case of antiques they'd be customs sealed with no further access once on the dock. But if they were classified as 'bric-a-brac'- Raite could come and go as he wanted.

He'd rung off. Got hold of a map. Saw that near the container berths was the Irish Ferries terminal – a convenient back door. But first he needed to turn the drugs money in the holdall into what the American buyer wanted.

The light turned amber. Raite swung the car across to the ticket barrier, took the stub, began climbing the ramps. On the almost deserted top tier he pulled in alongside a grey Ford. Killed the Porsche's engine.

The driver of the Ford was known to his colleagues as 'the Laughing Cavalier'. He gave a swift glance at the crumpled photo of Raite that lay on his knee. Leaned across. Cracked open the passenger door. Took out a pack of cigarettes from the inside pocket of his black leather jacket.

Raite, gaze flitting between windows and mirrors, reached backwards to wrestle the holdall into the front of the Porsche and onto his knee. Unzipping it, he regarded the bundles of used notes wrapped in heavy industrial black elastic bands. A green Irish passport lay on top of them. Raite opened it. A picture of himself with the name 'James Francis Walsh'. He lodged the passport in a nest of adhesive tape criss-crossing underneath the driver's seat of the Porsche. Near the gun.

Raite slid out of the Porsche and into the passenger seat of the Ford. Dirt, oil, tobacco, dogs. Clutching the holdall to his chest, he considered the Cavalier.

About forty, the Cavalier was skeletally pale. His round face that of a snowy owl with a persecution complex. On his knees was an extra-large padded envelope.

After a moment's hesitation, like ambassadors at early courts, they exchanged packages. The Cavalier opened the holdall and began to count the money. Raite carefully drew out of the padded envelope a squarish object double-wrapped in protective tissue. Inside the tissue was a thin, wooden board on which was an oil-painting. In the foreground, a troubled yet somehow insouciant young woman looked at him from across the centuries, her arms cradling a variety of dimly painted objects.

Raite stared at the monogram in the top right-hand corner; the date underneath. He touched these lightly with one finger. Then he began to consider the painting itself. The faded yet balanced colours emanating from the woman's flesh tones. He half-looked at the Cavalier. "Imagine when they were first put on?… Fresh off the palette."

The Cavalier, still counting, nodded. "Must've glowed."

"Looks *right*, anyway," said Raite.

"What they're doing," said the Cavalier, "these places… Scotland; places like that. Old mansions crammed full of stuff no one even knows *is* there, much less *what's* there…" The Cavalier's soft cockney accent was over-larded with West End art-dealer 'rah'. He was yet to look directly at Raite. Now, with a quick, expressionless glance, he continued, "They found one of these gaffs, drove up, booked in at some hotel in the Highlands a few miles away as a 'fishing party'…

Screwed the place… The geezer – old bastard who owned the stuff; about eighty – gave a list to the filth. But no *real* idea. He remembered some, which will be moved another way… But this, what you're buying?" He shrugged. "Far as anyone's concerned, you got it from a junk shop. Out of a skip… And it's kosher! Known! Mentioned in a few eighteenth/early nineteenth-century catalogues; couple of illustrations. But, like so much, dropped off the board. Sold privately to pay a debt. Buy a shag off some duchess… Who knows? But it'll come through. Microscopes, paint analysis, 'his' signature…"

"Monogram," interrupted Raite.

"Monogram," agreed the Cavalier, lighting another cigarette. "Which he *always* used. Whatever they throw will show green." He shrugged again. "In a way, it's just like buying from one of the big houses… Except we're honest."

Raite nodded. "Money right?"

The Cavalier patted the holdall.

"Something of Caravaggio?" asked Raite, gesturing towards the painting.

"Angles wrong," said the Cavalier. "Angles of light."

Raite lowered his eyes to the *Magdalen*. "Fancy her?" He grinned.

"Not that big on the religious types." The Cavalier threw his partially smoked cigarette onto the floor, grinding it into the wet cardboard. "Always got this hysteria thing inside them can get out of hand." He jabbed with his thumb at the painting. "Though her…"

"Yes," said Raite. "She's the one they all want to get at! 'Course, they have to go *via* the usual stuff –

Annunciations, martyrdoms, pietàs, resurrections – but she's the one! The Cagnacci? The Erhart? The ones in the nun's outfits. The de Maya? The Rosi where she's slumped on the steps – angel massaging her forehead? What's going on there?!" His voice rose. "The Giampietrino with the knockers? Would you ever get tired of sucking them?! The fact that she – the Magdalen – might have been doing a bit on the side with John the Bap?! Might even have been married to *Jesus*?!… Fucking Romney! Spent all his life painting dickheads; and so straight he went to bed wrapped in cellophane! But look at his shot at her!" Raite tapped the shadowy implements in the woman's arms. "Especially carrying the *Arma Christi*! Whips?! Chains?! Jar of *oil*?! Crown of thorns?! Hammers and nails?! Plus nudity an accepted option! It's out of their trousers like a conger eel 'fore they've picked up a brush!"… Into the now agitated silence, Raite added "All, naturally, at the far end of the gallery alongside Cano's Virgin squirting milk from her right tit into the waiting mouth of St. Bernard. The Child wondering about its dinner." Raite pulled at the Ford's door handle. Put one foot out onto the parking-bay concrete. "You always drive one of these?" he asked casually.

"You know how it is." The Cavalier lit another cigarette. "Wake up fucked. Head banging. Throat on fire. Saw this parked near my place. Blew on the door. Gave you a bell… Wasn't I was going anywhere important."

Raite blinked. Left the Ford. Climbed into the Porsche. Settled in the bucket seat. Touched various of the controls for comfort. Reached behind and lodged the painting. Waited for the Ford to move. Saw the Cavalier light another cigarette.

Raite started the engine of the Porsche and backed out.

The Cavalier watched him through the mirror. "Wanker," he muttered.

"Errand boy! Cunt!" shouted Raite through the windscreen of the Porsche as he simultaneously smiled and waved.

He turned towards the down ramps. Reached the exit. Paid. Moved out towards Euston Road. Put on his left blinker.

A traffic warden stood on the passenger-side pavement staring in rage and envy at the Porsche. Raite put the car into motion. Gave the warden the finger. Swung the car slightly towards him. The warden started backwards, slipped on the ice and fell. Raite howled. Floored it to the first set of red lights. Braked hard. Looked in the mirror. Saw the warden, still lying on the icy ground, unbutton a pocket for his notebook. Fuck! They'd trace the car right away. Why'd he done it? In a sudden rage, he banged the steering wheel with both hands. Glanced up at the green information board alongside the lights. Watford. The A1. Thing to do was get beyond Watford. After that – far as the Met went – another country.

The lights changed.

Raite took off.

SEQUENCE FOUR

SUNDAY, 7th FEB, 1982. 14.58
EXT/ DAY REHAB UNIT, GUILDFORD

The rehab unit was in a Georgian mansion situated at the end of a long drive. A carefully brushed white-gravel turning circle in front of the house. Three broad, shallow semicircular steps leading up to a heavy white-glossed front door. To one side of the door, a large, square brass plate. In its centre, a white bell push.

At the foot of the steps stood a Mercedes saloon; engine idling in neutral; passenger side facing the house. Through the side window, a finger belonging to Bogger Bone could be seen tapping impatiently on the dashboard clock which read 2.59 pm.

The front door opened and three figures emerged. A doctor in a starched white coat, stethoscope draped round his neck. A nurse in dark blue, with gold-rimmed spectacles, carrying a medium-capacity leather suitcase. The third figure the woman who'd crashed downstairs into Raite's art shop. Mrs Elizabeth Raite, ex-model, 'Just Liz'.

The driver's door of the Mercedes opened and Bogger stepped out. He was wearing a dark suit and dark glasses, and stood behind the bulk of the car, linked fingers resting on the roof, staring at the three figures at the top of the steps.

The doctor immediately felt under intense and dangerous scrutiny and decided to cut short the remarks he usually offered a departing patient. Careful not to glance at Mrs Raite's breasts one last time; to forget the notion of absently tapping one playfully with the end of his stethoscope. Besides, he'd had what he wanted from her during her initial heavy sedation. The nurse, seeing that Bogger had no intention of moving, set down the suitcase in front of the patient.

Mrs Raite smiled 'thank you' – then began, almost abstractedly, to rub the back of one of her hands with the fingers of the other. The backs of both hands were covered in heavy-duty plasters.

Like Pavlov's dogs, the doctor and nurse reacted immediately. The doctor carefully lifting the scratching hand away from the scratched. The nurse patting the scratched hand in gentle disapproval. Mrs Raite smiled again, picked up the suitcase, and walked down the steps to the car.

Now Bogger moved. Coming round to the passenger side to take the case and usher Mrs Raite into the car. Seen in full view, he appeared to be in his mid thirties. He stood about six foot two. Broad-shouldered; implacable. A peculiarity was his forehead. Like that of Beethoven – some other musicians – formed of thick, almost corrugated, bone. A forehead that could inflict a lot of damage. Bogger saw Mrs Raite into the car; closed the door on her. Turned and stared directly at the doctor and nurse. Both quickly moved back into the house.

Bogger walked round the car, climbed in, settled himself. Lit two cigarettes. Handed one to Mrs Raite. In unaffected East End, asked, "How was it, Liz?"

"Pure Glyndebourne…" said Mrs Raite "… Though without the usual riff-raff." Her voice crystal clear, yet soft and husky. A voice schooled to give orders. Marry a rich man.

Bogger shrugged indifferently. Took up a liquor flask from the footwell. Handed it to her. As she drank, he attempted to kiss her; to cup one of her breasts.

She pulled away, leaning against the car door. "Not now, Bogger!"

"Where to, Liz?" Bogger put the car into gear.

"Somewhere that doesn't smell of cabbage cooked by Austrian nuns!" She drew on her cigarette. Took out a prescription bottle of pills. Took another drink. Began scratching the back of one of her hands.

The car eased away.

SEQUENCE FIVE

MONDAY, 8th FEB, 1982. 11.00
INT/ DAY D.I. CRUST'S FLAT, SEFTON PARK,
LIVERPOOL

In the Sefton Park area of South Liverpool, in a ground-floor flat in a run-down, though once imposing Victorian house, a telephone rang with unstoppable determination.

Eventually, a large bulky man in his early fifties swung himself off a couch where he had been lying reading a book. The man was wearing a floor-length, dark blue woollen dressing gown. He had thick, tight, grey-grizzled curly hair. A large balloon-shaped head. A loose mouth with brown, snaggy teeth. Large, protruding, yellowy-green eyes.

The man stretched, then moved slowly across to a turntable and lifted the stylus off an LP playing stark, sombre music. Walked to a wooden partner's desk. Sat down in a captain's swivel chair covered in green leather. Stared fixedly at the still-ringing black Bakelite phone; then allowed his eyes to wander round the room. The ceiling was high, with an ornate off-white plaster rose in its centre. From the rose hung a length of flex supporting an unshaded light bulb. On top of a chipped white marble fireplace was a black slate clock with an enamelled face; its glass and one finger missing. In the hearth, a gas fire set to medium. Two wooden-shuttered windows overlooking an overgrown back garden. Between these windows hung three oil paintings of ballroom dancers frozen in strict tempo. The paintings stepped down diagonally. There were two lamps on the partner's desk, plus another on the low coffee table in front of the couch on which the man had been lying. All other wall, desk and floor space was covered in books; from dried-out, broken-spined, eighteenth-century leather boards – to modern paperbacks that would disintegrate if held over a saucer of warm water. Through a half-open heavy wooden door, the end of an unmade bed was visible. What could be seen of the bedroom walls was also covered in books. Two further doors led to a kitchen and a bathroom. Against the wall, next to the bathroom door, was propped a full-length mirror. Alongside the mirror – head height – was pinned a photograph of Rodin's *Balzac*. The flat was carpeted throughout in a dark, dense, industrial wool mixture that would show no stains. Overall, the impression of a life lived in semi-darkness and secrecy.

The phone rang on.

The man stood and stared into space. Sat down once more. Pulled an A3 artist's sketch pad and pen towards him. Opened it to a blank page. Picked up the receiver. "Crust," he said as he doodled a figure on a cross.

At the other end of the line, the Voice asked Crust how he was.

"Tired," said Crust.

"Right!… Three names coming to a condemned cell near you" said the Voice.

Crust wrote down 'Ronnie Raite', 'Mrs Elizabeth Raite' and 'Bogger Bone'. Fashioned an equals sign. Asked, "What's it about?"

"Basically? Mill plus in used notes."

"Belonging to?"

"Well. Ron's got it. But as to who it belongs to…"

Crust waited.

"… Ronnie Raite, we think, went to art college. Up near you; maybe Chester… I'll come to that. Then – late '60s, early '70s – served part of a picture-framing apprenticeship at some outfit down the King's Road. Sort of copycat Hecht place."

"Dodgy?" asked Crust.

"Handmade frames that weren't. Genuine gold gilding that wasn't. In reality? Helping well-off Chelseaite stupids polish their exam work… Well. You know the score. Boutiques, Beatles, bean stew. Hussar jackets, nose-hair, herringbone trousers. Chelsea Drugstore? Girls in bikinis and catsuits riding round on motorbikes delivering your every need sixteen hours a day, seven days a week?… Maybe you were back in the 'Pool by then."

"How'd he come to us? Raite?"

"Tried it on some amateur-pro type whose own stuff looked like vulture's vomit... But naturally shit-hot on bespoke frames and stuff."

Crust doodled a blank canvas on an easel.

"Wasn't life-or-death," continued the Voice. "So, by the time we got round there, both Raite's boss and the framing business had vanished. But though we missed his boss, we grabbed Raite. No arrest, just a 'talk'. 'Though he let us take his prints and mugshot. Like they sometimes do they don't know too much..." The Voice sighed. "If only we could always lift 'unknowing innocents' instead of 'knowing guilties'. Do wonders for our conviction rates... Anyway. Usual spiel from him: junior employee, no idea the gold wasn't real gold, boss cut the frames up in his own workshop, etc., etc. One thing, though..."

"What's that?"

"DC who questioned Raite said all the time they were talking Raite was totally bored – *except* when talking about paintings themselves rather than frames. Razor sharp, then."

"From round here, you said? Chester?"

"I'll get to that. In the end we sprung him. But he didn't go far."

"Oh?" Crust doodled a signpost with Dick Whittington. Bag over shoulder. Cat sitting behind.

"Just across the road," said the Voice.

Crust doodled a set of traffic lights.

"Own shop. Framing photos for the modelling set. Sourcing 'original paintings' for their flats... Next thing he's a photographer/amateur film-maker..."

"Blue stuff?"

"'Tableaux vivants' nudies. Definite S&M overtones. Other stuff, we think – but couldn't find. Anyway. Got Raite a sort of limited entrée. But, as naff paintings and photos will only take you so far with that sort of crowd..."

"Drugs?"

"Pills."

"This where the mill begins?"

"There's a sort of detour first."

"Oh?"

"En route. Ron met his destiny."

"Mrs Elizabeth Raite?"

"Victoria Elizabeth Rausenberg."

"From...?"

"Principality of the Home Counties. Old stockbroker stock... latterly old *failed* stockbroker stock."

Crust doodled a limousine. An arrow through it dripping blood. "That possible?"

"These days, Crusty, more and more is becoming possible..."

"Where's she fit in?"

"Looks, accent and connections got her a start in modelling as 'Just Liz'. But too demanding even for that crowd. Eventually just another well-known/well-screwed face... However! Ron has seen nothing like her before in his life!..."

"Looker?"

"Lads who questioned her said even if she'd been Irish they'd have hesitated fitting her up."

"But not for long?"

"Neither snow, nor rain, nor heat, nor flash floods, nor tube strikes!… But what a catch for ugly mug Ron! So he fed her enough uppers and downers to send her sideways, dragged her off to some registry office…"

"You've found it? The registry office? Checked it? What they put for their addresses? Occupations, etc.?"

There was a brief silence at the other end. "OK," said the Voice. "So Ron knows he's got his hands on a woman every bloke wants to shag – "

"Or murder?"

"That, too. He also knows it'll be no good explaining to 'Just Liz' about sourcing second-rate paintings for her sometime mates. He's going to need a fast, continuous, money stream… 'Science', in fact."

After a pause, Crust said, "I don't…?"

"Well. If him and his oppos could make false gold…"

"False happiness?"

"Speaking as the man who taught you all you know, I sometimes think we should have kept you down here. Yep. His false-gold bent-chemist pals… Big caravan gutted and rigged as a lab. Countryside near Brighton. Up and down to the Smoke. Till Ron noticed those long, straight, lovely South Coast roads…"

"Newhaven to Nirvana?"

The Voice laughed. "Kent to Cornwall. Yeah. So, another couple of caravan labs – all in Liz's name, naturally. And soon…"

"One million pounds?"

"At least."

"Bogger Bone?" asked Crust.

"East End nutter. Goes by 'The Clumsy Carpenter' –

he's broken so many legs. Arts-scene hanger-on. Known type. Became Raite's financial enforcer…"

"Fell for her…?"

"Like a guillotine blade…" said the Voice

"Local lad loses heart to wanton charmer?"

"Thousand miles in his bare feet, over broken glass, sniff her shit. Wiring pliers in one hand. Blowtorch in the other."

"We lifted them?" Crust asked.

"Well… The chemists and Liz…"

"Not Raite? Bogger?"

With a slight edge, the Voice said, "Crusty. You know the Met! Antler to antler every fucking day over packets of paper clips! Offices full of people, facing walls, coats over heads, muttering into phones. More holes than a Swiss cheese!… But! Got to be! Get the job done! Things to *work*!"

After a pause, Crust said, "What happened after the interviews?"

"Dropout chemists? Arses booted down to Parkhurst."

"'Just Liz'?"

"Lawyered-up straight away. Some pinstripe Percy demanding she be immediately hospitalised."

"Not *that* crazy?"

"Her type? None of them that mental they can't demand a bent brief."

"Or a hairy-arsed copper!… They're ever in real trouble!"

"She's got this thing she does. Scratching the backs of her hands. Fucking horrible! Plus, at that time, the way Ron had her, she couldn't have told you what way up she was

23

lying flat on her back. So we had to cut her *some* slack. But we kept at it and finally got to seriously question her…"

"And?"

"Lads who did the interrogations said – off the record – she did seem fairly fucked-up. Bandaged hands blood seeping through. Continually asking for her 'agent'! Naturally. Pair who questioned her reckoned she was some sort of nympho. But one who wouldn't just open up her legs for anybody."

"Meaning not them? What about Raite? The money? That is – why me?"

"Well. We did get a couple of things. Said one time he told her he came from up your end."

"This the Chester thing?"

"Seems pretty firm…"

"That what you think? He's somewhere up here?"

"That Ron always talked about dealing 'serious art'… But in the States."

"The money? The mill?"

"His missus claimed all that was handled by Ron. She herself had no idea such sums were involved."

"What she get?"

"Well. What with all the fancy lawyers… tentacles and black ink… Her assorted shrinks weeping crocodile tears… Her public-school character witnesses stilting round like parrots with sticks up their arses, lisping like fucking salamanders… Her old headmistress – wearing *jodhpurs*! – Carrying this big book on *Suffragettes* – Emily Wankhurst on the cover…"

Crust doodled a young Victorian woman carrying a placard inscribed 'VOTES FOR DRUGGIES'.

"… Judge – prob'ly her uncle – 'very much feared' that Liz's 'sheltered upbringing' meant she'd shown 'too much faith' in what 'others told her'. That a 'person of some worth' could easily be lost; wasn't 'mentally answerable'…"

"Her or the judge?"

"Released her into some private 'rehab facility' near Guildford. Final reminder from him to wear her Remembrance Day poppy…"

Crust signed his sketch 'Concerned: Cheltenham'.

"Naturally," continued the Voice, "No sooner she was in; three months later she was out. Few days ago, in fact. Picked up by Bogger."

"And Ron?"

"Knew he'd have to make a move. Us after him is one thing. Bogger's something else altogether…"

"Which leaves us…?" asked Crust.

"Ron's got this Porsche he swans round in. Been hidden one of them railway-arch lock-ups. Place you'd think couldn't store a kid's trike. But boot down the doors – there's a German armoured column… Anyway. 'Bout a week ago, Ron attempts to run over a traffic warden."

"So not all bad?"

"Barrelling out of some Euston Road car park, half six in the morning. Freezing. Dark. Raining like fuck. But the warden got a make."

"What was he doing there?"

"The angry wasp!?… Who can understand those fuckers?!"

"Raite!? A Euston Road car park! Half six in the morning?!"

"You tell me… Maybe that's where he was keeping the Porsche."

"For three months? With no questions asked?"

"OK. He was meeting someone."

"For what?"

There was a pause. "Anyway," said the Voice, "the calls went out and Ron's Porsche was spotted heading through Watford. After that, we lost him."

"Lost him?!"

"Communications, as usual. You know, Crusty, if the police could solve their communications problems, they could solve anything…"

"Even crimes?"

The Voice laughed, but with a touch of unease. "Look. You know what the lads at the Met think about 'oop north'. Cloth caps and clog dancing. Candle ends and Chorley cakes – whatever they might fucking be! And… well…"

In the pause, Crust sketched a Morris dancer. Then said, "So the three of them: Raite, Mrs Raite, this Bogger… Are?… Will be?"

"Thinking is, Raite's carrying around a big bag full of used notes. But his photo at all ports and airports. So… Even if he shaves his head / grows a false beard, it only needs one 'Can you open your bag, sir?' and he's fucked. Right?"

"No. He can't chance that."

"But he needs to get to the States. Now more than ever. So, if he can't fly…"

"Sea?" said Crust. "Ship?"

"Always difficult to police. How long Liverpool to the States?"

"Five days?" said Crust.

"We're thinking maybe these new giant container ships. Thousand places to hide. Slip on at Liverpool; off at New York... Hundreds of people around... Who'd notice?"

"Dock Police?"

"Pay some sailor to take it ashore? Someone knows all the wrinkles?"

"OK," Crust said. "Anything else?"

"Given he was born in the general area of Chester, we're thinking maybe he's holed up on the Wirral. Striking distance of Liverpool. M53 motorway through the Mersey Tunnel almost to the container docks – but still far enough away to stay fairly anonymous while setting things up..."

Crust doodled a ship. "You'll get me the stuff?"

"Files up there soon as... Look. I've a sergeant due in court needs setting straight on what he *really* saw."

"The bottom line?"

"Raite's got a mill plus belongs to us – the public, that is. Which we're looking for you to find for us – the public, that is..."

Crust doodled a confessional box. Penitent and priest. Priest with one hand behind his ear. "How confidential is this?" he asked.

"Basically, we're keeping it close. Cutbacks mean this is money *we* need!"

Crust stared silently into the phone.

"Crusty. Sooner or later it's going to be them or us... Better it's us."

"Any help?"

"Had a word with our mutual friend. That new HQ of yours at the Liverpool Pier Head."

"Fantasy Island?"

"Got you a plain-clothes DC. 'Busking Bill'. Played a guitar outside this pub they were dealing guns. Top collar. Says he made more busking than coppering. Totally solid. Be your runner. Watch o' nights... whatever."

"OK," said Crust finally. "Get me the bumf; let me know when Mrs Raite and Bogger leave London."

"Roger that."

The phone went dead. Crust thoughtfully closed over the sketch pad. Stood and stared into space. Walked over to the mirror propped outside the bathroom. Looked at himself. Then at the Rodin *Balzac*. Smiled his secret smile.

SEQUENCE 6

TUESDAY, 9th FEB, 1982. 11.30.
EXT/ DAY/ STANLEY ROAD. INT/ DAY/ BAYONETS
PUB.

Monday morning. Half-eleven. Mr O'Rourke turned left at the top of Flour Street onto Stanley Road. On the corner of the next street along stood his local, the Fixed Bayonets. The pub's signboard depicted a row of bayoneted rifle muzzles pointing across a stretch of savannah. In the background, palm trees and a tent. In the top right-hand corner, a lion resembling Salvador Dalí.

Mr O'Rourke shook his head. Pushed open the door which led directly into the public bar.

Curly, staring at nothing, was sitting at the domino table near the door. He immediately jumped to his feet. "Mr O! Fancy one? What'll it be?"

Mr O'Rourke settled himself as Curly moved to the bar. Curly was about five eight. Blue-eyed. A pale, pinched, Elizabethan face. Loosely curled blond hair.

At the bar, Mick the manager – 'the Militant's Militant' – moved across to serve him. Mick was tall and had very broad shoulders, one higher than the other – 'a lifetime of pulling short pints'. A head shaped like a coal scuttle. A very thin nose, broken many times during 'revolutionary' marches and fights; and which seemed to have been pressed into position by his minute, suspicious, green eyes. He leaned towards Curly. As he did so, the fumes from last night's brandy wafted over Curly. Supported on a solid wave of Mick's aftershave, 'Topsail Schooner'.

Curly waved a hand. "Mild and lager, Mick… Christ! Your breath!"

"Last night, comrade! Weekly NELLI meeting."

"Oh, yeah."

"You know, when I started the North End Liverpool Lightning Insurgents – NELLI – I gave everyone a unilateral veto. Now no fucker'll agree to anything and I can't get nothing passed. Might as well just go straight and join the commies; hard-left Labour; some other pansy outfit."

Mick turned to the optics. Drew a double brandy. Threw it off. Reached under the counter for his bottle of 'Tops'l Schooner'. The label on the bottle depicted a scantily clad handsome young sailor standing on a ship's yardarm in bare feet. One hand clasped round the mast. The other waving a glazed black hat towards the rising sun. Mick poured some of the lotion onto his hands, then rubbed it up and down the three-day stubble on his face.

Mick had come into pub management via a barman's job in the local Trade Union Bar – the 'TUB' – in Bootle. Late one New Year's Eve, he'd dug out some books of cloakroom tickets and used them to raffle off a battered upright piano that had come from a defunct colliery in South Wales. Telling his drink-sodden clientele that the instrument had once seen George Orwell play 'The Red Flag' for Aneurin Bevan. There were many present who maintained that Orwell – no matter how many mines he went down or plates he washed – was never more than one phone call away from his metropolitan claqueurs. But, given the occasion, all bought liberally.

The tickets sold, Mick had vanished with the proceeds. This led to another broken nose and the sack. But no money was ever recovered. His wife had then left him under unfathomable circumstances – but which somehow involved 'a dress'. Mick finally quit his council house with the largest rent arrears ever incurred by a Liverpool tenant.

With these rock-solid qualifications, he'd become barman – then manager – at The Bayonets. He'd then launched NELLI, considering that no other Liverpool political party presented a sufficiently radical programme. "Too much dialectic; not enough dynamite!" Premises were a disused ship-repair factory in Bootle whose watchman allowed access on Sunday nights. From here, full of Spanish brandy, Mick conducted his 'class war' against… "Your Rentier / Limp-Wristo Classes! Your 'RELICS'. Your Old Bleatonian, Old Oxphoneyan anti-working-class-bum-bailiffs."

Mick was alcoholic, misogynistic, misanthropic, and seemingly obsessed with what he understood to be the sexual preferences of the RELICS. On the other hand, he was a Liverpool FC supporter: could tell a good story: had a vivid imagination: and could quote the odd Latin tag. Therefore, 'a fella to be watched' in Liverpool extreme militant revolutionary politics.

Mick ran The Bayonets with his two Dobermans, Lenin and Marx; four-legged comrades released at closing time to drive Mick's fellow proletarians out onto the wintry steppes of Stanley Road.

As Mick began pulling Curly's drinks, he hissed, "What's this I hear about your mate accepting a handout from our fascist masters?"

"Just caught a whisper myself, Mick. I'll quiz his old fella I get back the table." Curly, waiting for his change, turned and gave Mr O'Rourke the thumbs up.

Mr O'Rourke nodded and gazed round contentedly. The Bayonets. His second home. Extended family. Militant Mick. The smoke. The noise. The lads down the end of the bar at the dartboard. The smell of old, cheap, too-often-washed clothing. The domino school. The young fella from two streets along trying to sell stolen sweaters in a T-shirt market. The crackly television with its ever-present white lines running across it; tuned permanently to the racing. The fact there were no women in the bar. And that the only non-white faces were those covered by oil, grime or house-paint. Everything exactly as it should be.

Curly squeezed-in with the drinks. They held up their glasses to each other. Both took a mouthful.

"That right, then? They're giving John money to open his own business?"

Mr O'Rourke shook his head. "I mean, Curl, he's been obsessed with that detective stuff since a lad. But never thought he'd confuse real life with fiction. Don't know what his mother would have said."

Curly put up two lightly clenched fists. "Same as mine when I told her I was thinking of turning pro – already brain-damaged beyond hope… Still, John's put his money where his mouth is, right?"

"You take along an idea for a business. If they like it, they give you forty quid a week for a year; help you get it off the ground…"

"But…?" asked Curly with a sour grin.

"Yeah. To qualify you've got to be drawing benefit for eight weeks and have a thousand pounds in hand."

"Which John's obviously got. The redundancy and that."

On the television, the race winner passed the post to a burst of noise both on the screen and in the bar.

Mr O'Rourke said, "Yeah, well. Anyway, he's there this morning signing the final forms. They're running things from the old Balliol Road dole office."

More applause from the televised race meeting. A grey top hat with a face like a sweating cheese holding a horse's bridle. Perched above, a tired jockey looking out over the crowds towards a hot bath and his money.

"A thousand pounds," repeated Curly.

"Or," said Mr O'Rourke, "they'll take a bank loan. Overdraft."

"But putting a thousand nicker of your own into a private tec business? I mean. What d'you think, Mr O?"

"On one hand, nothing more I'd like than to see him settled. Hardly ever goes out these days; never a peep about finding a girl…" Mr O'Rourke took a pull at his pint. "That right your Chris's back?"

Curly stared at his glass. "Finally left that other fucker after six years of hell."

"Maybe John's luck has turned, then?" said Mr O'Rourke.

"Maybe," said Curly neutrally. Adding quickly, "Maybe John'll drop by after he's signed up. Might even take me in with him… Another?"

Mr O'Rourke took out a note. Drained his glass. Handed both to Curly. "I'll put in a word for you. If he actually gets it off the ground…"

Curly stood. "Those places. Job centres and that. Fucking horrible. Really grim."

"Once you're sixty-five," said Mr O'Rourke, "it's the bus pass and a lie-in." He opened his *Daily Mirror* at the racing pages. "Fancy a bet?"

SEQUENCE 7

TUESDAY, 9th FEB, 1982. 12.15
INT/ DAY/ JOB CENTRE, BOOTLE.

The commission for decorating the job centre had been given to an 'industrial psychologist' named Will Whookey. Will's remit was to effect a decor that would produce calm and compliance among vulnerable and disturbed people, many with young children and no food or heat.

That morning, it appeared to be working. Everyone whispered. Distant phones rang in a discreet fashion, or simply stopped ringing as ten-pence pieces ran out in the far-flung, rotting, high-rise tower blocks designed by Will and his fellow visionaries. The people, too, on the job centre benches, seemed to embrace their roles. To be genuinely ashamed of being poor. No government could ask more of its suppressed class, or those employed with the unspoken agenda of maintaining that suppression.

There had been blips. A client who, notwithstanding Will's expertise, had set fire to herself in the foyer. Forcing Will into booking a 'Brazilian rainforest fortnight' to 'rationalise his karma'.

The very small room dedicated to Enterprise Allowance contained a tight group of six chairs which faced the door of a very small office. John sat in one of the chairs. Two chairs away sat a man who looked to be in his late thirties. A magazine in his hands with a picture of some sort of dog on the cover.

The man – self-effacing, yet somehow decisive – coughed and leaned over. "All very subdued?" he ventured.

"Not much to shout about," said John. "Not this side of the counter…"

The man immediately held out a hand. "Harry Rose."

As John hesitated, Harry asked, "Here for the scheme?"

John grinned. "Been there / done that / got the grant. Just the final forms now." He extended his own hand. "John O'Rourke."

As they shook, Harry asked, "Any hints?"

"Not sure," said John. "I mean, what're you…?"

"Merchant seaman," said Harry. "Chief mate, actually. Liverpool–New York container run from Seaforth. Just had enough. One way and another…"

"Thought you had to be out of work?"

"Taking a trip off," said Harry. "Unpaid leave."

"You're *still* working."

"Exploring possibilities." Harry nodded to himself.

"Live down that way, do you?" John asked. "Seaforth? Crosby?"

"Just the opposite. Wirral, actually. Place called West Heartwood. Bit the back of beyond, but handy for the motorway to Liverpool. Quite near the site of an old Iron Age village…"

"What'd they do there?"

"Got eaten by wolves… Caught the plague… Odd human sacrifice…"

"Saturday night, Scottie Road," said John.

Harry smiled.

"Wouldn't Chester've been nearer for you?" asked John.

"More at home in Liverpool. Went to navigation school here."

"One of the best, right?"

"First navigation school in Liverpool; mid nineteenth century, I believe."

"Thought so," said John in a satisfied tone.

"Truth is," continued Harry, "just more at home this side of the Mersey. *Ocean Seaspray*, she's called. Second-generation containers… Don't know if you've any interest? Maritime history…?"

Verbal diarrhoea merchant. Time to step in. "So, Harry! What you after?"

"Dogs." Harry tipped the cover of his magazine. *Track and Lights*. Below the title, a picture of a greyhound sitting up with half-bent ears.

"Greyhounds?"

"That's it."

"Want to breed them?" asked John.

"Save them. Highly specialised, you see. Fit for only one thing – racing. So once their careers are over – quite soon, given injuries, etc… usually at about three or four… then… well…"

"Greyhound pie?"

"'Fraid so." Harry shook a doleful head.

"But must be thousands of them…"

Harry nodded. "But even to save one or two; give them, well, a place to see out their days quietly…"

"Big dog man, then? Sort of childhood thing?"

"Quite sudden, actually. St. Paul on the road to Damascus."

"St. Harry on the road to White City?"

Harry laughed. "No. I was having a drink with my skipper on the *Seaspray*; Captain Barratt. Came from the great Cunarders…"

"Bit different to containers, then?"

" Plays on it a lot. His great Cunard days…"

John yawned before he could stop himself.

"… RNR during the war. Signals, Morse code, semaphore, flags… Specialised in lip-reading."

"Can't be much happening there?… 'Less you're a barman at closing time."

Harry sighed. "Bit confused, lately, too."

"That can't be too good. Running a giant ship."

"Trip before last. Our two QMs – quartermasters – Wally Jinks and his mate, Scouse MacGuinness. Whispering quietly on the bridge. Barratt tells me he's been reading their lips and they're planning to murder him. 'Poison his coffee'!"

"For lip-reading?!"

"I went over. Jinks tells me what he actually said was that Barratt was 'posing like a Toffee'. That's an Evertonian."

"I know," said John. "I am one!"

"Ah!" said Harry.

John relented. "Bit like my dad's three-and-fourpence story?"

Harry gazed at him.

"World War I. Messages passed down the line by word of mouth. This officer tells a squaddie to pass on: 'Send reinforcements; we're going to advance'. By the time it gets the other end it's 'Send three and fourpence; we're going to a dance'."

"I see," said Harry thoughtfully.

Miserable bastard.

Harry fanned himself with his magazine. "Anyway. This night we were having a yarn, as seamen do…"

John stifled another yawn. *Fancy being trapped on a ship with this. Those round-the-world voyages, whatever…*

"Barratt was talking of the 'ocean greyhounds' he'd been on. I thought, you know, ocean *greyhounds*. And then, for some reason… I don't know why…"

No wonder they mutinied. Murdered all hands.

"… Next time I was on leave, I got a book on them. Greyhounds. And what I read was… well… so peculiar and disturbing I thought, *They need help.*"

"You've got some, then?"

"Four. Sam, Bob, George and Dave."

"Not that much a dog family, us lot," said John. "More horses... But names like that? For greyhounds?"

Harry smiled quietly. "People who helped eventually found Cunard. Cunard himself. Robert Napier, George Burns, David McIver."

John took a breath. "Harry! You really think they'll give you money for this?"

Harry said, "I've had enough. Container ships. That bloody Atlantic Ocean! I was used to other things. India, East Africa, warmth, colour, time off in port to mooch around..."

"So why the change in the first place?"

"For the three-week trips – the sea was simply becoming unbearable!... But my family..."

"Go away themselves do they?"

"Worse than that."

John nodded. "Well. Not to upset you, Harry, but, truth be known, I don't give much for your chances. You being employed and everything..."

"Unpaid leave!"

"Still. Always gaps in the net for a few wiggle through... Slip round the track faster than the others, eh?"

A tall woman of about fifty, with a long grey skirt, long grey hair, and dark circles under her eyes appeared. She scanned the six chairs like Ahab looking for Moby Dick. "Mr O'Rourke?" she ventured, catching John's eye.

John sprang to his feet.

"Well, best of luck, John," said Harry. "By the way, what've you got...?"

"Private detective! My version of warmth, excitement, and colour."

"Maybe my dog scheme's not so crazy after all," said Harry thoughtfully.

John stared at him.

"Might even meet sometime?" Harry fixed John with a gaze that somehow demanded a response.

"I'll have an advert in the paper. You ever need a… well… a…"

"You'll be in Central Liverpool?"

John hesitated. "Yeah. Think so…"

"Stroll round Liverpool quite a bit on leave," said Harry. He pointed to the dog on the magazine cover. "Never know when you might spot one."

"That's for sure."

"Mr O'Rourke!" The woman in grey hefted her harpoon.

John adopted a simpering grin. Moved forwards towards freedom.

SEQUENCE 8

TUESDAY, 9th FEB, 1982. 13.00
EXT/ DAY. 'A' ROAD COUNTRY LAY-BY WITH RED
PHONE BOX

The Porsche pulled to a halt in a lay-by off the A1. One containing a telephone box.

Raite climbed out and headed towards the box. Reached forward to pull open its door.

SEQUENCE 9

John depressed the latch and pushed open the door of The Bayonets. He entered holding a red folder prominently under his arm, and immediately locked eyes with his father. Mr O'Rourke smiled tentatively. John held up the folder.

Curly jumped to his feet and shouted, "'Gratulations, mate! Pint?"

John nodded half-dismissively. Looked round the pub.

As he did so, his father stared at him closely. Then, ignoring his forebodings, Mr O'Rourke patted the seat beside him. "Come on. Sit down. Tell us about it! What was it like? What happens next?"

"When do we see the money?!" shouted Mick from behind the pumps.

SEQUENCE 10

TUESDAY, 9th FEB, 1982, 6.00AM.
INT/DAY BUYER'S GALLERY, LAS VEGAS

In a large underground art gallery/cellar, the Buyer, in a lightweight silk summer suit, put down the phone on his desktop.

A desk containing two heaps of financial contracts. One had many redactions and gaps where text had been excised from the bodies of the contracts. The other contained copies of the same contacts, entire and unspoilt.

The Buyer rose and walked down his gallery. Glanced at, then tapped a thermometer.

The wall covered with paintings of the Magdalen. All prime pieces.

Towards the further end of the gallery he stopped. Stared at the space between two early representations. Touched the wall.

SEQUENCE 11

MONDAY, 15th FEB, 1982. 13.00
INT / DAY CRUST'S FLAT

The Voice said, "Mrs Raite. Bogger. Mercedes saloon. On the M6 and prob'ly coming in on the M62."

Crust doodled a chariot. "Think they might know where he actually is? Have some sort of address?"

"Nah. They're winging it. Know about Chester. Heard him talk of America. Know he can't stay in London. Also figure he won't try climbing on a plane with a million pounds in a paper bag. Maybe even twig it'll be a ship… Her big thing is finding him. Unleashing Bogger. Getting the money. Giving Ron his final reward!… Files arrive OK?"

"Yeah. Read and registered."

"Met your plain-clothes yet? – Busking Billy?"

"Only after approaching two holly bushes. Beard like a rat peering through a bale of hay."

"But rock solid. What he'll do: pick them up at the end of the M62. Tail them. Let you know where they're staying."

"OK," said Crust.

"So," said the Voice. "Just me, you, and Busking Bill. You have to ring here – no messages of any kind. Me or nobody. OK?"

After a short pause, Crust said, "OK."

SEQUENCE 12

MONDAY, 15th FEB, 1982. 14.00
EXT / DAY: MOORFIELDS, CENTRAL LIVERPOOL
INT / DAY MOORFIELDS, JOHN'S OFFICE

John and Curly leaned into the winter gale blowing up off the Mersey as they walked up Moorfields.

"But a place like this. Top Liverpool address. Why so cheap?" shouted Curly.

"Just was," gasped John. "Area's gone down a bit now the shipping's gone." He pulled out a large roll of bin bags from his anorak pocket. "And needs a bit of sorting, truth be known."

"Still. *Moorfields*! Didn't they want references?"

"Saw the Enterprise Allowance forms; knew I was good for the money." John bent, breathless… "You know, Curl. 'Member coming here as a kid? Saturday afternoons. The foreign stamp shop. The Wizard's Den."

"All shit…"

"Yeah. The stamps worthless. The tricks all rubbish. Black face soap. Vanishing egg. Pharaoh's serpents…

Not one ever fucking really worked... But never thought I'd ever have a place here." John straightened. "Not far now. Just up here on the right. Nearly opposite the Wine Lodge... That night Everton won that replay? When they led that donkey in? Walked it round the bar. Blue-and-white roundels on either rump. Happy times, eh?..."

"Wasn't that the night you got punched in the face?"

Suddenly a dark blue police van ran up onto the pavement ahead of them. Five or six uniforms jumped out and charged up a short flight of steps into a building. John and Curly slowed their pace, awaiting developments. A policeman tumbled down the steps backwards, as if auditioning for the Keystone Cops. He rolled over, sprang to his feet, and waded back to assist in wrestling two large bikers across the pavement to the van. The bikers were hairy as coconuts, leathered-up, swathed in chains, and dripping with engine oil and hamburger grease. The heaving mass of men swayed back and forwards across the pavement.

John stared at one of the bikers who, as well as his two natural eyes, had a third tattooed in the middle of his forehead. Catching John's gaze, the biker shouted, "Fuck you looking at, shithead?!"

The other biker – matted yellow hair – struggling in a headlock – looked towards John and Curly. "Fuckin' hand, mate?!" he shouted.

As one, John and Curly turned their attention to the far side of the road until the various cries and shouts were cut off by the van's doors slamming, its engine revving, then roaring away.

"Nice neighbourhood," said Curly. "You've done well."

They walked a few paces further, then stopped at the worn steps down which the police and bikers had tumbled. At the top of the steps, a Victorian door frame. On one side of it, fixed to the outside wall, a number of old faded brass plates. John stared up the steps towards the door.

"Come on, John," said Curly. "Let's get on your place."

John looked at Curly. Then at the steps.

"You're joking?" said Curly.

"This is it."

"OK," said Curly. "OK. Let's see what we've got."

They walked down a narrow hall. Began to mount uncarpeted wooden stairs with spindly banisters.

Up past the first floor's 'Ace Audio'.

Up past the second's 'Acme Added Value Advertising'.

The third floor, where the office door simply had a picture of an open Bible. Underneath, 'This is a One-Story Building'.

Studio spaces created out of plastic and hardboard. All quiet as an old churchyard.

On the fourth floor, 'The Liverpool Drum Academy', the door to which was very slightly ajar.

Up from the fourth floor was a final flight of narrower stairs. The first of these creaked loudly under John's weight. He stopped. Turned back to Curly, still standing outside the Drum Academy. "I call this the Traitor's Stair," said John. "Early warning system. Let me know clients are approaching…"

Out of the corner of his eye, Curly saw the door to the drum academy open another half-inch.

John began to mount the stairs again.

Curly, following, deliberately put his weight on the Traitor's Stair.

The drum academy door opened a little further.

At the top of the flight, a dog-leg led to a final three stairs, then a small, square landing just big enough for a brown coir doormat with the inscription 'GOD BLESS THIS HOUSE' woven into it.

The door to John's new office was original Victorian heavy oak. A frosted-glass panel was set in its top half. On the glass, newly picked out in gold:

JOHN O'ROURKE
PRIVATE DETECTIVE

"Must've cost a few bob?" said Curly.

"Worth it, though, Curl. First impressions and that…"

"Yeah" said Curly. "First impressions. Always right unless they're wrong."

The door had been fitted with a hasp and a large new padlock. John took a key from his pocket and began trying to unlock it.

"John?" said Curly. "How you going to attract anyone up here?"

"Enterprise people went into that. *Yellow Pages*, flyers… and a poem I wrote for the *Albion*."

"Poem?" asked Curly.

John began to shake the padlock. "Why won't this key go in?! And these scratches? Where'd they come from?"

"The bikers, pal… Their squat, see!" The voice, from behind, was pure professional Scouse.

John and Curly turned with difficulty. Facing them was a small, round figure wearing a purple suede jacket with very wide lapels and lots of stains. A fur Davy Crockett hat pulled close round the ears. An orange open-necked shirt, tucked into the waistband of a pair of flared brown corduroys. All ending in a pair of stained green suede shoes. There was a scrap of dark blue silk tied round the speaker's neck. Above this, his face was the general colour and design of a blood orange; a face combining dirt, dissipation, stoicism and primal acuteness.

A dirty hand with heavily nicotined fingers was extended. Shaken by John. Then Curly. "Charlie," said the new arrival. "Charlie Um-Pah-Bah! Liverpool Drum Academy. Next flight down."

John nodded. "John O'Rourke. He pointed at the sign on the office door. "That's me." He pointed to Curly. "And Curly… my… well… you know…"

Charlie nodded. Patted his pockets. Looked puzzled. "Either of you lads got a smoke?"

Curly handed over a cigarette.

Charlie snapped off the filter. Threw it on the floor. Lit up. Drew heavily. Gave a hard cough. Looked quickly over John and Curly once more. Gave an indecipherable grin. "Yeah, the bikers…"

"Squatters, you said?" asked Curly.

"Yeah." Charlie pointed a finger at John. "Been coming here, on and off, couple of years now. Drinking and fucking around. Then away again. Heard them today, clumping up the stairs, poking and scratching with their blades at that new lock of yours. Gonna 'slice' whoever put it on…"

John and Curly exchanged glances.

"So," Charlie nodded towards John without looking at him, "I phoned the bizzies. Didn't even need to go out; find a call box… Because! No matter what! You always keep on the old dog and bone. Might have to go short on basics; cider and that. But a drummer like me, you got to be ready when the call comes!"

"Bikers?" asked Curly again.

Charlie nodded. "Not bad lads. Invited me up a few times; sample their home brew. Like drinking roadie's piss. This boss one – 'Arry some-fucking-thing or other; weird eye in the middle of his head – says he's an artist. Paints these pictures…" He looked at John. "You've seen them in there, yeah?"

"Yeah," said John reluctantly.

"Yeah," echoed Charlie. "Real nutjob stuff!… But! You know what surprised me? No biker parties. No young Judies running round stark bollock naked, tabbed-up on acid… Think this place was more so they could chill out after murdering some fucker; pulling a drug deal. There's about five of them in the gang. Like I say, they got back today; found your new padlock. Started going mental. So thought I'd do you a *favour*. Phoned the cops. Said a bunch of weirdos – *druggies* – were breaking into private property. So! A *favour*! Us being *neighbours*!"

He winked. Waited expectantly. Curly took out his cigarettes again. Charlie accepted one. Everyone stared at nothing.

Finally John said, "Right. Thanks, Charlie. Owe you one." He stroked a figure '1' in the air with his finger.

Charlie accepted a light. Blew a reflective plume of smoke.

"Much doing, then, Charl?" asked Curly. "Drumming and that?"

"Expecting a gig any time now. Reason I can't let anyone use the phone. So be grateful if you didn't ask…"

John said, "No sweat, Charlie. Be getting my own a day or so."

Charlie nodded. Took another drag. Leaned back against the panelling.

Curly said, "So who were you with, Charl?"

Charlie squinted, head on one side. "Started with Ted Tornado and the Twisters. Hate to piss on anyone else's bonfire, but it was Ted and myself put the 'beat' into 'Merseybeat'…"

"What happened?" asked Curly.

"Ted topped himself. A thousand chancers making it while he couldn't get a foot in the door."

"Know how he felt," said John. "Well, till a few weeks ago…"

"Plus Ted's drink problem," said Charlie, not breaking stride. "… Not being able to get enough!"

John and Curly laughed dutifully.

"Brewery promo where Ted threw himself in a vat. Got him out 'fore he sucked it dry, but the beginning of the end." Charlie took a lung-searing drag that ran the red tip of his cigarette down like a fuse. "Then Sam Sandstorm and the Sheikhs. Mostly playing the OPB – Orrell Park Ballroom. What a place!" He stepped back and lifted his air guitar.

"I've got you half-pissed,
I'm holding you tight,
'Cause you're the only good thing
In the Orrell tonight…

Finally went with Eddie Etna and the Eruptions. Named after Eddie's acne. Best fucking mate I ever had, Eddie! Well. Best non-Scouse mate… Because! Say what you like! If someone's not from the 'Pool there's always a bit of the Woollyback in them… Just can't help themselves. Am I right?"

John nodded slowly.

Curly said, "That name of yours, Charlie…?"

"Charlie Um-Pah-Bah?… OK! 'Member that old Del Shannon number – 'The Swiss Maid'?"

"Cracker!" said Curly.

"Was! Is! Always will be! But where the chorus goes, '*Um-pah-bah, um-bah-pah, um-pah-bah. Um-pah-bah, um-pah-bah, bah*' – well, that was me. Had it as a solo while knocking fuck out the skins!… Famous for it!"

John looked at Curly. "Great, eh, Curl?"

"Yeah," said Curly. "Some top names there, Charlie."

Charlie raised a grimy finger. "Now thinking management! You fellas ever come across a decent-sounding group?" He mimed holding a phone to one ear. Then waited, saucer eyes bright.

"Where you from, Charlie?" asked John casually.

"Anfield Road way… You lads?"

"Stanley Road… Go to school up there?" pursued John.

"All Saints."

"Yeah," said Curly. "Boxed in a few schools round there... Liverpool play-centres and that."

Charlie nodded. Winked. "Yeh. Thought you'd been bit of a scrapper. The build. The moves."

Curly smiled. "You know, there's this group of lads performs at St Joe's – this church club we sometimes go. Call themselves The Nurgs!"

"Like it!" said Charlie. "Makes you think."

"Of what?" asked John.

"Got this singer," continued Curly. "'Big Ned Nembutal', he calls himself."

"Like it more!" said Charlie.

"In fact," said Curly, "think they're booked for St Joe's Sat'dy after next... First week March. You're doing nothing that night..."

Charlie gave Curly a quick wink. "Cheers, Scouse!"

"Anyway..." said John.

"Yeah," said Charlie. "Mosey back down the drum academy. 'Less you're thinking inviting me in for a coffee or something?"

"Not today, Charlie," said John. "Too busy." He began trying to enter the key once more into the lock.

"Maybe seized with the cold?" said Curly.

"Altitude?" suggested Charlie.

"Maybe just pick it, John?" said Curly innocently.

Curly and Charlie exchanged winks.

John, face set, attempted to force the key. His fingers slipped and caught the metal. He stared at the white furrow in his flesh. The blood beginning to ooze.

Charlie peered into the padlock's keyhole. "Chewing gum," he announced. "They've bunged it up with chewy.

You'll need a new one. Maybe an anthrax shot go with it."

Curly laughed.

"Curly!" John looked at the lock. The key. His bleeding finger. "Curly! Nip down and find a tool shop; must be one round here. Get a junior hacksaw. New lock." John put his finger in his mouth and sucked on it.

"Yeah, but, John – "

"Just do it, Curl!"

There was silence.

Charlie said, "Prob'ly Curl doesn't know whether you're *asking* or *telling* him!… Place just round the corner, Dale Street, Curl."

"Chemist's, too," said John. "Get some plasters!" He stared fixedly at the lock.

"OK, mate. Take it easy." Curly nodded goodbye to Charlie and ran down, the Traitor's Stair creaking loudly.

Charlie said, "Fancy a cuppa my place? Rather than just hanging round here?"

John closed his eyes and pressed his head against the door.

"Yeah," said Charlie. "Haven't got another fag, have you?"

"Don't smoke," said John.

"Or a comb in your back pocket?"

John turned and looked at Charlie.

Charlie's eyes flicked up towards John's hair. "Yeah… Can see there's a bit of beach showing through the seaweed!" He whipped off his Davy Crockett cap. Ran a hand through his luxuriant, greasy black curls.

John closed his eyes and turned his head to rest once more against the door.

Charlie stood for a moment, then turned downstairs.

John stood, eyes closed, until he heard the stair creak. Opened his eyes. *Famous? For being another '60s refugee living on old vinyl and Valium? But like with all losers – keep your eyes closed, your head turned away, eventually they vanish.*

SEQUENCE 13

MONDAY, 15th FEB, 1982. 14.30
INT/DAY HOTEL ROOM, LIVERPOOL

The hotel was near the end of the M62. The door of its most expensive room opened and Mrs Raite and Bogger entered. Mrs Raite was wearing a creamy, off-white fur coat. Shoulder-length russet-black hair framed her heart-shaped face. A short nose lay at a slight angle to the perpendicular. Large, expressive, grey eyes. She shucked off the coat and threw it on the double bed. Underneath was a grey, fitted trouser suit, cut to emphasise her voluptuous, caricature-like, figure. Waves of intelligence, glamour and sex radiated-out like the solar wind.

She looked around the room. Sighed. Began to scratch at one of her plasters. Bogger stood just inside the door, staring at her. The two suitcases he had been carrying were on the floor; one on either side of him. A local newspaper clamped underneath his arm.

Mrs Raite sighed again. Walked to the minibar. Took out gin, whisky and a couple of mixers. She held out the whisky and a mixer. Bogger moved forward and accepted them without speaking. Threw the newspaper onto the bed.

Mrs Raite sat on the edge of the bed. Kicked off her black leather ankle-boots.

Poured gin and tonic. Swallowed half. Lay back, her drink in one hand. Eyes closed.

Bogger stood over her. Took off his jacket. Began to unbutton his shirt.

Mrs Raite opened one eye, which she fixed on Bogger. "We need to find him. Ronnie. I've a feeling there's not much time."

"We will, Liz. Get the money. Fuck him up properly... Long as he's here."

"Where else?" Mrs Raite stared up at the ceiling.

Bogger kicked off his trousers. Peeled down his shorts.

Mrs Raite idly scratched her plaster as Bogger seized the waistband of her trousers, dragged them down her legs and threw them to one side. She stared as his heavily muscled chest loomed above her. The thick, white-ridged knife scar. At one time, a vague turn-on. Now she idly ran a finger over it.

He plunged into her, grunting heavily. 'Lie back and think of England' was the old advice in such situations. Although her Virginia Water aunt used to say, 'Lie back and think of Le Touquet.'

She looked up into Bogger's straining face. Turned her head to one side. Saw the local paper lying towards the edge of the bed. Stretched out an arm and laid it across the paper.

Laughed as she thought of her grandfather referring to one of her early boyfriends as 'Dim as a Toc H lamp!'

Bogger, taking this as an expression of approval, redoubled his efforts.

SEQUENCE 14

MONDAY, 15ᵗʰ FEB, 1982. 15.00
INT / DAY/ LANDING OUTSIDE JOHN'S OFFICE. INT
/ DAY JOHN'S OFFICE

Panting with exertion, Curly finished sawing through the hasp of the padlock. Stepped back, flexing the fingers that had held the hacksaw.

John patted him on the arm. "Good lad, Curl! Now… Rome wasn't built in a day. Right?" He bustled into the office. Curly following.

Soiled mattresses. Broken glasses and cups. Cider/beer/British sherry bottles. Graffitied walls. Exposed plaster and lath. A doorless bathroom with a cracked sink and a filthy toilet. A large plastic home-brew bin whose contents had fermented into furry lengths running down the outside like the legs of a giant spider. Upended plywood desk. Doorless doorway to another small room; a purple velvet curtain hanging from nails across its entrance. Paintings and more paintings – propped up singly, and in groups, all around the skirting boards. Canvas, hardboard, cardboard. One – on board – hanging on a nail in the middle of the wall directly opposite the door.

"Christ, John!" Curly walked round stirring the clumps of the art with his feet. "What's all these?"

"Come on, Curl. You heard that Charlie fella say that one of the bikers – 'Arry some-fucking-thing or other -was a painter."

"Paintings? These?!" Curly pointed to the work on the nail opposite the office door. "I mean, look at that! One-track – dirt-track – mind."

They walked across and stood before it. Two female breasts, like two fried eggs, lay in the middle of the canvas. Between them was a large red eye. Above that, a halo supported by formless shapes, wings growing from their backs. Across the bottom, in large orange capital letters, 'CELESTIAL VISION'.

"I mean. What's the eye about?" asked Curly.

"You know, Curl… That biker we saw getting arrested. One with the eye tattooed in the middle of his forehead. Prob'ly that's the 'Arry that Charlie out there was talking about. Maybe it's… well… something he does with eyes…"

"Fuck's sake, John. What're the lads gonna think in The Bayonets? Your old fella?" Curly pointed to the almost undecipherable signature in the bottom right-hand corner. "Perv's even signed it!"

"Yeah," said John, peering closely. "It's him… Sort of squiggly ''Arry'; defo starts with an 'A'. Coupla squiggles. 'N'… 'Arian' rather than ''Arry', maybe."

"What sort of name's that?" Curly bent down and picked up a tea towel from among the canvases. A Beefeater in costume, holding up a halberd. The cloth full of paint smears and palette wipings. Curly gestured towards the beefeater. "Even this bent fucker looks more normal."

"You may be missing something here, Curl."

"Think so?"

"Arian," John mused. "Ever heard anyone called that?"

"Not in Flour Street," said Curly.

"Think it may be religious."

Curly pointed down to one of the works lying against the skirting board. " 'Specially where he's stuck that crucifix in that one!"

"In fact, I think it's the name of a saint."

"John! Let's have those bin bags."

John took out the bin bags. Curly peeled one from the roll. Reached up towards *Celestial Vision*.

"No!" said John.

"You're not leaving it up there?!"

"Just till I've done some… well… 'research'…"

"Or the Enterprise people come and boot you out on your arse!"

"Speaking of which!… Look, Curl. Can you hold the fort for a bit while I slip out; see this fella?"

"Fella?"

"Well… accountant."

Curly laughed. "Accountant?!"

"Part of the deal. To have an accountant. This one's just off Dale Street; says he won't charge for an 'initial consultation'."

"Won't charge you for talking to him?!… Wow!"

"Yeah. Well. Nothing for someone like you to worry about…"

"Someone like me?!"

"Curl. I – *we* – need to keep everyone happy. We're going to make a go of this."

"Well…"

"Listen! Fancy doing a bit of cleaning while I'm gone?"

"Cleaning?!"

"Tidying and that. Wipe a rag around…"

"Skivvying?!"

"Just a thought…"

"You're thinking of actually *living* here?!"

"Save coming in every day… Though just the odd night at first. Living and working space. Lot of that now. Flat *and* office… 'Floffice', I suppose…"

Curly spat on the filthy floor. Rubbed it in with his work boot. "Thing is, John. What's my position here?"

"Position?"

"Look. You need someone. That hacksaw… Flyers round the shops… 'Holding the fort'… Assistant?… Maybe partner?"

"Assistant?"

"Think that's fair enough. Otherwise… well… there's not much around out there. But from tomorrow I'll be looking…"

John smiled. "Mean that much, would it? Working for me?"

Curly swallowed. "Just fed up being a doleite… Able to tell people I'm doing something. Don't want no wages. 'Least not yet. Just a few bob expenses. Maybe a cut when the clients roll in."

"If they ever do…"

"Sure to, John. Fella with your nous. Your get-up-and-go."

John thought for a moment. Stuck out a hand. "OK, Curl. Assistant and chief bottle washer?"

They tentatively shook hands.

"Now," said John. "You going to do that cleaning?"

"Am I fuck!" said Curly. "But I know someone who will!"

SEQUENCE 15

MONDAY, 15th FEB, 1982. 15.20
EXT/ DAY. APPROACH ROAD TO WEST
HEARTWOOD VILLAGE / ROAD OUT FROM WEST
HEARTWOOD / CART TRACK UP TO PREFAB RAITE
IS RENTING

Coming in on the B road, scattered houses began to appear on either side. Then a sign:

WEST HEARTWOOD
30 MPH
PLEASE DRIVE CAREFULLY

Raite slowed. Place like this, there'd be no police. But a Porsche draws attention.

Like the warriors from the dragon's teeth, the houses began to increase in density. Then suddenly he was in a small Cheshire/Wirral market town. Usual set-up: the B road running into one end of an oblong 'town square', then out the other end. Although in the depths of winter, the square was crowded with people and cars. Gift shops, antique shops, produce shops. Homemade jams / hams / flimflams. An organic butcher's. Black-beamed, whitewashed B&Bs / pubs / hotels. Gentrification alive and well. Behind it all, the council estate to service those servicing the service industries. Further back again, the detached houses surrounded by walls and thick trees. Cotswold kitsch – but without the cachet.

"Cheshire," muttered Raite. "No wonder the cats smiled."

He drove carefully out of the square and back onto the B road. The houses thinned. A sign signalled the national speed limit. Another mile or so, on his left, the red telephone box. Next to it, the open gate leading to the ploughed field. Opposite, a weather-beaten board at ground level, lodged in the brambles. A yellow arrow pointing up an overgrown, rutted cart track.

Raite eased the Porsche onto the track. After a hundred yards or so there was a hard right. He was now out of sight of the road and on some broken, weed-infested pavement slabs. At the end of these, a 1950s prefab bungalow.

Raite brought the Porsche to a stop but left the engine running.

The prefab had cracks running up, down and across the walls. A battered front door. Dirt-encrusted windows on either side. From behind the windows, slanted, dirty brown curtains – watching like the eyes of a cornered fox.

Outside the front door, a Land Rover; a figure slouched in its driver's seat.

Raite eased the Porsche into a three-point turn facing back down the cart track.

From the Land Rover, the Countryman climbed down. Tweed pork-pie hat. Green Barbour. Tweed jacket. Gilet. Check shirt; mustard knitted tie; brown cords. Highly polished, heavy brown leather boots. *The Archers* via Shaftesbury Avenue. The Countryman stopped halfway towards the Porsche.

Raite killed the engine. Climbed out.

The Countryman took out a pack of cigarettes. Held them vaguely in Raite's direction.

Raite advanced smiling pleasantly. "Enough bad habits... You the one the estate agents put me on to? I spoke to on the phone?"

"Absolutely, squire!" The Countryman, not taking his eyes off Raite, made a strange gesture over the back of his head towards the prefab. "There she is."

Both regarded the house.

"A bit bare," said the Countryman. "Reflected in the rent, naturally. But – as promised – very, very quiet. Want to see inside?" He took a gold hunter from his waistcoat pocket. Flipped its lid. "Although actually... a little bit pushed."

Raite pulled out his wallet. "'Fraid those references hadn't arrived by the time I left."

The Countryman grinned. "Those in your wallet will be fine."

"Three months," said Raite. He counted the notes into the Countryman's fingerless-gloved hand.

The money was checked. Stowed in an inside pocket. The Countryman cleared his throat. "Ah! Chap who owns the property rang last night. Subject of wear, tear, breakages. Perhaps a month's deposit?"

"Not you, then?" said Raite. "Owns it?"

The Countryman carefully lifted one leg and shook a cleated boot. "Just his agent… Sure I mentioned it on the phone?"

"No," said Raite.

"Lives abroad… Far East." The Countryman licked one finger. Raised it as if to test the wind. "Know this area, do you?"

"Vaguely… Basic services still on?"

"Storage heater on low; keep the damp out. Made a note of the figures before you arrived. Hope you don't mind?"

"Anything else?"

"Well…" The Countryman gestured and they began walking side by side to the back of the property across more cracked, weed-infested paving slabs. They stopped as the Countryman pointed at the prefab's rear wall. A back door warped into its surround; its lock rusted and seized. Windows set in the wall on either side of the door. One of the windows had a piece of hardboard fixed over it. "Bathroom window's gone, unfortunately. Reflected in the rent, of course. I could get someone out to give you a price…"

Raite looked at him. Considered the window. "Two foot squarish?"

The Countryman stared.

"My old business," said Raite.

"Glazing?"

Raite began walking back to the front of the house, the Countryman hurrying after. They stopped near the Land Rover.

The Countryman licked his lips nervously. "All in all, I – we – feel a month's deposit…"

"Long as I'm not bothered," said Raite.

"Completely off the beaten track! No townie monkeys out here. Chap could do anything he liked here… *Anything!*… Hardly remember it's here meself."

"I hope so," said Raite, flattening his voice slightly as he took out his wallet. "The village? Many antique shops?"

The Countryman eyed the wallet. "Course, we'll never be like Stow. Stow-on-the-Wold! Place hardly the size of m' daughter's wedding marquee… Yet their own 'Antique Dealers Cricket Eleven'!" He gestured in wonder towards the heavens.

Raite opened the wallet. Took out the extra month's rent. Half-held out the notes. "Specialist dealers?"

"Well…"

"Perhaps replace a chair back?… Clarify a painting signature?"

The Countryman took out an ancient meerschaum. Peered into its bowl. Lit another cigarette instead. "Mmm… There is a chap. Bit off the beaten track himself, you might say. One Methuselah."

"That's his name?"

"Adds a certain something, no? A little je ne sais quoi?… "

"Especially if trying out for the first eleven."

The Countryman briefly showed his teeth.

A sound of dogs barking. Round the cart-track turn came Harry Rose with four greyhounds on leashes. The dogs stopped dead, pressing themselves, quivering, against Harry's legs.

The Countryman raised an arm. Shouted, "Trespassing, squire! Private property!"

Harry waved back. Prepared to move forward.

The Countryman moved swiftly across and reached into the Land Rover. Plucked out a shotgun from through the open window. "Trespassing!" he yelled again, but kept the shotgun barrels pointed towards the floor.

After one final, searching look, at Raite and the Countryman, Harry dragged the dogs around and vanished back down the track.

Raite turned an expressionless face towards the Countryman.

The Countryman fought to keep his extra rent – still in Raite's hand. "Merchant seaman chappo. Lives with his mother; big, rambling place the other side of town. Ship-owning family. Even keep a servant! Sort of people one never *really* knows how much money they have."

Raite didn't respond.

"He – the son. Usually away at sea – also some sort of dog fancier. Greyhounds! Rats on springs!"

"Sort who'll get the police?"

"These old families," said the Countryman quickly. "Money. Privilege… People like that do *not* want *any* attention under *any* circumstances! Sole purpose is keep what they've got while adding more to it. No. He's away for a month on his sea trips. Back again… Away again… Forgotten our existence in half an hour!" He dropped the gun through the Land Rover's window. Over his shoulder said, in an appeasing tone, "Methuselah?"

Raite nodded. Handed over the extra month's rent.

The Countryman took out a small notebook and pen. Drew a map. Showed it to Raite. Tore out the page. Handed it to Raite. Touched his hat. Climbed into the

Land Rover. Touched his hat once more. Bumped off. Turned down the cart track.

Raite stared after him. Walked towards the front door of the prefab.

At the junction with the main road, the Countryman saw Harry in the distance being pulled along by the four greyhounds. *No. Nothing to worry about there.*

SEQUENCE 16

TUESDAY, 16th FEB, 1982. 14.00
INT / DAY BAYONETS

In the Bayonets, Curly and Mr O'Rourke hunched over their pints. Mick stood behind the bar, polishing a glass and listening hard.

"Where's he sleeping?" asked Mr O'Rourke.

"This second room off the main one – small; really cramped. Plus the door's been ripped off."

Mick whistled.

"There a bathroom?" asked Mr O'Rourke.

"Only if you want to call it that. Take a sandblaster clean what's in there. Then a second cubbyhole with a hotplate."

"At least, though, he's got a bed?"

"One of those wire-framed ones with a palliasse. Rip Van Winkle wouldn't kip on it. Though John says he's getting a new one."

"But no door for the bedroom?"

"Sort of curtain pinned across it… Purple velvet."

"All sounds a bit Oscar Wilde to me," said Mick.

64

"Hasn't he told you any of this?" asked Curly.

Mr O'Rourke turned a page of his *Daily Mirror*. "He's not been home much lately. Says he's 'settling in'…"

Curly shook his head. "You wouldn't know what to think."

"You mightn't" said Mr O'Rourke and Mick simultaneously.

SEQUENCE 17

TUESDAY, 16th FEB, 1982. 14.30
INT / DAY HOTEL ROOM

Bogger, naked, was doing press-ups on one hand.

Mrs Raite lay on the bed with the local paper and a gin. "Bogger! At least can't you do it without groaning?"

Bogger sat back on his heels. "Make 'em moan. Make 'em groan." He grinned and winked.

Mrs Raite smiled blankly. "Listen.

Dogs, divorces, debts and cats.
Cars, canned peaches, Scotch in vats.
Humankind! Or Bite! Bark! Squawk!
We can find it! We're O'ROURKE!

A TODAY'S firm with TODAY'S approaches to TODAY'S problems!
But in a cheap way!

JOHN O'ROURKE, Private Investigator."

"Not too big on poetry, Liz," Bogger told her. "But sounds like prize bollocks to me." His press-ups were now on the first two knuckles of each hand.

"Your usual PI type is ex-police; armed services," said Mrs Raite. "This one appears… well…"

"Well?" Bogger pumped effortlessly up and down.

"Local… But also bizarre. That verse… Maybe a short talk?"

"OK. When we doin' it?"

"Just me, Boggs… Don't want to frighten him."

Bogger rose from his press-ups. "Not yet." He stretched. Shook his erection at her. It vibrated like a tuning fork. "Shower?"

Mrs Raite forced a smile. "Can't it wait?"

Bogger went to the minibar. Took out some drinks. "OK. These first. But then! Then we shower!"

"Grunt! Groan! Grunt!" said Mrs Raite.

SEQUENCE 18

FRIDAY, 19th FEBRUARY, 1982. 11.30
INT / DAY STAIRS TO OFFICE. INT / DAY OFFICE

John, second-hand electric fire under arm, crept quietly past the ever-ajar door of the Drum Academy. Trod carefully over the Traitor's Stair. Mounted the next couple of steps. Stopped. Inclined his head forward like a heron canvassing a particularly choice pond. There!… A faint noise. Like their old vacuum cleaner from Flour Street, described by his Father as 'You eating an apple, or an orangutan sucking its big toe'. Maybe Curly had finally got his arse into gear?

At the 'floffice', the new padlock was open; the door slightly ajar.

John pushed it a little further. Looked inside.

It *was* their vacuum cleaner, being used by Curly's sister, Chris. Wearing a blouse, jeans and an apron. Her blonde hair tied-up in a scarf. She stood on tiptoe, tense with concentration, clearing cobwebs from a high corner. John immediately pictured the cover of Brick Bradstreet's *No Alibi for Aphrodite!* Set in a Beverly Hills cosmetic funeral parlour, it depicted a blonde in diaphanous underwear suspended by gold chains from a chandelier, a diamanté wire basket of starving rats strapped to the top of her head. In the background, Brick, swathed from head to toe in bandages and only recognisable by his black fedora, was struggling his way out of a coffin.

Chris sensed him. Swung round. Switched off the machine. "Hiya, John!"

He waited until the vacuum ran down. "Hello, Chris… Long time no see."

One of her incisors was slightly crooked. If he fixed on this he could look at her face without meeting her eyes. Like Curly's, these were a glittering blue, catching and distributing light. She shook her hair free. It lay like a pale helmet around her head. That face and figure! Still. Rumours were she'd paid for them by her marriage.

"Your dad gave me a spare key." Chris grinned. "Curly's been coming home with more dust on him than a saint's sandals… I did knock…"

John nodded. "Most mornings I take a stroll. Paper; cup of tea…"

"Sorting your heating?" Chris pointed at the fire under John's arm.

John plugged in the fire. "Got it from the noticeboard. This place I go. Café des Artistes."

"Ooh la la!" said Chris.

"Fella who runs the Drum Academy put me on to it. Full of no-marks and dossers, but you can get stuff. Been here long?"

"Hour or so. You need some decent carpets. Pick up the dust easier."

"First thing I need's a decent mattress." John blushed.

Chris laughed. "Can't your old firm give you one?"

John gratefully echoed her. "Sort of thing my dad would say. How is he?"

"In The Bayonets quite a lot… Call in myself now I'm back. Militant Mick doesn't like women in the bar, but he doesn't say much, long as I sit quietly with your dad. Take an odd hand in the domino school. 'Sixes about'," she said in a gruff voice. "Your dad worries, though. Not hearing from you much; not even knowing if you've got that phone you mentioned." She stared at the desk where John's new phone sat next to a new directory and *Yellow Pages*.

John went into the box-room kitchen, switched on the kettle and began to take off his anorak. "Lot happening, Chris. Phone's only just come. 'Sides, I'd have to ring him at The Bayonets. Mick picking-up and going on about free calls for all workers when the revolution comes. Wanting to know what I want to speak to my dad about…"

"Mick!" said Chris, pulling a face.

"Chris? You ever hear anything about Mick's wife leaving him? Something about a dress?"

"Mick's wife's dress?"

"Just something I heard… Didn't hear… Though know I did…"

She stared at him.

"Chris. I've offered the old fella a phone for the house. Get it put in. Cover it for him. He just… well… said… if I let him put one in it'd be just one more excuse for me not to go there and see him." John shook his head sadly. Spooned coffee into the cups. "Curly mentioned you were back."

"About a month now." She grinned. Gestured round the office. "What made you go for this, John?"

He shrugged.

"I mean. I know about the detective books. But as a job?"

"That bedding factory…"

"'The Case of the Missing Fingers'…" Years ago, when things were easier, they'd laughed about John at the bedding factory.

"Still dream about them" John shook his head, "Those circular blades that cut the mattresses. Razor-sharp, and once the button was pressed they'd fly across, slicing the bed flock into lengths. Crap wiring, so everything shorted out every five minutes, the blades poised in mid-cut. Then getting sent under the cutting trestles to reset. Flock mattresses hanging round your head like rainclouds… Hardly see or breathe… The saws suddenly starting-up by themselves – and next thing you're in the back of a taxi heading for the hospital, one of your fingers wrapped in a bit of cotton waste alongside you in a drill box! Almost all of them – maintenance team – lost fingers… bits of fingers… At the end of your so-called 'apprenticeship', instead of giving you your indentures, it should've been one of your fingers stuck upwards on a saucer like a wax candle… Ceremony to be held in the glue room, all the women there laughing permanently with the fumes but refusing to work anywhere else 'cause of their home lives." He shook his head violently. "But you had to do it! Go under the machines! Talk of a union came up. Of having a rep… shop steward. Lads approached me. Got round to the owner; his son. Called me in. Orders falling. Going to be cutbacks. But if I went early there'd be twelve hundred quid redundancy. I know I shouldn't have taken it. But I'd had enough!" He gestured round the room. "Now I'm my own boss." He gestured towards a small vase of flowers on the desk. "That you?"

"Thought they'd cheer the place up a bit. Curly said it was a bit… well…"

"Yeah… Maybe should've done a bit more. But sorting the lease; business cards; the ad in the *Albion*…"

"The poem?"

"Just written to show I'm not your usual private eye!… Then the mess left by the last lot… Curly mention them, did he? How they left?"

"Black Maria removal van?"

"Yeah. Otherwise I would've suggested they clean up their own stuff… But I'm getting there slowly."

"Curly says you're maybe having Jimmy the painter in? Distemper the walls? Hang a couple of doors?…"

"Maybe put a few bob in. See how it pays."

"Oh! And I'd like to say thanks." Chris smiled. "Taking Curly in."

"Idea came from my dad... Someone to do the running around."

Chris's smile grew wider.

"Course, there's no money at the moment, so he's a sort of... well..."

"Unpaid partner?" suggested Chris.

"Associate assistant." John enunciated the words carefully. "But anything that comes up, he'll get a share. That's the deal!"

"He's very grateful... And so am I." She smiled and stared at him.

This was getting embarrassing. He quickly said, "Yeah... well... chance for all of us. 'Specially this place. Classy joint in its day. Old Liverpool... Antiquey bits and bobs..."

Chris's eyes flicked towards *Celestial Vision* on its nail opposite John's desk. A quick gesture to the other works round the skirting boards.

"Yeah," said John. "Left by 'Arry – Arian the biker. Thought I'd better hang on to them. 'Case he comes back."

She walked across. Stared at the signature on *Celestial Vision*. "'Arian'? Difficult to tell..." She stood there, smiling.

He stared back. One day! One day he'd have money! No longer have to explain himself. People'd just have to accept him or fuck off. All this 'question/answer! question/ answer! Niggle! Niggle! Niggle!... He realised Chris was staring at him. He coughed. Gestured at the painting.

"Actually, Chris, it *is* Arian. He's a saint. Looked him up. So this *Celestial Vision* is what's called 'devotional art'."

Chris stared. "Devoted to what?" With one foot she stirred the works lying against the skirting board. "There's an awful lot of it, John… this 'devotional art'."

"Just think it adds something."

"What if you get a client – maybe a woman – wants to talk about some fella following her… or her daughter?" She pointed at *Celestial Vision*. "And that's the first thing she sees?" Into the silence, she added, "I mean… what would your dad say?!"

John laughed. "Let's have some disinfectant."

SEQUENCE 19

FRIDAY, 19th FEB, 1982. 07.30 (E.S.T.).
INT / DAY BRIDGE, *OCEAN SEASPRAY*, ALONGSIDE
NEW YORK

Captain Barratt stood on the bridge of the *Ocean Seaspray*, looking for'ard through the great Perspex bridge windows towards the ship's bows. At the almost unbroken line of containers. Cranes putting the last few in place. Driving ice-laden rain. Wind 'like a whetted knife'. New York in winter.

In his head he heard: '…

Off the bows soft green palms waving.
"Ease the Helm there! Come about!"
'Neath the keel blue waters laving.
"Now lads! Walk the anchor out."

A tear started down his cheek. He took a silver flask from his uniform jacket's inside pocket. Tipped some of its contents into the cup of coffee he was holding.

SEQUENCE 20

FRIDAY, 19th FEBRUARY, 1982. 12.00
INT / DAY JOHN'S OFFICE

John stretched and put down the mop. Wrung out a cloth into the wash-bucket. "Coffee?"

"Be great, John."

He collected their two mugs. Walked into the bathroom and switched on the kettle. Decided it was time. "Chris? You don't mind me asking... What happened?"

She grinned. "Me and the ex? Usual. Started working overtime; then put himself on permanent nights. I stuck it for a bit... But with no kids to consider, just the odd black eye, I finally packed my medication and left."

John brought the coffees.

Her grin became fixed. "What really happened was religion." In an Irish accent she continued. "'Times *have* changed, girls. And the Church fully realises today's temptations and pressures. But *your virtue* is part of your personal integrity, and most men – *Catholic men* – will *rightly* expect...'" In her normal voice, she said, "So I kept my 'personal integrity', and he married me for the first night, before deciding he'd been the victim of serious religious sexual blackmail and I was the one to blame!"

John sipped his coffee. "At least, like you said, no kids."

"Not from want of trying. Something I really, really wanted... Course, by that time he was bored. So then all the tricks... Politics of degradation..."

John gritted his teeth. *Show a bit of interest; this is what you get. Always some hard-luck story.* "Don't they have them tests, now?"

Chris laughed shortly. "What if it was him? A 'real man' being told by a doctor – maybe even a *woman* doctor – he had no balls. Steak and onions and Sunday football all the way then! He was sweaty enough as it was." She rubbed her eyes as if she were tired.

John stared down at his cup. The moment seemed to go on and on. A knock at the door. *Thank fuck!*

Another knock and the door opened slowly. A head appeared. A hand holding a magazine. A vaguely familiar face smiling shyly, but with confidence. A body. "Hello, John. Remember me?... Harry?... Harry Rose?"

John stared; then stuck out his hand. "Job centre, right?... Harry Rose? Merchant seaman?"

Behind him, he thought he heard Chris mutter "'You're a card, Mr Spade'."

John turned to her. "Enterprise Allowance thing. Harry's in the Merch. Mate; chief officer... But wants to save greyhounds!"

Chris and Harry quickly glanced at each other. As quickly glanced away. Then seemed to edge towards each other without actually moving.

John laughed. Put himself between them. Shook Harry's hand again. "Assume you didn't qualify, H?"

"You were right. Didn't meet the criteria." Harry turned to Chris. "Dreadful place; dreadful." He stared down at the different copy of *Track and Lights* he was carrying.

Chris reached out a hand for the magazine. Looked at the cover.

John came beside her. Put an arm round her shoulder. "Yeah, Harry's one of them do-gooders, Chris. Saving our dumb friends. Though some of us have already got enough, yeah?!" He took the magazine from her, rolled it up and pointed it towards the kitchen. "Coffee, Harry?" Re-pointed the magazine towards Chris, then swung it once more to point at the hotplate cubbyhole.

Chris ignored him.

Harry said quickly, "I'll rethink it all next trip." Turned back to Chris. "On the *Ocean Seaspray*, out of Seaforth. Container run. States and back."

"Chris. Could you? That coffee?" John smiled grimly.

Chris asked, "So here fairly regularly?"

"Every three weeks," Harry told her. "New York–Liverpool. Though thinking of giving it up."

Chris looked at him.

Harry continued. "My skipper. Captain Barratt. Old school. Maritime literature buff. Said Masefield wrote it's not the length of any particular trip, rather the intensity of the experience."

Chris laughed.

Harry's eyes twinkled.

Chris, swaying slightly, moved off towards the kitchen.

John put the magazine on the desk. Stepped into Harry's face. "So!? H!?… What brings you this part of Town?"

"Recalling you inviting me to look you up?... I was in the area, and needing some advice..."

John grinned savagely.

"Rang *Yellow Pages*... They said you weren't in the present issue, but gave me the contact details you'd supplied."

"That's good." John nodded sagely. "Though, talking literature... That Masefield fella you mentioned... There's this poem by me in the *Albion* you might want to see..."

Chris came back carrying mugs of coffee. Handed one to Harry; one to John. "Chris," she said, holding out her hand to Harry.

Harry took it immediately. "John's partner?" he asked.

John grinned. "Just working off a favour for her brother. Chris takes the punters' minds off how much I'm charging. Speaking of which..."

Harry finally released Chris's hand. "Thing is, John, I found this place for rent on the Wirral." He half-turned to Chris. "Where the family home is. I live with my mother... and Anne. My mother's... well... maid."

"Maid?!" said John.

"Mother's considering a retirement home; possibly offering me the house for a greyhound sanctuary. Old stable block for the kennels. Maybe cash in my Merchant Navy officer's pension. But while I was out walking the dogs around West Heartwood I saw this property. Run-down, but potential... Just can't get in to see it."

"Estate agent trouble?" asked Chris.

"Didn't know you knew nothing about estate agents, Chris?" John smiled even more savagely.

"Absolutely," said Harry, his eyes fixed on Chris. "But I waited a bit too long – "

"As you sometime can," said Chris.

"… But having this trip off… being around as I will be for the next two weeks or so…" Harry stared at Chris. "thought I'd phone the agents myself. Who told me a short let has been negotiated…"

"He who hesitates is last, H!" John told him.

"… But after that, the owner might possibly negotiate an offer to buy. So thought I'd walk the dogs across; ask the new tenant if I could have a quick look round."

"And?…" Chris gestured for Harry to drink his coffee.

Harry took a sip. Gave her a thumbs up.

John coughed. Made a meaningless gesture.

"Got there with the dogs" continued Harry. "Almost too much for them. Strangely enough, greyhounds don't need that much exercise… Probably surprises you…"

"Fascinating," murmured Chris.

"Sort of old prefab, but plenty of land. Two blokes there; one possibly the new tenant. Porsche Carrera."

"Know them, do you, Harry? Porsches?" asked John.

"As a young man, some of my friends owned those sorts of cars."

"Maids to clean them every week?"

Harry laughed easily. "The other person… well… Maybe the owner's agent. Seen him about… Huntin'/shootin'/fishin'/gamekeeperin' type."

"You spoke to them?" asked Chris.

"Tried to. The agent pulled a shotgun."

"Oh, Harry!" said Chris, touching him lightly on the arm.

Harry faced John. "Look, John. Sailing for the States in two weeks. Friday 12th March. But I'll be around till then, and I was wondering if you could… well… look into all this? Would I be safe pursuing this place, or should I begin considering Mother's offer; the family house? Your usual fees, of course."

John pursed his lips. "Yeah… well… Nice to think of me, H! But here we're more… well…"

"Lord Lucan," said Chris. "The site of Atlantis… The lost chord."

Harry muttered, "Address; phone number." He fumbled out his wallet and extracted two business cards.

John stared. A seaman! Business cards! Most of the old shellbacks you sometimes still saw in the Bayonets couldn't hardly read. John took one. "Thanks, H… Mine haven't been delivered yet."

Harry offered the other card to Chris. She took it. Slipped it into her jeans pocket. Harry edged towards the door. Half-opened it. Looked back at John.

"OK, Harry. Got it clocked!" John told him. "And any time I'm over there…"

Harry stared once more at Chris. Looked at John. "As I said. Down to sail Friday 12th at the moment… In the meantime, either of you fancy a look around a state-of-the-art container ship? Drink on board?… Well, number's on the card." He slipped out, leaving the door open.

John walked across and closed it. "Maybe they don't have them on ships. Doors." He smirked. "Or just have maids close them after them." He shook his head. Held out his hand.

Chris stared at him. "What?"

"Want me to dump that business card? Mine's going in the bin." When she didn't respond, he continued. "What I don't understand is – why me?! What do I know about leases and that?!"

"Maybe Harry thought, *Liverpool male! Expert on everything! Ships, football, drink, women, greyhounds, land rentals!* He might've even wanted to help you out financially!" Chris picked up the bucket and mop and banged them down in the centre of John's desk. "You've advertised a service here!"

John lifted a forefinger, prior to addressing her, when there was another knock, loud and peremptory.

The door was flung open and a pair of eyes flashed from Chris to John. Round the room. Back to Chris for what seemed an instantaneous and complete assessment. Finally back to John.

John saw a dark, vivacious woman with bright scarlet lips, dressed in a black leather jacket. Black leather trousers, boots and gloves. A black leather bag, the size of a baby's cradle, slung over her shoulder. A raw intelligence / sexual projection / aggressiveness that immediately frightened him. Yet caused his heart to beat faster.

Mrs Raite casually unzipped her jacket. Beneath she wore a low-cut plum-coloured top. She breathed-in deeply, her bust expanding like an aircraft carrier's flight deck. A sweet, heavy perfume began to circulate the room.

"Just going," said Chris, staring at Mrs Raite. In a heavy Scouse accent, she added, "Next time I'll bring some carbolic, Mr O! Have a real clean-out!"

Under the woman's contemptuous stare, John helped Chris with her coat.

"You're a gentleman, sir!" said Chris. She swept out, leaving the door open.

John moved across to shut it. Then, conscious of his visitor's continuing scrutiny, moved behind the safety of his desk.

"Another satisfied client?" Mrs Raite's voice was like nothing John had encountered before.

He gestured to the other side of the desk and the battered canvas camp chair he'd put there for clients.

Mrs Raite began patrolling the office. Looked into the kitchen. The bathroom. Gave a theatrical shudder. Pulled across the purple velvet curtain to John's sleeping area. Finally walked over and stood considering *Celestial Vision*. Stirred the works round the skirting board with her toe. "You get many perverts?"

John picked up a pen. Opened his notepad. "You want me to find you one?"

"Bestiality."

John gestured incomprehension.

"Sitting on the steps outside. Magazine with a dog on the cover... Perhaps knows Ronnie."

Fucking Hell! Harry! Waiting for Chris to leave! "Client friend," said John. "Helping him negotiate premises for a dog shelter. Part of our charity arm... Saving greyhounds."

Mrs Raite turned back to *Celestial Vision*. "Collector?" she asked.

John nodded complacently.

"Visit many galleries?"

"Well..."

She gestured round the office. "Though disguising your *connoisseur* status?"

John flushed.

Mrs Raite smiled. "Ronnie's into art! His real obsession. Not the Porsches, not the 'films'. Never me. No. Just 'Art'! But just can't do it himself… A bad place to be." She peered at the signature. "Ar… i… an? Is that an 'i'?"

John nodded judiciously. "Arian. Known to his friends as ''Arry'. Yes. Arian. Religious heretic. See the halo? Didn't believe in the Trinity, so the halo signifies that while God is God, Christ was a bit less…"

Mrs Raite gave a short, sharp, bark of laughter. Moved one or two of the paintings against the skirting board with her toe. "I've seen some of these before."

"How?"

"It's called 'education'." Mrs Raite kicked at the paintings. "Copies from art books, galleries, old masters, young pretenders, old pretenders like Ronnie." She crossed the room and positioned herself behind the camp chair, leaning over it, and placing her arms on its arms. A lopsided smile that would fix her face in a male mind like a watermark.

John held out a hand. "John O'Rourke."

"Mrs Elizabeth Raite."

John sat. Steepled his fingers. Peered round the mop bucket Chris had thumped on the desk. "How can I help you, Mrs Raite?"

Mrs Raite slowly peeled off her gloves. She had large sticking plasters on the backs of her hands. She rummaged in her bag and took out John's poem ripped from the *Albion*. Read out the verse. "That you?"

John nodded nonchalantly.

81

"Are you on drugs?"

John gestured indefinably.

"I need someone to find my husband – Ronald 'Ronnie' Raite."

John stood. Raised a finger. "Before you tell me more. Coffee?"

Mrs Raite gestured for John to sit. He did so.

"My husband, after treating me both cruelly and *unnaturally…* is now refusing to pay alimony. Left London and is now up here waiting to *escape…*"

"Here in Liverpool?"

"The Wirral Peninsula."

John moved the mop bucket to one side. "But if you know where he is…?"

"Mr O'Rourke. The Wirral's a big place. Well. A big place full of small places. But also full of smart money…"

They stared at each other.

"How sure are you that he's on the Wirral?"

"When we were still married. Still a business…"

John raised the pen. "Business?"

"We once spoke of our homes – as you do between arguments. He told me – some poet or other – *Home's the place where – no matter what you've done – if you turn up – they've got to let you in.* Not that they'd let Ronnie in. Nor me. But also let slip his had been the Wirral… So that's where he'll be. Waiting."

"For someone to let him in?"

Mrs Raite nodded. "To America."

"America?"

"Where he imagines it will all be easy money and bang-at-it bimbos. The Yanks may think differently."

"Mmm…" John nodded. Scratched a few notes.

"So, the Wirral. And I need a quick result." The twisted smile once again.

"Is there a photo by any chance?" enquired John hopefully.

Mrs Raite delved back into her bag. Held out a photograph. A man leaning against a Porsche. *Porsches again…*

"About ten years ago?" John hazarded. "Five foot seven? Eight? Casual but sharp dresser… likes women… OK so far?"

He'd caught her interest. "That stuff? His height?"

"Porsches… Pretty low-slung. Won't be as big as he seems."

"Mmm…" Mrs Raite stared at John with wide eyes. "Bloody Porsches! Personal number plate, naturally: D-A-V-1-D."

"D-A-V-1-D?" said John.

"'DAVID'!"

"Thought his name was Ronnie?"

"The statue!" said Mrs Raite. "Michelangelo!"

John shrugged.

"Seventeen foot of throbbing, yet tremulous, testosterone. Another of Ronnie's 'How clever am I?' jokes."

John gestured incomprehension.

"The car in the photograph is a Porsche Carrera. *David* is made from Carrara marble!"

Fucking hell! What did Harry Rose say? Porsche Carrera! New tenant. The Wirral. Must fucking be! What was that village? West something… West… Heartway?

Heatwave? Heartwood! Cracked it already! Without moving from his chair! Go, O'Rourke!

She tapped the photograph with a blood-red nail. "The 'liking women' thing?"

John pointed. "That bit of a handbag. Edge of the print. Can't see who's carrying it but shows he likes women."

"Shows he likes something carries handbags," said Mrs Raite. "But you're right. It's me! Just out of the picture as usual!" From her bag she produced a white envelope. "Retaining fee – two hundred. Find him within a week – say, by next Monday – another hundred. Any longer I'll try elsewhere – and will want a hundred and fifty of this back!"

"And it's defo alimony? I mean, anything else I should know?"

The crooked smile.

"Mrs Raite? Why doesn't he just catch a plane to the States?"

"Planes give him a sinking feeling."

"So he'll be going by sea?"

"You know, maybe you've got what I hoped..." She leaned further over the chair. Held out the envelope. Large grey eyes with gold flecks. Eyelashes like sable paintbrushes.

John stared. Two hundred pounds, plus another hundred because he already knew where this Raite fella was. 'Course, only Harry Rose knew the actual address, and John couldn't ask him anyway, what with Harry now eyeing up Chris... And he would have to look as if he'd earned the cash. Go across there. The Wirral... Maybe a second-hand car. Someone in the Café des Artistes would know someone. He put out a hand and tentatively took the envelope.

Mrs Raite smiled knowingly. Stood and stretched provocatively. "Must push on. Bogger, you know…"

"Bogger?"

Mrs Raite made a gun of her first two fingers. Pressed them against the side of her head. "Though he seems happy enough at the moment. Thinking about the Spanish Inquisition, death camps, possibilities…"

John stared down at the desk. Yes or no? But three hundred quid! He took up his pen. "So! A few details?"

"Details?"

"Address," said John. "Telephone number, contact times…"

Mrs Raite leaned slowly across the desk. Took John's pen from his hand. As she did so, the front of her top fell away. On the palm of John's hand she wrote a number. "Where we're staying. Ask to be put through."

John stared, mesmerised.

She released his hands, straightened, then deliberately raised her top upwards from the waist. "Now you've seen them. Want to feel them?" She lowered the top slowly. Laughed a laugh the likes of which John had never heard before. She walked to the door. "Don't ring without a result. I'll be available eight to 8.15 every day this week. If Bogger answers, be understanding. Something of a rough diamond."

"Mrs Raite? Why me?"

"Initially, the verse… I admire people trying to better themselves." The lopsided smile. Then, "You like old movies?"

He stared at her.

"At school. Our girlish fantasies. Once we'd finished sampling each other's tuck boxes… *O'Rourke of the Redcoats*?"

"Think maybe I've… "

"Scarlet jacket… White piping… Glistening helmet." She sauntered out, leaving the door open.

Will no one ever close the door?!

John stared round the office. At the envelope lying on the desk. The number on his hand. He took the two hundred pounds from the envelope. Transferred it to his wallet. On his notepad, wrote, '£200 + £100 = £300'. Rechecked his wallet. Recounted the notes. Stood and punched the air. Grinned a knowing grin. Focused on *Celestial Vision*. Walked across and adjusted it. Walked to the door. Stared back round the 'floffice'. Grinned another knowing grin. Put out the light.

SEQUENCE 21

FRIDAY, 19th FEBRUARY, 1982. 19.30
INT / NIGHT CRUST'S FLAT

"She's consulted this private eye type." Crust doodled a keyhole through which was peering a disembodied eye.

"She take Bogger?" asked the Voice.

"No need," said Crust. "Some wannabe amateur… Tosser advert in the local paper."

"So why him?"

"Not sure. Someone who knows nothing and no one? No backup or clout but local so might touch lucky?"

"Be putting him under the pump? Bit of fear into his life?"

"Next day or so."

"Roger that," said the Voice.

The line went dead.

Crust, still holding the receiver to his ear, drew a speech balloon coming out of the far side of the keyhole. Inside the balloon he wrote, 'BOO!'

SEQUENCE 22

FRIDAY, 19th FEBRUARY, 1982. 20.00
INT / NIGHT. BAYONETS

In The Bayonets, at the domino table, Mr O'Rourke said, "A real one? A real client?"

"So our Chris said," Curly told him.

"Woman, too? Bit unusual."

"What?" asked Curly.

"Can't see any Judy round here going to a private eye."

"Just waltzed in, Chris said. Dead posh."

"But Chris *had* cleaned up? So this Judy wouldn't get a bad impression?"

"Still must've seen the paintings," said Curly.

Mr O'Rourke shook his head. "So, Chris and John. How they seem to be getting on?"

Curly said quickly, "More to the point, Mr O, how are *you*?"

Mr O'Rourke gestured to the racing pages of his paper. Around The Bayonets. "Anyway. He's coming tomorrow, John; collect his crime library."

Curly stood. Pointed at Mr O'Rourke's glass. "Another?... That'll cost him a few bob, getting them books into town. Have to be a taxi."

Mr O'Rourke handed his glass to Curly. "This new car he's just bought."

Curly stopped dead. "New car?"

"Someone in this *café* he goes to. Know it?"

"Fucking dump. Didn't mention no new car to me!"

Mr O'Rourke shrugged uneasily.

Mick, sensing blood in the water, moved behind the pumps. Pulled out the end of his shirt. Began polishing a glass.

Curly gave a twisted laugh. "Still. Haven't been down the office the last few days, so maybe just lost track a bit..."

Mick coughed. Shook his head. Gave himself a double brandy.

"He know you need a driving licence?" added Curly.

"He's got one," said Mr O'Rourke.

"What?!" Curly, unable to look at Mr O'Rourke, turned towards Mick, who began to whistle tunelessly.

"Took lessons when he got the redundancy," said Mr O'Rourke. "Said it would come in handy one day."

Curly stood staring downwards.

"Curl..." said Mr O'Rourke. "I mean. You know John..."

"I'm beginning to."

Mick struck the pub's brass ship's bell, inscribed

'*Marie Celeste*'. "Touch gloves. Come out fighting!" Gave a donkey-like bray of laughter.

"Yeah," said Mr O'Rourke. "Though really appreciates you're in with him… Really does."

"Course," said Curly. "We haven't got a phone in yet at home – though our Chris has ordered one – so really there was no way for John to let me know… about the car and that."

"Look," said Mr O'Rourke. "Let's have another… Get the bones out… or the crib board… have a couple of hands. I mean, John… well… This car, business… Well… Just probably forgot to let you know. Right?… Just probably forgot to let you know!… "

Mick struck the bell manically. "Women and children first!" He shouted "Women and children first!"

SEQUENCE 23

SATURDAY, 20th FEB, 1982. 11.00
INT / DAY METHUSELAH'S ANTIQUES

Raite entered Methuselah's Antiques to a grinding sound of 'Jingle Bells' from a plastic reindeer and sleigh alarm system taped to the top of the shop door.

Methuselah's had begun as a large car-repair workshop/garage. Tool racks and shelves still bolted to the whitewashed stone walls. Near the door stood two pairs of oxyacetylene bottles – now with their own price tags and World War II gas masks perched on top. In the centre of the floor, like a Hampstead Arts Council commission, was a large, rusting, manual, tyre-changing apparatus.

In Hampstead, there would have been a hand-milled Cornish slate plaque: *Sloughing Skins on Life's Eternal Wheel: A Brutalist Meditation:* Dame Tamsyn Twitchett-Twonks MA., RA., A.A.

Here, in Methuselah's, there was a torn piece of cardboard on which was scrawled, in red boot polish, '£15 o.n.o.'

Raite looked round.

Methuselah was bent over a sometime steel workbench, now doubling as the shop counter. A jeweller's loupe in one eye. The other fixed on Raite.

Raite strolled over.

Methuselah's shiny brown toupee had a straight fringe which rested just above what were now fully revealed as Methuselah's tiny, expressionless, crusted, red-rimmed eyes. Beginning between the eyes, and expanding out like a slice of pepperoni pizza, was a large, flat nose ending just above a rosebud mouth and tiny, pointed chin, from which sprouted a wispy, yellowish 'soul-patch' beard. Down either side of his nose, like poems in Braille, blackheads clustered in groups. Methuselah's clothing was a cut-down clergyman's cassock complete with black cloth buttons. Methuselah pulled on his beard and smiled, revealing overlarge false teeth. "Browsing, sir? Or perhaps already spotted something? If so, at Methuselah's, 'Negotiation' is our middle name!"

"Quite a bit." Raite swivelled slowly on his heels. "I've spotted quite a bit."

"Really, sir?"

"Export market," said Raite.

"Thought you had that 'container trade' look! We *are* talking America?"

"Warehouse in New York," said Raite.

"Then definitely trade?"

Raite nodded.

Methuselah threw a knobbly, much-beringed finger, skyward. "Then you, sir, will know how bad things are for us 'normal' dealers without your sort of access!... Business the way it is – I couldn't sell the Crown Jewels if they came inside a platinum dildo shaped like Rudolph Valentino's dick."

Raite took out a wad of notes from his pocket. "How much?"

"For...?"

Raite made a grand gesture.

"All of it?!"

Raite nodded.

Methuselah froze like a Komodo dragon, right down to the unwinking, encrusted red eyes. Exhaled a cloud of cinnamon-scented breath. "Cash?"

Raite nodded.

Methuselah paused. "If one might ask how one heard of us?"

"Walter Gabriel type. Land Rover and leggings."

"Ah!... Him!"

They paused, contemplating the possible consequences of even *knowing* someone like the Countryman. But the present opportunities were too good.

"So!" said Methuselah. "We *are* talking everything?!"

Raite nodded.

Methuselah began to rub his hands together. "Well, sir," he said eventually, "as one *entrepreneur* to another: you know some of this stuff is fake, right?"

"'I like to do a good fake now and then'."

"What's that?"

"Picasso story."

"Interesting case," said Methuselah. "Picasso…"

"A shop," said Raite. "Out of the way. Antique-look, working phone; shortest lease negotiable; half-decent painting for window dressing…"

Methuselah put one hand under the counter. Came up with a painting in a wooden frame. Signed. Dated clearly: 1926. A pale, fashionably dressed, slightly elongated woman strolling across grass among attenuated pale trees. "*Green Park*," he said.

Raite turned it over. The backing paper was lifted; the frame nails loose.

"Thought there might be another behind," explained Methuselah. "Felt heavier than it looked."

Raite stared into space. The *Magdalen* framed behind another painting? Finally he nodded. "OK… Some half-decent stuff for the living room of this hovel I'm renting. Rug, lamp, another painting, etc. Right sort of handyman to fit an intercom; deadlock to the front door. All done yesterday."

Methuselah crossed his hands in front of his chest. Bowed slightly.

"And two shipping containers."

Methuselah stared.

"For all this." Raite waved casually around. "And more!"

"More?!" Methuselah copied Raite's gesture.

"Second- and third-hand throw-out office furniture," said Raite.

Methuselah squinted one eye.

"Desks with locked and jammed drawers. Locked heavy-duty filing cabinets that won't open – but have no keys anyway."

"Lost me now, sir. But!… Is one actually expecting to sell these… ah… ah… ah… 'mid twentieth-century white-collar artisan artefacts' – to a New York clientele?"

"Jam-packed as solidly and awkwardly as possible in the containers. Delivered ASAP to the Seaforth Container Terminal in Liverpool, using the new shop address. There's a ship – *Ocean Seaspray* – sails in two weeks: Friday 12th March for New York. To be consigned to her."

"Little time, much effort!" mused Methuselah.

Raite laid the bundle of notes on the counter.

Methuselah picked up a quill made from an oil-soaked seagull's feather fitted with a biro refill. "Now, sir. Under what name?"

Raite considered.

"He who has two names has two weapons," said Methuselah.

Raite hesitated.

"I wasn't always Methuselah," said Methuselah.

"Mr Porsche," said Raite finally.

"Like the car?"

"To the last umlaut."

"No," said Methuselah sadly. "I wasn't always Methuselah."

SEQUENCE 24

In Flour Street, Mr O'Rourke sat poring over the *Albion*'s 'Deaths' column.

The kitchen door opened. John entered. "Anyone you know?" he asked, pointing at the paper.

His father shook a disappointed head. "Tea?... Can of mild?"

"Better be tea." John coughed self-consciously. "New car and that."

Mr O'Rourke rose. Took the teapot to the geyser. "Got your books down from your room. Put them in those boxes in the hallway."

"Yeah. Tripped over them."

"Can't you be grateful for anything?!" said Mr O'Rourke shortly as the teapot filled. Then, more moderately, "Curly said you had this Judy came to see you?"

"Out-of-town London type, wants me to find her husband. Alimony thing. Thinks he's hiding out on the Wirral till he does a flit to the States." John handed over the photo of Raite.

"The Wirral?" said Mr O'Rourke, handing it back.

"So she says."

"What do *you* say?"

"Well. Rang round a few places. 'Mr Ronald Raite'. No joy."

"A *few* places? Has the Wirral shrunk?"

"Thing is, I sort of know roughly where he is; place called West Heartwood. Near the motorway leads to Liverpool and the docks."

"Not the one leads to Speke Airport and a plane to America?"

"His missus says he's afraid of flying. Avophobia."

"'Avophobia'?" said Mr O'Rourke.

"So it'll have to be by sea."

"So how did this West Heartwood come up?"

"Bit of a long story." John tapped the side of his nose. "But when I rang directory enquiries... 'No such subscriber exists.'"

"Let's think about it," said Mr O'Rourke, "while we load-up your reference library."

They walked into the hall. Looked at the six cardboard boxes. John opened the front door. They stepped into the street. John's car was standing at the kerb. Squat. Malign. Pronounced list. Hand-painted in magenta/plum red/crimson/diarrhoea brown. Old rust already showing through the new paint.

"The *Baker Street Express*," said Mr O'Rourke. "How much?"

"Two twenty... Bargain. This café I go. Owner's mate's emigrating. Six months tax. New MOT. New battery."

"It's you needs the MOT. Christ, John! It's got more miles on it than a Poor Clare's rosary!"

John pulled a piece of bodywork from the door. "Dad! I'm on forty quid a week from the Enterprise Allowance." He gestured back to the hallway.

They dragged the book boxes to the boot of the car.

"Spiders'll have to get themselves rehoused…" Mr O'Rourke lifted a hand to signify a pause for breath.

John lifted the lid of one of the boxes and gazed down at the top book – *Flesh for Sale!* The cover showed Brick hanging by the belt of his trench coat from the end of a flagstaff that protruded through a skyscraper window. Clinging to one of his legs was a young woman with hair of iridescent yellow wearing a short skirt and half a blouse. The skirt had ridden up above her waist to expose a purple suspender belt and matching briefs. Leaning out of the window, glaring down, was a man with a yellowish complexion wearing a pair of dark glasses with lenses like frying pans. One hand holding a giant syringe dripping thick bright green liquid.

John stared at the purple briefs. Twitched involuntarily, thinking of Mrs Raite.

They manoeuvred the boxes into the boot. Lowered the lid, tying it to the back bumper with a piece of string.

"Fancy a sit inside?" John asked. He helped his father into the passenger seat, then walked round and climbed into the driver's seat.

"Christ, John! It's freezing! Why is this window open?" Mr O'Rourke tried the winder, which turned aimlessly.

"Fancy a spin?"

"My bad foot's cramped… Does this chair move back?"

"Top of my to-do list. Now. Just listen this engine. Specially tuned for me." John turned the key. There was a whirr, then silence. He tried again. "Needs a minute… Just flooded."

"As Noah said."

John stared out of the window. Retried the starter. The car whirred again.

Mr O'Rourke said, "John. Life's too short."

"Dad. Just want to take you round the block, so you can tell the lads you've been in it."

"Who'd be interested?!" said Mr O'Rourke shortly. Then, seeing John's disappointment, "So! This Ronnie Raite…"

John shook his head. "Like I said, I've rung and rung but no one's heard of a new subscriber called Raite." He retried the starter. "Course, engine might need a bit of running-in…"

"Let's see that photo again. We're waiting for lift-off."

John took out the photograph given to him by Mrs Raite.

His father looked at it. "What's that he's draped over?"

"Porsche. Loves them. Children he's never had?"

"How d'you know he's never had any?"

John tried the starter again. There was the hint of a mechanical cough.

Mr O'Rourke said, "Alimony, you said?"

"Yeah. Though can't see how someone like her got shacked up with someone like him. She's something else, Dad! She really is."

His father tapped the photograph. "I don't believe it for a minute."

"What?"

"Alimony… And why you? Why not some big agency? That shithouse of an office you're in. 'Far as she knows, you couldn't find your way out of a paper bag."

"She saw my poem in the *Albion*!" said John sharply. "Sensed what I have to offer. Plus, this film – *O'Rourke of the Redcoats* – seems I remind her of its star. Sentimental stuff."

"Yeah. About as sentimental as a bosun's fist."

John stared. "Come on," he said, pressing the starter. "What have you got?"

"You've picked a queer business." Mr O'Rourke looked him fully in the face.

"I won't have one at all if I can't come up with Monty Macho." In the silence, John struck the car keys with his fingernail.

Mr O'Rourke sighed. "I don't suppose there can be many with a name like that – even on the Wirral."

"Dad! What have you got?!"

"Mr Porsche?" said his father. "Noted car fanatic."

John turned the key. The engine spluttered into life. "It works!" he shouted.

"Occasionally," said Mr O'Rourke.

SEQUENCE 25

SUNDAY, 21ˢᵗ FEBRUARY, 1982. 16.00.
INT / DAY CRUST'S FLAT

"A car?!" said the Voice.

"More 'Frank's pram'." said Crust. "Parking it behind his office building… Old wartime bomb site." He doodled a rocket ship on a launching pad, fire and exhaust gases coming from its tail.

"Things moving, then?"

"Could be…"

"Busking Bill?"

"Permanently parked up other side of the bomb site from O'Rourke's. Plenty of wrecked lorries, other old cars, trailers, old fridges, general shit in between. Bill's OK… Got his sleeping bag, fags, plastic pineapple with removable lid to piss in…"

"Oh, to be young again," said the Voice. "Back in the field."

Both laughed.

SEQUENCE 26

MONDAY, 22nd FEBRUARY, 1982. 16.30.
INT / DAY JOHN'S OFFICE

John picked up the phone once more.

"So what makes you think he's calling himself 'Porsche'?" asked Curly.

John placed one finger alongside his nose. "Elementary, my dear Curly." Began to dial. Mouthed, 'Coffee' in Curly's direction.

Curly stared blankly for a second, then picked up John's cup off the desk and slowly moved towards the kitchen cubbyhole.

There was a knock on the door.

Curly stopped dead.

John put down the phone. In a no-nonsense voice, shouted, "Come in!"

The door swung slowly forward – but no one appeared.

John and Curly stared at the gap. At each other.

Then a large figure wearing a railwayman's overcoat filled the door frame. A balloon curly grey head. Loose-snaggle-toothed mouth. A slow all-encompassing gaze.

John saw authority. Stood. Smiled accommodatingly. "Afternoon, sir!" Walked round the desk. Extended a hand. "John O'Rourke. Private investigator."

"Detective Inspector Crust. Public nuisance." Crust walked across and stood before *Celestial Vision*. Pointed at the paintings round the skirting boards. "Yours?"

John scratched his ear. "Came with the lease. Done by the last tenant. Actually a squatter who sort of left them here."

"Not technically theft, I suppose." Crust stirred a group of paintings with his toes. "After Renoir... After Magritte... After a night on the plonk." He lifted down *Celestial Vision*, closed one eye and tried to read the signature. "'A... r... i... an'?"

"Arian," said John. "Signature used by this squatter, 'Arry. Religious heretic."

Crust turned over the painting. "Cheap frame. Buy cheap, buy trouble." He rehung it. "Got a kettle?"

John said, "Curly...?"

Curly again hesitated, then sauntered into the cubbyhole. The tap ran.

Crust pointed to John's chair. John sat.

"No," began Crust. "No. I'm not your ordinary 'scuffer'. Three packs of smokes a day. Double beef curry and chips every night, washed down by a bottle of Scotch. Even got OU credits!"

The kettle began to whistle.

John cleared his throat. "What is it, Inspector? I mean, what do you want?"

"To be liked, I suppose. Most coppers do… Except those that very definitely don't. A type you wouldn't take to at all. Nor them to you!"

Curly came back with two cups of coffee. He handed one to John; the other to Crust. "Milk's gone off."

Crust took a sip. Opened his greatcoat. Yellowy shirt. Pale blue knitted woollen tie. Set-of-handcuffs tiepin. "I'll give an example. Nothing more memorable than a good example. Years ago, we'd trawl the streets of Liverpool two a.m. – just after the clubs let out. 'Why am I being arrested?' they'd shout. As if two in the morning wasn't enough. Back at the Bridewell, lads'd say, 'Bend your truncheon round the bastard's head, Sarge, that'll quieten him down!' or 'Kick him in the bollocks, Sarge! Give him something to scream about!' But that wasn't my style, so not even my own kind respected me! Though in the end they did. Know why?"

Curly and John stared.

"Promotion! Everybody respects and likes the boss. At least, if they've any fucking sense they do. They listen to him carefully; answer his questions truthfully. And my question to you is…" Crust turned to John. "Why are you here?"

"Like yourself. I fancied being a boss."

Crust shook his head. "I assume it's me and my kind paying your wages?"

"Who's paying yours?" asked Curly.

Crust pointed his cup towards Curly. "Where's he fit in? Young Dombey? Actually, it's two novels: *Dombey and Son and Dombey and Daughter.*" He held out his empty cup towards Curly.

Curly remained motionless.

Crust moved leisurely across, took one of Curly's hands and put the cup in it. Closed Curly's fingers round the cup. Walked back across to look at *Celestial Vision*. Turned back to John. "Nothing official... not yet. No 'sworn statements'; 'Accompany me to the station'. Just a bit of info. Want to tell me about her?"

"Client confidentiality," said John.

"They say policing's moved to a new era. But those lads I mentioned... Still a few down there at the Bridewell."

"Thatcher's seen to that," said Curly.

"Me, though?" said Crust. "I prefer 'swamp with enquiries', 'check licences', 'ring the Enterprise Allowance Board'. And suddenly. Bang!... Back to the bedding factory!"

After a pause, John said, "Wants me to find her husband."

"Fucking hell!" muttered Curly.

"Alimony stuff," John added.

"Find him where?" said Crust.

"She says he's on the Wirral. Where exactly? Well, that's my job..."

"*Our* job!" said Curly.

"The plan?" asked Crust.

"Ring around for him."

"Why didn't I think of that?!" said Crust. Straightened *Celestial Vision* slightly. Left without closing the door.

"Think anyone'll ever shut that door?" asked John.

"He doesn't think the painter's called Arian," said Curly.

"So much for the Open University."

Curly said, "Know why I really gave up boxing?"

John stared.

"See the way his hand closed round mine?" Curly smiled. "My hands... My physique. Never going to make heavyweight. And if you can't be a heavyweight..."

John shrugged. Picked up the phone again and dialled directory enquiries.

"What town, please?" asked the operator.

"West Heartwood, Wirral."

"The name, please?"

"Mr Porsche. He'll be a new subscriber."

There was a pause. John and Curly stared at each other.

"I'm sorry, caller... " the operator began.

John snapped, "I said he'll be a new subscriber!"

After a pause, the operator said coldly, "That number is ex-directory."

John mumbled an apology as the connection broke. Looked at Curly. "He's there, Curl! He's actually there!"

Curly stared respectfully. "Gold, mate! Gold! You done it. Hats off to you on this one, partner."

They grinned at each other. Shook their heads and laughed.

"Time for a pint?" asked Curly.

"Yeah! And my shout! The boss solved it; the boss gets them in! Tell you what..." John gestured expansively. "Charlie Cup-of-Char!"

"Charlie...?"

"OK, fella's a bum – his no-mark music career – but today's the day the *Donnelly* docked, right?"

Curly grinned brightly. "Right."

"We'll give him a knock on the way down."

"Right."

"I mean. If you can't help those haven't got what you've got, who can you help?!"

SEQUENCE 27

WEDNESDAY, 24ⁿᵈ FEBRUARY, 1982. 16. 45
INT / DAY HARRY ROSE'S FAMILY HOUSE

The other side of West Heartwood to Raite's prefab, Harry Rose stood before the door of his mother's 'sitting room'. He drew breath. Knocked. Entered.

His mother sat cocooned in a nest of pillows on a well-stuffed two-seater brocaded couch standing on a large oriental carpet. Opposite her was her 'Ottoman ottoman'; a television on top. Against one wall an eighteenth-century sideboard. Next to her, an occasional table with a radio and magazines. At one time the table would have held books. On the walls, five paintings in gold frames. Two were nineteenth-century ships: one a sailing ship; one a sail-assisted steam vessel. The other three oils were portraits. A Merchant Marine captain standing on a poop deck at the top of the ladder up from the main deck, leaning on an ornate cane and gazing out with an iron face; his equally iron-faced mastiff at his side. The other two portraits were early twentieth-century 'university vice-chancellor/wing commander' school. Ship's business rather than biscuits. Managerial class. Guarding the interests built by the iron-faced captains. The room was very hot. Harry's mother wore a shawl.

Harry seated himself next to the television on a Victorian nursing chair. Stared down at the designs in the carpet. How many times had he done this? His mother muted the television. Began flicking between Harry and the screen.

"I was wondering…" he began. "The possibilities we discussed…"

"Yes. And I feel… well… it's just too big now… a lot of unnecessary bills. Made some enquiries… Nursing homes in Chester… "

"Yes… Yes…" Harry's eyes remained fixed on the carpet.

"Not immediately, though perhaps sooner rather than later… And my wants – needs – all, I think, getting a bit too much for Anne…"

Now Harry looked directly at her. "And Anne…?"

"I'll arrange a small flat. Chester. Near her relations. An annuity… Speaking of which… Our seafaring arm… We've been talking about investment."

"Their advice?"

"Shipping is still fine. But perhaps – again – sooner rather than later – containers?"

"Where it's all heading…" said Harry.

"Naturally, your name came up. Command? Or you might consider early retirement? Sit on one or two of the boards?"

"I'm not going for command, Mother. I've had enough of people being ordered about."

"Surely you don't intend to end up as – what did your father call them? – a 'professional mate'?"

"I'm looking at things *I* might want to do…"

"Your dog project? *All the virtues of man and none of the vices.* Was that Byron?"

Harry shrugged. "I'd have to ask Captain Barratt… Though with him it would have to be sea dogs."

They smiled tentatively, but with an undercurrent of warmth.

"No," said Harry. "Still trying to get to see that vacant property…"

"Why not let me? One or two calls…"

"I'd rather do it myself."

"Though with this place now being empty from next year…"

"That's definite, is it?"

"Rose Hall House… Of course, we lost the first Rose Hall in the Crimea."

"Went with all hands," said Harry. "Widows and children left with nothing."

"So… Your project. Perhaps run from here? The old stable block for the kennels?"

"We could certainly think about it."

His mother went still. "You're hiring staff?"

"Perhaps someone to handle day-to-day chores while I'm setting things up."

"Who is he?" asked his mother.

Harry looked up once more. "A private detective I've met… His assistant. I mentioned the idea. She seemed quite interested…"

Out of the stillness. "What's her name?"

"Chris… Christine, I suppose."

"Liverpool?"

"Very much so."

"I see," said his mother. They stared at each other. "Perhaps – when your plans are more advanced – you might like to bring her here to look round?"

"Thank you. I'll certainly bear that in mind."

"And I'll look into you going on one or two of the boards. If we're moving into container ships, who better to advise than yourself?"

Harry stared at her for a moment. Stood. They nodded to each other. Harry began to leave.

At the door he turned. "That annuity for Anne. It *will* be index-linked?"

SEQUENCE 28

WEDNESDAY, 24nd FEBRUARY, 1982. 19.15
INT / NIGHT MERCEDES OVERLOOKING MERSEY

Bogger sat in the driving seat of the Mercedes, Mrs Raite next to him. Parked up overlooking the Mersey. The river was dark and quiet. A few ships' lights up and down the seaway. The Birkenhead Ferry churning water as it manoeuvred alongside the Liverpool Landing Stage.

"Don't mind me asking, Liz – What's it do for you? This sort of thing?"

"No idea. You'd need to talk to some of my psychiatrists."

Bogger stared out through the windscreen. "Fucking dump, you ask me. Thought it was a big port?"

"A hundred years ago we'd have been looking at a forest of masts and men."

"So what happened?"

"Americans wanted dropping off nearer London… Liverpool beginning to consider itself irreplaceable…"

"Which no one is, eh, Liz?"

"Certainly not to the person who replaces them."

"Scouse chancers," said Bogger. "All them strikes you read about… Good day's work'd kill them."

Mrs Raite sighed. "We need to get back. O'Rourke left that desk message; he's ringing at eight."

"Think he'll've got anywhere?"

She shook her head. "Meet him, you feel he couldn't solve a two-piece jigsaw with Einstein leaning over his shoulder… But… well… a feral intelligence. Plus he's smelt money… Plus he wants to please me… And be told what to do…"

"'Oh, Jeeves! Peel me a grape!'" said Bogger in an affected voice. He began to massage the back of her neck in a slow, intimate fashion.

"Someone's got to give them orders," said Mrs Raite tiredly.

"'Them'? Who's 'them', Liz?" Bogger's massaging hand tightened slightly.

"Who's 'them' Bogger? Why, 'them's' 'them'! That's who 'them' is." She removed his hand from her neck. Gestured towards the gear lever.

Bogger obediently turned on the ignition.

SEQUENCE 29

John, Curly and Charlie sat in a pub near Moorfields. A smallish, deserted room off the main lounge. The three of them the only people in it, sitting round a table. In front of them, half-empty pint glasses and a full ashtray. Charlie stubbed out the cigarette he was smoking. Picked up the packet. Offered it to Curly and they lit up. John glanced covertly at his watch. Twenty to eight.

Charlie was detailing life on the rock 'n' roll road for Curly. "Yeah. Me 'n' Eddie, back of the roadie's van, always heading for the next gig and fame. Jars and a joint; girls waiting with open arms and legs…"

"Wow!" said Curly. "I mean, you hear tales…"

"Yeh. Groupies. All went like rabbits! Trying to hide in the van, the dressing rooms, props trunks, motorway services, that one in my bass drum case…"

Curly whistled.

"Begging for it! Stick to you like shit on a shoe till you said yes. Sex, drugs 'n' rock 'n' roll!… As for the Liverpool–Hamburg Scene…"

"All at it over there as well, were they, Charl?"

"Know the only German word I remember, Curl? 'Oma'! 'Grandmother'! This old doll we were all poking. Looked just like him; Omar Sharif… Right down to the moustache…"

Curly laughed. Slapped his knee. Drank. Pulled on his cigarette.

Quarter to. John stood. Mimed putting a phone to his ear. "Mrs Raite…"

Curly gestured at the table and the drinks. "Won't need me, will you, John?"

"Naw. Keep Charlie's memory company. All those exciting times he's had."

John finished buttoning his coat. Gazed idly towards the lounge door. The table next to it had been empty a few moments ago. Now there was a figure sitting at it in front of a half of bitter. Hippy type. Dirty brown duffel coat, hood pulled up about the ears. Jeans. Cowboy boots. One arm round a guitar; the other hand holding up a book in front of his face. The book dropped. A pair of eyes ringed by black bags. Face full of whiskers. A lazy stare. The book was lifted up again.

"I'll put a couple in for the two of you on my way out," said John. "We did good today!"

Curly gave him a double thumbs up; Charlie a knowing wink.

John moved towards the door to the main bar. As he passed the hippy's table he looked at the book. The cover showed the Devil on a surfboard riding a wave. One arm flung back; the other brandishing a trident. The title: *Surfing for Satan*. John stopped. The arm came from round the guitar. The book was lowered again. Another lazy stare; two fingers raised. 'Peace, man!' mouthed the hippy. Book raised once more. Arm back round the guitar.

John turned and looked back at the table he'd just left. Curly and Charlie, their heads together, laughing, stopped as one to look towards him. Their faces set. Blank.

John turned away to make his phone call.

SEQUENCE 30

In the motel, Bogger was sitting in an easy chair facing a low coffee table. On the table, a pack of playing cards laid out for patience. Mrs Raite was on the bed, propped up against the pillows, holding a drink.

Bogger drew his bathrobe aside to examine the underside of his penis, which resembled a Dead Sea Scroll. "Sort of itch, Liz… Most blokes, it's just pimples from pulling on it too much and not washing their hands."

The phone began to ring. Mrs Raite gestured towards it with her glass.

Bogger rose. Picked up the receiver. "Yeah?"

John's half-apologetic voice. "Er… Mrs Raite there, please?"

"Who's this?"

"Mrs Raite, please?"

Bogger pursed his lips. "Who are you, Nobbs?"

"John O'Rourke."

Bogger shouted, "O'Rourke geezer!" Waggled his penis at Mrs Raite.

Mrs Raite eased herself off the bed and took the receiver. Bogger went to the minibar. Poured a whisky. Moved over behind her. Began kissing her neck.

"O'Rourke?" said Mrs Raite, adjusting the receiver so Bogger could listen.

"Good news, Mrs Raite… Look. How about I call you 'Liz'?"

"Oi!" shouted Bogger.

"Yeah… Right… OK…" muttered John.

"Well?" asked Mrs Raite.

"Mrs Raite, your husband is now called 'Porsche' and living in West Heartwood on the Wirral."

"Excellent!" said Mrs Raite. "The address?"

"Er… Yeah… Well… Exactly *where* in West Heartwood is the next thing I need to work out. This call is more to bring you up to date."

"My very own palm tree."

"Fucking calendar!" shouted Bogger.

"Mrs Raite, you said to find out where he is. I've done that, so just wondering… That extra cash?… If I've qualified yet?"

Mrs Raite said quietly, "Yes and no. Ultimately… not quite. You'll need to go across there. The actual address; the set-up."

"I'm not sure about that," said John.

"I am."

"OK," said John. "If that's how I get the extra hundred?"

"Yes, that's how you get the extra hundred." Mrs Raite broke the connection.

Bogger nuzzled the back of her neck. "Want me to pay him a visit, Liz?"

"Not yet."

Bogger pulled aside his bathrobe. "How about being a good doggy? Something for Bogger's bone?"

Mrs Raite stared down. "Sometimes it seems it's me who's barking mad."

"Always an answer, Liz." Bogger pulled the dressing gown from her shoulders. "Always got an answer!"

SEQUENCE 31

In the office, John sat holding a cup of coffee. He bent to one side. Put a second bar on the electric fire. Leaned back and stared at *Celestial Vision*. Closed his eyes. Saw Mrs Raite raising her top. Opened his eyes. Took out his wallet. Counted the money again.

There was a sort of thump on the door which swung open to reveal Charlie clutching a can of cider. Another sticking up from his pocket. "All right, mate?!"

John hurriedly closed the wallet. Put it back in his inside pocket.

Charlie stared. Grinned. Rubbed his thumb and forefinger together. Pulled out the second can and made as if to toss it to John.

John held up one hand. "Working, Charlie! Back sharpish from the pub, aren't you? They put the towels on early or something?… Where's Curly?"

Charlie looked round the empty office. "Yeah. See you're busier than ever. Curly needed to go see his ma." He walked across and fingered the purple curtain that concealed the doorway to the bedroom. "'Left Bank of the Mersey'." Poked his head into the bedroom itself. Came across and stood before *Celestial Vision*. Turned to face John. "That right you used to try out mattresses for a living?"

John stood. Adjusted his anorak. Switched off the bars on the electric fire. Charlie drained the can of cider. Placed the empty on John's desk. Opened the second can.

"There *is* a bin, you know, Charlie."

Charlie took a drink. "Heard your Hoover the other day. Crept up thinking might've been the bikers back... Ones I saved you from..."

"So I could buy you more pints?"

"Knew it couldn't be you doing any cleaning, but stuck my head in anyway. Saw this blonde... Curly says it's his sister."

John shrugged. "Known them since they were kids."

Charlie nodded. "Clocked she's a bit younger than you... Fancy your chances there?"

"Got herself mixed up with this deadbeat husband... Now? Both of us just taking stock."

"Yeah?"

"But... yeah. Maybe I might say we're getting serious..."

"What would she say?"

"You ever get to know her, Charlie, you can ask her. And now..." John zipped his anorak.

"Just thought I'd stroll up; check you're OK. I might even've been a punter."

" 'Cept they usually knock. Wait till they're asked in."

Charlie took another drink. "Yeah... well. You know where I am. You ever need me..."

John laughed. "Think it'll ever come to that, Charlie? Me needing you?"

"Personally, La?... I'm sure of it!"

SEQUENCE 32

SATURDAY, 27th FEBRUARY, 1982. 23. 00
INT / NIGHT SHADY SADIE'S ESCORTS, CENTRAL
LONDON

The Manageress stood behind the counter. A very attractive blonde of about forty dressed in a business suit. A discreet walk-in office in Central West London. In front of her on the counter, a stack of business cards: 'SHADY SADIE'S ESCORT SERVICES'.

Down the phone, the Cavalier said, "Mainly known as the Cavalier… That's confidential, of course."

"Of course," said the Manageress. "And where would our escort be going?"

"Sort of up here… My place… Mansion House way."

"What's that like?" asked the Manageress.

"Piccadilly Line. Not too far in; not too far out. Not too cheap; not too expensive. Not too violent; not too lavender… Handy for the football…"

"And you still found us?"

"Got a few cards from telephone boxes. Didn't really feel right, so talked to this friend of mine who said maybe call you."

"I'd know your friend?"

"I can't tell you that, but both of us know George Manchell. I've got to say, you've a very pleasant voice…"

"Thanks. Appreciated. What age would she need to be?"

"Well, I'm something of a young late thirtyish… So maybe…"

"Early?… Mid twenties?"

"Sounds OK."

"Short or long visit?"

"I was thinking a few drinks, so maybe an overnight."

"Should be OK. Preferences?"

"Brunette. Bit of spirit. Curvy. Why don't you choose? Sure you've got impeccable taste."

The Manageress gave a low laugh. "Still here after five years so must be doing something right… OK. There's a girl called Florence might suit. Thing is, being Saturday all our overnights are booked – mainly for weekends. I can get you someone else now – quick visit. Then Florence on Monday. How's that sound?"

"I'll go with it. And you? Get any time off yourself?"

"Sorry," said the Manageress. "Spoken for. Well spoken for."

SEQUENCE 33

MONDAY, 1ˢᵗ MARCH, 1982. 11.30
INT/ DAY JOHN'S CAR. EXT / DAY WEST
HEARTWOOD

Like a bloodclot travelling through Caligula's brain, the *Baker Street Express* stopped, started, juddered, scudded and shuddered its way across West Heartwood town square. Feeling its way through a multitude of vehicles both backing in and backing out while performing three and four-point turns both on and off the pavement. Simultaneously, the village's booming geriatric population staggered backwards and forwards across the road in all gradations of absent-mindedness, bloody-mindedness, Alzheimer's and Parkinson's.

Curly, on a provisional licence, was driving the *Express*. John was navigating using an out-of-date road atlas. John wore a Paddy's Market Tattersall check sports jacket with brown plastic patches sewn onto its elbows. A blue pullover. A pair of brown cavalry twill trousers. Black rubber-soled shoes. A white shirt and black tie.

Curly had on jeans, a white T-shirt, a leather jacket, work boots, and a Liverpool FC scarf knotted round his neck.

"Half eleven," said John, consulting his watch. "That Mersey Tunnel's a killer this time of day… While as for Birkenhead!"

"Yeah." Curly ground the *Express* to a halt once more. "All them roads dug up… Like those photos of Berlin after the war."

"Plus that fuck-up at the tolls!" said John.

In a loud, aggrieved voice, Curly said, "How should I know you need the right money?"

"There was that sign, Curl. 'No Change Given'?"

"I was too preoccupied. That Woolly in that beat-up Morris Minor behind us… Right up my arse. No wonder I got confused."

"Yeah. Any closer he'd've been on the back seat asking for a fag. I turned round; give him a good staring-at. Big hat pulled down. Dark John Lennon specs. Big, tangly beard! Sure I'd seen him before…"

"Be from New Brighton," said Curly. "Somewhere like that."

The *Express* haemorrhaged forward once more. Reached the far end of the square. Still no parking space.

Curly turned up a side street and found a spot halfway along. "This'll have to do." He shook his head. "John? What exactly we doing here?"

"Waiting to spot Raite. That square has got to have half a dozen pub-type hotels."

"And…?"

"He'll be in one… Or we'll catch him going into one."

"Yeah?"

"Curl, the fella's a player! Tell by that photo. What do players do? Put themselves about! Pump barmen for info. Chat up barmaids…"

"He's a player wants to stay a player, which means, far as I can see, his missus not getting her hooks in him. He's not going to be putting nothing about."

Busking Billy's Morris Minor crept into the street and parked down and away from the *Express*.

John shrugged. Pushed open his door, which dropped six inches to rest on the pavement. "Ready?" he asked.

Curly gestured. "Mate! Look at my gear. At least you've got that sports jacket. I'd be well out of place. How about I stick here; read the paper?"

John shrugged. Swung his legs out onto the pavement.

"John. You really think this is about maintenance? Alimony?"

"Curly." John stopped halfway. "I don't care! What I think is that this is about her paying me – *us* – good money! This is about a *chance*."

He eased himself out the rest of the way. Relodged the door. Headed back down towards the square. Passed the Morris, glanced in. Same bloke from the Tunnel tolls. Dark anorak. Woollen cap pulled low over his head and some fucking paper or other up in front of his face. Guitar on the back seat. Had he seen him before? Someone like him?

John swung into the square. Came to a stop. Gazed around. Opposite was 'The Three Jolly Friars'. Nothing that looked like an entrance. He strolled across and spotted an arched passageway leading to a cobbled yard. *Right. Give that a miss!* The next gaff seemed more normal. 'Black Bess's Highwayman's Bothy'. John stepped up to the main door. Beams and whitewash. A parchment covered in italic writing in a glass case stuck on the wall. John looked at the tariff. At least they'd got the name right. Highway fucking robbery. Still…

He pushed inside. A reception desk. A blonde in a sheer white blouse. A smile of stellar intensity which faded rapidly as she assessed him. Behind her head, a sign: a silhouette of a levelled pistol pointing to 'Dick Turpin's Cave'. With a burning face, John turned, left the hotel, stared blindly round, then hurried back through the square and up the street where the *Express* was parked. He passed the Morris. The driver lying-back, newspaper over his face.

John climbed into the *Express*, tight-lipped with anger and shame. He slumped down wearing an expression of puzzled, but knowing, resignation. That born on the face of Velasquez's *Jester Named Don Juan of Austria*.

"How'd it go, mate?" asked Curly.

John shook his head. "If only this was one of Brick's…"

"John… "

"… Raite would come strolling round the corner right now. Yeh… 'Some call it expertise – Brick knows it's 'tecspertise'."

Curly pointed through the windscreen. A postman with a bag was pushing letters through doors.

"Yeah. They're called postmen," said John.

"Who know everyone's house and that? Who's new to the area…?"

John stared. "You know, Curl… Just had the same thought myself. But how do you talk to a Woolly? I mean…" He stared a moment, then exploded out onto the pavement and up the street behind the postman. "'Scuse me, mate!"

The postman turned. About fifty. Red cheeks and nose. Obviously some sort of 'old arse'. Peaked hat. Padded coat. Bundle of letters in one hand. He pointed at them with the other, thinking John might be claiming some mail.

"No, pal. Not letters. Look, I'll level with you. Been on the Old King Cole some time now. Finally got this start as a private eye…"

The postman blinked.

"Tracking down this fella been giving his missus a hard time. Really needs her alimony. Pay the bills. Feed her kids."

The postman nodded sympathetically.

"Know he's in the area; just can't get an address. So wondering…?"

The postman waved the bundle of mail. "What name?"

"Porsche," said John. "Like the car."

The postman thought. "No… Not on this round."

John spoke faster. "Antiques? Pictures? Anything, really…"

"There's a new shop," said the postman.

"Shop?"

"Recently rented. A painting in the window, on an easel. Swirls of cloth round it. That sound like it?"

John clapped the postman on the shoulder. "Mate! Exactly like it!"

SEQUENCE 34

MONDAY, 1st MARCH, 1982. 14.00
INT / DAY KITCHEN, FLOUR STREET

Mr O'Rourke, John and Curly sat in silence at the kitchen table in Flour Street. Mr O'Rourke turning the pages of the newspaper. Empty cup in front of him.

Chris was at the sink making tea. "So what happened next?" she asked, swinging the pot under the geyser.

John hunched over. "Acting upon information received…" he began in a gruff voice.

No one moved.

Curly, with controlled excitement, said, "Well, once we got the info off the postie, we ended up down some side street. This antique shop. Sort that's… that's…"

"Never open unless it's shut?" said Mr O'Rourke.

Curly and Chris laughed. John's gave a begrudging smile.

"Found a space," said Curly. "Parked up. Took a stroll past. Nothing but this painting on an easel."

"What was that like?" asked Chris.

"Bit different to those in John's office."

" 'Floffice', eh, Curl?" John smugly corrected him.

Curly turned quickly. "John! Don't ever! – Ever! – use that word again while I'm around!"

There was a paralysed silence.

"Pink cloth round it," continued Curly. "White card. That copperplate writing. Three hundred nicker – total con!"

"You'd know, would you, Curl?" asked John.

Chris brought the teapot to the table. Took off the lid for a final stir.

"At least it wasn't *Celestial Vision*!" said Curly.

"Yeah, well. The more I look at *Celestial Vision*, the more I come to value it for what it is!"

"You and all the other *Men Only* readers," said Mr O'Rourke.

More laughter. Chris went to a wall cupboard. Brought three cups to the table.

"Seem pretty much at home here now, Chris?" said John.

"Least she hasn't forgotten where 'here' is," said Mr O'Rourke.

Chris began pouring, milking and sugaring.

Curly said, "Anyway, John says to have a look round the back. I did, but all the buildings were really old and sort of higgledy-piggledy cramped; couldn't really tell which was which…"

"Any name over the shop?" Chris interrupted.

Curly shook his head.

Mr O'Rourke said, "Not even 'Mr A. Ferrari' or something?"

More laughter.

Curly said, "Talking about cars, though. There was this beat-up old Morris at the Mersey Tunnel, and then John said he thought it was parked up where we were first parked. Then, while looking at Raite's shop, it comes past again."

"See who was in it?" asked Chris.

"Beardy-weirdy-hippy type. Gave us a right looking-over as it sailed past."

"Felt I knew him," said John. "Or maybe just reminded me of Mikhail."

"Who?" asked his father.

"Mikhail Musteekoff, Mad Mandolinist of Minsk."

"Oh, him!" said Curly.

"One of Brick's," said John.

"Minsk?" said Mr O'Rourke. "In Russia?"

"See," explained John, "Brick's up for anything. No job too big or small. One day his hand's up someone's chimney feeling for their canary…"

Curly turned a laugh into a cough. Mr O'Rourke and Chris stared down at the table.

"… Next thing he's in Inner Outer Mongolia chasing Mikhail Musteekoff and his nuclear warhead samovar."

"Outer Inner Mongolia?" said Chris.

"Chris! *Inner Outer* Mongolia! Where Mikhail's bunked-up with his two judies – Valentina Vasilina, Viper of the Volga. And Natasha Nutski, Knoutmeister of Nizhny Novgorod. All living in this yurt made from the skins of Abominable Snowmen, playing duets on zithers, drinking yak-butter tea… "

"John!" said his father loudly.

After a dead silence, John continued. "Talking of which…" He winked at Chris and tapped the side of his empty cup.

Chris, in a light voice, said, "Maybe it's your turn, John! Maybe a cup of antifreeze. Power-steering pie… There's one in the fridge."

Smiling grimly, John leaned back and pulled open the fridge door. Empty except for a tin of condensed milk with thick, yellow, snot-like crud round its edges, and a packet with a few curled-up rashers of bacon.

"Something wrong?" asked Mr O'Rourke as all stared into the fridge. "Just don't eat as much as you get older."

"Leave it to me and Chris, Mr O," said Curly. "Soon get it soojied out and stocked up."

John went red. "That's on me!" he said savagely.

Everyone stared at nothing.

"Big thing," said John tightly, "is finding Raite's *actual* address. Not just the shop!"

His father said, "How?"

Chris gave a bright smile. "Maybe sleep on it. Tomorrow's another day."

"As is next Sat'dy!" said Curly excitedly. "St Joe's!… So get on your dancing shoes!"

"St. Joes?" said John "We really got time for that sort of thing?"

"Well, yeah" said Curly. "We promised Charlie."

"Charlie?" said John.

"When he helped out with the lock. We told him about The Nurgs being on first Sat'dy in March… Invited him along… Must remember, Mate!?"

"Charlie?" Said Mr O'Rourke. "Who's Charlie?"

"No. I don't remember no invites," said John tightly.

"Charlie Um-Pah-Bah," said Curly to Mr O'Rourke.

"Rock 'n' roll drummer," said Chris. "Great fella. Sometimes slips up to see me when John's out."

"Which you didn't think to mention?" asked John.

"Which I didn't know I had to," said Chris with her smile.

"Top skinsman in the old days…" said Curly quickly.

John laughed loudly and shook his head.

" Now looking to get into management," continued Curly. "Find a group. So, the Nurgs being on at St Joe's on Sat'dy…"

"'Um-Pah-Bah'?!" said Mr O'Rourke.

"Maybe not *just* your type, Mr O," said Chris. "But I know you'll like him."

"Hear that, Dad?" asked John.

"'Um-Pah-Bah'!" repeated Mr O'Rourke. "What sort of name's that?!"

"What's it matter?" said John. "Weren't you listening? You're going to like him!"

SEQUENCE 35

TUESDAY, 2nd MARCH, 1982. 10.00
INT / DAY CRUST'S FLAT

"Smart move," said the Voice. "Asking the postman."

"Maybe too smart," said Crust. "Like how he even found West Heartwood in the first place. Bloke you'd think couldn't find his arse holding its cheeks with both hands…"

"What else Bill say?"

"O'Rourke pumps the postie. Gets some info. Bill follows them in his Morris. Ends up outside this backstreet shop. Painting in the window. Price the other side of common sense."

"And?"

"I made a few calls," Crust continued. "Bloke took the shop lease is called Methuselah… Antiques dealer."

"You're going over?"

"Wouldn't miss it for a big clock."

"Swinging brass pendulums?" asked the Voice.

SEQUENCE 36

TUESDAY, 2nd MARCH, 1982. 10.30
INT/DAY CAVALIER'S FLAT

The Cavalier, lying in bed, still half-drunk, watched Florence wriggle into her briefs. "Cash's on the dresser," he slurred. Picked up the vodka bottle from the side of the bed. Took a gulp. Reached for the cigarettes.

Florence moved across to the dresser. The top drawer had a key in it. Standing with her back to the Cavalier, she picked up her money with one hand and gently pulled open the drawer with the other. Some bundles of notes in industrial rubber bands. Something that looked like an illustration torn from some old book – some sort of painting? And look! Same initials as hers! On top, the crumpled photo of Raite used for identification by the Cavalier.

Florence counted her money slowly as she pushed the drawer back with her stomach. Turned and began to count it again.

"Problem?" shouted the Cavalier from the bed.

"Just hoping for something for the service, lover."

"Fifteen per cent!"

"And very grateful, sugar."

The Cavalier took another swig from the vodka bottle. "Hey, Florence? Thought about a modelling career?"

"Not that kind, sugar. My mum and everything…"

"Gets the mags, does she?"

Still thinking, Florence clipped on her bra, slipped on her top, pulled on her trousers. Stepped into her heels. Picked up her fur coat. *Keep it light.* She walked across the room and stood before a painting hanging on the wall. "What's it mean?"

"Whatever you want it to."

"It got a title?"

"Yeah. *See You Next Time.*" The Cavalier swung himself off the bed.

She shrugged into her coat. He followed her to the door of the flat and opened it – but left the chain on. Stared at her. He'd sensed something.

She grabbed his penis. Tugged it playfully. "Ding! Ding! All aboard!" Forced herself to stare into his eyes. "How about tomorrow?"

He hesitated. Shook his head. "Nah. Like to spread it when I've got it…"

"Your loss."

"As they say in the VD clinics."

"At Sadie's we've all got certificates. From a *real* doctor!"

He unhooked the chain. Half-opened the door. Still staring questioningly.

"Chains and locks," she tried. "Got something valuable tucked away?"

His stare intensified. Fuck! She'd given him it. She tried to make herself look smaller.

"That outfit you're with," said the Cavalier. "Shady Sadie's. Said I should give them a ring… How you came across…"

She knew there was fear in her eyes. "Pleasant and obliging, I hope. Give the customer what he wants. That's what they tell us."

She nodded; slipped past him and down the hall in one movement. Thank God he hadn't been totally sure. Was still half-pissed.

She flew downstairs. Walked easily and casually across the road. He'd be watching from the window. Why the fuck had she mentioned valuables?

After a hundred yards she turned down a side street. Up ahead was a phone box. She slid inside and picked up the receiver. Waited a moment to put her thoughts in order. Dialled.

SEQUENCE 37

WEDNESDAY, 3nd MARCH, 1982. 12.30
EXT / DAY – METHUSELAH'S ANTIQUES

Methuselah stood outside his shop with a mug of coffee. He looked upwards. Took a hip flask out of his pocket.

Took a swig. Raised the flask to the 'FOR RENT' sign. Stepped back another pace.

The weight of an unmistakable hand on his shoulder.

He slumped slightly. Then, without turning round, "Just hoping for a few worry-free years. Costa del Delighto. Chest and liver's well fucked with the smokes and drink. Bit of sun and sangria. Nice older bird…"

"As it stands…" said Crust from behind Methuselah's back. "What I know. You haven't broken any law!"

"So what is it?"

"That shop you rented… Name of Porsche?"

"That's all I've done. Leased the shop for him, bought him two containers, filled them with junk, sent them to the Liverpool container port…" Methuselah turned and faced Crust. Licked his lips nervously.

"His private address? Raite's? Porsche's?"

"No idea," said Methuselah.

"Then what I need is…" Crust paused. "Who sent him to you?"

Methuselah licked his lips again. "This bloke. Bit of this; bit of that. Calls himself an 'agricultural advisor'."

"Looks like what? Hangs out where?"

"County knob look. Tweeds and Widow Twankey. Fitzrou Arms, Main Square."

"Well, if that's the case…"

"Yes?" whispered Methuselah.

"… Then fuck off wherever. Because if I'm happy, so are you."

SEQUENCE 38

The Countryman sat at a small circular table for two in The Fitzrou Arms. Half-pint of bitter in front of him. A small notebook held-up close to his eyes. Running the stub of a pencil up and down columns of figures. Although the bar was relatively empty, he had put a battered leather satchel on the second chair to discourage intruders.

He sensed someone approaching the table; then saw a hand come to rest on top of the satchel. Without taking his eyes from the notebook, the Countryman said, "Sorry, squire! Seat's taken! Friend of mine joining me shortly."

The hand picked up the satchel. Dropped it onto the floor. The Countryman's head shot up to see Crust staring down at him.

SEQUENCE 39

FRIDAY, 5ᵗʰ MARCH, 1982. 11.00.
INT / DAY CAPTAIN BARRATT'S CABIN, *OCEAN SEASPRAY*

Captain Barratt sat in one of his cabin's armchairs. Wearing dress blues. Staring into space. His face a Rembrandt self-portrait of that painter's 'seen-too-much' school. Before him, an occasional table on which sat a glass of rum, an open book, and his sextant in its original pre-war case.

He rose, went to a port and looked out at the heaving Atlantic. Grey. Wild. Gloomy. He recited softly:-

"'… I suppose that you think 'cause my trousers are tarry,
And because that I wears my long hair in a tail.
While landsmen are figged-out as fine as Lord Harry,
With breast-pins, and cravats as white as old sail…'"

Barratt repeated, "… *'as white as old sail'.*" Sighed. Returned to his armchair.

There was a knock.

"Come in?"

His white-coated steward entered.

"Kenny! How goes it?" Barratt's voice was slightly slurred.

"Chief officer asked me – should I be passing – could I let you know the Liverpool pilot's ordered for tonight at the Bar."

"Perhaps the chief officer could have found time to tell me himself!? Let him know that, will you?"

"I will, Captain… And of course, we've got Mr Rose back next trip."

Barratt opened the sextant case. "Know what this is, Kenny?"

"Sextant, Captain?"

Without removing the instrument, Barratt held the case towards the steward.

Kenny came across and looked at it. "Beautiful, Captain. Really beautiful."

"My mother bought it me. My first trip. Long time ago now… Know why I'm showing it you?"

"I don't, Captain."

"Because shortly, Kenny, the only place to see one will be a museum."

"That's a shame, Captain. A real shame."

"That's all, Kenny."

The steward walked to the cabin door.

"Oh, Kenny?"

Kenny turned.

"At standby for the pilot. Let the chief officer know to call me himself!"

"Captain." Kenny left, closing the door quietly behind himself.

Barratt leaned forward over his book. Stretched out a questing hand for his rum glass.

SEQUENCE 40

FRIDAY, 5th MARCH, 1982. 11.32.
EXT / DAY STANLEY ROAD. INT / DAY BAYONETS

John, file under arm, looked at his watch. Twenty-eight minutes to twelve. Began banging on the door of The Bayonets.

The bolts came off. Mick's head poked out. Red-rimmed eyes. Breath like a blast furnace. "Fuck's sake! It's only twenty-five past!"

John exposed his wrist. "Twenty-five *to*!" Brushed past. "Come on, Mick! I really need one after those Enterprise dickheads."

Mick muttered something. Walked down the bar and

round through the counter flap. Took a bottle of Tops'l from under the counter. Poured some into the palms of his hands; rubbed them over his head and face. Positioned himself behind the pumps. Pulled a test measure into a half-pint glass. Held it to the light. The beer was reddish, with what looked like threads of fat in suspension.

"Fuck's sakes, Mick! You're not going to serve that to *people*?"

Mick tried the next pump. Another test. Then a full pint. Put it in front of John. Rang up the sale. Tapped John's *Daily Mirror*. "You're aware, tovarich, that Thatcher and her arse bandits go through the papers every day cutting out stuff about people like us? King Arthur and his Knights of the Coal Table."

"Our hero…"

"*Times, Daily Mail, Telegraph, Express, Sun* – TDTES: Thatcher's Dirty Tricks Expresso Bongo Scumbags! What we need to start doing ourselves. Cataloguing the Tories with their 'cake and arse' parties. So-called 'royals' all knobbing each other."

"Why don't we?"

"No money, comrade. I mean, I take a collection at NELLI every Sunday night; hardly enough for the next week's booze."

"Give the Queen a ring. She's got plenty."

"Fucking Von Scroungerhoffs. Parading round in their brown-hatter uniforms and medals. Haven't been enough wars cover the number of bottle tops on their pigeon chests… Uncle Joe would know what to do there."

"Like he did with a few million others."

"As the man himself said – 'One death? A tragedy. A million? A statistic'. Yeah. Hand out a few bottle tops and titles. Unquestioning obedience and arse-licking for life! What a great fucking con!"

John drank. "Wouldn't accept one yourself? Services to brewing?"

"Wrong, comrade! But only to get down to meet them… See, come the rev, your rentier / limp-wristos – your RELICS – your Old Bleatonians and Oxphoneyans – will know their time's up. So invite people like me to go down to their arse-bandit Boy Scout hangouts. See what we'll take to leave them alone…"

John drained his glass, put it down, tapped its side.

Carrying it to the pump, Mick continued. "Only thing is, one of the lads at NELLI was saying, first time you're down there… The 'don't bend down' half-crown?"

John shook his head.

"You get invited to one of their gaffs – Eton, Oxford and that – first thing you see on the marble floor's a half-crown piece. All shiny and new. Have them minted special – once they know you're coming."

"Don't bend down to pick it up?"

"Up your exhaust pipe like O'Reilly's rat! Specially if it's Pluckingem Pissouse! Because – behind the nearest marble pillar – someone will be waiting – kecks down to his knees…"

"Any particular one?"

"Could be any of them, mate!… All brought-up to bat for both sides – case they miss out some sort taxpayer handout. I mean, look at them. A Kraut! A Greek! A fucking Greek! You know what that means?! 'Stern torpedoes away!'" Mick turned to the optics. Gave himself a double brandy. "You know, I almost feel sorry for that Judy of his. He probably wouldn't even recognise her face 'cept for the stamps!"

"Stamps?"

"Licking them for the letters to his old German wartime pals in South America... Fucking hell! Ruled by a sausage gobbler and an olive picker. Millions from our taxes for doing fuck all!"

John laughed. "Taxes, Mick?!"

"Course I don't pay taxes! But what with claiming the dole... Still getting a bit from the UAB – as was... Hardship allowances... This place... Constantly needing false addresses. While them – born on feathers – sitting in their fucking castles."

"Every Englishman's home, Mick..."

"You know they got about a dozen? Palaces and castles? While kids all over this country's freezing and starving in pre-war slums?! They're taking the piss, comrade! Taking the piss! I mean, even their spiritual leader – biggest bloodsucker of all – Count Drac – only had one! Plus them 'grease and slaver' gaffs for their knob-hound hangers-on while I can't get a decent-sized council flat to store those stolen container ciggies... And who forks out every time there's a bit of pointing needed to the battlements? Oil for the drawbridge? Water for their moats; row their punts up and down? There's not one ever paid a gas bill their slimy fucking lives! Know what they're doing right now?... Now as we speak!?..."

John shook his head. Swigged his pint.

"… Sitting in their marble boudoirs, looking at each other out the corners of their eyes, wondering how they're still getting away with it!… Laughing that much they're pissing into each other's hands…"

A couple of lads strolled in. One called for two pints of bitter. The other asked if there were any darts behind the bar.

Mick stiffened. "Darts?!… You from round here, pal?!"

"Easby Road, mate!"

Mick made his way across to inspect them more fully. John drank from his second pint. Read his newspaper.

Down the bar, Mick handed over a set of darts.

"Oi, mate!" said one of the two. "This arrer's got a flight missing."

"Write to Robin Hood!" advised Mick.

He came back to the pumps and began pulling the darts-players' pints. "Fucking darts! When the world's workers are going up in flames."

"Had something about them, though," said John. "Those Monday darts-match nights; late '50s, early '60s. 'Fore everyone had a telly and that. 'Fore you arrived on the scene…"

Mick stared at him.

"Yeh" continued John "Only time women were officially allowed in the bar of The Bayonets… Yeh, 'member fighting for my place in the first team!"

"Instead of at the barricades, you mean?!"

"Tradesmen mainly. The first team. Printers, fitters and toolmakers; painters and decorators. The odd labourer who'd worked his way in. Shirt, ties, jackets and polished shoes. Eight a side. Eight-foot-six oche. Double to start and finish. Afterwards, sandwiches from silver metal trays. Away side 'always' served first. No eating for the home side until the away side began. Sing-song to finish. Mainly Hank Williams. 'Your Cheatin' Heart', 'There'll Be No Teardrops Tonight', 'Settin' the Woods on Fire'… sometimes finishing on 'Now is the Hour'- some sort of emigrant parting song, I think that was. We used to sing at my grandma's every Christmas… Happier times, Mick… Happier times."

"You cunt!" said Mick as he took the two pints down the bar.

Yeah. An old-days Bayonets darts match. Sort of thing where he could've invited Mrs Raite – Liz. Introduce her to the lads, so she could get a look at everyone; everyone get a look at her. Give her a chance to make her mark…

Mick came back down the bar. Rang up the money. Slammed the cash drawer shut.

One of the two at the dartboard shouted, "And another two if you would, pal!"

Mick began pulling a further two pints. Turned an enraged face to John. "How the boss class'd love you! You and the other Monday-night drones queuing up to throw their Jim Pikes into a dartboard instead of into the bloated arses of the plutocrats. I'd bar you on the spot if it wasn't for the paltry few bob you bring in here."

"We've all got our memories, Mick."

"Some shorter than others. Like what it was like in Flour Street on ration books after the war… Gogol's muzhiks – Dead Souls – had more spirit than you, you fucking capitalist arse-rag."

John said quickly, "Tell you what, Mick. Give us another pint and yourself a brandy!"

Mick stared at him, then gave himself a double brandy. Threw it off. Left off pulling the two pints for the darts players. Stared unfathomably at John. Then said, "Thinking about getting a barmaid. That sister of Curly's?... Chris?"

"Totally straight... You'd have no worries there."

"Suppose I could ask her. Maybe you could?"

"It's your pub, Mick."

"That last one. Maggie O'Crimm. Daughter of Corny O'Crimm; NELLI stalwart. Hand in the till her first night. Starts crying when I pull her. 'Just borrowing my bus fare, Mick'... Lives three streets away! Forced her hand open. Like trying to open an oyster with a banana. 'Bus fare?!' I say. 'Where you living now, Maggie? Australia?' Thing is. Lots of meetings coming up at NELLI. Those ciggies... twenty-foot container... five million fags or so... moving them to Wales and Scotland. Then this picketing we're starting on this container ship due in today. *Ocean Seaspray.*"

"What's that about?"

"Bosses getting too big for their jackboots." Mick sighed. "Containers've really fucked up the docks. Threats of redundancies. Even *the sack*! Imagine! Being able to *sack* a *Liverpool docker*! It's back to the Dark Ages! All our hard-earned rights vanishing as we speak! 'Work-On By' Sundays. 'Loss of Doss' payments?"

"Any chance of those other two bevvies, mate?!" shouted one of the darts players.

"All right! All right! Hold your fucking horses!" Mick took the two pints down the bar. Accepted the money.

Rang it up. Turned back to John. "Maybe I need get elected to a legit political party. Get myself on 'excees' like all the other conniving cunts!" Mick bared his brown, broken, crooked teeth. "Only thing I'll get elected to here is a nervous fucking breakdown and early grave." Mick gave himself another double brandy. Threw it off. Picked up a pint glass. Held it at arm's length; contemplating it like Vindici the nine-year-old skull of Gloriana. About the same length of time since the glass had last been washed.

Suddenly Mick shouted " 'The Scouse Barman!'
He pulled his final cloudy pint
Proposed a final toast
Then died. Then met the Father, Son,
And then the Holy Ghost,
Who cried, 'Come in, Scouse Barman!
We've watched you do your best
The Spanish House, The Yankee Bar,
The Legs, The Throstle's Nest.
The Lighthouse and the Roundhouse,
The Griffin, the Dominion,
Those North End bucks,
Their docker's hooks,
Who worked you rack-and-pinion.
Who had you bleaching pipes and pumps
And washing down the vinyl,
The spewed-up pies, piss, ciggie stumps,
That clogged-up each urinal.
Who watched you fight and battle
Each night at throwing-out
Jammed in the door. Flat on the floor,
An ashtray in your mouth…

But that's all in the past now,
For here's your harp and berth
No more the jukebox blast now
That deafened you on Earth…
And there's a throne. Sit down and rest,
'Least, 'til the towels come off!
For tonight's the 'Pilgrims Piss-Up'
And we're shocking short of staff!'"

John nodded in admiration. "Never realised, Mick. One of us!"

"Us?…Who the fuck's 'us'?"

"Poets. See that one of mine in the *Albion*?"

"Load of shite… And don't you go mentioning this! Understand?"

"But, Mick…"

"Never mind… 'But fucking Mick'! Word gets out I'm one of them 'laureates', this place'll be full of Tory fudge-packers piping my arse ev'ry time I bend-down pick-up a crate." Mick belched. "Maybe you or your old fella have a word with Chris? That barmaid's job?…"

John shrugged non-committally.

Mick pulled him a fresh pint. Passed a forefinger over the top, signalling 'on the house'. "This 'private eye' scam of yours?"

"Mick, it's no scam. Just trying to get something off the ground."

"You mean like your car? Can't even get off the fucking pavement!? Thing is, lads at NELLI think this 'tec business could be handy for hearing stuff…"

"Stuff? What sort of stuff?"

"Useful fucking stuff!"

"Useful…?"

"To *us*! Your *fucking class*!"

"Mick…"

"And. In return. NELLI will be on the *qui vive* for anything might push a few bob your way. *Quid pro quo!* Look after each other?… Right?!"

"Right…" said John eventually.

"So. From now on. Anything you need, you knock here first! The Bayonets! Uncle Mick!… OK?!"

As John stared at him, Mick said in a flat voice, "*Carpe diem*, brother! Seize the day!"

SEQUENCE 41

FRIDAY, 5th MARCH, 1982. 18.00
INT / EVENING CRUST'S FLAT

"A painting," the Voice said. "Raite's turned the money into a painting."

"Makes sense," said Crust, reaching for his drawing pad. "Given his previous."

"Bought from a bloke they call 'The Laughing Cavalier'."

"Dodgy dealer school?" Crust began sketching the Frans Hals portrait of *The Laughing Cavalier*.

"New breed that's twigged that art's safer / cheaper / cleaner than Securicor vans."

"How'd he come to us?… This 'Cavalier'?"

"Few years ago. 'Found' a Corot in Portobello Road Market."

"Where actually from?"

"Norfolk country house that got done while Lord and Lady Fuckbrains were off 'wintering' in the Caribbean."

"Just can't get the slaves," said Crust.

"Norfolk" said the Voice "One million years BC."

Crust drew a dinosaur.

"One of our lads began by driving ambulances up there" continued the Voice. "Reckoned the surgical trolleys had hair growing round the wheel arches."

"They get anything else?"

"Other paintings, silverware, porcelain… Corot was the pick."

"Owners couldn't identify it?"

"Lord and Lady F? Wouldn't know a Corot from a can of peas…

Crust drew a face-shaped can of peas with a lorgnette

"… Only info was from an old insurance policy" continued the Voice. But as no one ever robbed houses like theirs – not then, anyway – it was just down as 'Camille Corot, Landscape'. No dimensions; description… Norfolk sent us the info, thinking it would end up in the Smoke."

"While meanwhile…?" asked Crust.

"Exactly! While meanwhile, the gang who ended up with the stuff had no real idea what to do with it. What, if anything, was it worth?

"And… ?"

So they ask round the East End. Hear about some local wannabe spends lots of time in art galleries…"

"Without being murdered by his own family?"

"Has this natural understanding. And naturals are… well… Look at George Best!"

"Look at his bar tab…"

"They invite him in. Like him. Name him 'The Laughing Cavalier'. Show him their haul. He picks out the Corot. They tell him to sort it / report it. The Cav knows about Bond Street. Wraps the Corot in last night's chip paper; takes a stroll down there. We'd circulated it, but just as a 'Corot landscape'. Bloke on the desk in Bond Street's suddenly got this pure jellied-eeler in front of him with a Corot. Asks can he have the Cav's name and address – which the Cav actually gives him."

"Unbelievable!" said Crust.

"Both you and I know how easily people can fuck up, they get a whiff of serious money. Desky says they'd be *delighted* to value – possibly *dispose of* – the painting. But the Cavalier needs to leave it to be 'assessed'."

"At which point…"

"Yeah. Right out the door. Onto the Tube…"

"We go round there; address he gave?"

"That night. One-room flat. Cavalier right on the offensive. Why's he being hassled for owning a painting he bought in Portobello Road Market? The bloke who sold it to him – who he'd never seen before – said he'd picked it up at a house clearance."

Crust sighed. "What'd he say he paid for it?"

"Four quid… Says it was his beer money for the day and he almost didn't buy it as it might've been a forgery."

"We confiscate it?"

"You serious? Seems as soon as he gets back from Bond Street his nerves are so shattered he falls into the nearest boozer…"

"… And meets another bloke who offers to take it off his hands?"

"Twenty quid. So that was the end of that one!"

"Heard of since?"

"Nah. Onto the Continent… Then anywhere."

"And us?"

"Getting our own Art and Antiques bunch. But it's new. So taking time."

"Be strolling into the National Gallery lifting them down from the walls, next," said Crust.

"*Art!*" said the Voice. "More shit for us to deal with!" Then, "You know the old 'Pearl & Dean' – Queen – has her own 'picture hanger'?"

"Christ! Where'd they find him?"

"'Member that gents' in Regent Street? Green and white tiles; black railings? Our lads permanently at the urinals waving their todgers round waiting for a bite?"

Both laughed.

"Also heard – one of her personal protection crowd – she has someone wear-in her leather shoes for her. Case they pinch the royal bunions."

"Those boots we first got issued," said Crust. "Like rowlock leather! 'Member them?!"

" 'Member my verrucas like lily pads.'"

There was a moment's shared nostalgic silence as Crust doodled the sole of a human foot with a lily-pad-shaped verruca in its centre. Then, "How'd we finally link them? The Cavalier? Raite? The painting?"

"There's this sex outfit," said the Voice. "Shady Sadie's Escorts. They get a call from the Cav. to send over one of their girls. Florence."

"All domes and curves?"

"An overnight. Next morning, the Cav, still pissed, tells Florence her money's on the dresser. Being a nosy bastard, she opens the top drawer. Bundles of notes. An old copy of some painting. A photo of someone she later identifies as Raite, which we think the Cav was carrying for recognition. But then Florence somehow lets the Cav know she's seen the stuff… immediately crapping her crotchless French knickers."

"Mutually exclusive proposition," said Crust. Into the silence, "OU philosophy…"

"Not joining the other side, are we, Crusty?"

"'Know thine enemy'."

Another uncertain laugh. "… Now. The Cav's got no violence on his sheet…"

"… But knows a man who has?"

"Florence understands this. Rings a DS she's had a bit of mutual with since her early days down the Cross."

"'White PVC and no knickers' period?"

"'Cept in winter. Keep her ankles warm. Anyway, she's frightened and asks him for help…"

"Which was…?"

"Money to go stay with her cousin up in Manchester."

"Manchester or the Cavalier. There's a choice?" Crust doodled a cloud. Rain coming from it.

"Tells our DS she's tired of her 'life of glamour'," continued the Voice, "and wants to retrain as a nurse… You know, Crusty. You accept terrible things as a nurse. Probably why so many marry coppers… Plus shift patterns mean you never have to see each other. But after Sadie's… well… well… Good luck to Florence!"

"So back to the Cav again for us?"

"Two of the lads, same evening; friendly call. See if he'd had any more thoughts about the four-quid Corot."

"'But now we're here…'" said Crust.

"Exactly," said the Voice. "'Mind if we have a quick look round; maybe spot a bargain *we* might like to buy?'"

"And?"

"'Certainly,' says the Cav. 'Just give my brief a quick ring…'"

"Soon won't need briefs," said Crust. "The crims'll have their own law degrees."

"Top ones already have," said the Voice.

"Cupboard bare, I suppose?" said Crust.

"Dresser still there. Top drawer still there. Nothing in it."

"*Still Life with Egg on Our Faces*?"

"'Cept now we know the money's a baroque *Magdalen Bearing Arma Christi*."

"That last bit…?"

"Stuff used at the Crucifixion. Nails, whips, crown of thorns, etc."

"But it's gen?"

"Art and Antiques had Florence in. She said the painting had initials in the top right-hand corner, and a date. Couldn't remember the date, but the initials were the same as hers: FF, Florence Foresham. Also used, seventeenth century, by Filipo di Fredi. Noted for his 'sublime attention to facial expressions, use of light and shadow, and meditations on all aspects of the Crucifixion'. They showed her that mugshot I mentioned Raite let us take. Which she identified it as being the same bloke as in the photo in the Cav's top drawer.

It's him all right – Raite. The Cav's offloaded a baroque masterpiece onto him for the drugs money."

"How big is it?" asked Crust.

"Thought you'd never ask… About twenty by twenty-four inches, they reckon."

"OK," said Crust, drawing an ornate frame and scribbling '20 x 24'.

"Want a photo we got?" asked the Voice. "The Cavalier's?"

"Ever likely to come up here?" asked Crust.

"Liverpool?! Gouge his eyes out first with a palette knife."

"Let's leave it. Someone I'll never see. No. I'm down there, I'll pick one up."

"I'd like that. See you again… Man who taught you all you know." After a pause, the Voice asked, "Busking Bill?"

"O'Rourke and his mates were in some pub. O'Rourke left; the other two stayed. Talking about some church club 'do' they're all going this Saturday."

"You can have two pints on expenses."

"Crime never pays."

" Never stops!… OK! onward and upward! Serve and suspect! Touch the blue!"

SEQUENCE 42

FRIDAY, 5th MARCH, 1982. 19.50
INT / JOHN'S OFFICE

John sat in his office. In front of him, on the desk, yet another cup of cold coffee and the blank pages of his diary. He stared at *Celestial Vision*; flashed once more to Mrs Raite. Stretched out a hand to pick up the phone, then brought it back to his lap. He took the phone on his lap. Put his feet up on the desk. Put his hand on the receiver once more.

As he did so, it began to ring.

"Evening, John," said Harry Rose.

"Harry!" said John. "What's new?"

"Well. Realise it's a bit late. But rejoining the *Seaspray* Monday – sailing next Friday 12th. But also need to go down the berth tomorrow – Saturday. Be coming into Liverpool by train to Central Station and thought we might meet for that drink we mentioned?"

John thought for a moment. Rustled the leaves of his empty diary. "Yeah. Cancellation here... so I've got a space... Been thinking myself we should get together."

"How about lunchtime? That pub opposite the station on the corner?"

"Just make a note. 'Lunchtime beer. Harry'."

"And... er... I was thinking, John. Perhaps Chris might like to join us?"

John gave an easy laugh. "You know, Harry, for a moment there I really thought it was me you wanted to see."

"Not at all, John. Always interested in the views of someone like yourself..."

Like yourself...?

"... But when I rejoin officially on Monday, *Seaspray* starts loading in earnest. Some vintage cars going on the Ro-Ro deck – 'Roll-on/Roll-off' – accessed from the stern. The more valuable cargo: classic cars; machinery too big for the containers themselves..."

Blah – Blah – Blah – as fucking usual…

"… Which is why I'm going there tomorrow. Look at the cargo specs; word with Captain Barratt… Sure I mentioned him?"

"*Night to Remember* again?"

After an indecipherable pause, Harry continued. "And as she… ah… Chris… seemed quite interested…"

"… In Ro-Ro decks?"

"… Greyhounds… Their treatment… That look round the ship I mentioned?"

"OK, Harry, I'll see what I can do."

"Or I could come to your office?"

"Going back to my dad's. There's this dance tomorrow night…"

"Dance?!"

"Parish club… Catholic thing."

"Oh! Chris going?"

"Not sure… Obviously you can't."

"Oh!?"

"Like I said, H – 'Catholic thing' – so you can't go. Don't ask me why. I can't even explain it to myself… Just take my word."

"If you do see her, please give her my best regards."

"Sure. And now, Harry…"

"Of course. See you tomorrow about midday."

John put down the phone. Stared at *Celestial Vision*. Lifted the receiver again.

SEQUENCE 43

In the hotel room, Mrs Raite sat on the bed in her underwear, painting her toenails bright red. Her hands were free of plasters. The skin on their backs was corrugated, scored and raw. Covered with ointment. At the coffee table, Bogger played patience, looking through the undealt stack for any cards he needed. The pack had a different female nude on the back of each card.

The phone began to ring.

After a glance at Bogger, and a sigh, Mrs Raite rolled off the bed and walked provocatively to the receiver. Bogger eyed her hungrily.

"Hello?"

"Mrs Raite? John O'Rourke. Look, I want to speak to you…"

Mrs Raite rolled her eyes in Bogger's direction. "Mr O'Rourke, I'm pressed for time. Just give me the address."

Bogger came over and brought an ear near the telephone, simultaneously cupping one of Mrs Raite's breasts in his right hand.

"Mrs Raite? What's exactly's going on?"

"Isn't that what *you* are being paid for?"

"Why are you really looking for your husband?"

"Do you have the address?!"

"This policeman – Crust – where does he come in?"

"Policeman?!" Mrs Raite began scratching the back of

the hand holding the phone. Blood oozed. She gestured Bogger towards the minibar.

"I'm not happy about this, Mrs Raite. Finding all this stuff for you. Getting nothing back…"

"'All this stuff'? Really?"

"And don't like the way you talk to me, neither!"

"Good luck or good judgement."

"What's that supposed to mean…?"

"Simply. That between the worst professional and the best amateur is a bridge that can never be crossed?" Mrs Raite accepted a glass from Bogger.

"Yeah. Well. As far as pros go, you've probably got them all licked."

A long, stretched silence. John's feet could be heard hitting the floor as he sat bolt upright.

"Mrs Raite… It's just that… Look, maybe I shouldn't have said that."

"You can tell that to Bogger."

John said quickly, "Mr Raite – your husband – yes, he's on the Wirral. This small village. I don't exactly know the address yet, but I'm meeting a contact tomorrow who has it. At which time I'll want that other hundred you promised."

"You're still meeting Bogger," said Mrs Raite, and put down the phone.

Bogger put a lit cigarette between her lips. Began grinding himself into her rear. "Getting a go at him, am I, Liz? Though why you hired a tosser like that in the first place…"

"I thought – him clumping round over there – Ronnie would somehow hear. Maybe make a move we could pick up on. But he's actually *found* Ronnie. Your classic *idiot savant*..."

"What's that?"

"Mostly moron – but a smattering of distinct ability"

"Met 'em. Talked to 'em. Fucked 'em over."

"Plus a policeman now seems to be involved somehow..."

"Liz. Any cop with brains is on the take! We'll piss rings round all of them. Reckon this O'Rourke's really got Ron's address?"

"Close enough to try to start striking deals." She began scratching the back of her other hand. "He knows it's not alimony... And now a local plod... Maybe it's coming up from London... We'll need to move on this."

"He say anything else?... O'Rourke?"

"Besides telling me I'm on the game!?" She fixed her eyes on Bogger. Lifted her chest.

Bogger hugged her like a starving bear. "Don't you worry, Liz. He'll come to me in the end. Him *and* Ronnie. They all come to Bogger in the end."

"He's smelt money. Maybe got ideas..."

"So've I – for him!"

"Friday, today... If he gets that address tomorrow I think he might try to pay Ronnie a visit himself. Maybe Monday... Yes... Maybe over there – the Wirral – Monday."

"How so?"

"For the O'Rourkes of this world, work always begins on a Monday... When it begins at all."

"I'll fucking gee him up!"

"And as he has to go through the Mersey Tunnel..."

"Yeah?"

"…That's where we'll be waiting. From 9am."

"Then, doll?"

"Follow him to Ronnie's. Where you do him!"

Bogger grinned. Slowly reached across and took her by the hair. Began pulling her towards him. "But first, love… I do you!"

"Bogger… Bogger… Not too rough! Promise?"

He began to force her over the chair. "You like it rough, Liz… You know that."

"At least… the bedroom…" she gasped, struggling.

"No, doll, here… Here and now. I give you what you want all the time, your way, Liz. So now I do you! My way!"

SEQUENCE 44

FRIDAY, 5th MARCH, 1982. 20.10
INT / NIGHT – JOHN'S OFFICE

John sat staring in fear at the phone in his hand. He replaced it gently on its holder. Rose to his feet and backed against the wall near the window. He pulled back the curtain slightly and peered out into Moorfields. Hurriedly put on his anorak. Made a quick adjustment to *Celestial Vision*. Opened the office door. Peered carefully out onto the landing. Switched off the light.

SEQUENCE 45

SATURDAY, 6th MARCH, 1982. 10.30.
INT / DAY FLOUR STREET

Saturday morning. Mr O'Rourke limped deftly round the kitchen, cleaning and listening to local radio as he put breakfast together on the stove. John, yawning, stumbled in, and sat at the table.

Mr O'Rourke slipped bacon between the two slices of fried bread he'd been keeping on the go in the frying pan. Put the sandwich in front of John. Turned on a new electric kettle.

John yawned, "Thanks." Picked up the sandwich. Opened it. Removed a piece of fat from the bacon.

"Good to hear you come in last night" said Mr O'Rourke "Not expecting you or anything… Something happen?"

"Just thought… well… might be a bit of company for you…"

"Speak for yourself," said Mr O'Rourke. "Best time I've had in years lately." He opened his paper at the racing pages.

John took two mugs to the new kettle. He wouldn't ask where it came from. There was also a new small mirror on the wall above the sink.

Mr O'Rourke ran his pen slowly down a list of runners. "All set for tonight, then?" he asked. "St Joe's? Few pints. Bit of a dance?… Father Malachy's latest music discoveries?"

John stood. Came round the table. Leaned over his father's shoulder, gazing down at the runners. "Get many there, these days?"

"Saturdays? Still just about a decent turnout. Not like it used to be, though." Mr O'Rourke marked off a horse. "But Chris being around again'll bring in a few hopefuls."

John paused. "Anyone she seems interested in? Talks to?"

"You'll see tonight." His father rose. "I'll just get a wash and a shave. Nip out for a bit of shopping for tonight's tea. Tomorrow's dinner… How about The Bayonets at one?"

"Can't, Dad. Got this meeting in town! Possible case breakthrough."

"Got to be today, has it?"

"Yeah. He's sailing again next Friday."

"Sailing?"

"That fella, Harry Rose, I mentioned from the job centre… That chief mate."

"Where's he fit in?"

"Comes from West Heartwood. Legal property stuff I'm advising him on… And just might have Raite's address… Complicated."

"Can't put him off? Seems a long time since we had a pint."

"Not possible. This Raite case… The bonus…"

"Bonus?"

"I mean… yeah… Mrs Raite said there might be an extra few bob if I find his address for her chop-chop!"

"Curly know about this bonus?"

"Not sure… Prob'ly mentioned it. Yeah, Harry, chief mate – not a bad fella. Even invited me down the ship for a few bevvies."

"No time for that, either?"

"See, he's just in central Liverpool today. Having a

word with his skipper till he rejoins properly next Monday. 'Fore they sail next Friday. So got to be today lunchtime."

"That the same as dinner time?"

"Yeah. Interesting fella. Chief officer. Seen a few things…"

"So's a lot of seamen from round here. Maybe even a few more than him."

"Yeah. But… well… chief officer and all that obviously brings… sort of different perspective."

"Perspective's what it's all about… But you'll be back for teatime? I was thinking of getting a couple of chops."

John frowned thoughtfully. "Could be. Should be… Then St Joe's, right?"

His father stopped at the kitchen door. "By the way. That new kettle. A present from Chris and Curly… As was the mirror."

"Yeah… Mirror seems a bit small."

"Thought it might be." Mr O'Rourke turned out into the hall for his coat. The front door banged.

John took his mug and plate to the sink. Stared into the mirror. Shook his head at his reflection.

Definitely too small.

SEQUENCE 46

SATURDAY, 6th MARCH, 1982. 13.00
INT / DAY PUB OPPOSITE CENTRAL STATION

The pub was crowded. Shoppers. Visitors. People out for a drink on a Saturday afternoon. John and Harry were squeezed in at a small cast-iron-legged, wooden-topped table near the door, pint glasses in front of them.

"No longer married, then, John?"

"Certainly split up – but whether there's been a divorce? Actually, Harry, she's mentioned you a few times."

"She has?… Like another pint?"

John held up a finger. "Sure it must be my turn… Keeps coming back to how dangerous it must have been…"

"Dangerous?"

"That fella pulling a shotgun on you when you were looking over that location for your greyhounds scheme… Where was it again?"

"West Heartwood, outside this prefab. But I've now had another offer. My mother's going into a retirement facility and has offered me her house. Stable block I could perhaps utilise as kennels…"

"Stables, eh? Wonder what the poor are doing this year? Anyway, stables or not, Chris is going to quiz me tonight. Sure of it. Once she knows I've seen you… So what exactly happened again? Where exactly was this prefab? Then maybe we'll have that pint you just offered…"

SEQUENCE 47

SATURDAY, 6th MARCH, 1982. 21.00
EXT / NIGHT STREET OUTSIDE ST JOE'S. INT/
NIGHT ST JOE'S

At 9pm, Busking Bill's battered Morris pulled up about a hundred yards from St Joseph's Church Social Club. Crust climbed out. Closed the door. Stretched. Walked round the vehicle, looking up and down the road. Tapped on the driver's window. "Have a break. See you Monday."

Bill stuck up a thumb. Drove away.

Crust strolled back along the pavement towards the club which was situated in a '50s brick annexe attached to the Victorian building which comprised St Joe's School. Further on again was the church itself.

Inside the open front door of the club was a vestibule with a trestle table and folding chair. An elderly man, with a bald head like a wrinkled yellow onion, sat on the chair reading a hardback. Soft grey flannel shirt. Green polyester tie. Ratty tweed jacket. Ratty grey flannels. Pair of carpet slippers. Gas-bottle heater next to the table. Glass of scotch. Open 'visitors book' with half a dozen or so scrawled signatures.

Crust, putting his finger to his lips, showed his warrant card. The man half-rose. Hesitated. Sat down again.

Crust lifted the book the doorkeeper was reading: *A History of Ireland*. "'They went into battle singing but they always died'," he said.

"So they did. Mainly on behalf of the British Army... Which later thanked them by shooting them down in cold blood!"

Crust raised one eyebrow slightly. Moved past the table and through a set of push doors into the club itself. Edged into the shadows near the entrance.

A large rectangular room with a bar almost filling the length of the long side opposite the entrance door. At the left-hand end of the bar, two doors – 'Ladies' and 'Gents'. At the right-hand end, steps leading up to a raised stage. Along the bar, small clusters of men. A priest, right of centre towards the stage, laughing and joking with the chosen few. A group of four young men further towards the stage steps, clutching pints, heads together in close conversation; all wearing skintight jeans and skull-and-crossbones headbands. One was appreciably taller than the rest; his headband red and white rather than black and white. On the stage, a large drum kit. Amplifiers; three guitars leaning against them. An upright piano with its keyboard turned to the back wall.

In front of the stage, a small dance floor. Ranged around the dance floor – and radiating back from it – a number of tables. Family groups packed around them, some with children in their late teens. Crust knew, given the tangible air of combined Irish feyness and fecklessness, he'd have been immediately identified. He stood still and focused on John's party – seated at a table halfway between the entrance and the bar. Curly. An older man – the father; Mr O'Rourke? A girl in her late twenties – Chris; Curly's sister?

Like an iceberg in fog, Crust began to drift along the back wall silently; but always with an eye on the O'Rourke table. There appeared to be a certain amount of stress there. Stares and glares. *Four pints, they're anybody's.*

SEQUENCE 48

SATURDAY, 6th MARCH, 1982. 21.15
INT / NIGHT ST JOE'S – O'ROURKE TABLE

"So let me get this right," said Curly. "This dinner time you were in town bevvying with this Harry Rose fella?"

"Curl!" John took a drink from his pint glass. "…
Cheers, everyone!… Curl! Chris must have told you how
he turned up at the office wanting me to check out this
place he was interested in renting to look after clapped-
out greyhounds?…"

"West Heartwood," said Chris.

"Where we were yesterday?!" Curly shook his head,
stared down at the table. "But where you never mentioned
fuck-all about this Harry Rose?!"

"Curly!" said Chris.

"Yeah. Women present!" said Mr O'Rourke.

"Yeah, OK, Curl," said John, "which maybe I should
have."

"So why didn't you?"

"Because last night he rang to tell me he now doesn't
want the property thing sorting because he's found
somewhere else."

"Where?" asked Chris.

John stared at her. "Well, no concern of ours –
but maybe taking over his ma's house… Stables or
something… That he can use for the mutts."

"Stables?!" said Mr O'Rourke.

"That's definite, is it?" asked Chris.

"So," said Curly, "if your business with him was a
non-starter – why go meet him anyway?"

"Because he asked if I wanted a drink and a friendly
lunchtime chat."

"*Lunchtime*!" laughed Curly.

"I *can* have friends don't spend *all* their lives in The
Bayonets, I hope," said John.

"What's wrong with The Bayonets?" asked Chris.

"You told me it had to do with the case," said Mr O'Rourke. "You seeing this big 'chief mate'!"

The whole table glared at John.

The barman dropped the stylus onto an LP on a turntable behind the bar. A deafening, tinny rendition of 'Blanket on the Ground' throbbed from the speakers. People slowly began to stand and leave their tables for the dance floor.

"Strange, though," said Curly, "it happened to be this West Heartwood place!"

"To be honest, Curl, just didn't put the two together in my head."

Chris began fingering a beer mat. Turning it in her fingers. "He say anything about going down the ship, John? That drink?"

"Drink?!" said Curly. "Ship?! What's all this?!"

"Look!" said John. All eyes riveted on him. "Harry Rose and his dogs have got nothing to do with nothing. There's just Raite, and the alimony and…" He raised his face to look directly into Crust's eyes. Crust nodded encouragingly. "… Crust," John finished quietly.

Crust took a step forward. Bent his knees. "Evenin', all!"

"Look what the cat's dragged in," muttered Curly.

Crust pulled a spare chair from the next table and placed it between John and Curly. He didn't attempt to sit. Leaned in, hands on its back. Winked at Chris. "Anyone for a pint?"

"Family group," said John.

Crust smiled. "Hopefully not the Borgias… Any intros?"

John gestured round the table. "My dad... Curly you know. Curly's sister, Chris."

"Nice to meet you, Mr O." Crust offered his hand, then pushed it forward towards Chris. "And you, Miss...? Mrs...?"

"Between husbands." Chris allowed her hand to lie limply in Crust's for a moment.

Crust nodded. "While I'm between arrests... Disraeli, was it, said, 'every woman should marry, and no man'?"

Chris edged slightly closer to Mr O'Rourke. "Reader, are you?"

"When there's no overtime going." Crust produced a crumpled banknote. "Table or counter service?"

"Counter," said Mr O'Rourke. "They like to know who's in."

Crust held out the note to Curly. "Go on, son – on me!"

Curly stared at him without moving.

"Curl, could you? Just as a favour?" said John.

Curly stared ahead. "Look, John, I'm here for a few drinks with our Chris, you and your dad. And while I do the running around at work, this is right outside of that." He stared at Crust. "What's wrong with him getting his own in?" He swung towards John. "Or even *you* getting a round in for once?!"

Crust nodded approvingly. "Kelly, I appreciate what you're saying... But I need to talk to your boss. And far more comfortable – for him – I do it here."

Chris leaned across and took the note from Crust's hand. Held it out to Curly. "Curl... would you?" She put a hand on Curly's forearm.

"Yeah... Well." Curly took the note. Rose slowly. Slouched towards the bar.

The record crackled, hissed and scratched its way to its end. The dancers returned to their tables.

The compère, in a green tweed suit, a green tie, a cream shirt, and a pair of brown brogues, freed himself from the group around the priest, climbed up the steps to the stage, moved across to the mic and began fiddling with it while performing a short, spirited dance like a leprechaun with an itchy back. He spoke into the mic but nothing happened.

"Try turning it on!" shouted a voice from the audience.

The compère began tapping and shaking the mic.

Curly returned with a tray containing three pints, a gin and tonic, and Crust's change. He gave the gin and tonic to Chris and a pint to Mr O'Rourke. Left John and Crust's pints and the change on the tray. Gestured with his thumb over his shoulder. Charlie Um-Pah-Bah arrived carrying a triangle of three pints. These he carefully set down near the edge of the table. Drank half of one. Stepped back. Began to play air guitar:-

"How many stairs must a man fall down
Before you call him a cab?
How many 'g's of the white stuff sniff
Before he ends up on a slab
In the lab?
And!
How many hits must one group have
Before they get known as 'The Fab'?
Smart answers, my friend, will only get you chinned!
Smart answers will only get you chinned!..."

In the background the compère climbed down off the stage and went to consult with The Nurgs. Now a glowering group at the foot of the steps leading up to the stage.

Curly gestured their way. "Charlie's here to see The Nurgs. Maybe make them an offer."

"Charlie," said Chris, "this is John's dad, Mr O'Rourke – Frank. And Inspector Crust."

"Detective Inspector Crust," said Crust.

Charlie whistled. Took another mouthful. Pointed a finger at John. "Here to lift him?" he asked Crust.

"Not yet." said Crust.

Charlie raised his glass to Crust. "Yeah. Looking over these Nurgs in honour of Eddie! Eddie Etna and the Eruptions." He mimed pulling pimples from his face. "Who! Though a Woolly! Died for rock 'n' roll. Tonight, though, what I need to know is! Have these Nurgs got what it takes?! Are they worth the froth off your pint?!" He strummed his air guitar.

"Maybe ring my private guru,
Magic carpet all-girl aircrew,
File their nails and trim their hairdo,
Do what bop-a-wop-a-girls do…"

Turned to Curly. "Ready to rock, amigo?"

"Yeah. Let's get back to the bar. Some fresh air…"

Charlie finished his first pint. Picked up a second.

In the background, one of The Nurgs was up onstage with the compère. The Nurg adjusted the mic, shouted, "Testing! Testing!" then made his way back down the steps to his bandmates.

Charlie downed his second pint effortlessly without lowering the glass. Burped. "Had one knocked over once!" Played a few air-guitar chords. Pointed the arm of his imaginary guitar at Crust. "Hear what happened when St Patrick drove the snakes out of Ireland?… All swam to Liverpool and joined the police force!"

Curly laughed loudly.

Picking up his last pint, Charlie led Curly to where The Nurgs were standing. Moved into their orbit. Clapped Big Ned on the back. Produced a banknote and began waving it at the barman.

The compère, glass of whisky in one hand, walked to the drum kit and struck one of the cymbals with the bottom of his glass. The noise from the audience increased. The compère gripped the microphone. Stared out at the audience – willing silence. The Nurgs wandered up the steps onto the stage. One picked up a guitar. Plugged it into an amplifier. Fiddled with some switches. Played a crashing chord that brought absolute silence. Sat on another amplifier. Put his head in his hands.

The compère cleared his throat. "Ladies and gentlemen! While we're all enjoying yourselves, and each other's company, and before we hear from Big Ned Nembutal and the Nurgs – one of who you've just heard invoking his musical muse – a word about this year's parish outing to Lourdes…"

Big Ned and the other two Nurgs began hooking up. The drummer, dressed in a zebra skin, began to insert himself into his equipment.

The compère took a sip of his drink. "Quizzes and dances and sponsored events every Saturday to help the old and ill to get free places on the coach! Saturday being today, for those who aren't sure… Hopefully with everyone returning with something from *The Shrine* – some, praise be to God, cured! Others with good and holy tales… Mrs Rooney, for instance, coming back last year with her usual extra-large flask of Lourdes water. Customs fella points at it. 'Holy water!' cries she. Customs fella opens it for a sniff. 'Gin!' sez he. 'Another miracle!' cries she!"

One or two people laughed. Someone groaned loudly.

The compère shook his head. Finished his whisky. Clapped his hands. "So! Without further ado, folks! Father Malachy's answer to the Beatles! Big Ned Nembutal and the Nurgs!"

The compère lurched away towards the steps. Big Ned grabbed his crotch; shook it at the compère's departing back. The tinny country music began again. People silently stood once more. The music abruptly stopped.

Crust slipped into the chair next to John.

Big Ned gripped the microphone. Released it. Took a clear plastic bag from his pocket. Shook something from it onto the back of his hand. Inhaled loudly. Began to cough and sneeze.

"Where's he getting *that* these days?" said Mr O'Rourke in Crust's direction.

Crust shook his head slightly.

"Irish snuff," said Mr O'Rourke.

Big Ned gripped the microphone again. "One of our own to start. 'Just Another Night', written by our drummer, the one and only Bobby Mac!"

From inside the drum mountain came rolls, thumps and clashings. Ned pursed his lips moodily. Stuck his thumb into his half-unzipped fly. The noise from the drums continued. Ned's hand went from his fly to his nose; a finger shoved up one of his nostrils.

Another shout from the audience. "Don't pick me, pal! I'm not playing."

Loud laughter and conversation all round. Two or three full glasses in front of most of the male drinkers. At the centre of the bar, the priest had a large whisky clutched in one hand; someone's coat lapel in the other.

Big Ned poked his head inside the drum kit, still holding the mic near his lips. "Come on, Bobby! Fucking behave!"

After a final roll and smash on the cymbals, there was silence.

Ned faced the audience again. "Yeah! Right! Thanks, Bobby! Letting us know where you're coming from! Though after that twenty-first do last week, does anybody really want to?! 'Just Another Night'!"

The group struck individual attitudes and began walking up and down the stage to a long, slow introduction. Guitar bodies wedged in their crotches. Guitar necks pointing up towards the ceiling.

Crust nodded affably to Mr O'Rourke. "Interesting group. Winsomely sentimental?"

"Sound like two Harrison boats," said John's father.

"Still. Nice and slow to dance to… You and Chris, maybe?"

With a final crashing chord, Big Ned fell on one knee facing the audience.

"The days run together.
There's no change in the weather.
There's no time for the future,
And though she might suit, you're
Looking out for the next one,
So another pretext's gone
For escaping the time clock,
Getting clear of the bedrock.
And it's…"

There was a pause as Big Ned dropped the mic. Everyone took another drink, or lit up a cigarette.

"…Just another night,
Bored and feeling low.
Smoke a joint of hash!
Lick a line of snow!
Score a gram of H!
Maybe do some speed!
Drop some LSD!
Cut yourself and BLEED!"

The group now pointed their guitars at the audience from between their legs. Threw the necks of their instruments into the air towards fame! Money! America!

"So. That dance with Chris?" said Crust to Mr O'Rourke.

"Maybe a bit advanced for me…"

Chris reached over. Took Mr O'Rourke's hand. Pulled him up and out onto the dance floor.

John looked at them. His father in the suit and tie he wore religiously for anything he considered even slightly religious or official. Chris in jeans and a loose top. The faithful milling and moving about under a slowly spinning coloured mirrorball.

Crust said, "Maybe *The Raft of the Medusa*; maybe *The Eternal Verities*."

"Another two Harrison boats?"

Crust lifted his pint. "The Chopin waltzes might be waltzes; but there's a big hernia waiting you try dancing them."

"Yeah. Thanks," said John. "Wouldn't have thought of that."

"Bit of a beauty," said Crust, nodding towards the dance floor and Chris.

John's drinks began to find their voice. "Yeah... Even as a kid... Always a bit different."

"That old Abbott and Costello horror-film exchange," said Crust. "'Went something like 'In half an hour the moon rises and I turn into a wolf.' 'You and twenty million other guys.'"

John nodded judiciously. "Yeah. Though for me... well... always felt we had this sort of understanding."

Crust took another sip of his pint.

"But then she met this other fella. Tradesman, of course. Chris's not the sort to marry a labourer or anything – but..."

"No good? This bloke she married?"

John watched Crust waggle his large, bug-eyed, floppy head in what seemed to be sympathy and agreement. Maybe he was wrong about Crust. Especially here in St Joe's. Warm. Comfortable. The few cans he'd had at his dad's. The few pints here. Dim lights. Laughter... Maybe

Crust had feelings like everybody else. Just didn't know how to show them. "Yeah," he said. "Bit of a bastard. And heard there might have been the odd bit of 'physical'. Though Chris's not the easiest person. Got this mouth on her…"

Crust took another sip.

"… But a really good heart under it all." John raised a hand to his eyes. "You know, Inspector, some of them seem to target the ones like her – the 'bit special' ones – just to destroy what's in them."

Crust said, "All these new rights they've got… The old days. St Anne Street. Copperas Hill. I'd give the con on the door a wink to drift away for five minutes. That's all it takes. Five seconds you know what you're doing!" He raised his glass. Took another sip. "OK, John. Couple of years ago there was a flourishing drugs racket along the South Coast. Not static, so difficult to nail down. Ronnie and lovely Liz…"

"Yeah. Liz, too," said John. "Also special. But in a different sort of way."

"… Mobile homes rigged as laboratories. Chemistry degree dropouts with problems… Not as many as they ended up with."

John closed his eyes. "Five seconds? That's fast! Even for a big fucker… fella like yourself!"

"Million pounds – maybe more – before we caught them."

John's eyes shot open.

Crust nodded. "Everything in Liz's name, so did the time. But not a lot. And not in your common jug."

"Insane asylum?"

"'Extenuating circumstances' would've got Crippen off. Gets out expecting half the cash; a loving husband… Half the cash, anyway."

"Why would anyone leave someone like Liz?"

Crust stared. "John! I'm going to give you Raite's actual address."

John shook an admonishing finger. "The prefab, right?"

Crust stared harder. John put one finger against the side of his nose. Gave a sly smile.

"OK," said Crust. "Thing is, does Mrs Raite know about the prefab yet?"

John again put a finger against the side of his nose. Gave a sly smile.

"*Don't* do that again!" said Crust in a tight voice.

John coughed and took a drink.

"See, John, that mil. belongs the taxpayer! Needs to be found. So we need Raite 'started'. Out in the open. I'm sending you in Ucca…"

"Ucca?"

"Undercover—"

"*Disguised*, eh?!"

"No. Just to pretend you're a dickhead. Thick as a plank. Couldn't spot your shadow with a searchlight behind you… Can you manage this?"

John ran his tongue across his top lip. "What's in it for me?"

"Few bob, maybe. Sort of 'citizen's reward'."

John took a quick drink.

"Plus my goodwill," continued Crust. "Handy, you're staying in this game."

"That's a promise?"

"We'll need the layout of the place. The money itself if you can spot it…"

"How big is that sort of cash? I mean, would you get it in your ma's shopping bag?"

"Largish holdall. I'd mention a wall safe behind a painting except prefabs don't exactly have walls… We need him disturbed; off balance… Think you can do that?"

"Totally convinced! Er… can I mention Mrs Raite?"

"Bogger might be better! Put some extra fizz in Ron's lemonade."

"This Bogger," said John, clearing his throat slightly, "ever met him?"

Crust smiled. "Not what he was…"

"No?"

"Getting on a bit. Wants to put his feet up; settle down with Liz… But got this rep, so has to plough-on murdering, maiming, raping…"

Big Ned struck a final exhausted pose in the front centre of the stage.

"… Just another night,
And you've won the race.
Now the moon's too bright,
Doesn't know its place!"

With a series of discords the group began to stroll slowly round the stage, winding down the song and bumping fists. Dancers began drifted off the floor. 'Blanket on the Ground' began once more. Chris and Mr O'Rourke started heading back. Stopped to talk to another couple.

John picked up Crust's empty glass and looked at him.

Crust shook his head. "Driving... Now, Raite has two shipping containers arrived or about to arrive at the Seaforth Container Terminal for New York. Ship sailing next Friday."

"*Ocean Seaspray*, right?" John said complacently.

Crust stared at him.

"Chief officer's an old pal of mine... Introduction you want one. Get you on board for a drink?"

Crust shook his head as if bothered by some sort of insect. "Now! These containers are filled with assorted worthless shit – bit like your office – among which we think he'll try and plant the mill. Not immediately, but before she sails. So he'll be in and out of them; the containers."

"Hang on! Bundles of notes? Not going to be difficult to spot. And if those nosy customs bastards..." John snapped his fingers. "Know what I'd do? Something smaller... diamonds?"

Crust smiled. "Could be... So we may just let them go – the containers. Over in America 'interception and confiscation' is more liberal, especially regarding Limey antique dealers. But we need him 'started'; made aware..."

"What of?"

"That he's been found! And if you can find him..."

"And am working for Liz and Bogger?"

"Exactly."

"But even if I get in, how'll I get him to open up to me?"

"Shared interests?" Crust suggested. "Maybe art?"

John frowned. "Art?" He drank half of his father's pint.

"John. What's in his shop window?" said Crust patiently.

"Oh, yeah."

"Mainly I want him off balance! Thinking Bogger! Thinking panic!" Crust pointed at the dance floor.

Chris and Mr O'Rourke now threading their way back. Behind them, at the stage end of the bar, Curly, Charlie, The Nurgs – all talking excitedly at once.

Crust stood abruptly. Began buttoning his overcoat. "Right! Regards to the folks. One thing. Raite. He's as slick as a greased door handle, and under the weird hair is a head full of rusty nails!"

"That's two things," said John complacently.

Crust stared across the dance floor. "I'm not totally opposed to ambition. But it can lead to other things. In your case – don't let it. Don't compromise me – my integrity – or I'll come for you. Properly… Get there Monday morning. About eleven…"

"Why eleven?"

"Because I say so!"

Crust turned away. Moved purposely across to the door and out into the night.

John smiled. Stood. His father and Chris arrived back at the table.

"Went well, then?" asked Chris.

"Anyone fancy a curry after here?" John stared at her.

"What's going on?" asked Mr O'Rourke. "What did he want?"

"Dad!" said John dismissively. "Let's not spoil the evening… Complex stuff's just gone down."

Mr O'Rourke immediately turned and walked to the bar. John shrugged. Looked to Chris for an explanation.

"John, can I say something?"

John made a gesture of consent. Took a further mouthful of his dad's pint.

"Curly thinks you're not… well… treating him properly. That you took him in as a partner. He's upset… It means a lot to him, working with you."

John took her hand. Tried to look contrite. "Let's discuss it over a meal," he said. "Grab a 'fast black' into town. Find a restaurant; discuss Curly."

She hesitated for a moment, then nodded.

Gotcha!

He stood and held her coat. As she turned to slip into it, he permitted himself a smile of triumph. Glancing towards the bar, he saw his father, Curly and Charlie all staring across with expressionless faces.

Fuck 'em! He threw back his shoulders. Took Chris by the elbow. Began to thread his way towards the door.

SEQUENCE 49

SATURDAY, 6th MARCH, 1982. 23.30
INT / NIGHT MAIN OFFICE, CONTAINER
TERMINAL, SEAFORTH

All movement in and around the containers and the terminal was controlled from a substantial, newly built, four-storey control centre situated on the dock itself, just back from the berths. From the building's top floor – picture windows on all sides – everything happening on and off the container estate could be monitored.

Ships, cranes, containers, the approach roads, security checkpoints, and barriers and perimeter fencing.

The top floor also held the office of the container terminal's manager; and that of his cargo planner. About midnight, the manager stood looking down onto the deserted, icy, windswept berth; the silent ship. In his sixties, he wore a creased suit and white shirt. Merchant Marine tie and lapel badge. Worn, highly-polished, black shoes.

The door to the planner's office opened and the planner came into the main office. Thirties, well-cut sports coat and slacks, woollen polo neck, suede shoes. He was carrying a coffee mug. He picked up the manager's mug and made his way to the kettle and coffee jar. Switched on the kettle and addressed the manager's back. "Right! Now ready to start loading first thing Monday."

"Good of you to come in so late."

"Things need to happen as they should." The planner brought across the two coffees. Stood next to the manager. They both considered the bleak, freezing dock; the ship's stern with its open Ro-Ro door.

"Ever miss it?" asked the planner, picking up a set of binoculars from the window ledge.

"Mainly miss being young. Tying up alongside Calcutta. Up The Hong Kong Bar. Meeting a ship-wife live in my cabin the three weeks or so until we sailed. 'Dance of the Moon Maidens' at Cochin… Never see that again either." The manager gestured to the freezing scene outside. "You'd need to have sailed in tankers miss that lot out there."

The planner focused on the approach to the gates. "Pickets are setting up."

The manager picked up his own set of glasses and looked towards the approach road. Small figures gathered round braziers holding teas, coffees or cans of beer, jumping and slapping their arms with the cold.

"Even they must realise it's now Canute and the tide!" said the planner. "That there *must* be redundancies?"

"Some realise that, where they come from, retirement kills more men than hard work ever did."

The planner made a noise in his throat. "Hard work?! Pull the other one!" He swept the dock with his glasses. "Progress takes its toll; always has! Galleys to sailing ships, sailing ships to steam cargo… Now containers. Manual dock labour is over!"

"You're a university man?" asked the manager.

"Economics."

"There's a policeman been on the phone," said the manager. "Name of Crust. Detective inspector."

"Don't tell me they've actually solved the missing container of cigarettes?"

The manager shook his head. "Not yet."

The planner laughed shortly.

"It's about two other containers. Be coming on site probably Monday. Manifest over there on the desk. Belong to a bloke called Porsche…"

"Naturally."

"… To do with antiques."

The planner shook his head.

"This policeman, Crust, wants them somewhere in full view of the office and everyone on the dock. Placed under a confluence of lights."

"OK. I'll sort it Monday." The planner raised the binoculars once more to look at the pickets. "Midnight Saturday and look at them! Think they have some sort of lives?"

"A lot of these men," said the manager carefully, "… this *is* their life. This and their back-to-back terraces. They don't have gardens. It's this or the pub – not much of a choice; nor for their wives… the ones I really feel sorry for."

The planner shrugged. Looked closely at the faces of the picketers; any he might later be able to identify.

SEQUENCE 50

SATURDAY, 6th MARCH, 1982. 23.40
INT / NIGHT 'BOMBAY DUCK' RESTAURANT

Inside The Bombay Duck, the voices were quiet; the wallpaper flock; the doorman's uniform that of a nightclub bouncer, plus red turban and cummerbund.

As Chris and John entered, a waiter hurried across holding a number of fanned-out menus while gesturing forcibly towards a table set in the window. Here Chris would be in full view of male passers-by who hadn't yet decided how to finish their evening.

Chris took a seat. John followed. The waiter put two menus on the table and asked John if he would like a drink. Did not look directly at Chris.

"Might try a lager," John said to Chris. "Round the evening off. How about you?"

"Gin and tonic, please."

"And two chicken curries, mate!" Without having looked at them, John held up the two menus in the general direction of the waiter.

Chris plucked one from his hand. Opened and scanned it. Asked for some dish unknown to John.

The waiter nodded. Scratched something on his pad. Turned back to John. "Kingfisher? Cobra?"

"Yeah," said John. "A great country, India – all those animals and birds under threat!"

"They're brands of beer!" said Chris abruptly. "Bring him a Cobra!"

The waiter, face expressionless, bowed and left the table.

John and Chris, as one, gazed out onto the main road. Its progression of late-night merrymakers lurching along towards clubs where they might possibly gain admittance. Places where they might urinate. Vomit. Pass out.

An Indian in a white mess jacket came to the table. Put down the drinks. "Your gin and beer, sirs. The food to follow immediately."

John gazed at the label on the bottle of Cobra. Wondered how safe it might be to drink. Under what circumstances and conditions it had been brewed.

"To an interesting evening at St Joe's." Chris raised her drink in his direction.

John raised his own glass. Took a mouthful. *Not too bad.* "You seem pretty much at home here – ordering and that. The lingo and what have you…"

Chris smiled. "My ex was a great one for chats over the chapattis before it became punches over the porridge."

She smiled more broadly. "Sorry, John. Just catches up sometimes. Strangely enough, usually after times when I've actually half-enjoyed myself. Like tonight…"

Half-enjoyed? "Yeah, well… Did my best, Chris. Man can't do no more."

"… Though it's starting to bother me less now I'm doing my usual day-to-day things back at my mum's."

"In your own time, Chris. Just glad to be here with you."

Chris nodded half-heartedly, then immediately seemed to change her mood. With soft, appreciative eyes she said, "Makes a lot of difference to have someone who tries to understand. Who's willing to listen."

What did the lads in The Bayonets say? 'Women! Can't live with them; can't live without them! Just don't take them to Anfield or Goodison!' That old story of the fella outside the ground offering the spare seat next to him for sale. 'Usually come with the missus – but she's being buried this afternoon'.

John laughed out loud.

Chris stared at him.

John shifted slightly. "Yeah. Nice to be trusted… Bring us even closer."

Chris said quickly, "So! The case! Getting any nearer?"

John paused. "Got his address – Raite's."

"Crust give you it?"

"Had it already figured. Case I needed to give it to *him*!"

"Oh?"

A different Indian materialised. Small. Corpulent. Very large eyes. Thick, curled hair. He bobbed at the knee, and laid down two plates from a silver-coloured salver. "One curried chicken, one vegetable jalfrezi, two naan bread. You are wanting more drink, sir?"

"Still got this, thanks," said John.

The waiter looked at Chris. She shook her head. The waiter bobbed again; then bobbed away.

"Yeah," said John, "complicated all round. Well. A million in drug money…"

Chris looked up, startled. "Drugs?!… A million pounds?!"

Fuck! John held up a calming hand. "Chris. Just think one of Mick's scams, only bigger… Though all on the q.t., though, for the time being… OK?"

"And Curly?"

"Sort of in and not in… Tricky."

"Does he know all this? Drugs? Money?"

"Well, not everything…"

"John, I don't want him involved in this."

John patted her hand. "You leave it to me." He took another mouthful of Cobra. *No. Not bad stuff. You wouldn't drink it on a regular basis, but still…"*

"John! I'm serious about Curly."

"Chris! I look on him as my own brother! Even brother-in-law?!"

Chris picked up her gin. "It's just… well… anything happened to Curly, my mum would never get over it."

John tapped the side of his head. "Got it! Make extra sure he's not exposed. 'Sides, don't think Crust goes much on him. Know he's your brother, but that mouth of his…"

She looked at him closely. Her mood seemed to change once more. "Yes. I can see that. That your policeman *friend* mightn't take to someone like our Curly…"

"No," John burped. "It's me who's more the 'fingers-on' man for Crust."

"Unless under a bedding machine in your old factory. When it's…"

"… Fingers-off?"

They both laughed. Chris, looking relieved, stirred the contents of her plate gently with her fork. "How will you approach him? Raite?"

"Art… maybe antiques." He yawned.

"Tired?"

"Yeah… Not done a lot, but somehow feel dead beat all the time."

"Emotional strain. Like when I was trying to force the divorce through; get the papers signed." She laughed apologetically. "There I go again!" She finished her gin. Her eyes began to shine.

John looked out of the window. A bus had stopped in the middle of the road directly outside. In front of it, two figures were weaving backwards and forwards in a drunken struggle. From the top deck of the bus, semi-comatose men stared down through the restaurant window. One caught John's eye and showed him a balled fist.

"Sometimes, you know, Chris, I wonder myself what's going on? What it's all about? Like in *Tarantula Tap Dance* when Brick's imprisoned in this hut in the middle of this jungle. Wrapped in barbed wire. Seated on a mound of skulls. Sticks of dynamite tied round his neck. Two windows; one either side of the hut. A candle on a table burning down towards the dynamite fuse. A moth flies in one window, circles the candle, flies out the other. Brick mutters into his secret micro-recorder. 'Brick's last testament. We enter from nowhere. Circle round a few times. Exit back to nowhere. Over and out.'" John shook his head. Shovelled a forkful of chicken curry into his mouth. Took a swig of Cobra. Looked towards Chris's left hand gently stirring her still-untouched food – food he'd be paying for! No wedding ring! He was sure she usually still wore it. Was she telling him something!? He suddenly leaned forward and grabbed the hand. "Notice you're not wearing the old wedding ring, Chris. That mean you're finally calling it a day on him?"

He pulled up her hand to his lips to kiss it, causing her fork to jerk some jalfrezi onto the floor and into his face.

Chris stared at him. His curry-stained lips. The piece of chicken between his teeth. The jalfrezi blobs on his forehead and cheeks.

He squeezed her hand hard. "Know what we need, Chris? A holiday! Crust mentioned these mobile homes Raite had. Then you the bedding factory and the fingers! Fella there lost his left index. Took his missus on a caravan holiday."

"John… "

"So I thought, *I've never had a weekend in a caravan!*"

"I have!"

He dropped her hand. Took a sip of his lager. A waiter came and gently mopped the food from his face.

Chris's eyes softened. "John, I couldn't have another man like that yet. Not if he came on a gold plate with an apple in his mouth. You see this crew standing round the walls? Extras from *King of the Khyber Rifles*?"

"Very colourful." John looked at the scraps remaining on his plate. The empty beer bottle and glass. Chris's almost untouched food. All costing money and fuck-all to show for it.

"You ever wonder what they do to their wives when they get home?… John!? Can we get our coats?"

SEQUENCE 51

SUNDAY, 7th MARCH, 1982. 10.00
EXT / DAY STARBOARD ALLEYWAY, *OCEAN SEASPRAY*

Sunday morning. Everything quiet on the berth. The *Ocean Seaspray* lying starboard side on to the quay. Bows facing the tidal locks and River Mersey. At a point roughly halfway along the *Seaspray*'s starboard alleyway, running down from the ship to the quay, was a fitted gangway with a hand winch set at its top for its raising and lowering. At the top of the gangway a small boarding platform. There were safety guide ropes round the platform and down both sides of the gangway.

From a companionway door near the head of the gangway a sixtyish man stepped out over the combing and onto the deck. Quartermaster Wally Jinks. Jinks was dressed in a heavy navy duffel coat, a black woollen Monmouth cap, and black fingerless gloves. He had a two-and-a-half-foot-square blackboard tucked under his right arm. His left hand gripped a wooden vegetable crate. He walked to a point opposite the head of the gangway. Bent and placed the veg. crate on the deck against the ship's steel bulkhead where it would automatically meet the eye of anyone mounting the gangway to board ship.

Wally laid the blackboard on the ship's rail. Took a piece of white chalk from one pocket. From the other a can of beer. Popped it. Took a glug. Put the can on the rail alongside the blackboard. On the blackboard, still flat on the rail, he wrote with the chalk:

S.S. *Ocean Seaspray*
Liverpool for New York
Sails 11pm, Friday 12th March

He erased and rewrote one or two of the letters, interspersing these corrections with mouthfuls of beer, then lifted the blackboard from the rail and propped it on the crate. He stepped back onto the gangway platform to admire and judge the position of his handiwork. How it would appear to those *shoreside fuckers* who would be constantly on-and-off the ship looking to lift anything that wasn't nailed-down until the *Seaspray* finally sailed.

He picked up his beer. Leaned forward over the rail, slowly scanning for'ard and aft along the quay. His gaze lingering on the ship's ropes; and also resting briefly on an engine-room discharge sputtering white-foamed cooling water into the dock.

Wally upended the can to his mouth, draining its last dregs. Squashed it in his hand. Threw it down the side of the ship.

SEQUENCE 52

On a day overcast almost to the point of darkness, steel-tipped rain lashed the *Express* as it lurched up the muddy lane to Raite's prefab, its one working wiper dragging back and forwards like a maimed lab insect. Rounding the bend to the house, John eased on the brake. Stopped the car a hundred feet or so from the front door. Put off the lights.

"'For sale. One cowshed'," said Curly looking towards the pre-fab.

"At least no sign of Beardy in the Morris," said John. "Though there was that other set of lights I thought was following us; big Merc, looked like."

"Didn't clock them, mate."

"You wouldn't," said John, "gassing on about Charlie and music management."

"Expanding field."

"Like bankruptcy!… Ready?"

Curly picked up a newspaper from the floor of the car. "Best of luck, mate."

John stared. "You're not coming?"

"Someone'll need to live to tell the tale."

"OK," said John. "Quarter of an hour, then come and get me."

Curly winked. "What's left of you."

John climbed out of the car and started towards the house. The sunken gravel-cum-tarmac drive was full of water pits. Raised, cracked, humps of concrete. The house was dirty. Filthy windows. Drawn, heavy curtains. No wonder Harry Rose had decided on his old girl's place with its stables.

John reached the front door and stared at the new intercom system. A recently cut deadlock keyhole. He pressed the buzzer.

The intercom crackled. "Yes?" said a flat voice.

John took a deep breath. "Mr Porsche? John O'Rourke. Passed your shop in West Heartwood; saw that painting in the window. That Judy walking through those trees. Sort of thing the wife might like; birthday and that. No name, so I went the town hall; got your address from the electoral register. Pretty soon, her birthday. Why I've gone to these lengths..." He broke off and stared at the microphone.

There was a short pause, then the sound of a double lock coming off. Then the door opened a few inches on a thick chain. "Back, please..."

John stepped back for inspection. The chain came off and the door opened. Raite was wearing what John immediately classified as a 'smoking jacket'. Silk. Broad, shiny lapels. Big, deep pockets. Tasselled cord round the waist. Wow! Top posing gear!! One of Raite's hands was in a pocket, from which a handle protruded.

Following John's eyes, Raite drew out a claw hammer. "Boarding a broken window." He smacked the head of the hammer into the palm of his other hand. Still looked as if something else – something bulky – was in the pocket.

John stepped back. Raite did likewise. Gestured for John to enter.

John found himself in a dirty, freezing-cold, bare concrete hallway. A couple of odd scraps of torn lino. Raite closed the door. Put on the chain. Turned the deadlock. There seemed to be four rooms off the hallway, which ran the length of the house to the back wall, where there was what looked like a seized-up fire-exit door. Raite, still holding the hammer, opened the door to the first room on the left and gestured with his head for John to enter.

Another world. Newly painted walls and floorboards. A painting under a spotlight. Two heaters. A 'Turkish' carpet. Very warm.

Raite gave an affable smile. "Coat?" He took John's anorak, openly patting the pockets. Placed it carefully on the varnished wooden boards near the door.

The rain outside increased its intensity, spattering loudly against the dirty, impenetrable front window.

John gazed round uneasily. "Nasty weather," he offered.

"'*Blow, blow, thou winter wind...*'" said Raite. Still smiling. Head cocked to one side.

John made a gesture of conceding to the better man and smiled back.

"Drink?" asked Raite, pointing the hammer towards a cut-glass decanter on a tray with four tumblers; the whole on a table with spindly legs and lots of scratches.

John nodded slowly, then more quickly. He could easily get used to this.

SEQUENCE 53

MONDAY, 8th MARCH, 1982. 11.15
INT / DAY MERCEDES IN FIELD OPPOSITE CART
TRACK TO RAITE'S PRE-FAB

The Mercedes was parked behind the hedge in the open field opposite the bottom of the cart track.

"Don't like it, Liz. Someone else with an 'in'. What'd he say again?"

Mrs Raite opened the window. Flicked away her cigarette. Had a scratch. "Bogger! For the last time! The motel desk clerk said he'd been rung by someone who wouldn't leave a name but said to tell 'Hansel and Gretel' – giving our room number – that Ronnie was living up a lane opposite a red public telephone box on the road out of West Heartwood. Where O'Rourke would be about eleven."

"'Hansel and Gretel'?" said Bogger. "What the fuck's that about?"

Mrs Raite shrugged. Lit another cigarette.

Bogger leaned across to light it. "That fucking copper, maybe? That O'Rourke mentioned?"

"Possibly…"

"Why?"

Mrs Raite shrugged again.

They stared through the hedge towards the bottom of the cart track.

Harry Rose staggered past the opening of the track. His four Cunarders straining at their leashes; one stopping to urinate, bringing the party to a halt. Harry wearing a large black sou'wester and a suit of oilskins.

"Scott's Emulsion," said Mrs Raite.

"What the fuck's that?" asked Bogger.

"My grandfather used to give it me as a child. Build me up."

"And did a nice job!" As if by rote, Bogger leaned over and squeezed one of her breasts.

Mrs Raite stayed perfectly still, her face blank.

Harry and the dogs set off once more.

"Walking dogs in this fucking weather!" said Bogger. "What's wrong with them up here?"

"Anything to do with dogs," said Mrs Raite, "automatically excludes anything to do with common sense – or women. Page one – Home Counties bible… You know, Bogg, although patently impossible, I felt I knew him… Something to do with tongues."

Bogger glared at her.

"Or maybe he's involved, too," said Mrs Raite. "I feel it's getting that way."

"I fucking hope so!" said Bogger viciously. "I fucking hope so!"

SEQUENCE 54

MONDAY 8th MARCH 1982. 11.25
INT / DAY RAITE'S PREFAB. EXT / DAY RAITE'S
PREFAB

Raite raised the heavy crystal glass. "'To nights we'll never remember with friends we'll never forget.'"

"Nice one," said John, taking a trial sip from his own glass.

"Twenty-year-old malt," said Raite.

"'Like angels' laughter tickling your tonsils,' as my old Irish Gran used to say about her Christmas port," said John. Then, "Got one of them cash 'n' carry cards, have you?"

"I don't vote, Mr O'Rourke. Do I look like an idiot? Never on an electoral list in my life."

John smiled. Took another sip. *Fucking hell! How heavy are these whisky glasses? Say what you like, the Raites of this world know how to live. Size of that gold watch! Surprised he can get his arm up to his mouth... Two electric fires! Both on! No wonder he needs drugs money! But that claw hammer? That lump at the bottom of his pocket!...?*

"Working for Liz?" Raite looked at John over the top of his own glass.

John immediately nodded.

"She has this address?"

John shook his head.

"Madame de Maintenon meets Madame Defarge meets Lady Godiva meets Lady Macbeth meets Lady Loony!" said Raite.

"Mmm..." said John.

"But a masturbator's dream."

"Er..."

"Frankly, Mr O'Rourke, you wouldn't know what to do with a woman like Liz."

"Why not tell me?... Then we'll both know."

Raite stared at this. Then remarked "Married yourself?"

John shook his head again. Tipped his glass forward. Raite half-filled it.

John sipped. Said in awe, "Like having a hot-water bottle inside you."

"Fiancée?... Girlfriend?"

"Sort of..."

"I look forward to meeting her."

Just as if.

"Jack..." Raite intoned. "Jack London said a man who can forgo drink and women can live very cheaply... Poor Jack!"

"Brick says 'sex' is a four-letter word," said John. "Brick Bradstreet. Guy with the gimlet eye and the two-tone golf shoes."

Raite nodded. "Self-preservation, sex, instinct of the herd: the three great driving forces of human nature. Money helps, of course. Doesn't buy happiness; just a far better brand of misery. You know what sex was like between Liz and myself, John?... May I call you John?"

"Ron! Call me anything you like, long as you don't call me early!"

Raite's smile tightened for a moment. "You know how long I've been celibate?" he asked.

John tipped the almost-empty glass vaguely in Raite's direction.

"But, like Lazarus, I will arise!" Raite gave John a top-up. "The painter Mataran," he continued, "declared himself finally free of sexual desire at the age of eighty-two and never painted another decent canvas!"

John drank half his whisky. "Bit like Inspector Crust... Weird stuff."

"Inspector Crust?" Raite made a sweeping gesture with the hammer.

Fuck! "This plain-clothes copper. Checked me out when I first set up. Nutter. Bit like Lazarus: holding himself back. No real emotions or anything."

Raite lifted a finger. Left the room. John stared round. Moved across to look at the painting above the empty fireplace. Shook the spindly table. Quickly topped up his glass while keeping an eye on the door.

Raite oiled back carrying a white envelope. Held it out.

John took it and flipped the flap with his thumb. Banknotes.

"Three hundred," said Raite. Held up the decanter. "Perhaps I've insulted you? – offering you money?" Extended a hand as if for the return of the envelope.

John held out his glass. Kept the other hand, holding the envelope, close to his body. "What's it for, Ron?"

"This policeman – Crust?… Told you what?"

"Drugs. Missing money and that. See what I could find out…" John gestured around the room. "We all need a few bob, Ron, right?" He drank, then suddenly swayed forward. *Fuck!* Too much, too fast. But stuff like this! For nothing! Make the most of it while you can. *'Make the most – before it's toast!'* John smiled at nothing. Shook his head. Laughed out loud.

Raite stared even more carefully. "John, towards the end of the '60's, many of my friends developed problems; became sick. Liz, too, unfortunately."

"Don't deserved…" said John in a thickening voice. "Not Lizsh…"

"So. A 'People's Pharmacy'…"

"Poor Lizsh!… Any background, Ron?… For my records."

"London 'modelling' ultimately… Her past? Shrouded in Home Counties mystery. Windlesham whispers; Sunningdale secrets; Berkshire banking practices…"

" 'Down South', then? Posh?"

"*O Sancta Simplicitas!*" said Raite. "'Holy Simplicity'! As Huss observed to the old peasant woman stoking the fire."

"Bit King Billy? – Chilly? – Was he?… This Huss?"

"Being burned alive for his beliefs… No. Liz exhibits a sense of privilege and high entitlement. A 'hoity-toity fucking bitch' in the patois. But came to me for help, spark plugs flashing in both ears. Yes, I gave her drugs; perhaps wrongly. Paid her account in some *very* expensive reclamation yards. Even gave her marriage!"

"Wasn't enough, eh, Ron? Yeah… Can see she's maybe that sort! Even though I'm not one to judge people myself."

"John, as far as women go, there are only two sorts. Those a man can marry. And those he can't."

John swayed forward. "And what's Lizsh, Ron?"

"To keep her stable I had to increase production to cater to her whims. Money flowed. Needed collecting…"

John nodded sadly. "Don't tell me, Mate!… Bogger?"

"Who could wring blood from an iron girder."

"Yeah. Heard about him. What's he really like, Ron?" John tipped his glass.

"Think Goya's madmen," said Raite, "but without the good humour!" He poured another inch or so.

Miserable bastard! "Goysa, yeah."

"Unfortunately, cracks appeared. Think Piranesi's prisons…"

"You got arrested?"

"Not personally."

"But Liz got done?"

"And blames me. Would see me emasculated. Shot with the arrows of the St Sebastian. You've seen the Zurbaran?…"

"Not yet, Ron… But one day… one day… "

"Reminds me a little of you at this moment…"

"And wanted Bogger roast your nuts as well, I suppose?"

"That, too."

"Thing is, Ron, I'm supposed to give her this address…" John tilted his glass hopefully.

Raite tapped the envelope in John's hand. Poured more whisky. "John, I'm leaving shortly – America." Tapped the envelope again. "Muddy the waters. Feign ignorance… just *don't* reveal this address!"

"Ron. You got to see I got pofesshinal commits… commitments?" John tightened his grip on the envelope. Swayed. Lost interest. Looked round. Lurched towards Raite's painting. Put one hand on the wall next to it. Screwed up one eye to view it from close quarters.

Raite followed, carrying the decanter. John turned to face him. Gestured uncomprehendingly at the painting.

"Yes," said Raite. "Easily mistaken for a dish of sacrificial entrails. In reality, early Plonksby. *Reclining Nude with Jam Sandwich.* Piers Plonksby. Knightsbridge

School. Good colour values. Interesting planes and masses. Investment possibility, even though its only genuine aspect now is the signature."

"*Reclining Nude with Jam Sandwich*; early Plonkshby." John peered at the unreadable scrawl in the right-hand corner. "Same problem... Arian's writing."

"Arian?"

"See, Ron. Bit of a collector myself... Heard of *Celestial Vision*?"

"Mmm..." Raite tipped the decanter once more.

"Signature gnarled-over like this one... But defo 'Arian'. Big halo... Big thrippenny-bits... Heretic... Father and the Son... Not the Holy Ghost!" John gestured helplessly. "Catholic stuff, Ron. Complicated." He took a sip. Raised a thumb.

Raite nodded. "Given current forgery levels, soon only written and attested provenance will matter!"

"That place in France?"

"Work bought from the artist in his studio, fully documented before being sold onwards. Provenance, in fact, will become the new signature... You bought directly from Arian?"

John pursed his lips. "Not exactly totally truthfully exactly. Look, Ron! Been doing a bit of reading... public library. Ron, would you say yourself painters are mainly nutters?"

"Of the three fine arts – literature, painting and music – I consider the potential for mental illness – only too rife among all three – is much greater for painters."

John held out his glass hopefully.

"Take Beethoven..."

John jiggled his glass up and down. "Wouldn't be a drop more, would there, Ron? Get me back to the car? Usually I wouldn't ask, but it's fuckinge… fuckinbg… fucking freejing outside."

Raite emptied the last of the whisky into John's glass. "Say Beethoven came back…"

"Sort of Lazarus again?"

"… Or Shakespeare. Asking for the return of their works."

"Got me there, Ron."

"Some issues, but no one would seriously contest their basic rights to the contents of their manuscripts. But if Alexander the Great reappeared; demanded the return of the countries he'd conquered? The cities he founded?"

"Well…"

"More to the point. If van Gogh came back, asking for his canvases?"

"No chance."

"Correct! Paintings are different from music or literature. Like land, they revolve around a specific *type* of ownership."

John staggered. Grabbed a lapel of Raite's jacket. "Ron! Ron! *Da-doo-ron-ron…*"

"You know why?"

John waggled his head.

"Somehow a painting – more than, say, a novel or symphony – seems to be part of an obligate symbiotic relationship between the artist, his psyche, and the purchaser's pocket and psyche…"

"… Deep depths, Ron! Deep! Deep! Depths!"

"… That is, if Beethoven or Schubert hand over a manuscript – it's simply a collection of papers… But a painter handing over a canvas resonates on a far more visceral level where the relinquishing of the canvas becomes a splinter hewn from the soul of the artist – which then becomes liable to stress fracture… I hope I'm not making a relatively taxing concept too simple?"

"You just tell it like you see it, Ron! Don't give a fuck about me!"

John sipped the last of his drink.

Raite plucked the empty glass from John's hand. Picked up his anorak from the floor. Opened the door to the hallway.

John struggled into the anorak without releasing the envelope. "Yeah, right, Ron… Time's up. Maybe you 'n' me?… Some Sat'dy night?… Bayonets?"

Raite blocked John's exit. Touched the envelope.

"Yeah," said John. Slid the envelope into his inside pocket. "Yeah, I'm in, Ron."

Raite smiled. Stepped back. Gestured up the hall towards the front door.

"Yeah. Though, 'fore I go, Ron… Mind I use the toilet?… Just won't last back the 'Pool without a slash. Where is it, mate?… Down the hall?"

Raite took John's arm. Led him to the front door. Opened it. "Gardening, they say, is a contract between man, nature, and God. So go outside and fulfil that contract!… Piss on a flowerbed!"

John closed one eye as he attempted to step down onto the concrete path.

Raite, helping him, said in a low voice, "John!"

John stopped, swaying.

"I hope you don't mind me mentioning, but there's probably at least one good charity shop in the village. You may end up looking like *The Leader of the Luddites* from the 1812 engraving; but the labels will be half-acceptable."

"Wosthat mean, Ron?"

"It means there are four things that will tell you all you need to know about any man. Car! Shoes! Watch! Wife!"

John was given a slight push and lurched forward into a puddle. Behind him, he heard the door close and the bolts go on. Simultaneously, his boots filled with freezing water and the whisky struck home.

He began to walk slowly, legs apart, back to the car. His old Gran he'd mentioned to Raite – what was it she used to say? 'Sure, and what if the rain does run into one of the holes in your brogans? Doesn't it just run out another?!' That and her fucking 'soda bread'! Like eating lumpy wallpaper paste... Why did every day feel more of a struggle *just to stay sane?* As he gazed ahead to locate the *Express*, he stepped into a second puddle. He raised his face to allow the rain to beat on it. Shouted, "Car... Shoes... Wife... Watch!" Opened his arms; face still upraised. *But what have I got? Wreck of a car! Boots full of holes! Chris and Liz both fucking me off! A watch with no second hand!* He pulled up his sleeve. Held up his wrist. "No second hand!" he shouted. "No fucking second hand!" He wiped his eyes, which were suddenly full of tears. Looked down. Why were his feet so cold? Lifting one leg, he shook off the shoe. Fell over. Knelt and emptied the water out of the shoe. Held it to the sky. Staggered to his feet and kicked off the other shoe. Threw both towards the prefab. Staggered onwards towards the car. Gripped the door handle. Pulled. Lost his grip. Staggered back and sat in another puddle.

Curly hopped out and helped him to his feet. "Christ, mate! What'd he do to you? What's happening with the shoes?"

"Crurl! I'm buying a pair of chukka boots!"

"Yeah. Right!… That polo club just opened Stanley Road." Curly struggled to get John into the car.

"Talking malted Scotch!… Lirature and art…"

"Talking broken biscuits!" Curly lodged John in the front passenger seat. "Won't be a minute!"

John grabbed at him. "Don' leave me, Crurl. Not now…"

Curly shook him off. Collected the shoes. Climbed into the driver's seat.

John leant across, attempting to take the steering wheel. "Jack London! Woke one morning. Eighty-two. Couldn't get it up any more…"

"Should fucking hope not – at that age! Dirty bastard!"

"Crurl… Only genuine from the provinces. The fucking *provinces*!"

"John, just get your head down while I get us home, OK?!"

John sank back in the seat. Rested one hand over the anorak's inside pocket and the envelope. Gave a loose-lipped, sly grin as his head fell on his chest.

Curly started the car.

SEQUENCE 55

MONDAY, 8th MARCH, 1982. 12.00
INT / DAY RAITE'S PREFAB. EXT / DAY RAITE'S
PREFAB

From behind the curtains, Raite watched the *Express* lurch away. He picked up a *Yellow Pages*. Went to 'Second-Hand Cars'. Drew a ring round 'Bazza's Birkenhead Bangers'.

Holding the *Yellow Pages* over his head as an umbrella, he left the prefab and walked round the back of the building to where the Porsche was parked. Unlocked the door and put the keys in the ignition and documentation in the glove compartment.

Walked back into the house.

Put his finger on the number for 'Bazza's Birkenhead Bangers'. Picked up the phone.

Outside, distant thunder rolled.

SEQUENCE 56

MONDAY, 8th MARCH 1982. 12.15
INT / DAY MERCEDES IN FIELD

Tucked behind the hedge in the field opposite the path to the prefab, Bogger and Mrs Raite watched the *Express* turn out and along the road leading to the motorway and Liverpool.

Mrs Raite wrestled her mule-pannier bag from the footwell and rooted out some make-up and three pill bottles. She took a pill from each. Lit a cigarette. Began to work on her face.

Bogger said, "Reckon that's them gone, Liz?"

Mrs Raite nodded. Bogger drove carefully out of the field and slowly up the cart track.

As they came in view of the prefab, Mrs Raite said, "Round the back."

Bogger edged the Mercedes down the side of the building, stopping near the Porsche. They surveyed the back of the bungalow with its rusted, jammed-up rear-entrance door and its newly boarded-up kitchen window.

Mrs Raite pointed towards the Porsche. "Let's start there."

SEQUENCE 57

MONDAY, 8th MARCH, 1982. 12.25
INT / DAY *EXPRESS*. EXT / DAY *EXPRESS*

Just before leaving the country road for the motorway approaches, Curly bumped over a dead stoat and jolted John awake.

John started uncomprehendingly. Grabbed his stomach. "Curl! Stop! Quick! Quick!"

Curly skidded the car to a halt.

John kicked open the door. Hung out, vomiting and retching. Climbed out. Bent over the verge to vomit once more. Groaning. Then, his back to the car, pulled out Raite's envelope. Checked it. As he held it, Crust's cold voice came into his head: *Don't compromise me – my integrity – or I'll come for you. Properly.* John retched once more. Stood. Stared into space. What if Raite got lifted by Crust? He'd be sure to blab that he'd paid-off John. And Crust would come for him. Yeah… The Raites of this world would come and go, but Crust was the big turnstile that led to steady work. And the three hundred? Sort of thing a finickity fucker like Crust might see as a bribe. Be a real bummer… giving it up. But long term…?

John slipped the envelope back into his pocket. Made his way back to the passenger door. Fell into the seat. Closed his eyes.

"Ready, mate?" asked Curly.

"We need to go back."

"Back to Raite's?… Why's that?"

John, eyes still closed, said, "Just do it, Curl… OK?"

Curly stared, then began to try to turn the car in the narrow lane. Another car pulled in behind, its driver watching them with a slight smile. Finally, after a cheery wave from the other vehicle, they began to head back.

John opened his eyes. Stared ahead through the windscreen. "I got something from Raite."

Curly stiffened slightly.

"Envelope… Money… Worked it on me while I was half-pissed."

"How much?"

John took the envelope from his inside pocket. Laid it on his knee. "No idea. Handed it me I was leaving."

Curly shot a sideways glance. "Didn't think of mentioning it earlier?"

"Fuck's sake, Curl. I've been passed out. Fucking bladdered. Conned by Raite's whisky…"

"So what's it for?" asked Curly.

"Keep my mouth shut; maybe lay a false trail... What it really is, I suppose, is, like, him offering a sort of way forward."

Curly smiled. "'Stead of a way back, you mean?"

John swallowed his anger. "Curl. We're still on the bottom. I'd like to get off it."

Curly glanced across. "I don't see that, John. Sure, not doing brilliant at the minute, but we've got a bit of a start. And let's face it, it was never going to happen overnight."

John gritted his teeth. "You're missing the point."

Curly grinned. Held out his hand to receive the envelope.

After a second's hesitation, John placed it onto his palm.

"And no idea how much?" Curly asked again.

"Didn't even open it," said John. "Otherwise – fella like Raite'd easily accuse me of lifting some."

"So what's he really want?" Curly hefted the envelope.

"Buy me, I suppose."

"And you're kicking him into touch! That's great, John." Curly laughed. "For a minute there, you had me worried you thought Crust might find out!" He tossed the envelope back into John's lap.

John picked it up. Gave it a quick squeeze. Slipped it back into his inside pocket. "Nearly there."

"Ten minutes or so" said Curly, "Then maybe we can fuck Raite off for good!"

"All he deserves!" said John.

SEQUENCE 58

MONDAY, 8th MARCH, 1982. 12.50
EXT / DAY REAR OF RAITE'S PREFAB

Mrs Raite and Bogger stood next to the Porsche. Both of its doors were open. Bogger was holding the documentation from the glovebox. "As phoney as he is… Rag down the petrol tank, Liz?"

"You're sure the money can't be in the car?"

"Doors open? Key in the ignition? Nah. It's inside where he can see it."

Bogger bent. Picked up a sharp flint. Ran it down the side of the Porsche. Mrs Raite nodded. Gestured towards the rear wall of the prefab. They moved across.

The back door was warped into its surround; the lock rusted and seized. They considered the newly boarded-up kitchen window. Some dirty shards of glass still protruded from old putty. New, and fitted from the inside, was what looked like a heavy square of wood wrapped securely in heavy-duty plastic. Mrs Raite reached inside. Pressed on the board and its plastic sheeting. Looked towards Bogger.

"Liz, even if I could get through, noise I'd make, Ronnie'd come down and beat my brains out with something."

Mrs Raite gestured towards the car. "One more quick look. Then the front. But remember, Bogg, he's got to be able to talk! Yes?!… He's *got* to be able *to talk*!"

SEQUENCE 59

MONDAY, 8th MARCH, 1982. 13.10
INT / DAY CONTAINER TERMINAL OFFICE

The manager and the cargo planner looked at the groups of containers mounting up around the berth. Two being slightly isolated from the others.

"Porsche's two?" asked the planner.

The manager nodded.

"Going to ring that policeman?"

"Crust? Yes, suppose so." The manager looked down and out over the containers, the dockers, the ship, the berth, the fence, the gatehouse, the pickets with their braziers, coffees and cans of beer. The nearby docks with their scant ships. The traffic and pedestrians on the dock approach roads. The smoke and haze over Liverpool itself and its clamorous, entertaining, radical, football, Tory hating, and strike-obsessed population. He sighed. "You know, I read once – in a book – 'If only the world could be ruled by merchant seamen'."

The planner laughed loudly as he moved towards the coffee cups and kettle.

SEQUENCE 60

MONDAY, 8th MARCH, 1982. 13. 15
EXT / DAY RAITE'S PREFAB

On the doorstep, Mrs Raite pointed at the intercom.

"Fuck's sake, Liz!" whispered Bogger. "What do I say? 'Come on out, Ron; meet the knuckle brothers'?"

"You're O'Rourke!… Just needing another word."

Bogger cleared his throat. Pressed the intercom button.

A few seconds' pause. The same flat voice. "Yes?"

Bogger spoke with breathy nasality. "John O'Rourke. Something I forgot…"

"Wait!"

Bogger grinned. Mrs Raite nodded approvingly. The locks and chain came off, and the door began to open.

Bogger kicked it inwards and grabbed Raite by the lapels of his smoking jacket. "Out you come, Ron!"

As Bogger dragged out Raite, Mrs Raite shouted, "Able to talk!"

Bogger's corrugated-bone forehead broke Raite's nose – though not hard enough to immobilise him permanently. Simultaneously, he kneed Raite in the groin and hit him with a vicious, open-palmed right hand across the face, which put Raite on the ground. Raite curled into a ball, and Bogger, like a mechanical toy, began to circle him, kicking him half-heartedly.

Mrs Raite grabbed his arm. "The money, Bogger! The money!" Made a duck-quacking gesture with her thumb and fingers.

Bogger laughed. Winked at her. Leaned over Raite's inert torso and put a foot between his shoulder blades. Stuck two fingers up Raite's broken nose and pulled back his head. Raite began to make screaming, seal-like honking noises.

"Right, Ron! Where's the dough?" asked Bogger jovially.

Turning away to light a cigarette, Mrs Raite saw John's car creep into view around the top of the cart track. "Bogger!" she yelled.

Bogger let go of Raite's head, which banged on the gravel, and moved casually between Mrs Raite and the *Express*. Curly erupted from the driver's side. John exited slowly, positioning himself behind Curly.

"Leave him to me, John," shouted Curly, beginning to circle Bogger.

Bogger, in a high, girlish voice, repeated, "Leave him to me, John! Oh! Leave him to me!"

Mrs Raite walked over to John. Swiped him across the head with her bag and its punching power of half-a-dozen tins of beans. John fell to his knees.

To the sound of excited barks, Harry Rose appeared with his four greyhounds, drawn back to the property for another look as he re-hashed his encounter with Raite and the Countryman.

John raised himself shakily on one knee. "Harry! Phone! Bottom of lane! Police"

Harry immediately turned back down the track.

Mrs Raite swiped John again with the bag. Inside which, a large ceramic pot of *Aztec Lust* – in the shape of an Inca god – put John once more on his back. She turned to where Bogger and Curly were still dancing and sparring. Curly jumping in and out, Bogger awaiting his chance to get to grips. "Bogger!" she yelled.

Bogger lunged towards Curly with a kick that Curly blocked. Somehow Bogger moved behind the kick and caught Curly with a punch to the head. Curly staggered, slipped and fell. Mrs Raite rushed across and grabbed Bogger by the arm.

"Liz!" he said. "For fuck's sake!"

"Later, Bogger! Later!" She pulled him away and they vanished around the side of the prefab.

Curly helped John to his feet and began to steady him. The Mercedes, engine revving, appeared from behind the prefab and lined-up facing them. Through the windscreen they saw Mrs Raite shout something to Bogger, then punch him on the upper arm. The Mercedes veered away towards the cart track.

John and Curly approached Raite and began trying to bring him to his feet.

Amid much barking, Harry appeared once more at the head of the track. He dragged the dogs across. "My God! Ran us into the bushes... Who are they?!"

The greyhounds began sniffing Raite. "That'll do, you fellows!" said Harry. He crouched next to Raite's bloody face. "Oh, Lord! And this one?"

"Your elusive tenant," said John.

"Not you attempting to ask him to vacate the property, I hope?" Harry's voice was strained.

"His ex-wife's boyfriend asking him to vacate life." John took one of Raite's arms. "Curl, give us a hand."

They raised Raite to his feet and began to shuffle him towards the *Express*. The bloody mouth bubbled, then spoke. "Where? Where...?"

John said, "You need attention, Ron."

"No hospital..." Raite stopped dead. "No hospital... Just nose... bruises."

Harry lifted Raite's chin. "Might be right. Worse things happen on a big ship."

Raite moaned. Waved a hand at him.

"OK," said John. "Let's head the office. Sort him there."

"Sort him how?" asked Curly.

Raite suddenly began to vomit and shake. At the car, he was eased onto the back seat and covered with John's anorak.

"OK, Harry," said John. "We'll take it from here. And thanks. Saved the day, showing up like that... Still sailing Friday?" He turned to Curly. "Harry's chief mate on the *Ocean Seaspray.*"

"Yeah. Heard of you," said Curly.

Harry nodded. "Spoke to old Barratt this morning. I'm officially rejoining tomorrow now. Tuesday." He sighed. "'Fraid he and Jinks have been at it again." Harry turned to Curly. "Captain Barratt's something of a lip-reader."

Curly looked Harry over carefully. Tightened the knot in his Liverpool scarf.

"Barratt swore he saw Jinks saying to the other QM, 'We'll put him over once we're in the bay.' He confronted Jinks, who claimed what he actually said was 'We'll be in clover; these new rates of pay'... Oh, well..."

John gave him a thumbs up. "Yeah. Great. And hopefully see you shortly, Harry. Maybe take-up that invite come down the ship?"

"Accompanied by Chris, of course," said Harry easily.

"Chris?!" said Curly.

"John's assistant," said Harry.

From the back seat, Raite groaned and stretched up a beseeching hand towards Curly who slammed the door on it. "*I'm* John's assistant, pal!" he told Harry. "Sometimes even his partner, depending on what's needed!... Chris?... Chris is my sister!"

"Then you and I may be seeing more of each other," Harry said amiably.

"How?" asked Curly.

Harry looked to where one of the dogs was eating Raite's vomit. "George!" he shouted, and was soon pulling on leashes, issuing orders and threats, and shepherding the greyhounds back towards the head of the cart track.

John and Curly checked Raite snoring, snorting and snuffling on the back seat.

As they settled in the car, John attempted a disinterested voice. "Think they might be waiting? Mrs Raite and Bogger? Ambush us and that?"

Curly's voice was tight. "What's all this about our Chris?"

"He – Harry – met her in the office. Sure I mentioned it..."

"Did you fuck!"

"Yeah. Well. Seems to fancy her. Obviously got no chance..."

"Not only him!"

From the back, Raite groaned loudly.

"Our Chris needs a break after that other fucker," said Curly. "Won't let me have a go at him. But no one else is gonna fuck with her! Know what I'm saying?!"

John stared ahead through the windscreen.

"It's OK, John," said Curly. "They're well gone. They've made their point."

"What's that?"

"That we're out of our league. That Bogger. I'd have a go. But can't do it. Him."

"Can't do it…?"

"Like you never could with anyone!" said Curly shortly.

You're gone, Curl! You don't know it yet. But you're gone!

A quick flash of lightning. A few seconds later, the crash of thunder.

"John! For fuck's sake! Let's get back to the office!"

John opened his mouth. Closed it. The envelope! The three hundred quid. Still in his pocket. Well. No need for a decision now, Raite being the way he was. Though maybe, while he was dazed, a bit of probing about the million? John sighed as he thought of Brick's truth serum in *The Dead Don't Sweat*. What was the formula, again? Brains of giant squids. Lemon juice. Baking powder?… some other stuff? He sighed once more.

Curly put the *Express* into gear.

SEQUENCE 61

MONDAY, 8th MARCH, 1982. 14.00
EXT / DAY FIELD OPPOSITE CART TRACK. INT /
DAY MERCEDES

On the other side of the main road, from behind the hedge, Bogger watched the *Express* lurch away, then walked back to the Mercedes and climbed inside. "All gone, Liz. Back up? Turn the joint over?"

Mrs Raite helped herself to a cigarette and pills. Took off her gloves. Began to scratch. "Police?"

"Dog Man didn't give the phone box a look," said Bogger. "And the last people O'Rourke and Ronnie want are the heavies… What is it, Liz?"

"Something feels off." Mrs Raite drew heavily on the cigarette. Blew the smoke upwards towards the roof of the car.

"Maybe Ron's took the dough with him?" Bogger offered. "Brought in them two Scousepots on some sort of deal?"

"Even Ronnie's not *that* deranged. No. It's still in there."

"You say so, Liz…"

"I do."

"Then let's go find it!"

SEQUENCE 62

MONDAY, 8th MARCH, 1982. 14.10
INT / DAY CRUST'S FLAT

"They're on the berth, then?" asked the Voice.

"Two highly desirable containers; property of an arsehole." Crust doodled a container with a clown's head and hat growing out of its top.

"How about the painting?"

"No idea."

"Has he still got access now they're on the quay?"

"Yeah… Consigned as bric-a-brac, so access till it sails."

"You'll be having a look yourself?"

"If they let me in."

"We're the police, Crusty. We can get in anywhere."

"Except the hearts of others," said Crust.

"There you go again!" said the Voice.

SEQUENCE 63

MONDAY, 8th MARCH, 1982. 14.20
EXT / DAY RAITE'S PREFAB

The Mercedes now stood directly outside the open door of the prefab. Bogger and Mrs Raite emerged from the building onto the step.

"It's not in there!" said Bogger.

She stared at him.

"Liz. We did everything but take up the non-existent fucking floorboards. Look at the state of my hands. State of my clobber, fishing through those manky cupboards!"

Mrs Raite rubbed the backs of her hands. "So, back to the Porsche…"

Bogger shrugged. "Which means the door panels coming off, the seats out, the whole fucking shebang… Because there's no way the cash can be in one lump inside that car!"

Both tensed as a clanking came from the cart track. Eventually a flatbed car transporter appeared and stopped in front of the prefab near the Mercedes. Its driver, a bulky figure in blue overalls, wound down the window. A cigarette stub flicked onto the gravel. The door opened and the driver climbed out. About five feet tall. Well-developed upper chest and arms. Heavy steel-toed work boots crunching on the wet gravel as he surveyed Mrs Raite; Bogger; the general prospect. Then Mrs Raite again. She responded by lifting the strap of her bag from her right shoulder and passing it over her head to her left shoulder. The strap, now lying across her chest, pulled tauter the already taut material of her coat. The driver gave her a knowing smile.

She smiled back brightly.

"Over here, China," said Bogger.

The driver looked at him. "A'right, pal? Looking for a fella called Raite. Bazza's Birkenhead Bangers." As he said, 'Bazza's', he directed a thumb at his own chest. "Here for the Porsche… Cash!" He patted one of the top pockets of his blue boiler suit. Smiled again at Mrs Raite.

Again she smiled back brightly.

Bogger moved a few paces forward and fixed Bazza with a stare.

Bazza held it for a time, then looked to one side.

"I'm afraid you've missed him," said Mrs Raite in a husky voice. "But I'm *Mrs* Raite. And no sooner arrived here with my chauffeur, Carstairs," gesturing towards Bogger, "than my husband had to fly to Zurich. A life-and-death meeting with some *gnomes*." Her smile widened.

"Gnomes' Mush!" said Bogger, running his eyes up and down Bazza's five-foot stature. "You understand?!"

Even huskier, Mrs Raite enquired, "Perhaps you could clarify the arrangements?"

Bazza stared at her, then Bogger, then back at Mrs Raite. "Well… I'd come and pick up the car; take it back with me. Said he didn't particularly want to meet me – just push the money through the letter box and he'd leave the paperwork in the glovebox and the keys in the ignition."

Mrs Raite took out the keys. Jingled them. Gestured to the rear of the prefab. Through the wind and icy drizzle, all three walked around to the Porsche.

Bazza pointed at the scratch made by Bogger. "He didn't mention this."

"Juvenile delinquents," said Mrs Raite as the rain lashed down. "Even in this halcyon spot. Although I'm sure my husband would be happy for us to reach an agreement with you on his behalf…"

Bogger, who had moved silently behind Bazza, said, "There you go, son!"

Bazza jumped. Bogger moved to stand beside Mrs Raite.

"The money?" she said.

Bazza hesitated.

"The money," said Bogger.

Bazza reached into his boiler-suit pocket and pulled out a roll of greasy notes secured by a thick rubber band.

Bogger walked over and took it from his hand. "Am I gonna have to count this?" he asked, pushing his face into Bazza's. "I fucking hope not!"

"What about the scratch?" said Bazza to Mrs Raite, refusing to look at Bogger.

"What I think," said Mrs Raite, "is that my husband – always incredibly generous to the less fortunate – gave you a good – probably excellent – deal. I also feel – and I hope I'm not misjudging you, Buzza – that, sensing this, you've arrived a little short. 'Just can't lay my hands on it'.

'Bank wasn't open', etc. A shortage you promise to push through the letter box sometime in the future."

"While fucking off with the boxmobile!" said Bogger.

"So I think," continued Mrs Raite, "that the money you *didn't* bring will more than pay for any repair. Where did my husband tell you he was going?"

Silence.

"Oi! Cloth ears!" shouted Bogger.

"He didn't," said Bazza. "Maybe to another life-and-death situation… Or maybe he just wanted to vanish for good himself…"

Mrs Raite smiled and held out the Porsche keys. Bazza came across and took them.

Mrs Raite breathed in deeply. "And now…"

"Yeah?" said Bazza with a flicker of hope.

"Now *you* can vanish for good!"

"Back to the other fucking gnomes." Bogger made a gesture of dismissal.

After a moment Bazza turned and began to walk away towards the front of the prefab and his transporter.

Mrs Raite said, "You're right, Bogg. Not the car. Ronnie would never allow serious money near a Neanderthal like that."

"Then where is it? We're talking about a largish holdall here."

They stared at the rear of the prefab. The rusted, warped back door. The boarded-up kitchen window. The broken paving flags. The acres of rainy, cold countryside, under any of which the money might be buried.

From around the front of the building they heard the engine of the transporter fire.

SEQUENCE 64

MONDAY, 8th MARCH, 1982. 14.55
INT / DAY BAYONETS

Monday afternoon. Quiet. Everyone's wages gone after the weekend. Couple of old-timers sitting at tables staring in front of themselves, reading newspapers, or looking up blankly at the eternal white bands moving across the black-and-white TV screen. Mr O'Rourke at the domino table near the door, marking up his final selections for the late afternoon race meetings. Mick, idly smoking a Capstan Full Strength, spat a piece of tobacco from the end of his tongue into a clean glass waiting to be filled with beer.

The door opened. Chris entered, her face set.

Mr O'Rourke immediately to his feet. "Chris! What's up? You OK? Fancy a Babycham?"

"I can bring it in the parlour," Mick said, moving across. "She feels a bit *out of place* in the bar!"

Chris shook her head. "Thanks, Mr O. Curly just rang me at my mum's. They're the other side of the Mersey Tunnel and something's happened. They're bringing that Raite fella back to John's office and they want me there to help."

"Raite?" said Mick. "Who's that?!"

"How'll you get down there?" asked Mr O'Rourke. "To Moorfields?"

"Curly said John said for me to get a taxi and he'll pay."

"Fucking hell!" said Mick. "Have the Martians landed?!… And who's this Raite!?"

Mr O'Rourke said, "I'll come out and wait with you,

Chris." He took his half-full, mostly flat glass to the bar. "Put this behind for me, will you, Mick?"

"You know we close in a few minutes?"

"Then I'll get it after the betting shop at half five."

"What about the germs risk?"

"You'll think of something to tell the health inspectors." Mr O'Rourke pulled on his mac.

Mick stared at him. "You old arses! Sit here all afternoon with one fucking pint, using my heat and electricity! Then the betting shop! Also warm, cosy, and free. Your usual tanner-each-way double; then back here till bedtime, cadging drinks and crisps and nuts off the workers! Bleeding your fellow proletariat dry! *Dies irae*, friend! Beware the day!"

Mr O'Rourke held open the door for Chris. Turned to face Mick. "But isn't that what the revolution's going to be about, Mick? Food and warmth for the old and needy? Free Latin lessons?"

The pub door slammed shut on its spring behind them.

Mick stared at it with hatred. Drew a finger across his throat.

SEQUENCE 65

MONDAY, 8th MARCH, 1982. 15.40
EXT / DAY PARKING LOT BEHIND JOHN'S BUILDING
INT / DAY BUSKING BILL'S MORRIS MINOR

The back door to John's office building stood open. John, Curly, Chris and Charlie were supporting Raite from the *Express* across the waste ground and into the building.

From the far corner of the car park, behind the burnouts and the abandoned shells, Busking Bill checked his watch and made a note.

SEQUENCE 66

MONDAY, 8th MARCH, 1982. 1600
INT / DAY PRISON LIBRARY.

The prison library was part of the 'Education Corridor'; a stretch of rooms devoted to literacy and numeracy. 'Going on Education' didn't pay as much as 'the workshops'; but it was better than nothing.

The library, once a large admin office in the days when there was money for such fripperies, was walled out with bookshelves. Plus four free-standing, double-sided, heavy bookcases. Six foot high; eight foot long. All positioned at carefully considered strategic angles to the door. Plus three free-standing 'Christmas tree' revolving bookcases containing only paperbacks.

From behind the various bookcases, inmates' heads would sometimes appear suddenly. Have a quick look round. Vanish again.

To the right – immediately you entered the room – was a largish desk. This was stacked with books and open boxes of borrowing records. There were also trays with request slips and index cards. Various items of stationery.

The Librarian was about fifty-five. Usual 'lifer' outfit. Heavy blue-denim twin-pocketed overshirt. White T-shirt underneath. Blue jeans. Soft shoes. Silver hair. Spectacles. A benign, scholarly, expression. From the care with which he handled the books, indexes and records, he obviously loved his job. He had been found guilty of the murder of his wife -though no body had been recovered. As he confided to one or two of his intimates, "Eight years they've been looking for her – but they're not going to find her."

'Arry the biker entered. He and the Librarian greeted each other; the Librarian careful not to stare at the eye in the centre of 'Arry's forehead.

The Librarian picked up a hardback from a pile. "Here's that one on naive erotic art, 'Arry. But no joy on *Vlad the Virgin Impaler*. Got as far as No. 3 Governor as 'sociological research', but knocked back in the end."

"Win some, lose some," said 'Arry.

The librarian stamped the erotic art. As he amended 'Arry's borrower's card he said, "They're still thinking about *The Sex Life of the Marquis de Sade*… You'll be OK with the two on Hitler – standard reading in here now… But no go again, for some reason, on *Understanding the Ku Klux Klan*."

'Arry said, "Cancel them – I'm getting out!"

"For fuck's sake, 'Arry!" said the Librarian. "You're only just in! Here's me thinking I've found a new star customer! What's the score?"

"Cop who arrested me; my brief says he's had a breakdown and fucked off to North Wales. Some fucking hippy-type commune or something… But it was all bullshit from the start! I mean, how can you get done attempting to break into your own squat?"

"It's a joke," said the Librarian.

"Should never've even been on remand. Usual fuck-up and my brief not doing fuck all till he saw the money."

"'Arry? You being a biker – what's the diff between a vacuum cleaner and a lawyer on a motorbike?"

'Arry closed one of his two functioning eyes and shook his head.

"The mo'bike's the one with the dirtbag on the outside."

'Arry stared hard at the Librarian. "Know how many lawyer jokes there are?"

"Those fuckers?! Millions!"

"No," said 'Arry. "None! None, mate! 'Cause all those so-called 'jokes' are true fucking stories!"

"Bastards!" said the Librarian. "Take that one of mine. I'm in here on this phoney charge that I murdered the missus. See. She just never thought I was good enough for her. So what she's done is fucked off to Spain with some driving instructor or estate agent. Some cunt like that. If only she could see me now! A librarian! That'd turn her piss green. But, like a fool, I admitted I'd had a bit of aggro with her just 'fore she vanished; plus all the neighbours and her relations grassing me. Next thing, I'm up for her. Course, with there being no body – as there can't be, her being in fucking Spain or something…"

'Arry yawned.

"Yeah… Waste of time even talking about her. But what it meant was, there being no body, and me getting life, I get top legal aid. Appeals, counter-appeals, motions for, motions against… All of which moolah goes right into the pockets of that fucker supposed to be representing me, who obviously doesn't need another client – he's got me! I'm putting his kids through private school! That's what I'm fucking doing!"

"Cunts. All of them," said 'Arry. "Real job'd fucking kill them!" He raised the naive erotic art volume in salute prior to leaving.

"So what's next, you get out?" asked the Librarian.

"Pick up some of my paintings I left in the squat."

"If they're still there," said the Librarian.

"They better fucking had be!!" 'Arry walked to the door. Turned. Gave a Nazi salute. Shouted '*Seig Heil!*' Raised his two index fingers and laid them horizontally, knuckles outward, one across each eye. Each finger – between the first and second joint – was tattooed with a further eye. The effect was of someone who had covered his eyes but still had you under scrutiny. He strode from the room, index fingers still pressed to his eyes, as if he were able to look through them.

As the Librarian continued to stare at the door, an inmate's head slowly rose above the top of one of the angled bookcases. The inmate and the Librarian regarded each other. The inmate's head slowly sank back down.

SEQUENCE 67

MONDAY, 8th MARCH, 1982. 19.00
INT / NIGHT CRUST'S FLAT

"Been talking to the cargo planner down the container terminal," said Crust as he doodled a top hat and a big cigar with coils of smoke in the form of a dollar sign. "Paperwork's been cleared on Raite's containers. Ready to go Friday, elevenish – give or take a strike or two…"

"What sort of shape's he in? Raite?" asked the Voice.

"Walking wounded, says Busking Bill. At least we know where he is. Laid up in the House of Usher."

"But he'll be able to get around? Get to the painting?"

"Unless it's already in one of the containers," said Crust. "Hidden among all the crap."

"What d'you think?"

"That, like Descartes, the only thing I'm sure of is that I'm thinking I'm having this conversation."

"Wait 'till I take that up the canteen" said the Voice.

SEQUENCE 68

TUESDAY, 9th MARCH, 1982. 11.00
INT / DAY JOHN'S OFFICE BEDROOM

Raite moved his head slightly. Winced. Looked at his watch. 9am Tuesday. In bed in a room he didn't recognise. Dingy, small, cheap. Facing him, a doorless doorway, its opening covered by a purple velvet curtain suspended on nails. The *Magdalen*. Could they? Would they find it? Surely they'd still be looking for paper money? No; should be OK. *Fucking Bogger!* A dull throbbing pain swelled in his skull. His nose was blocked with dried blood, but all his limbs were mobile. Nothing broken. He groaned and leaned over the edge of the mattress, and a few drops of bile spilled from his mouth.

Then John was standing over him holding a plastic bucket. A woman with him. Blonde. Fit. Very fit!

Raite tried to speak but it was all too much and he fell back. In seconds he was asleep.

SEQUENCE 69

TUESDAY, 9th MARCH, 1982. 13.00
INT / DAY RESTAURANT, CENTRAL LONDON

The Cavalier sat with the Companion in a pub/restaurant off Oxford Street. Two empty white wine bottles on their table. Another, three-quarters full, in an ice bucket. Two empty plates with scrunched-up napkins/cutlery. No food left on either.

"So…?" said the Companion.

The Cavalier positioned an ashtray in front of himself. Poured two fresh glasses of wine. Put the bottle back in the ice bucket. Lit a cigarette. "This Florence must have rung the filth almost right away. I sort of saw it coming and got everything out and somewhere safe."

"How long?" asked the Companion. "'Fore they arrived?"

"Late same afternoon. Two of them – rat-a-tat-tat! 'Anybody home?'"

"How'd they play it?"

"Back to the Corot. Fucking thing's haunting me like something out of Edvard Munch!"

"Escort agency, you said?"

"Place called Shady Sadie's."

The Companion nodded he had the name. Then, his smile just still there, "How'd she get onto things? This Florence?"

"Her money was on the dresser. Had her back to me. Must've slid the top drawer open as she picked it up..."

The Companion waited.

"... Money from my cut in there. The illustration of the painting from that old book. Raite's photo..."

"Everything, then?"

"I know. I fucked up." The Cavalier stubbed out a half-smoked cigarette. Lit another.

"Seems quick? Them getting round to you?" The Companion gently waved away a hovering waitress.

"She was frightened. Been in one of their pockets. They'll have brought her in. Grilled her. Bundles of notes? Picture of a painting? Photo? Of who? A bell'll've rung somewhere. You know yourself... Always some Leslie Welch-type memory-man copper got stuff lodged in the back of his mind. The Corot will have surfaced. My mugshot. You know how they somehow manage to put stuff together you never think they'll get to..."

The Companion nodded, still just smiling.

The Cavalier drained his glass. Stubbed out his newly lit cigarette. Lit another. "Yeah... My fault."

"What were they like? Pair that turned up?" asked the Companion.

"That sort of jumpy acuteness bent coppers have."

"Offer any sort of deal?" said the Companion casually.

"Didn't give them a chance. Told them, 'Help yourselves... But just need to ring my brief.'"

"That did it?"

"Eventually. Still, not what I wanted. My name back in play. They're getting a hold on art redistribution now. Training up their own experts."

"I heard. So…"

The Cavalier looked at the Companion warily.

"So," continued the Companion, "before they train up too many, start fucking about with our livelihood, maybe we all need a break."

"Reckon?"

"Country life… mountains… big isolated houses."

"Bit of fishing?"

"Old friends… Help with the catch…"

The Cavalier gave a relieved laugh. "OK! I'll drink to that!" He held up his empty glass. "If there was anything in it!"

The Companion smiled and lifted the bottle from the ice bucket. With his other hand he covered the Cavalier's. "It can't happen again."

SEQUENCE 70

WEDNESDAY, 10th MARCH, 1982. 15.30
INT / DAY KITCHEN FLOUR STREET

In Flour Street, John and his father faced each other across two mugs of tea. John played with the salt cellar.

"Seeing Raite getting hammered by that Bogger scared me… Curly too!" he added quickly.

"I keep telling you, you're out of your league." Mr

O'Rourke turned over a page of his paper. "What's the damage?"

"Broken nose. Bit of a kicking. Everyone thinks it's fairly superficial."

"A superficial broken nose?"

"Eyes sort of black, blue and yellow… Them things live in the jungle? Come out at night?"

Mr O'Rourke tapped his *Mirror*. "I'll be doing the Quizword later."

"Actually, thought we might drift into town. Let you meet him."

"No thanks." Then, seeing John's face, "Who's there now?"

"Curly, 'fore he goes to his ma's. Then Chris, till I get back. Fancy it? Give you a chance to size him up?"

"Yeah. Might be interesting, meeting someone like that… Once!"

John took a sip of tea. Stared down at the table. "Can't help wond'ring 'bout the money, though…"

"The 'alimony'?"

"Yeah, well," said John, "there's a bit more to it than that…"

"Oh?" Mr O'Rourke began marking off horses.

"Million pounds," said John.

Mr O'Rourke's eyes shot up. "A million pounds?!"

"Drugs stuff."

"A million pounds?! Drugs?! Someone like you?! Are you *mad*?!"

"Yeah… Well… I need help."

"You need a doctor! Is Curly in on this? Chris?"

John shook his head. "Don't want to worry them.

Thing is, he was supposed to have it in the prefab."

"Said who?"

"That copper, Crust. But when we brought him back to the office he was empty-handed. I mean…"

"… Not the sort of money you'd leave for a passing tramp to find?"

"Been trying to think what he might have done with it."

"You've got to get out of this!" Mr O'Rourke stared into John's eyes. "Give back what you've had from them!"

John stared back. "No!" he stated flatly. Then, in a more conciliatory voice, "Like I said, I need help."

His father stared down at the column of horses. Wetted a thumb. Turned the page. "Could he have buried it in plastic?" he said. "Bit of tarpaulin or something? What's round there? Where he lives?"

"Fields and shit. So yeah, maybe… Although…"

"What's it like? A million pounds?"

"Not sure. Maybe a biggish holdall?"

"Couldn't hide that in an old prefab," said Mr O'Rourke. "Even on the Wirral, where money's their leading currency. Unless…"

"Yeah?"

"Changed into something smaller? Gold? Diamonds? Something he could move easy… You say you got inside his place for a talk?"

"Yeah."

"What about?"

"Paintings, mainly." John made a frame with his hands; looked through it. "One there – *Reclining Nude with Jam*

Sandwich; early Plonksby. Knightsbridge School!... My own acquisitions..."

His father stared at him.

"Arian's *Celestial Vision*! And... Got to say... Raite fella seems to know his stuff. Planes and masses... Investment implications..."

"Implications you'll be able to discuss with the bikers. They show up looking for what's theirs?"

"Nah. Seen the last of them. Lazarus, of course..."

Mr O'Rourke consulted the racing pages. "What meeting's that at?"

"... Waiting to burst from his tomb of sexual impotence."

"I just hope there's not another war."

"Full of shit? Yeah! But interesting. Pity he's off to the States."

"The States?"

"Antique dealing other side of the pond. Two containers of objets d'art going across this Friday on the *Ocean Seaspray*. Harry Rose – that mate of mine..."

"Objets d'art?"

"Dad..."

"You didn't think to mention them? These containers? Antiques? Paintings and things?"

"Come on, Dad..."

"The million? How's that going across?"

"On the plane with him?"

"A holdall with a million in notes? His photo under every desk? Yankee customs?" John's father stared at him. "Remember Mr Porsche?"

"I remember us coming up with the idea."

"So what about Mr van Gogh?... A painting?... Something he could turn the money into? Hidden in the middle of a container full of other crap? No one the wiser! Some of that art stuff goes for millions! God forgive their silly sense."

John stared. "Yeah! I like it! He's bought a painting! We could be on to something here."

"Bet your copper friend, Crust, will be. A container full of crap to hide an even bigger piece of crap."

John stared at his father. "OK, look. Come and meet him; see what you can figure. There's a million up for grabs here, Dad!"

"Belonging to who?"

"Well..."

"John! Don't even think about it. You can get murdered in Liverpool for fifty quid... A million pounds?!"

"Dad! For me? Just to see what you make of him. Then maybe a trip across the Wirral. Mooch round his gaff... See what we can find."

"We'll be taking Curly?"

"Curly's going his old girl's... I did mention it. 'Sides... Look, Dad... things between Curly and myself are..."

"Then who's keeping an eye on things there now?"

"I told you! Chris."

Mr O'Rourke stared at John. John caught his thought. As one, they jumped from their chairs.

SEQUENCE 71

WEDNESDAY, 10th MARCH, 1982. 15.40
INT / DAY JOHN'S BEDROOM, MOORFIELDS

Raite opened his eyes again. Looked at his watch. Twenty-to-four. He swung his legs over the side of the bed. Someone had taken off his shoes. He slipped one on. Groaned. Stood. Groaned. Walked slowly across to a mirror hanging on a nail. Inspected himself. Groaned. Walked slowly back and sat on the side of the bed once more.

SEQUENCE 72

WEDNESDAY, 10th MARCH, 1982. 15.45
INT / DAY DRUM ACADEMY

Charlie, clutching an A4 brown envelope, burst inward through the door of the Drum Academy. Inside was a square room with badly plastered walls. In the centre, a battered, bare wooden desk with a chair behind. Desk and chair stood on a square of cheap, stained red carpet. In the back wall, two further doors painted bright yellow – 'Rocker's Lair' and 'Practice Room'.

On the immediate right, coming through the outer door, flat against the wall, a large, free-standing white fridge. Charlie put the envelope on top of the fridge and opened its door. Inside, the wire shelves were crammed with bottles and packs of cider. Charlie took out a six-pack. Split one off. The label read 'Dr Pippin's XXXX Cider'. It depicted a jolly Pickwickian farmer pressing a stethoscope to the bole of an apple tree whose branches brushed the ground under the weight of their glowing fruit. An ornate banner round the label bore the inscription 'An Apple a Day!'

On a nail hammered into the wall alongside the fridge hung a 'church key' – a steel beer-can punch. Charlie used it on the can. Drank. Belched. Drained the can. Threw it on the floor. Stamped on it. Looked up towards John's office. Took down the brown envelope. Kissed it. Split off another can from the pack. Punctured it. Had a glug. Opened the envelope. Took out a set of contracts. Kissed them. Looked up through the ceiling once more towards John's office. Began to read...

SEQUENCE 73

WEDNESDAY, 10th MARCH, 1982. 15.55
INT / DAY JOHN'S BEDROOM / OFFICE.
EXT / DAY MOORFIELDS

Raite stood. Lost his balance. Fell back onto the bed with a cry. There was a quiet knock, and the curtain was pulled aside to reveal Chris. Raite stared at her. Smiled. Waited.

Chris smiled back. "Mr Raite, I'm Chris. A friend of John's... That is, my brother Curly is his partner. Your poor face... What was his name who did it? Bogger? The boys were saying you didn't have a chance."

Raite shrugged. "Too much time in 'the galleries'. Not enough in the gym."

Chris nodded sympathetically. "Curly used my skipping ropes more than me."

Raite stared. Bondage? Fetishism? Didn't look the type. But there'd be some weakness. *One thing you can always depend on with the working class – gullibility.* He adjusted the crotch of his trousers. "Any banks round here, Chris? Access my accounts?"

Chris smiled. "Surrounded by them... All probably being robbed."

Was she serious?

Her smile intensified. "Maybe I could get you a coffee?"

Raite shook his head abstractedly. Suddenly he felt incredibly horny. Had Bogger's beating somehow stirred his sex drive into hyperactivity? *Adler, Jung – the Freudian well hung!* A sharp bark of laughter.

Chris stared. "Mr Raite?"

Sitting on the side of the bed, he raised a hand. "Could you, Chris? Still feeling a bit groggy. And please call me Ronnie."

She offered her arm. He put his hand under it, pressing against her breast. She manoeuvred him into the office. Sat him in the client's chair.

He touched her hair lightly. "Honey blonde... Can't get that out of a bottle."

Chris moved away quickly. "Needs a bit of a touch-up these days."

Raite gave a low laugh. "The old 'touch-up'."

Chris maintained her smile. "I'll make that coffee. John'll be back shortly. Help you get sorted..." She turned away into the kitchen alcove.

Raite looked round quickly. On the desk, a couple of newish-looking keys on a ring. Front door? Office? He slipped them in his pocket.

Chris came back. "Kettle's on the boil."

Raite rose. Walked slowly to stand before *Celestial Vision*.

"Part of John's 'collection'." Chris laughed briefly. "Came with the lease. As did…" She gestured around the skirting boards.

Raite stirred them with his foot. "Rubbish. Though careers have been made on less."

"John says a lot of them remind him of Brick Bradstreet." Chris gestured to the three-tier bookshelf against the wall behind John's desk and chair.

Raite walked across. Crouched with a groan. Pulled out a battered paperback. The cover illustration was that of an observer standing on a landing in a sleazy tenement house. A set of shadowy stairs falling away to the left. The foreground was the back of a man wearing a long black overcoat and a slouch hat; his hands plunged into the coat pockets, his shoulders hunched. Facing the man was a half-open doorway in which stood a demure, chestnut-haired girl wearing a terrified expression and a transparent pink silk negligee into which someone had stuffed two basketballs. Through the gap in the door, the end of a battered sideboard could be seen. On it a lamp cast lurid shadows. The title was *Roxy Needs Her Rent*.

Raite held up the book. "'The guy with the gimlet eye and the two-tone golf shoes'?"

"John's obviously mentioned him… Anyway, like I said, he'll be here shortly."

Raite stood. Walked round the desk. Positioned himself in front of her. Held out the book. She stretched out an arm and took it.

"John and I met through art," Raite told her. "A painting he saw in my atelier window."

Chris smiled.

"'Atelier'? Studio... Even teaching studio."

"Thank you," Chris said, with what appeared to be becoming simplicity.

"Said he wanted it for his wife." Raite bared his teeth.

"I'm not John's wife, Mr Raite... And nobody else's!"

"Though not short on offers, I imagine?" He smiled.

Chris smiled back.

Raite stretched. Groaned once more. "Should have kept up the old 'TM' – Transcendental Meditation. Ever been to India, Chris?"

"Only via a teabag."

He stared at her.

"You're bleeding again," said Chris quietly. She handed Raite a tissue.

"Bogger?" he said, dabbing his nose. "Simply a large, clumsy machine. What you see..." He gestured towards his swollen nose, discoloured eyes, split lips and gravel marks. "... Simple surface damage. Amateur open-cast mining."

"I worry," said Chris. "John... my brother Curly... I'm not sure they understand what they're doing."

Raite shrugged. Walked back over to *Celestial Vision*. Took it down and turned it over, testing the fixing clips with his fingers. Shook his head sadly. "The old 'Psychosexpathic School'. Though with – here – a touch of becoming *jeu d'esprit*, I feel… Yet if the art establishment decreed it a masterpiece…"

"Art establishment?" said Chris for want of anything better to say.

"'Connoisseurs', dealers, fixers, gallery and museum boards… Van Meegeren?"

Chris shook her head.

"His own work ignored by the critics, Meegeren began forging Vermeers before, and during, World War II. Crudely incompetent, yet everyone bought in. Bowing before Meegeren's 'finds'. 'Finds' painted in his own… well… back room."

"Atelier?" suggested Chris.

Raite stiffened. Flexed his fingers. "Even Göring acquired one. After the war, the Dutch wished to try Meegeren for treason – selling Dutch masterpieces to the Germans. His defence? He'd done them himself. The art establishment couldn't afford to hear this. Some swearing that even if the paintings *were* forgeries they were *genuine* forgeries! Meegeren offered to knock up one in his prison cell, and did. Göring claimed he couldn't believe anyone could sink so low."

"Sounds quite a character…"

"Meegeren spoke of one particular painting. How critics, academics – 'crackademics' – came from all over the world to view it. Planes arriving every hour, on the hour… After his fall, this painting just ceased to exist. Those who had thronged the streets to stand in awe before it – now passed by on the other side as though it was a wayside tomb. But, as Meegeren observed, 'the painting hadn't changed'."

"You're very knowledgeable," Chris said softly.

Raite waved this aside impatiently. "No. Art is now a big provider for the privileged. Mainly women, I'm sorry to say…"

Chris smiled.

Raite flexed his fingers once more. "… Finally having unstoppable entry into fashionable universities, something's then got to be found for them – the BBC being already stuffed with their male counterparts. No!!…" Raite's voice rose "Get a 'fine art' degree, suddenly you understand painting. And with the usual educational and social nepotism, positions suddenly open in galleries, museums, on the boards… 'glamateurs'.

"Mmm…" said Chris, glancing at the wall clock.

Raite looked at her.

"Just wondering where John's got to."

Raite shook his head in a frightening, angry, twisting motion. Stared at Chris. "I'm getting out!"

"Of here?" asked Chris hopefully.

"America! Video. Art films!…" He gestured towards *Celestial Vision* and what lay around the skirting boards. His voice took on a raw, loud, note. "All this! The rest?… Just post-dated cheques on the walls of the rich." He stood before *Celestial Vision*. "Ah!… Here's a nice Bank of Coutts – note the patina!… An interesting Hoare! Some fine greasy fingermarks… An intriguing countersigned Rothschild!… Art, Chris, is the rich exhibiting their money. Far better if they simply hung the cheques themselves. At least then they'd know what they were looking at." He lost his dazed expression… Rubbed his chin. "John got a spare razor?"

"Mr Raite, your face... Perhaps if you waited a few days?"

"Razor, Chris!" said Raite tightly.

Without speaking, Chris walked through to the bathroom. Brought back a plastic disposable razor. Held it out to Raite. Wearing a slight smile, he reached out and took her wrist. She gently tried to pull away. He tightened his grasp. She relaxed. He suddenly let go.

"America, Chris... Possibilities... Their new Rome to our old Greece... "

At a loss, she enquired innocently "Do you paint yourself, Mr Raite?"

His hand flashed out venomously. Once more took her wrist. This time she actively tried to pull away.

Without any change of expression he resisted her. "What I've come to understand, Chris..." He slapped her face lightly. "Is that the only works worth collecting are those where the collector has known the artist. Has had psychological... even *psychic*... interaction with the artist. The artist's sufferings. Because, where any buyer has *not* known the artist intimately, there will always be elements beyond the reach of even the most technically knowledgeable connoisseur." He smiled. Touched her cheek where he'd struck it. "You been to America, Chris?" He tightened his grip round her wrist. "Don't say via a Coke bottle!"

She swallowed. Gave a sudden jerk. Almost broke loose. They stared into each other's eyes.

"California," he told her quietly. "Wouldn't take long – someone like you. Learn how it's done..."

"John's bringing his dad to meet you."

Her casualness told Raite it was true. He brought up the plastic razor. Stroked her neck with it. "Sharp but cheap." Dropped the razor. Took down *Celestial Vision*. Waved it in front of her eyes. Then held it before his crotch. "A kettle to the boil…?" he suggested. said

"Lava to Vesuvius?" she suggested back.

A hard, open-handed slap. She rocked on her feet. Stared at him with calm eyes. He punched her in the mouth and she staggered back and fell, hitting her head on the side of John's desk. Lay still. Raite grabbed the Beefeater tea towel off the table and stuffed it in her mouth. Stood astride her legs. Tore at her blouse and underwear. Dropped to his knees. Began to unfasten his belt using one hand. *Celestial Vision* in the other. Shouted, "Lazarus!"

The slightest of knocks and the office door crashed open.

Charlie stood there singing "*Seventy-six large whites and a lemonade / Two packets of crisps and a…*" In his left hand the remaining ciders in their pack. In his right, the contracts in their brown envelope, and the steel can opener.

Dropping the ciders and envelope, Charlie moved forward with the opener.

Raite pulled the towel from Chris's mouth and lurched forward towards Charlie – flapping-towel in one hand – *Celestial Vision* in the other.

As they closed, Charlie swayed one way – Raite going with him. Charlie swayed back trying for Raite's eye with the opener.

Raite raised the painting and deflected the opener so it took off some of his ear lobe. With a howl, he ran through the office and down the stairs and stumbled down the front steps into Moorfields.

A taxi was puttering along.

Raite jumped into the road waving *Celestial Vision* in one hand – the tea-towel in the other. The Beefeater and his halberd now mostly obscured by blood.

The taxi driver decided he'd stop. Before him he saw what he considered 'a genuine headcase' – but one could easily have money. True, his face was pretty fucked up. True, he was dripping blood and holding some sort of perv painting in one hand; the other waving a tea towel with what looked like a picture of Superman holding up a skinny alien with a head shaped like an axe.

Raite climbed into the cab. "Go! Go! Go!"

The driver lit a cigarette. "Where, Ace? Go where?"

"West Heartwood! The Wirral! Right away!"

The driver considered. If it was just another Liverpool 'wannabe', he could always run his cab into the nearest cop shop yard – let those idle fuckers sort it out. But a genuine fare to the Wirral? Top dollar! He nodded, feeling his way. "Sure you don't want the Royal Hospital for the ear? Walker Art Gallery for the picture?"

"West Heartwood, the Wirral! Urgent family matter!!... Just GO!"

"What I mean, Ace – is anyone *after you*? Jacks or that?... I mean. Face like a pan of burnt chip fat. Blood everywhere... That painting – where's that come from? Load of shite but I can't be done for 'aiding and abetting' – I've got a wife and kids... Not all us cabbies have time to go on *Mastermind* – pick up loads of poke answering questions on the Brontë Brothers or Lord Byrom!... Four Horsemen of the Acropolis!..."

"An accident," said Raite, tea towel alternating between nose and ear. "Shall I get another cab?" He shot a glance towards John's building's open door. How long did he have?

"Yeah! The Wirral," said the driver. "Tempting. But only if I can pick someone up on the way back!"

"Double," said Raite. "I'll pay double! But I need to stop off at an artist's supplier. A chemist. A camping outfitters. Won't take long."

The driver whistled. Nodded. "OK, Ace! This once. Double fare. But don't spread it round. Everyone'll be after the same deal." He hawked a ball of phlegm into his throat. Gobbed out of the window. Put the cab into gear.

As they reached the corner they swung wide to avoid the *Baker Street Express* coming the other way. John and Raite stared at each other. Raite grinned triumphantly.

John ran the *Express* onto the kerb outside the office. Jumped out as the engine stalled. Began to run up the steps into the building, his father trailing behind.

SEQUENCE 74

WEDNESDAY, 10th MARCH, 1982. 17.30
INT / NIGHT CRUST'S FLAT

"So…?" asked the Voice.

Crust sketched an ambulance. "So they took her the Teaching Hospital. Suspected concussion. After he smacked her, she caught her head on the desk going down."

"She'll be OK to talk tomorrow?"

"Not sure how much she'll know… Think we'll maybe leave that…"

"How'd you find out?"

"Busking Bill. Heard the sirens from that back lot; went round the front. Three-ring circus. Ambulance crew could've – should've – walked her down. But being Liverpool, had to be a stretcher. Didn't strap her on properly, so falls off at this bend in the steps."

"Bill spot anyone in the crowd?"

"Usual waders and peckers. Someone in a Merchant Navy uniform he thought looked a bit out of place."

"Might be worth a sniff" said the Voice. "Who called it in?"

"Bloke called Charlie Um-Pah-Bah," said Crust.

"Old Scouse moniker?"

Crust drew a shield. Quartered it. In one quarter, a football rattle. The second, a ship. The third, a pint glass. The fourth, the nude figure of a woman. "Rock 'n' roll drummer; next floor down from O'Rourke. Gone up to O'Rourke's with a few cans; celebrate some record deal he's made. Walks in just as Raite's dropping his trousers. Cuts Raite with the beer-can punch. Saved her."

"Talk to him?" asked the Voice.

"Again, is it worth it?"

"And Raite?"

"Grabbed a passing taxi." Crust doodled a black cab. Question mark on its radiator.

"Plate?"

"No one got it. But pound to a pinch of shit he's heading back across to the Wirral… I think the painting's there and he went to collect it."

"You and Bill going over?"

"Waste of time. He's got to bring it back to the container…"

"Make sure you give him our best," said the Voice.

SEQUENCE 75

WEDNESDAY, 10th MARCH, 1982. 19.00
EXT / NIGHT RAITE'S PREFAB

Outside Raite's prefab, the taxi driver sat smoking and staring towards the open door. They'd found an art shop going through Wallasey. Raite had emerged from it with a very large, shallowish plywood box. Then a chemist for some lint, sticking plaster and ointment. Finally an army surplus store from which Raite had emerged dressed as a textbook rambler.

"What happened to that other gear you was wearing, Ace?" the driver had asked as they finally headed for West Heartwood.

"Left it in the shop."

"Didn't think of your old mates, then? People like me who've done you a few favours? Even though it was covered in blood… So what's with the box?"

"Artist's field kit! Thinking of doing some landscape work… Of course, for that sort of thing one also really needs a wide-brimmed sun hat."

"Yeah," said the driver as the cab, headlights on full beam, rocked down the dark country lanes; icy conduits of wind and freezing rain. "Yeah, 'course. Should've realised…"

SEQUENCE 76

John sat at the kitchen table, waiting for something – anything – to happen.

His dad's new phone rang. John answered hesitantly.

"John? John? Is that you?"

"Yeah…"

"It's me. Your dad. You on that new phone?"

"Dad! What's going on? Where are you?"

"Teaching Hospital, off London Road. She's seen the specialist."

"And…?"

"Given her something and she's sleeping. Keeping her in overnight. Maybe home tomorrow, but prob'ly Friday."

"How's she look?"

"Paler than a banshee's bodice."

"Fuck!… Shall I come down?"

"Curly and the rest of her family are here."

"Not blaming me, are they?"

"Who else have they got?"

"How was I to know Raite was a couple of wires short of a light bulb?!"

"Just leave it till tomorrow; let things cool down a bit."

"Think I should have a word with Curly?"

"You want to end up in the next bed to Chris?!… Afternoon visiting's four till six. Come in about five-ish tomorrow. I'll see it's all clear."

"What are you doing?"

"Stay another couple of hours, then head home. Maybe stop off The Bayonets for a pint."

"Shall I meet you there?"

"John! It's already the talk of the wash-house!"

"What is?"

"Your fuck-up!"

"Dad!"

"Right! Going back to the ward. See you later."

Mr O'Rourke rang off. John stared down blankly at the Formica tabletop. The phone rang again. *Christ! Not the old fella again. Maybe Chris has died.* He stretched out a tentative hand.

"That you?" asked Crust.

How's he got this number? Coppers. Get where Epsom salts wouldn't.

"That you?!" demanded Crust again.

"Yeah," said John. "Yeah... That Inspector Crust?"

"You being funny?"

"How d'you get this number?"

"Had it from the start. Your number."

"You know about Chris?" asked John. "That bastard Raite?"

"Yeah. Hear she's in shock but stable. Meaning she'll need some support for a bit, right?"

"Well..."

"Thing is, John, we think we know where he's going now."

"America, you said. With his containers."

"And once over there. With American law enforcement involved... So... Well... Now essentially police."

"I'm not sure..."

"Did I mention a citizen's reward? We're really grateful for your input so far, but now you maybe need to look for something else. I'll help you with that."

"Inspector Crust… Look… Can we talk about this?"

"Yeah. Catch up eventually…"

"Maybe about a painting?"

"That one in your office? *Celestial Jism*?"

"Or the other one?"

"Other one?"

"Just been talking to my dad. This *Albion* reporter caught him at the hospital. Was my place really full of sex paintings? How did he – my dad – feel about Chris and me settling in together in a 'biker orgy den'? Wants an interview. Photographs of the paintings. Started me thinking about Raite maybe moving a painting rather than a suitcase of money…"

"OK," said Crust after a pause. "Maybe we should talk. What's tomorrow – Thursday? What're your movements?"

"Enterprise Allowance in the morning; Chris at 'late afternoon visiting'. Maybe get to the hospital about five."

"There's a pub I sometimes use – London Road, not too far from the Teaching Hospital. Say, six o'clock? Give you and Chris a bit of time together for you to trot out your excuses for what you've done… By the way, heard there was some bloke outside your place today wearing a Merchant Navy officer's uniform…"

"Where'd you get that?!" demanded John. "Who've you been talking to now?"

The phone went dead.

SEQUENCE 77

The driver tapped the meter. What the fuck was Raite doing in there? And what was actually going on? Posh accent; dump like this? And that banging he'd heard…

The driver grinned and waved as Raite re-emerged, still carrying the plywood box, but not that horrible painting he'd brought. Or was it inside the box? Leaving the front door open, Raite walked across and climbed into the cab.

"Where now, Ace?" asked the driver.

"Back!" said Raite.

"Moorfields?" asked the driver. He consulted his watch. "Yeah. Wine Lodge well open." He prepared to engage the gears. "I hear some banging, Ace?"

"Knocking out one of the back windows."

"Yeah. Course, ventilation." Pointed at the open door of the prefab. "Talking of which. Gonna put the wood in the hole?"

Raite stared at the driver. Left the cab. Walked back across to the open front door. Took out his penis. Urinated into the hallway. Came back and climbed into the cab. "'Reflected in the rent!'" he said in a humorous voice.

SEQUENCE 78

WEDNESDAY, 10th MARCH, 1982. 19.32
EXT / NIGHT REAR OF RAITE'S PREFAB

At the back of Raite's prefab the wind and rain now whistled through the boarded-up back window which was now a gaping hole. The *Penitent Magdalen* having been finally removed and put inside the artist's field kit box.

SEQUENCE 79

WEDNESDAY, 10th MARCH, 1982. 20.30
INT / NIGHT JOHN'S OFFICE – DRUM ACADEMY

Charlie and Curly stood in John's office. Chairs knocked over. Mat rucked-up. Paintings scattered about and trodden on.

Charlie pointed. "Bizzies've even pulled down his purple curtain."

"He's a respectable businessman now," said Curly. "Standards to be upheld."

Curly then suddenly laughed. Stuck out a hand to Charlie. "You saved her, mate. Fuck knows what would've happened if you hadn't showed."

"Forget it." Charlie shook Curly's hand. "She deserves a medal just talking to a wanker like that in the first place. Look! Fancy going down my place? Bit of relaxo? Can of cider?"

Curly pointed at the wall where *Celestial Vision* had hung. "Least the Rembrandt's gone."

"Raite ran out waving it," Charlie told him. "Meant I couldn't get a good go hooking his eye out with the opener."

"Pity!" said Curly.

Charlie clapped him on the shoulder. "One of those things."

They made their way downstairs, Charlie jumping up and down on the Traitor's Stair.

"Gonna go down; close the front door?" asked Curly.

"Bizzies might come back" said Charlie. "Then this reporter…"

"Reporter?"

Charlie pushed open the academy door. "Tell you about it inside."

Entering 'Reception', he opened the fridge and took out a six-pack. Gestured towards the left-hand door in the back wall leading to the 'Rocker's Lair'. "Let's get it on!"

SEQUENCE 80

WEDNESDAY, 10th MARCH, 1982. 20.35
EXT / NIGHT MOORFIELDS

The cab came back to rest opposite John's office building. The front door was still open.

"What now, Ace?" asked the driver.

"Quiet hotel. B&B. Cash up front. No questions."

In the silence, the taxi valves clattered away.

"OK," said the driver eventually. "I can do that. Thing is... That double fare... And now sorting out hotels and that..."

Raite had the field kit box on his knees. He opened it. The inside had been stripped of its wooden separators. Face up was *Celestial Vision*; the *Magdalen* still in its back-prefab- window polythene sheeting underneath. On top, a brown envelope. Raite passed the envelope through the hatch.

The driver opened it. Half a dozen or so black-and-white glossy photographs. "Fucking hell, Ace! Who's this?!"

"Name's 'Just Liz'. Model I used to know."

"Those two fellas she's with! Todger on that one! Where'd you find a pair hung like that?"

"Soho... She ever re-launches her career – sort of thing she might want to buy back!"

SEQUENCE 81

WEDNESDAY, 10th MARCH, 1982. 20.40
INT / NIGHT DRUM ACADEMY.

The Rocker's Lair hosted Charlie's sleeping and recreational arrangements. Black-painted floorboards loosely covered with old betting slips, newspapers and empties. Against one wall, Charlie's bed – two mattresses stacked one upon the other. On the top one, a rumpled double sleeping bag and a couple of greasy pillows. Alongside the mattresses a long, low table. On the table a number of overflowing ashtrays, a radio, and a stack of glossy magazines covering Charlie's interests. The wire from the radio led to the room's one electrical outlet, low down on the wall at the head of the bed. Into this was plugged a triple adapter. Into this, a series of further single adapters, double adapters and extension leads. Connected in turn to toasters, kettles, toasted sandwich makers, lava lamps and broken TV sets. Plus assorted record decks and speakers. All the adapters and extensions had black-and-brown scorch marks on their white plastic casings. There were lots of exposed wires.

The walls of the Lair were again roughly plastered. Their only decoration a poster showing the corpse of Elvis Presley. Across this someone had scrawled, in neon pink, 'Returned to Sender'. That was one half of the room. The other half was Charlie's work/entertaining space. A large overstuffed armchair plumped-up with '60s psychedelic cushions and tie-dyed 'ethnic' throws, standing on a bright orange circular rug. In front of the chair was a low, wide, kidney-shaped table. On the far side of the table, a second, guest, armchair. The centre of the table – directly opposite Charlie's chair – contained his 'gear'. A battered, flat tobacco tin with hand-painted abstract decorations. A hand mirror with a plastic playing card lying on it. A pouch of rolling tobacco. A packet of jumbo-sized cigarette papers. A box of cook's matches. A box of standard matches. Three lighters. A pack of twenty 'tailor-made' cigarettes. A oversized glass pub ashtray full of bits of cigarette-packet cardboard for use as roaches. Crumpled and discarded cigarette papers. Screwed-up betting slips. Pill bottles with and without pharmacy labels. The right-hand side of the table held Charlie's provisions. An extra-thick sliced loaf. An industrial-sized lump of cheese with a knife sticking out of it. A block of corned beef covered in yellow fat. A carton of margarine. On the left-hand side, a record deck connected to two speakers. Stacked to the left of Charlie's armchair were three cardboard boxes holding his record collection.

Charlie raised a can to Curly in the opposite armchair. "Cheers, oppo."

"Cheers, Charl!"

Both drank. Lit cigarettes.

From a pocket, Charlie drew a bag of marijuana. Threw it on the table. "Top skunk!" he said. "Can't offer you no coke at the moment. But that'll come... Right!... Three, five, or seven skinner?"

Curly shrugged in incomprehension.

"Let's make it a five. Get the party going." Charlie finished his first can. Opened a second. Began building a joint. "Like I said. Saving your Chris. Least I could do. Those press bastards, though... That reporter I mentioned?"

"Yeah. You said... So what was that about?"

"First thing he asks? How much clothing your Chris still have on? Was Raite bollock naked? When I was lunging forward with the 'razor-sharp opener', did I think of James Bond? Did I get my feet tangled in Chris's black, lacy, torn-off bra? What size would I say it was? Could I pose for a photo waving the opener above my head, 'so it catches the light'?" Charlie licked the seal on the joint. "Course, good for business one way..."

"Chris being nearly raped?!"

"... But in another way, people find out where you are. Fines... Outstanding warrants... That paternity thing..."

Charlie sighed. "The price of fame! Yeah. Maybe we need to close the front door after all. Do it in a minute." He lit the joint. Took a deep toke. Coughed heavily. Leaned forward, head bent. Waved the joint towards Curly. Looked up when it wasn't taken from his fingers. Rasped, "Here you go, Curl… Get a lungful of this!"

"Mate. I don't!"

Charlie stared uncomprehendingly.

"Don't take drugs," Curly clarified.

"Curl! You're puffing away on a tailor-made and swigging a Dr Pippin's! The fuck d'you think they are?"

"I mean your sort of drugs."

"Curl! You're almost in the music business. Those fuckers spot any weakness – like not schmoozing along – be onto you like a dog into a butcher's shop! 'Sides, what Mary-Anna is – essentially – is the 'drug of peace'! Ask any medic or bizzie who they'd rather see coming through the doors've A&E half-eleven Sat'day night?… Some poor bastard had four or five J's and stepped off a bus platform thinking it'd stopped – like we've all done… Or some hard-case had ten pints of wife-beater… Fell through a shop window… And is now out to prove a point!" Charlie took another big toke. Held his breath. Groaned. Exhaled. Handed the joint to Curly.

Curly took it.

"Right. Just like you're smoking a straight. Big one now – right down into your lungs – then let it go up into your head. Don't exhale till I give the word!"

Curly took a bit hit. Closed his mouth. Began coughing without opening his mouth until the smoke finally exploded out.

"Good start," said Charlie. "And another!"

"Charlie…"

"Fuck's sake, Curl! Get with it!"

Curly took another big drag and handed back the joint.

Charlie hit it again and again – watching Curly closely "Feel anything?" he asked

"Not really… No…" Curl suddenly looked down as if listening for something.

"Time for another." Charlie began searching his pockets while singing in a heavy French accent, "*No cee-gar-ettes… No! I have no cee-gar-ettes!*" Became aware of the pack on the table. Began to build another joint.

Curly raised his head and stared loose-lipped at Charlie without saying anything.

Charlie drank more cider. Leaned over the side of his chair to his record boxes. "The King or the Master?" he asked. "Elvis or Roy?" Brought up a record. Laid it near the turntable. Started the turntable. Drank some cider. Unscrewed a pill bottle and took two pills. Stared fixedly at the revolving turntable. Lit up again. The neck of the joint had not been closed off properly, and some burning shreds fell onto Charlie's T-shirt. He staggered to his feet, beating at his front. Began to play air guitar.

"I sparked up on the train going west,
Went on the nod and burned my chest.
They gave me heroin to ease the pain.
Can't wait to climb on that old choo-choo again!"

Fell back in his chair. Half-staggered to his feet holding the joint across the table. "Curl! Curl!"

Curly raised a blurry head. "Wha's it, mate?"

Charlie waveringly offered the joint. Curly took it. Sucked in another big hit. Equally re-waveringly offered it back.

Charlie snatched it back. "Yeh!... Fucking heroin!? That third wife of mine?... Goes on this week-long heroin bender. Wakes up. This Judy next to me I never even seen before. Seems I married her two days earlier. Some sort of pagan do... Ended up dumping her out the van at some motorway services. That's heroin for you!"... He shook a warning finger at Curly. "Also bad for you medically!" He picked up the playing card from the mirror... "Coke's the real deal, Curl. Speed if you're skint! Maybe opium once we find our feet. The 'rooms? Mushrooms? Just your heart banging away and hearing loud footsteps following you all the time. Acid? Not for someone like you, Curl. You might never come back... No! It's the old nose candy for us."... Charlie staggered to his feet. Gestured round the Lair. "Be like mounds of white builder's sand all over the floor. " Charlie pointed to the revolving turntable. "The Nurgs!" Staggered and fell. Crawled behind his chair. Felt under the edge of the orange mat. Pulled out the brown contracts envelope. Crashed down in his chair again. Held up the envelope. "Our big chance, Curl! And I'm bringing you on board! Though should've been Eddie!" He drank heavily from his can while simultaneously beginning to cry.

Curly mumbled something.

"Me 'n' Eddie!" sobbed Charlie through his tears. "Loved ballads, see. Songs with a story! In the van, drinking, drugging, screwing, singing our way through Marty Robbins. Jim Reeves… Always finishing with 'El Paso'… What a fucking song! Eddie even did his own version using names from some woollyback place down south he came from." Charlie staggered to his feet. Pointed his air guitar.

> *"Down in the West Sussex town of East Grinstead,*
> *I fell in love with an Edenbridge girl.*
> *Night-time would find me in Verity's Chip Shop.*
> *Steam would rise up*
> *And Noreema's hair curl.*
> *Bluer than skies were the eyes of Noreema;*
> *Bluer than skies in the warm Sussex breeze.*
> *So, ev'ry night, though she had bad ex-zee-ma,*
> *I'd spend my dole on fish, chips, mushy peas.*
> *One night a wild young slabber came in…*

Yeah. Eddie could take off almost anything. But never wrote nothing of his own, so we just did covers!" Charlie collapsed back into his chair. Took another hit. Finished the fourth can. "If you can't write your own stuff, mate, you might just as well put on the Leonard Cohen and reach for the razor blades. How many bands have I known, Curl…?"

Curly muttered something. Held out a hand. Charlie picked up the empty cider can. Tipped it to his mouth to make sure it was empty. Put it in Curly's hand. Curly upended the can to his mouth. Let his arm and the can fall into his lap. Nodded off again.

"… Bands even had the Beatles *open* for them – but could only do covers. Where are they now? All packing supermarket shelves. While the Beatles!... But! The Nurgs!" Charlie put the vinyl record on the turntable. Stared at it revolving. Dragged a number of scribbled-on music manuscript sheets from the brown envelope. Pencil and red pen scrawls. Shook his head. "Totally original and totally right for today's market. Fuckers can do anything." He threw up a finger. "But only with the right management! Which is!? US!" He finished the fifth can. Threw it against the wall. Opened the last. Made a half-hearted gesture of offering it to Curly. Began to drink from it. "Yeah. Music's funny. Some read it but can't play it. Some write it but can't read it. Some can play anything on any instrument without knowing nothing about it! The Nurgs, though..." He waved the sheaf of manuscripts. "Even now there's enough to start looking at a first album. 'Ants Up Our Arseholes'. That one they sang at that club of yours: 'Just Another Night'? Perfect for would-be suicides – big market these days. Then two cracking ballads – 'I Rang Up Dr Frankenstein'...

I rang up Dr Frankenstein.
He said, 'We need to drink some wine.
Some vintage, deep, dark, rich and red.
The sort of stuff would raise the dead!'

Pure gold! Lots of people – dealers – roadies – interested in bringing back their dead girlfriends. Plus a really good twist not in any of the Frankenstein films! Natch for Radio 1 – *Top of the Flops... Radio Cluck'nburg... Desert Island Divs...* This other one though they've got. 'Ballad of Torn-Ears Tom and D-Cup Dan'!?... No...

No Radio 1 there. *Crop of the Slops. Desert Island Dicks.* Not on your fucking life! Where's that music?!" Charlie held the stylus over the revolving LP. Scratched it up and down until he found the right track. Roy Orbison began to sing 'Crying'. Charlie slurped from the sixth can. Pointed to the empties. "Christ! We're almost out. You greedy bastard, Curl!"

Curly muttered something.

Charlie lurched to his feet. "Just get another pack. Lock that outside front door… Cunts coming-in trying to steal our gear." Swaying, he lit a straight. Staggered to the door of the Lair. Turned. Pointed a trembling finger at Curly slumped forward in the guest armchair. "Don't go anywhere!"

SEQUENCE 82

WEDNESDAY, 10th MARCH, 1982. 21. 45
INT / NIGHT RAITE'S ROOM B&B

Raite's hotel room was small and square. A table with a chair. A bed. A battered dresser. Stained carpet. On the table was the artist's field kit box. Resting across it, *Celestial Vision*, face up. A pair of pliers and a roll of heavy-duty adhesive tape.

Raite picked up *Celestial Vision* and turned it over. The cardboard back had been removed and replaced. Numerous strips of the tape held the new back in place.

He hefted the painting. Checked the hanging screws were in tight. Hefted the painting once more. Laid it in

the field kit box. Closed the box. Put on his climber's
waterproof.

SEQUENCE 83

John and his father sat at the kitchen table. There were
two cans of mild on the table. Two glasses, both half-
full. In front of Mr O'Rourke, a newspaper. In front of
John, a book.

"Dad?"

"Yeah?"

"Say you wanted to get on the container berth?
Unofficially…?"

Mr O'Rourke looked up. Poured mild from the can
into his glass. "On behalf of who?"

"You know…"

"John. Containers are after my time."

"But there'll be a way, right?… Getting stuff out
unofficially?"

"There's always a way." Mr O'Rourke wetted a finger.
Turned over a page of his paper.

"Mick? I suppose he'd know?"

"How to tie you in pipe-cleaners before selling you
two tickets to the Titanic." Mr O'Rourke wetted his finger
again. Turned another page.

SEQUENCE 84

Charlie stood in front of the fridge, a six-pack of Dr Pippin's in his hand. His eyes were closed and he was propping himself up with an arm against the fridge. "Fuck!" he said suddenly. "That front door!"

He reached to pull open the academy door. Stopped and listened. Feet on the stairs. He closed the door to a crack and applied his eye.

Raite appeared carrying some sort of big, shallow wooden box. The Traitor's Stair creaked as he made his way up towards John's office.

Fucking hell!

Behind Charlie the door of the Lair opened. Curly staggered into reception. "Charl? What's going on? Feeling a bit... bit..."

Charlie moved across the room. Pushed Curly hard back into the Lair. Curly staggered back and fell on the floor. Charlie quietly closed the Lair door on him and went back to the door of the academy.

A moment or so later Raite came down, still carrying the box. The Traitor's Stair creaked. His shoes pattered quickly down and out.

What the fuck was all that about?!

SEQUENCE 85

Harry Rose sat at the desk in his cabin. In front of him, a writing pad and fountain pen. On the pad, four or five lines. He sighed and opened the bottom drawer of his desk. These days a mate on a ship like this had his own small drinks/ entertainment area. But old habits die hard and the first move anyone ever made after a long day was towards the bottom drawer of their desk; or down the side of their bunk mattress.

Harry took out his gin bottle. Moved across to his fridge for a bottle of tonic. Made up a drink. Closed his eyes. Took the gin and tonic to his writing desk. Took up the pad. Read aloud.

SS Ocean Seaspray
Alongside Liverpool
Wednesday 10th March

Dear Chris,

As we're sailing in two days, I hope you don't mind me contacting you like this. We're almost loaded now but I wanted to try and see you before sailing to perhaps discuss the greyhound project, so arranged some time off this afternoon to go to John's office. However, when I got there I saw an ambulance and...

He put down the pad. Took a drink of gin.

There was a knock on the door.

Harry covered the pad with a cargo manifest. "Come in!"

Quartermaster Wally Jinks. "'Scuse me, Mr Mate… One of them dockers has snagged his hand on a wire. No more'n a scratch and shouldn't have been anywhere near it – but you know what they're like. Stick their hands up the Devil's arse, thought there'd be anything there for them… Gave him a plaster, but these days all needs to go in the accident book so needs countersigning."

"Wally, I'm not long off. It's the coasting second mate on now."

"Yeh. Knocked on his door. *'No answer!' came the stern reply.*"

"I see."

"Maybe he's slipped across the road? Seven Stars? Forgot about the time?"

"That where he is?"

"Well… I suppose with the dockers knocked off for the day, and him – coasting second – leaving us shortly… When's the sailing second rejoining anyway, Mr Mate? If I'm not asking out of turn?"

"Tomorrow, supposedly. All back to normal then."

"Yeah. 'Coasting mates'. I've spent longer on a wave most of them have at sea. Yeah, some fellas know a good screw they see one…"

Harry stretched. "Right, Wally. Let's get that accident book sorted." He stood, disturbing the cargo manifest.

Wally's eyes shot to the writing pad. "Finally got a girl?"

Harry inclined his head slightly. "Well…"

"Yeah. Often said to Scouse MacGuinness I couldn't understand how you'd got away with it. Decent-looking. Good job. No sign you're a bit 'hard a-starboard' or anything…"

Harry gave a cautious grin. "Early days yet…"

"Yeah," said Jinks. "Get married and learn how to become a miserable bastard, same's the rest of us."

"OK, let's get up the bridge; get it written up."

"Mr Mate? Just one more thing…"

Here it comes.

"Just that the skipper – Captain Barratt. This lip-reading thing and always thinking I'm out to get him… Me and Scouse MacGuinness in the QMs' mess room the other day; if you can call a broom cupboard a mess room. Few coconut macaroons and a mug of tea. I looks up towards the window – if you can call a 'torch glass' a window – and there's the skipper staring at my lips as I'm explaining something to Scouse…"

"Wally…"

"Scouse MacGuinness – reading man; almost sat his third mate's ticket one time; real brainbox – thinks I might be developing one of them 'traumas'. That I might be able to apply for 'paid mental sick leave' for an 'indefinite period'."

"The captain, Wally… I hear he might be retiring soon."

"Natch'ly, I don't want to get the union in, but…"

"Wally! That accident with the finger you put a plaster on. Must be good for… well… at least two hours overtime?"

SEQUENCE 86

THURSDAY, 11th MARCH, 1982. 13.30
EXT /DAY SEVEN STARS PUB, CONTAINER
TERMINAL

Opposite the container terminal berth, on the other side of the dual carriageway, was The Seven Stars. In front of the pub was a lay-by; and at the lay-by's end, a left turn into the pub's car park. In the lay-by, two saloon-model private-hire taxis, their drivers sitting on the bonnet of one of them, smoking. Watching the passing show. When the pub closed at 3pm they would be there to provide transport to late afternoon drinking dens along the Dock Road – or in Liverpool itself.

A blonde walked into the pub. One of the drivers made a fist, then swung his forearm between his legs.

John drove the *Express* slowly past the lay-by, peering myopically through the dirty windscreen before making an even slower left turn into the car park, clipping the pavement as he did so.

The taxi drivers stared at the *Express*, then at each other.

SEQUENCE 87

THURSDAY, 11th MARCH, 1982. 13.40
INT / CONTAINER BERTH OFFICE

The container manager stared down at the berth. "He's back."
"Raite?" asked the cargo planner, laughing.

"This time with a big, shallow box thing. Never seen anything like it. Not even that bloke intending to sleep with his vintage Jag on the Ro-Ro deck – case someone stole its wire wheels."

"Wasn't here myself then," said the cargo planner, "but didn't they get them anyway?"

"Three," said the manager. "They stole three."

"So why three?" asked the planner after a pause.

"Liverpool overkill," said the manager. "Or maybe they heard he had a couple of spares."

SEQUENCE 88

THURSDAY 11th MARCH 1982. 13.41
EXT / DAY SEVEN STARS CAR PARK

The car park was relatively deserted. Very few dockers and seamen owned cars. Standing next to the *Express*, John stared across at the container berth, the terminal enclosed by a seven-foot fence of steel palings that seemed to stretch all the way back to Liverpool.

He walked round the front of the pub.

The two taxi drivers were still sitting on the bonnet, talking in low voices, their heads bent. John walked on towards the main entrance, nodding to the drivers, who ignored him.

At the entrance of The Seven Stars he turned to look once more across the dual carriageway at the container berth. Behind the fence, non-stop activity. Giant spindle-legged cranes, warning sirens sounding, moved slowly backwards and forwards, lifting and shifting containers onto a large ship which lay stern on to the road. The *Ocean Seaspray*. Harry's ship.

John stood trying to memorise what he was seeing. The cab drivers now openly staring at him. One spat loudly. John looked away. Pushed open the main door.

"Fucking wanker," said one of the drivers.

"'Written all over him," said the other.

SEQUENCE 89

THURSDAY, 11th MARCH, 1982. 13.45
EXT / DAY CONTAINER BERTH

Raite exited his container carrying the artist's field kit box. Made a show of checking its catches. Closed the container doors. Began to fiddle with the locks. Glanced out of the corner of his eye up towards the top floor of the terminal office block.

SEQUENCE 90

THURSDAY 11th MARCH 1982, 13.50
INT / DAY SEVEN STARS

The bar of The Seven Stars was noisy and jostling. Clumps of dockers arguing about football, working conditions, football, politics, women, football, working conditions, the price of beer, working conditions, football, women, politics. Clerks and office staff from the terminal. Seamen in and out of uniform. Marine engineers in white boiler suits.

John moved to the bar. A group of four Scandinavians laughing and joking with three girls who must have spent the night on board. Scattered about, further single women and women in pairs, all ready for action. Unpaid helpers wandering about collecting glasses. Minesweeping unfinished pints. Waiting for the unfailing generosity that would eventually include them in a round.

An older man – a docker in a belted blue boiler suit, an old mac, a flat cap and a muffler – sat in a window seat with a pint of mild; a newspaper in front of him. John sat opposite with his half of bitter. The man had been staring into space. Now he caught John's eye, nodded, and pointed down at the newspaper.

John smiled. "Seen it, thanks, pal."

The man nodded. "From round here?"

"Stanley Road. Trying to find an old pal of mine… Freddie England?"

The man shook his head. "Heard the name… But no. Can't place him."

"'Cross the road, are you?" asked John, gesturing out through the window.

The man nodded. "Just grabbing a dinner-time pint."

"Yeah. Maybe's Freddie's over there. Maybe drift across; see if someone knows where he is. All right to get on the terminal, am I?"

"Could've been a few weeks ago. But then they got them fags out… You hear about that?"

"Nah," said John. "Must've missed that."

"Now you'd need your card… or a pass."

John stared across at the cranes moving about like drunken giraffes. "Size of those bastards."

"Spiders, they call them. Those giant, straggly legs… Terrifying walking under them when they're moving."

"Many accidents?"

"Used to be. After a few deaths, the *Albion* ran an article. Bosses finally fitted warning sirens."

"Must make it a lot easier, though?" said John. "Containers? All that 'handball' in the old days… 'Member the states my old fella used to come home in. Covered in all kinds of shit from ships' holds… Even asbestos, he told me."

The man smiled and nodded.

"Course, the old fella'd bring home odd tins of this and that. Lemonade bottles of overproof rum if they'd broached a cask…"

The man's pint was untouched. He seemed to be listening, though at the same time somewhere else. Not deliberately rude… Just something…

John sipped his half. "Though I suppose once the containers are sealed you're pretty well done for if you've forgot to put something in?"

"Depends what it is," said the man. "Some come on already sealed by customs – Christ knows what's in them. But if it's not so valuable… well… seems you can put in stuff till the day you sail." He moved listlessly. Definitely on edge.

"Yeah… Right… But if it *was* valuable – antiques or that?"

The man looked at him squarely. "You talking about that bloke's been coming down messing around since

269

Tuesday whatever? Two containers? Always wanting stuff in and out?"

John met the docker's gaze. "Look, pal. I'm a private detective, but my old man was a docker all his life. Frank O'Rourke?"

The man nodded.

"That fella you just mentioned," continued John. "He's bad news."

The man stared at him.

"Hurts women. He's got hungry kids who are going short and that. I'm chasing him for alimony. He's got assets, but they're in one of them containers."

The man coughed quietly. "Frank O'Rourke?"

"Flour Street, Stanley Road," said John.

The man nodded.

"Spot anything yourself?" asked John pleadingly.

"To be honest, pal…" The man folded his paper. Stuck it in his pocket. Pushed his pint away with two fingers. "Yeah. Lads were saying, bit of a weirdo. Well… 'antiques' that's enough. But – see – he's marked his gear 'bric-a-brac'; means he can get in right up to sailing. Couple fellas've seen inside. Old office desks. Filing cabinets. Heaps of this, heaps of that. 'Like a madwoman's shite' as this mate of mine put it… On and off the Ro-Ro deck, too… Almost like he's looking for attention…"

"He can't help it." John picked up a heavy ceramic ashtray and made as if to hit himself on the side of his head with it. After a moment, "Any idea if he took anything in? Brought anything out?"

"Went in this morning with this box… Big, shallow thing. Told one of the lads some sort of painting kit artist types use when they're painting in the country. Banging round in there all morning." Suddenly the man bent and began to cough deep and low. He leant forward on the table to steady himself. A few nearby stopped talking to stare.

"You OK, pal?" asked John. "Anything I can get you?... Water?"

The man looked up. "Got sent for this morning. Doctor's. Test results..."

John drained his half-pint. Looked around for help.

"... Been having to get up in the middle of the night; go the lav quite a bit. So in a way I knew... Anyway. It's there."

John attempted to look confused.

"What you mentioned... Asbestos and stuff... Those ores... some of them still smoking and smouldering while you were shovelling them into sacks in the holds. No masks or anything. Few days of that, you'd need to go behind the shed; cough your guts up. Sometimes blood and stuff..."

John cast a quick glance towards the door and safety.

"... Anyway, that's me fucked," said the docker. He looked directly at John, eyes haunted and glassy.

John stood. "Look, pal, I've got to go. Thanks for the info. And I'm really sorry about the other."

The man smiled. "I always fancied going up in an aeroplane."

John stared in mounting panic.

Holding John's eye like some sort of lifeline, the man said, "Don't know how the missus will cope. Luckily the kids are grown up; fairly settled – well, much as they can be, way things are these days. But the missus..."

John nodded. "Yeah. Must be grim. Look, I need to report in and that…"

"Right," said the man.

John hesitated. "Sure I can't get you nothing? Another pint? Meat pie?"

"I'm fine, son. You get off… And best of luck with your case! But you'll need help to get on that dock if you don't belong. You know anyone?"

John stared. "Mick…" he muttered.

"Good Liverpool docker's name," said the man. Gave John a thumbs up.

John reciprocated. Scurried towards the main entrance.

Outside, one of the taxis was just pulling away with Raite in the back seat. Raite sensed John's presence and swung round. Smiled. His taxi joined the traffic on the main road towards town.

John stared at the driver of the second taxi, his thoughts in turmoil.

"Fuck are you looking at?!" said the driver.

SEQUENCE 91

THURSDAY, 11th MARCH, 1982. 15.15
INT / DAY CABIN OF ROGER DRUMMOND,
COASTING SECOND MATE, *OCEAN SEASPRAY*

Harry knocked on Roger Drummond's cabin door. Roger was the *Seaspray*'s coasting second mate.

The 'coasting crowd' joined when the 'sailing crowd' went on leave. Took the ship round the coast, discharging and loading cargo. Left when the sailing crowd returned to take the ship out on its next trip. Coasting mates came in two types: those who came by public transport wearing their uniform trousers and a sports jacket, with their uniform jacket, 'steaming bonnet', and sextant in a brown paper bag. And those who arrived by taxi with three suitcases full of uniforms, 'going-ashore' gear, 'toiletries'.

Harry knocked once more and entered to the "Yes?!" from inside.

The arrival of container shipping with its one-week turnaround had effectively curtailed shoregoing time for crews. To compensate, shipping companies had provided previously unheard-of accommodation standards which also tempted people to remain on board – therefore on call – for extra, unpaid, duties. Roger's cabin had the latest fittings. A comfortable couch and armchair. A writing desk with drawers and a leather-covered drop-down lid. A fridge. Bookshelves. Decent carpet. A double wardrobe. Its own shower and toilet. Two open leather suitcases sat on the floor, clothes spilling over their sides.

Roger sat in his armchair, can of beer in hand. A gash bin, three-quarters full of empties. A case of beer with its lid torn back near his chair. Roger had the face of a wasted cherub. Puffy cheeks. Watery blue eyes. Curly blond hair, the latter mostly hidden by his uniform cap, which he was wearing back to front. Black uniform trousers, top two buttons undone. A white shirt, top two buttons undone. A black tie hanging round his neck like a horse's halter. He'd kicked off his black rubber-soled work shoes and socks and had his feet on another, unopened, case of beer.

Harry spoke expressionlessly. "Just wondering about those chart corrections?"

Roger waved an arm towards his desk, covered with cargo manifests, charts, books, newspapers, ashtrays, empty cans and letters. "Fancy a beer, sir?"

Harry smiled. Shook his head. "Captain Barratt's a bit anxious…"

Roger held up the can. "Just finish this. Then full ahead the chartroom! Full sea speed all pencils, protractors, projectors…"

"If you would…"

Roger drained his can and threw it in the wastebasket. Absent-mindedly opened another. "El Capitano Barrattski," he began. "Ever talk to you about Wally? Wally Jinks? That old quartermaster?"

"Not really…" said Harry.

"Told me he thinks Wally's trying to murder him. Through lip-reading… That's a new one! Then onto tales of the *Berengaria*, *Aquitania*, *Queen*s during the war. RNR whatever…" Roger drank. Burped. Stared at Harry.

"Those chart corrections?" persisted Harry quietly.

Roger swished the can next to his ear. "Almost done… But with the sailing second due back imminently, thought I might leave them to him."

"Yes, well. There's a complication there."

Roger stiffened.

"His wife's pregnancy. Not back now till late tomorrow… If at all."

Roger froze. Groped for another can. "If at all?!"

"Captain Barratt asked me to let you know the office want you to be aware that you may have to do the voyage."

"Do the voyage?!" Roger pulled off his hat. Began to fan himself. "I can't do a *voyage*. I'm not mentally prepared."

"The office feel you are." Harry gestured to the open suitcases showing and assortment of uniforms and 'shore-going gear'.

Roger sighed. "Just in case I'm invited anywhere. Or fancy a trip up the road to a dance at the Seamen's Mission... 'Member those Catholic Mish dances? Girls you actually *could* take home to meet Mother? Now your average mission belle is worse than we are... And all down to containers!!"

Harry nodded sympathetically.

Roger made an all-encompassing gesture. "Ever thought of getting out?"

"Crossed my mind..."

Roger drained the can. Lobbed it in the bin. Opened another. "That Merchant Navy and Airline Officers' Association we're all part of." He took a swig. "Going round ships flogging insurance policies to people like ourselves; sign anything once they've had a few. Trouble is, no sooner on board, first thing you hear is 'Have a beer!' Yes?"

"More or less..."

"Situation like that, easy to get carried away, overstep the mark... Especially with the 'ginger beers' – engineers! Those fuckers and drink! Excuse my French! You could vanish into their accommodation and never be seen again!"

"The old man really wants those corrections, Roger."

Roger waved his can. "On it as we speak."

Harry forced a smile. "Look, Roger, I worked through lunch but would really like to slip into Liverpool for an hour or so; a friend in hospital. But don't really want to bother the old man. Can you look after things here for me? The dockers finish at five today."

Roger smiled slyly. "Your wish is my command, O Chief Officer."

"But try and do something with the chart corrections, will you?"

Roger held up his beer can with one hand. Pointed the other upwards. "My feet already – figuratively – on the companionway stairs!"

SEQUENCE 92

THURSDAY, 11ᵗʰ MARCH, 1982. 15.30
EXT / DAY BAYONETS. INT / DAY BAYONETS

Half three. The Bayonets door shut and locked. John banged hard. Then again. Then again. Heard Lenin and Marx barking, then scrabbling off the bottom of the stairs leading up to Mick's flat. Throwing themselves against the door.

The bolt came off. The door opened a crack. The dogs fought to get at John.

Mick said, "Fucking you! Thought it might be Special Branch, all that fucking racket. Hang on I sort these pair of bastards…"

The door banged shut. John pressed his ear to it. Heard Mick cursing and kicking the dogs. More non-stop barking. The door to the flat slamming.

The main door opened again. Mick glared at him. "You realise half three till half five's my only time off till I open this shithouse again?"

John's father had told him, 'Ask a man for a pound, he'll chase you. Tell him you need his wisdom and know-how, he'll slip you two quid without thinking'. "I need advice, Mick," John began solemnly. "Someone with his finger on the pulse; who knows the road. And… well… couldn't think of a better person than you."

Mick's already narrowed narrow eyes narrowed even more. He cracked the door a foot or so. Gestured John inside. Slammed and relocked it. Straight behind the bar for a double brandy. "Nothing for you as we're officially closed! Right, let's hear it!? And remember 'Comrade Mick understands!'"

"I need to get on the container berth."

"What for?"

"This case I'm on… But it's confidential…"

Mick's all-embracing affability vanished. "Not fucking here, it's not!"

They stared at each other. Mick pulled a glass of bitter – put it in front of John. Took a bag of crisps. Shook them at John to signify that he should begin. Began stuffing crisps in his mouth.

"Thing is, Mick, there's this client I've got…"

"That London Judy Curly mentioned?"

John smiled grimly. "Yeah. Hired me to find her husband. Alimony."

"That where they're handing out the alimony now? The container berth?"

"Well… There's also this painting…"

"Yeah. Heard about them. Them and your purple curtain! 'Backs to the walls, lads!' Still don't see the connection."

"This alimony money… Sort of tied up in this painting her husband's shipping to the States in a container of antiques."

"Might've fucking known… More art shit. No wonder she's fucked him off. And all going down on the *Seaspray*, is it?"

"See, I need to locate the painting inside one of his containers to half-inch for his missus. So need to get on the berth myself."

"You?! Blag your way onto the terminal?! Break into one of the boxes!? Cunt like you couldn't break into song… Plus those boxes are customs sealed."

"Got through locks before, Mick," said John. "Had to break into my own office once."

"Yeah. That hacksaw you didn't pay Curly for!" Mick threw off the remains of his brandy. "OK. Be back here fourish; we'll take a trip down there."

"Thing is," said John, "supposed to be visiting Chris about five. Then another appointment at six."

"Won't take long. You'll be at the ozzy by half five – *if* she'll see you. You leaving her alone like that!" Mick came round the bar. "Right! Shoot down your old fella's. Cup of tea. Your arse back up here!" He walked John to the main door and took off the bolts. "This painting? Worth a few bob?"

John didn't answer.

"Don't worry, tovarich. Sort all that later… Once it's in our hands!" Mick opened the door. Peered up and down. Pushed John out. The bolts went back on.

SEQUENCE 93

THURSDAY, 11th MARCH, 1982. 16.00
EXT / DAY PRISON CAR PARK

The parking lot in front of the prison was a large, flagged square bounded by a low wall containing the necessary openings and exits. Inside this square were assorted warders' and visitors' cars.

Today, four motorcycles – flying pennants and colours – cruised round. Idly weaving in and out of the cars.

The prison's main gate opened, and all four machines stopped.

'Arry emerged from within the prison carrying a brown paper bag. He walked across and climbed on the back of one of the machines. The bikes made one more circuit of the parking lot – klaxons and horns blaring – then pulled out of the exit and away.

During all this, no staff appeared.

SEQUENCE 94

THURSDAY, 11th MARCH, 1982. 16.02
EXT / DAY STANLEY ROAD. INT / DAY TAXI

John was back outside the Bayonets. A black cab pulled into the gutter alongside the kerb, its engine remaining running. The driver was bulky, double-overcoated, shapeless. Two woollen Liverpool FC scarves wrapped round his neck and head.

The pub door opened and Mick emerged wearing a fawn trench coat with large shoulder epaulettes. It had been so long since John had seen Mick outside of the Bayonets that he'd forgotten the landlord had any outside gear at all. Certainly none like this. Looking at the trench coat, the story about Mick's missus' dress flashed into John's mind.

Mick gestured for John to open the door of the taxi. He did so. Mick climbed in. John followed. The taxi pulled away with the usual clattering of dirty valves. Mick and John sat next to each other on the rear brown leather bench seat. Mick, stinking of stale cigarette smoke, brandy fumes, and Topsail Schooner, adjusted his trench coat over his knees as a woman adjusts her skirt.

John stared.

"Like a photo?" asked Mick.

"Just the coat, Mick. Very smart. Military, like…"

Mick pursed his lips. Pulled at the skirt of the coat again. Gestured towards the driver. "Jimmy Egan," he shouted. "Jimmy! It's O'Rourke."

Jimmy's head went up and down inside the scarves.

"Jimmy's Intel. Ops. at NELLI," said Mick. "Knows a bit about you!"

This hung in the air as Mick lit two Capstan Full Strength and passed one forward over Jimmy's shoulder. Jimmy accepted with a grunt.

Mick blew out a stream of smoke into John's face as the cab chugged along Stanley Road and through Bootle. "Thing is, John," he said eventually, "been a few questions lately."

"Questions?"

"Lads at NELLI. Wondering where you're coming from."

"Just Flour Street, Mick."

Mick smiled grimly. "Point is. What exactly the fuck are you?!"

"Me?"

"How d'you see yourself? Sewer-rat saboteur commie? Aristotelian negotiator? Crypto-fascist with Nazi longings? Radical peacenik? Polemic predator? Revolutionary by stealth? Utopian apparatchik anarchist? Or just a simple betrayed socialist? Lads are interested… Am I right, Jim?"

"You're not wrong, Mick," confirmed the driver.

John grinned. Waved a casual hand. "How about a 'nothingalist', Mick? Someone just trying to get by?"

Jimmy gave a sort of groan.

"'Nothingalist'?!" Mick blew smoke into John's eyes. "I mean, all hands know you're an Evertonian – fuck knows why! But don't even seem to get up Goodison any more?"

"I used to, Mick. But as you get older… My dad… Life, I suppose…"

"For lots of fellas, Anfield and Goodison *is* life!"

"Then the redundancy… trying to manage on the dole…"

"Yeah. The redundancy. That fucking bedding place. Everyone on Stanley Road walking round with holes in their backs."

"How's that?"

"Springs poking through those cheap fucking mattresses of yours."

"Nothing to do with me, Mick… Just a maintenance fitter."

"Sold out the shop floor, some say. Even heard the word 'scab'."

Jimmy groaned.

"Mick," explained John, "the place was finished. About to close. Thought I'd take something from the boss class 'fore it did."

Mick lit another two Capstans. Passed one over the front seat. "I mean. Don't you owe nothing to your old fella?"

"The old fella?!"

"Permanently creased with worry at your goings-on. Laying all the wrong 'bones' in the domino school. The limp getting worse, that he suffered in his fight against your RELICS – your rentier, limp-wristo Old Bleatonian, Old Oxphoneyans!"

"He did get that compo."

"Yeah. But from who?! The shipowner? Together with a get-well card? The only card any Liverpool shipowner ever sends is a fucking dole card! Liverpool fucking shipowners! May their heads slow-roast in Hell, their mouths stuffed with salt! As for your dad's compo. How far did that take him?"

"How about up to The Bayonets? Where he pissed it right back into the capitalist system buying booze for all hands, including you!"

Mick's face went white. "No, mate! Any profits from The Bayonets go right back to that same RELICS brewery class – most powerful of the powerful – who then portion off their pub managers with a slave pittance! Don't get smart with me!"

"Mick, I'm just…"

Jimmy swung the cab left at North Park/Knowsley Road for the run down to the container terminal.

"Now! You support Militant, right?" asked Mick. "Bring down Thatcher and her Tory arse bandits?"

"Course I do. Everyone in the working class does."

"You'd be surprised. What with all the brainwashing. 'Right to Buy' and a pension you couldn't feel in your arse pocket if you were wearing an Old Bleatonian boy scout silk jacket with a slit up the back... And we all know what *that's* for!"

"Mick! I'm from Flour Street! What else can I be?!"

"So what about that poem in the *Albion*? Seen by some as you moving your political core towards all that South End Liverpool liberal arts poetry shit... Plus your hair's getting too long, which everyone's noticed but 's too polite to mention." Mick leaned across and brushed a lock of John's hair to one side.

"Mick. My office is in Central Liverpool. Nowhere near the South End."

"Fuckin' poets! Look what they done to Jimmy..."

Jimmy groaned.

"I mean. Jimmy was a *checker* on the *Liverpool Docks*! A *checker*! A licence to steal cases of salmon!... Almost hereditary... sort of 'inalienable right'! Like your Von Scroungerhoffs, Bleatonians and Oxphoneyans able to walk into any East-End working-class boys home near Westminster demanding the 'speciality of the day'!... But look at Jimmy now! All muffled up 'cause he can't face the world. Know what happened? His missus fucking happened! Liberal South-End Liverpool arts poetry shit happened! That right, Jim?"

"You're not wrong, Mick."

"His missus?" asked John, puzzled.

"Goes the housy-housy – bingo – whatever they're fucking calling it now. Runs out of cash. Home early. Puts on the telly. Wrong channel. BBC 2! Some fucker talking 'drama'! Plays, that is…"

John nodded.

"Yeah. Thought *you'd* know. What *she* thought, fuck only knows, but starts asking – *demanding* – Jimmy takes her to see a play. Poor Jimmy's almost in tears. What sort of wankbiscuit *drama* could a fella like him – like any of us – watch without wanting to kill themselves?! Gets the *Albion*. Sees this *Scaffold* advertised. Immediately thinks of some poor working-class bastards being strung up by the bankers and the boss class. Maybe it's even about Albert."

John frowned.

"Albert Pierrepoint! Last official hangman! Fucking hell! Even you must have heard of *him*?! So could be a good laugh if nothing else. Anyway. Jimmy and his missus head into town. When they get there, though… Tell him, Jim!"

"I can't, Mick! Can't talk about it!"

"Ended up under the doctor!" said Mick. "Permanent sick note. Checker's job snatched off him."

"There *was* them copper ingots that Safmarine boat, Mick…"

"Jim! The afternoon them ingots went missing, I had you in a poker school in Stan Waters' with five lads from NELLI! We could have beaten that, you'd listened to me." Mick turned to John. "So, we fiddle his taxi exam and get him a plate, 'cause what else can he do?... And 'though now he knows all about plays and shit – think he'll ever get a job at the BBC or Arts Council? If only you were a *bender*, Jim! Be banging your door knocker off tomorrow morning!"

Jimmy groaned.

"Come the rev, though, we'll fucking sort it!" declared Mick. Then, in a hopeless voice, "Except we won't!"

"How's that, Mick?" asked John.

"'Cause your RELICS will always be one step ahead!" Mick lowered the cab window. Gobbed into the road. Turned to John. "You know the worst thing ever happened to me in my whole life?... The very worst?"

John shook his head.

"'Member that Militant Trade Union Bar I ran on Derby Road? The TUB?"

"The piano?... The raffle and that?"

"Piano?" said Mick. "I don't remember no piano... Piano, Jim?"

"No. No piano, Mick."

Mick pushed his face into John's. "I'd think before I spoke if I was you, cunthooks!" He lit two more cigarettes. "Yeah... This night, about one in the morning, just serving a last few pints and there's this shouting and yelling from the gents'. Big Denny McKevitt's only got his 'pork sword' stuck in his zip."

Jimmy groaned.

Mick threw up one finger. "Immediate action! Grab his bell rope with one hand; yank down his zip the same time. More screams than a boss hearing his chauffeur wants time off to bury his mother!... Thing was, though, I'd had

285

to *touch another man's half-yard*! Haunts me! But only shows the power of your Old Bleatonians / Oxphoneyans and Cambridbudgernerigigans. See, people like us, when we meet another fella we shake his hand... But them?! Well, see, they go these schools where they bunk together. 'Dorms', they call them. No sooner lights out than they're out of bed on the marble floors and grabbing each other by the old one-eyed Portuguese porridge pump! Time they leave they know ev'ry pimple on each other's tonsil ticklers – all ready to be blackmailed into doing fucking anything for each other, rest of their idle fucking lives!"

At the beginning of the approach road to the terminal were a couple of men in overcoats with clipboards and pens.

"More trapdoor terrorists," observed Mick.

Jimmy groaned in horror.

In John, sudden rage overtook common sense. "How, Mick?!" he almost shouted. "How can you know two ordinary-looking fellas like that are homos?!"

"Maybe their cashmere overcoats?"

"Cashmere?"

"They're fucking shining!"

"Sure that's not the drizzle?"

"Collars and ties. Leather shoes, gold fountain pens! Am I right, Jim?"

"You're not wrong, Mick!"

Along the side of the approach road nearest the fence were the braziers and pickets. Small groups of hooded, anoraked, figures. Rubbing hands. Drinking tea, coffee or beer. Mick tapped Jimmy on the shoulder. Jimmy stopped the cab opposite the braziers. One of the hooded figures raised a hand. Mick raised one in return. The picketeer continued to stare at the taxi.

"That's Billy piping you," said Mick.

"Billy?" said John.

"Billy Curtin."

Chris's married name.

"Chris's ex," confirmed Mick. "Who's heard you're now trying to get your leg over with her."

"Not any more."

"Wise move. Billy's a shop steward with English Electric on the East Lancs Road. English Elecky's got special links with Militant. Billy's a fella with lots of friends..."

In the cab, the only sound was the muted clatter of the engine valves.

Mick turned sideways to face John fully. "Although I'm wasting my time, there's a couple of things I need to say to you."

Jimmy sat rock-still, staring forward.

"What some of us think, looking at your fucking goings-on, is you don't know what you're part of here. This is North End Liverpool, for your information. It isn't part of Lancashire, isn't part of England... It isn't even the capital of Ireland, as some clever cunts say. It's North End Liverpool – capital of itself! And if we didn't critically need the handouts from the arse bandits at Westminster, we'd have fucked them off years ago! Liverpool's always been a working-class city. Exploited as such. The docks! Ford and its brain-mush assembly lines! The odd few, like you, get a trade, but most fellas are born to handouts and die on handouts. First they took the ships – Cunard to

Southampton… You know how much Cunard and his like made out of this place? What life was like for people like us on the so-called 'great liners'? Those fucking stokeholds! Dying in puddles of sweat and third-degree burns from keeping those fucking boilers fed so those cunts on the upper decks could have more ice in their cocktails? Cunard sitting up to beg in London drawing rooms to buy his kids a rentier-class leg-up?! Plus the coffin ships? Try reading Samuel Plimsoll, mate!… James Hanley… *The Last Voyage… Greaser Anderson…* instead of all that snot-gobbling detective shit of yours!"

Mick tapped Jimmy's shoulder. Jimmy took the cab almost to the glass security office in the middle of the road – then suddenly swung it round and they exited back along the slip road and the main approach road, then onto the dual carriageway, across to The Seven Stars and into the car park.

"Nice one, Jim!" said Mick, lighting up two more cigarettes.

On the other side of the carriageway, fencing-in the berth, was the long stretch of unbroken seven-foot steel palings.

Mick banged John hard on the head with his packet of twenty Full Strength. Pointed across the carriageway in the general direction of a paling bearing a short diagonal slash of white paint. "See it?"

"One with the paint?"

"From there, you count along, away from the gates, another twenty-three posts. That, and the one next to it, are loose at ground level. Move them to one side, you can slip through – *comprende*?"

"What about clobber, Mick?"

"Wear a heavy check woollen shirt. White crew-neck vest underneath. Jeans. Heavy-duty boots. Woollen hat. If you're thinking of getting into a container you'll need something for the lock. Maybe that hacksaw..."

In the silence, no one moved.

Eventually John said, "Thanks, Mick. I owe you one."

Mick smiled enigmatically. Tapped Jimmy on the shoulder. Jimmy released the clutch. The taxi began to move.

"Jimmy'll drop you the Teaching Hospital," Mick said. "Give Chris our best."

SEQUENCE 95

THURSDAY, 11th MARCH, 1982. 17.30
INT / DAY TEACHING HOSPITAL

The foyer of the Teaching Hospital was totally awash with people. As if Christ had agreed to appear in person to heal all the sick of Liverpool – and been rewarded with a full turnout. All types, ages and sexes, thronged the mosaic floor – in all manner of dress and deportment. In suits, tracksuits, smocks, frocks, shoes, sandals, trainers, dresses, hats, gloves, scarves, tights (with or without designer holes), leggings, jeans and jerseys. They stood, sat, crouched, limped, walked, shuffled, hobbled-by in splints, swung-by on crutches, were manoeuvred in wheelchairs or rushed through on trolleys with ancillary hospital staff running alongside holding up bags of fluid. Some of the less afflicted sauntered about, taking in the passing show while eating hot dogs dripping with fluorescent ketchup and baby-diarrhoea mustard. Others chain-smoked and coughed into sodden, gluey handkerchiefs. Some drank coffee or tea that was almost solid sugar; or worse, full of sweeteners. Visitors in relatively stable physical and mental health stared round like observers newly posted from reality, more and more terrified with each passing moment by the thought of ever becoming ill themselves. From time to time, like battleships cutting through a jumbled fleet of fishing smacks, doctors blazed through the milling crowd, often tagged by patients in flapping dressing gowns listening humbly to any remarks thrown back at them by these white-coated Übermenschen; unaware that these omnipotent beings were themselves bowed beneath the weight of their own fallibility, the ever-rising mutterings of *provable* malpractice suits, and the problems of getting their money into these new 'offshore' accounts. The whole ensemble a Thatcherite reworking of Jan Bruegel's *Christ In Limbo* by way of Pieter Bruegel's *The Triumph of Death*, by way of 'The Demons' from Grünewald's *Isenheim Alterpiece*.

John, traumatised by recent events, stood frozen just inside the never-still revolving doors, trying to plot a course across the foyer to the lifts without drawing attention to himself. If only he were Brick! His mind drifted to *The Bride Wore Size Tens*. Brick as an ageing altar boy. The occasion: a Mafia nuptial Mass. Brick there to poison the chalice from which the groom would drink. A machine gun under his cotta; three frag grenades in his thurible. On the altar – two cardinals, five archbishops, ten bishops, fifteen priests, a cloud of nuns, and a host of other altar boys. The congregation a shoulder-to-shoulder ménage of hitmen, lawyers, accountants, CIA, FBI, Secret Service, newshounds, film producers and Las Vegas showgirls; all patting each other on the back, shaking hands, comparing guns, and exchanging telephone numbers.

John began edging round the walls, but the building's design was such that a patch of open floor would have to be crossed. Then someone fell off a bench in a fit.

The crowd, finally engaged, formed a silent circle around the kicking figure on the floor.

John saw his chance and pushed into an already overcrowded lift. The lift thrummed and hummed upwards, its passengers staring at their feet.

On the seventeenth floor, John walked out to face another row of benches containing more patients / visitors / relations. All again smoking, coughing, complaining, eating or drinking.

On the ward he had to pass the nurses' station, where two trolleys were being racked up with enough drugs to neutralise King Kong. Hard currency for the coming night's staff v. patients truce.

John entered the ward, and made his way towards where he could see Chris's blonde hair. There was a plaster and lint at the hairline over her right eye.

"First tonight." She smiled at him. "Visitor, that is."

John smiled back. Held out chocolates and tulips. On the side table there were already a few cards and bunches of mixed flowers.

"Tulips!" Chris raised herself slightly. "My favourite! Such lovely shapes and colours." She smiled again. "John,

I really appreciate them, but would you mind giving them to Mrs Bird over there, behind you? She's been really kind to me, listening to my troubles and everything – though she's got plenty of her own."

John turned and looked at the bed facing Chris's.

In it, living up to her name, was a small, thin figure of a woman of about seventy. She had a beaklike nose and small, bright eyes that twinkled. She waved a weak hand at him.

"Sure," he said. Then, in a low voice, "No visitors, then?"

"Steve – her husband – is around, but they live out on one of the estates. He came in the first night – she's really ill – and there was a gang of youngsters waiting for him to leave for the hospital. Once he'd gone, they broke in and ransacked their flat. He has to stay at home now or they'll have nothing left at all. He just *can't* visit her."

"She tried the police?"

"Said they'd keep an eye, but…"

John nodded. "Maybe Crust could put it on his list."

He took the flowers over to Mrs Bird. The old woman's chest heaved as she tried to thank him. John smiled. Arranged the tulips in a vase containing some dying daffodils. Gave an inane grin. Squeezed Mrs Bird's hand. Walked back across to Chris, unconsciously wiping his hand on his trousers.

"Some of her days are better than others," said Chris. "Her chest is terrible, and now they think she might have an infection… She's over seventy, you know."

John nodded. Made a sympathetic face.

Chris patted the bed. "How are things at the office?"

John sat. Gave a quick smile. "Should never have left you there. Deserve what everyone would like to give me – a punch in the mouth."

"John, it's done. Forget it."

"Plus it should have been me, not Charlie, who saved you."

"Just glad it was anybody."

"He sends his best wishes – Charlie."

"Send mine back. All confusing, really. What happened. Can't remember most of it."

"Confusing is right. Charlie even thought he saw Raite again."

"When?"

"Later, after you'd been brought here. I went home with my dad. The police were well gone, leaving the door of the office open as you'd expect. Lock's gone missing, of course – more expense! Charlie tidied-up up a bit, then went back down to his own place; talk things over with Curly. Charlie says he dropped-off with exhaustion and woke hearing someone on the stairs. Poked his nose over, and thought he saw Raite going down and out the front door. Seems pretty sure."

There was a pause. Chris said, "Everyone's been so good…"

"That's what we're here for," said John, and held out his hand.

She slowly took it. They looked at each other, both sets of eyes blank.

SEQUENCE 96

"So where is it?" asked the Voice. "The Porsche?"

"Place called Bazza's Birkenhead Bangers," said Crust.

"Do him just on the name!"

"That what you want?"

"What we want is for its paperwork to vanish. Then the car itself."

Crust doodled a rabbit coming out of a hat formed from the top half of an open sports car.

"How about the painting?" continued the Voice.

"Difficult to say. Raite's in and out of his containers, most recently with an artist's field kit box. Football pitch size."

"Reckon he had the painting in it?"

"Or wants us to think so…"

"Worth lifting him now?"

"If it's stashed somewhere else, we'll lose it. He won't give it up." Crust doodled Raite on a rack.

"So…?"

"Think it all depends whether he goes with the ship. If he does, that's where it'll be. Work it off in New York one way or another…"

"And you?" asked the Voice.

"He goes, I go."

"Can you get at it? On the ship?"

"This cargo planner at the berth – 'friend of the bobby' – tells me Raite's two containers'll be on the Ro-Ro deck that's set flush with the bottom of the ship."

"That a 'yes'?"

"Could be… We thinking of an arrest?"

"Thing is," said the Voice, "he's arrested, a lot of stuff could come out…" A pause. "You'll be taking a gun?"

"Not sure."

"As the one taught you all you know," said the Voice carefully, "a gun may be necessary." Another pause. "And O'Rourke?"

"Seeing him sixish tonight. Sign him off. But let him know there's a bit of cash…"

"Bogger and Mrs Raite?"

"Christ knows."

"Remember I mentioned if we could sort police communications, how much easier the job would be?"

"Yeah."

"One crime usually definitely beyond communications – *or witnesses* – someone goes overboard at sea at night…" A further pause. "Course," continued the Voice, "Bogger and Liz find out what Ronnie's planning – someone drops a coin – might decide to make the trip themselves…"

"Like when I Hansel-and-Gretelled them with Ronnie's address?"

"Hello, sailor!"

SEQUENCE 97

THURSDAY, 11th MARCH, 1982. 18.05
EXT / NIGHT TEACHING HOSPITAL CAR PARK

From the Teaching Hospital it was about ten minutes to Crust's pub in London Road. John stood outside the hospital's main gates for a moment to collect his breath, and thoughts, then turned right.

Harry, carrying a very large, ribboned bouquet of flowers, slipped out from behind a vehicle and headed towards the hospital's main entrance.

SEQUENCE 98

THURSDAY, 11th MARCH, 1982. 18.20
INT / NIGHT CRUST'S LOCAL

Crust's local was, like The Bayonets, Victorian. A narrow bay-windowed frontage crammed between a clothing store and a furniture 'emporium'. The pub's door lay behind a tiny tiled vestibule angled back from the road. An easy place to miss.

Inside, immediately to the right, was the bar stretching three-quarters of the way back to the rear of the pub. At the back of the bar, an ornate Welsh-dresser type of overmantel, its cupboards and shelves stretching almost to the ceiling. On the left-hand side, a cracked red leather bench ran down the pub. In front of the bench, cast-iron tables with a few scattered chairs.

Unlike at The Bayonets, there were local women in the bar. Mostly elderly and poorly dressed; some with husbands, lovers or grown-up children. Plus a table of six or so women in pink overalls sitting around a large white-iced cake with a bar of soap shaped out of blue icing rising from its centre. The cake surrounded by empty Babycham bottles, laughter, and muted screams. A few single men in suits. Medical, clerical and ancillary staff from the hospital and university. Building-site labourers. All washing away the taste of the day. An impression everyone knew everyone else.

John positioned himself halfway down the bar and tried to attract the barman's attention. Felt someone looking at him. Turned. It was a large woman planted firmly in a broad-bottomed bentwood chair in a far corner of the room. Unguessable age. Swathed in black shawls. Pair of dock gateman's boots. In one outstretched hand, a half-full pint glass. In the other, a bottle of Mackeson Stout. On her head, a white 'biddy bonnet'.

John decided he'd wait outside for Crust. As he turned to go, the barman, tall, black-haired, and of Modigliani angularity, raised a finger towards the far end of the pub. John looked towards this shadowy region furthest from the street door. Three worn wooden steps led up to what seemed to be a small railed-off snug. He edged down the bar and climbed them.

The snug had a cracked red leather circular bench running round the back wall. Two wrought-iron tables with wooden tops. Sitting on the bench in front of one of the tables was Crust. The other side of the table, a chair. On the table, two empty pint glasses and two whisky glasses. Crust was holding a book backed in brown paper. He laid it down, print to the table, pointed to the chair, rose and walked to the top of the steps. "Tom!" he roared. "Two pints of bitter."

"Lager," said John.

Crust resumed his seat. Surveyed John. "How was she?"

John shrugged. "Getting back to her old self."

"And you?"

"Feel bad over what happened to her. Then not managing to get in to see her last night..."

"Not family. Though I'm sure you'd like to be." Crust stared down at the table with a crooked smile.

He's had a few. "Even now, staff wouldn't tell me anything," John tried.

"'Medical Professionals'. And as all professions are conspiracies against the public, the less the public knows the better. No, no one'll talk to someone like you." Crust half-raised a finger. "But they'll talk to me! 'Cause, while they have their powers, I've a greater one! The power to take away their liberty! A terrible power! Though I'm delighted I've got it!"

Tom climbed the steps and put the drinks down in front of Crust. "Two pints, gents!"

Crust picked up one of the glasses and held it to the light. "I hereby pronounce this horse unfit for work!"

Tom shook his head. Picked up the empties. Walked back down the steps. Crust laughed. Raised his fresh glass and waited until John did the same.

"Voltaire, I think it was," began Crust, "said if we knew the private lives of our physicians we'd stone them in the streets. But it's not French literature here – it's paintings. Or is it money?"

Fuck! John still had Raite's envelope. The three hundred quid. Did Crust know somehow? *Fucking coppers.* And if Raite was caught? Would he give John up? Should he mention it?

Crust was staring him in the eyes.

John stared back. "I don't think there is any money. Not any more."

"Oh?"

"Got a decent blimp round the prefab, like you wanted. Saw nothing looked like a big holdall, though plenty of other expensive stuff. Fancy carpet. This painting on the wall… Raite went on about all that; painting and stuff."

"Expert, is he?"

"Well. Got that shop and that…"

Crust took a swallow. "You saw every room?"

"Much as I could. All pretty cold and miserable 'cept his den. Dark, too. Boarded-up back window. Dump, really. No, what I reckon is that drugs cash is now a painting."

The door opened with a bang. Crust's eyes flicked over John's shoulder, then back to John. "The one in the 'den'?"

John shook his head. "Nah. Early Plonksby. Knightsbridge School. *Reclining Nude with Jam Sandwich.* Blonde piece lying naked on a couch. Not that I'm an expert yet, but didn't seem that special…"

Crust stared at him. Asked casually, "Period?"

John frowned. "How could I tell something like that? If she was on the rag?"

John started slightly – as for a fleeting moment he registered an expression of homicidal rage flash across Crust's features.

"Evening, Mr Crust." A low voice insinuated itself into the conversation from just behind John.

"No," said Crust. "Was it a modern painting?"

"Bit of a miserable evening," said the new voice. "But maybe spring's round the corner…"

John turned to look. Male. About five foot four. Mid to late fifties. Wiry, yet soft in build. Hair grey and close-cropped but still thick. The face, cancer-pale, triangular and finely boned with large, deep-set, dark blue eyes. A day's growth of white stubble. A worn, shiny pinstripe suit; trouser bottoms and jacket sleeves both turned up. John felt the suit had once belonged to Crust. A buttoned-up grey flannel shirt. Old, scuffed black leather shoes. A chesty wheeze. A faint acrid smell John could not identify. Strangely, an overall impression of natural reserve and elegance.

"Minty," said Crust, "I'm busy…"

"Just thought I'd say hello, Mr Crust. Freezin' out. Had my new mac pinched, too."

"That'll slow your sex life a bit."

"That one Father Merryman gave me… Got left in the confessional. Should've seen what was in the pocket!"

"Seen anyone that chest of yours, yet?" asked Crust.

"Doctor just keeps prescribing bottles of linctus. Cost a fortune I wasn't exempt."

"Not from me, you're not." Crust took a mouthful. "Any point in all this?"

"Just dropped in to see my ma. In the bar on the last of her bottle of Mackie's Stout. Tom said you were up here, so came to pay my respects."

"Tell Tom give you another couple of bottles. You and her."

"Thanks, Mr Crust," said Minty. "Thing is…"

"Yeah?"

"Thing is, Mr Crust, our Joey's due out week on Friday – "

"For a short time, he probably is…"

"… And me and me ma need to visit him to explain how his room's got let while he's been inside. But what with me ma's stomach, them buses… Fiver'd cover a taxi, Mr Crust."

Crust took out his wallet. Withdrew a five.

Minty accepted it. "Hope you don't mind me saying I pray for you at early Mass every morning, Mr Crust!"

"I'm almost finished here, Minty," said Crust. "Have one with your ma, then come back up."

Minty nodded. Gestured at John. "So who's this with you, Mr Crust? Me ma'll want to know."

"That, Minty, is another great detective like myself."

Minty burped softly. "'Scuse me." Began to thread his way down the snug steps.

Crust said, "Born fifty thousand pounds up the social ladder, he could have been anything."

"Yeah" said John, "A real winner!… So? What d'you think, Inspector? My painting idea?" He drank his pint to within half an inch of the bottom of his glass. Tipped it casually towards Crust.

Crust used one finger to tip the glass back. "I think

you've done enough. Played your part. That citizen's reward I mentioned…"

"Just thought that… well… if that dough *is* now a painting, and he's putting it on that ship, maybe someone should be there; keep an eye on things?"

"If it *has* become a painting," said Crust.

"Can't be nothing else," said John. "Mix with his other stuff… Smuggled off the other end…"

"Even so," said Crust. "We can't have you on this."

"But I'm the one found him. Worked out it's now a painting!"

"Something like this," Crust said, " is now between us and the States. You just can't be there. But you've been noticed… So much so, we're going to trust you with a bit of real police work."

"What's that?"

"Raite's Porsche."

"Thought that'd been discounted."

"As regards the money. But it was sold on. And we want the paperwork."

"Why?"

"Tie up the case. That sort of thing…"

"So who's got it? The car? The paperwork?"

"You're meeting him tomorrow."

John stared.

"See, John, each time you push the door a few inches, you're nearer to being inside. That's what you want, isn't it? To be inside? On the team?" Crust touched John's glass. "I won't get you another as you're driving."

"I got dropped off," said John quickly.

"Even so. Need you at your best tomorrow. So maybe an early night at your old man's? Then that lay-by on Scottie Road just before the Tunnel entrance! Half ten tomorrow morning. The Porsche's in Birkenhead."

"What will I be doing?"

"Like last time." Crust smiled. "Acting gormless."

John stood. Stared at Crust. Crust laid his hand on his book. Stared back.

John walked down the three steps to the bar. Minty was sitting with the elderly woman in black with the biddy bonnet. Everyone staring, though no one looking at him. In complete silence he made his way down the bar and out onto London Road.

As John left, Minty stood and wandered back up to the snug. Sat facing Crust in the seat vacated by John. Tom arrived with two double Scotches and two halves. Put them down. Left.

Minty took a sip from his half. "You OK, Mr Crust?"

"One of those nights."

"We all have them."

"Trip on a ship, Minty…"

"This weather?!"

Crust took a sip of whisky. "Busman's holiday."

Minty studied Crust's face. "Got Father Merryman's number, you really need to talk to someone…"

"You ever had a holiday, Minty?"

Minty shook his head. "All that strange food. Even worse, I hear, you go abroad. Plus having to use a strange lav. Say what you like, Mr C, nothing beats your own khazi… Though me ma went on one once. Holiday. Charity job… Even got herself up onstage for the 'Knobbly Knees Contest'."

"Seeing something like that," said Crust. "Would somehow make everything else worthwhile... Bring you anything back?"

"Usual towels and light bulbs. Towels were awful thin."

"Christ! Didn't have a bath, did she?"

"Got twenty into the spare case she brought. Even managed a layer of light bulbs on top. That's how thin they were. Working class exploited again."

"It's just life, Minty."

"So where you going? This ship thing?"

Crust shook a perplexed head.

"Don't mind me asking, Mr Crust – you been listening them requiems of yours again? Death music and that?"

"They're real, Minty! Early requiems, written by those who'd seen it first-hand. Loved ones dying in agony. No morphine – unbearable pain." Crust raised his whisky. Minty followed suit. "The other stuff? Johann Sebastian Metronome? Fritzy-Frotzy Mozart? Chest-Out Beethoven? Masturbation by Moonlight Chopin, Schubert, Schumann, Mendelssohn? Bombs-Away Berlioz, Brahms, Wagner? Back-to-Basics Berg and Schoenberg and your minimalist twats, who all should be done for loitering with intent."

Minty nodded. "Course, me and me Ma are more Radio 2. 'I'll Walk Beside You', 'Boys of the Old Brigade', 'Rose of Tralee', 'Bonnie Banks o' Loch Lomond', 'Rock with the Caveman', 'Indian Love Call'... Then the old Liverpool ones... 'Has anybody Seen Our Cat?'... 'Don't Forget to Genuflect'... Minty sang softly :- 'Don't forget to genuflec' / Don't forget to curtsey / Don't forget to wash your neck / In the River Mersey...'"

"Know why this is my local, Minty?"

"He never charges you for a round?"

"Near where I started. Copperas Hill; St Anne Street."

Minty nodded.

"My first station had this sort of big basement room. Desks. Linoleum floor. Tea urn. Couple of cons, heads together, working up their notebooks. Plato, I think, said, 'Not even God can call back time.' Those cons could've showed him... Then this big, moon-faced Irish sergeant, typing away with one finger. Round the walls, those big black chest-high heating pipes; sort we had in schools..."

Minty nodded. "Everyone trying to get next to them in winter."

"They had this crim. tied to one of these pipes. Arms stretched out like he was being crucified. Every now and then the big sergeant would get up and walk over. Punch the crim in the guts, hard as he could. 'Ready to talk yet?!' he'd shout. Then get back to his typing. I knew right away we all belonged."

"Fella tied to the pipes think that?"

"These wet-eyed social worker types – 'Police brutality!', all that shit. Maybe a pair of them down some back jigger one night having it off on taxpayer expenses. Suddenly, two 'jigger rats'. Stanley knives, lead pipes. Know what your wet eyes want to see then? More than anything in the world?"

Minty shook his head.

"That same big Irish sergeant charging down with his extra-long special hardwood truncheon." Crust took an angry drink. "Where was I?"

"Floor's yours, Mr Crust!"

"Course, you weren't properly blooded till you'd gone to a council flat, middle of summer. Some old biddy croaked in her chair pulling on her nylons. Melting out for the next three weeks, purple and covered in flies; big green and blue ones. Fucking smell all the Vicks Vaporub in the world can't mask…"

Minty nodded. "That cat they found in me Nan's gas cupboard…"

"Mist from the pit… Exhalations from the abyss…"

"You've a right one on today, Mr Crust."

"Something developed a long, long time ago to keep us away from dead bodies." Crust took a swallow. "Lots of the lads would turn up in an old pair of flannels, cheap jacket, then just burn them. 'Cause if it was a bad one, all your Johnsons dry cleaning in the world couldn't handle it. Wouldn't let you in the shop with it… But you know what I thought about that smell, Minty?"

"Go on…"

"What *I* thought – sniffing it in like the kids in the advert – was not *Ah, the gravy!* but *Ah, the gravy train! Ah, the fucking job security!* But ever ask yourself what honest coppers like myself have to put up with in the name of job security? Those lying fuckers in Parliament…"

"Thought someone like you'd be a bit above politics, fella like yourself. Though, yeah, everyone hates them bastards."

"And yet…"

"What's that, Mr Crust?" Minty took another sip of his whisky. Began on his half.

"Minty, what's the two things any ordinary fellas – normal fellas… "

"… Everton supporters."

"… Want every Monday when they get home from work?"

Minty made a gesture of incomprehension.

"Like you were saying before. Their toilet flushes. Their bin's been emptied. Now, someone's got to organise this… Which we call 'politicians'." Crust stood and began buttoning his railwayman's coat. "No one normal is ever going to want to do this; become a shit remover or bin emptier. No. Needs a special sort of mental type… And in return we have to watch them send our children off to war; sell arms to fuckers who use them to burn and rape women and children. But those empty bins? Clear toilet bowls?" Crust sighed. "You're right, Minty. I need a holiday!"

"One of them camps the old girl went to?"

"No, Minty. One where your old girl has never been! Where there's not only enough towels to dry myself, but enough fucking light bulbs to do it by!"

Crust slowly made his way down the steps to the bar. Stumbled slightly off the last one. Lumbered and shuffled to the street door. Left without looking back.

SEQUENCE 99

Raite stood at the ticket-counter in full rambling/hiking/ climbing gear; his artist's field kit box across his back. Near the entrance of the booking hall, two policemen looked on in a cursory fashion. Raite knew he wouldn't present as Irish terrorist material, but still wanted to get in and out as quickly as possible.

He put the Irish passport on the counter. "A cabin if possible…"

"And for tonight?" The booking clerk looked as tired as the decor and lights.

"Painting-and-sketching holiday," said Raite in a loud academic rasp. "Finally wangled a sabbatical. West Coast. The bays, Clew Island… Rock formations and flowers. Light and shadow and movement of the sea as winter turns to spring."

The booking clerk picked up the passport. Looked at the photograph. Looked at Raite. "James Francis Walsh?"

"Mayo forebears… " said Raite.

The clerk looked at the photo and Raite again. Closed the passport. Slid it back to Raite. "One inside berth," he said. "Only wish I was going with you."

SEQUENCE 100

FRIDAY, 12th MARCH, 1982. 11.00
INT / DAY JOHN'S CAR. EXT / DAY BAZZA'S GARAGE

Once through the Tunnel, the *Express* drove through Birkenhead, then crossed the bridge dividing the West and East Floats. Great open spaces of water catering for the last remnants of the Blue Funnel and Ellerman fleets.

Crust pointed down a long, straight road. John drove at a steady thirty.

Crust said reflectively, "Birkenhead"... Then, "Slow down. Coming up on our right!"

Bazza's was a large, circular yard. Entrance through two wooden gates thrown wide open – hanging from the remnants of two brick pillars set in a brick wall that was crumbling away to nothing. Through the gates the view was of weed-infested, churned-up, dirt. Scattered about were vehicles in various states of disintegration. At the back of the yard, an open-fronted garage/workshop. Behind this, a glimpse of a closed shed. Between the front gates, what seemed to be a crumpled car mat on a chain.

Crust, having stared intently, remarked admiringly, "Got to hand it to him. It's all there. Even to the Alsatian in the oil puddle!... Keep going a bit, then U-turn. Park a hundred yards or so from the gates."

John did so.

Crust produced a roll. "Four hundred. Which I'll be checking... Your liking for undocumented cash." He handed the notes to John. Smiled a knowing smile.

John coloured. "What's it for?" he asked, fingering the used notes.

"I need to know that Raite's Porsche is in that shed behind the workshop. Bazza needs to think you're there for a car. Flash the cash. Get into the shed. Leave the rest to me."

John ran his hand through his hair. "What do I say? Do?"

Crust laughed out loud.

John felt frightened. "Can't you just arrest him? Get his books and that?"

"Solomon couldn't sort the stuff he'll have in there. Plus search warrants, court orders... etc. No. I'll be appealing to a more basic side." Crust climbed out. "Don't make me wait too long. *Don't* fuck up!" He banged his head on the roof of the *Express*. Stepped back.

John pulled away. Put on the left blinker. Turned into the yard. The Alsatian lifted its head. Began to bark. Made a tired run at the *Express* – but was pulled up by the chain. John stopped near the workshop and climbed out. From the workshop's open doors Bazza approached smoking a cigarette. John put him at thirtyish. Small but powerful. Thickset with a mop of curly black hair. Dark eyes. A round, open face with high cheekbones. Ready for trouble, but not looking for it. Navy-blue boiler suit, beer gut straining against it. Black leather boots with exposed steel toecaps. All visible parts covered in oil.

Without speaking, Bazza walked around the *Express*, throwing a few half-hearted kicks at the tyres and peeling off strips of rust. Came and stood directly in front of John. "My advice, pal? Get rid!" His upper lip looked raw and sore. "Yeah," he said, catching John's gaze. He pointed at his cigarette's filter. "Bet you thought I was a Tranmere supporter? Smoking a tailor-made with a Tampax on its nose?... Thing is, see, under this van last week, Woodbine on the go got stuck to my lip; way they do in this fucking freezing cold. I didn't notice, what with fucking about with this exhaust pipe. Come up for air; pull it out my mouth; took half my fucking lip away... How'd you find me?" He looked towards the gate, across which a woman was pushing a pram.

John licked his own lips. "Just driving past. Spotted the yard; thought maybe time for a change."

Bazza nodded encouragingly.

John gestured towards the *Express*. "Doors won't lock properly. Window-winder troubles. Though a very handy car..."

Bazza shook his head. Rubbed his hand across his eyes.

"Just thought you might have something maybe part ex?"

"How much you looking to spend?"

John produced the roll of notes. "Four hundred."

Bazza stared intently at the money. Stuck out his hand. "What's your name, friend?"

"John."

"Bazza!... Well, John, got something in only yesterday. Special. Belonged to this old nun. Only used it to go out for cat food. Then ran over it. Her cat. So had to be put in a home. The currant bun." Bazza pulled out his cigarettes. Held the packet towards John.

"I don't, thanks," said John.

"One of them vegetariums?" Bazza lit up. "Maybe a coffee?" He gestured towards the shed at the back of the garage.

John decided to explore his part. Gestured towards the *Express*. "Be safe here, will it?"

Bazza laughed. "You got it insured, right?"

" 'Course."

Bazza stepped back slightly, looking at John carefully. Finally said, "Mr. Cruncher'll keep an eye on it. *Cruncher!!*"

The Alsatian raised a weary head. Barked once.

"Best days are gone," Bazza said. "Though nothing wrong with his teeth… Few he's got left. Poor old bastard!"

Looking once more at the four hundred in John's hand, Bazza gestured with his head and led John round the back of the workshop to the shed. Corrugated-iron doors. Heavy locks. A small locked wicket. Cruncher began to bark loudly. Bazza stabbed a finger at John not to move. Walked quickly around the workshop towards the front yard.

A few moments later he was back. "Spooked! Just too old. Bite the balls off a bulldog, I first got him. Now just snores and farts… But I couldn't let him go."

"Got a mate feels the same," said John. "Though it's greyhounds with him…"

"And yourself?" Bazza unlocked the steel wicket gate. Gestured John through. Inside the garage were four cars under covers. A workbench and tools down one wall. A pit and hydraulic lift. Bazza switched on an electric kettle.

"Just no time," John told him. "Shifts and that. Couldn't walk one."

"Where's that, John? Work?"

"Bedding place. Assembling mattresses."

Bazza laughed. "Get to try them out?" He walked to the nearest car and dragged off the sheet. What lay beneath looked to John like the *Express* – perhaps older – hand-painted in bright yellow gloss. Bazza shook his head in admiration. "Like I said. This teacher -"

"Nun?"

"Yeah. Nun that taught. Yeah. In a home now, but loved this car. Cried when I boxed her off with the cash." Bazza shrugged. "Gave her over the odds – but that's just me – sort of fella I am. Told me it hadn't even been out in the rain. Broke her heart but she knew it had found a good home."

"What's the mileage?"

"Hardly anything… But even so, it wouldn't matter. These things?… Twice round the clock, pistons'd still be shining like a council clerk's arse." Bazza opened the driver's door. "Fucking hell! I told that bastard apprentice not to fit that new eight-track! Plus the tapes!"

"How much?"

"There's the kettle… I'll make that coffee." Bazza suddenly snatched up a spanner and hurled it the length of the workshop. It clattered among a mound of spare parts, wheels and tyres. "Fucking rat! See it? Size of a badger!"

They walked to the kettle. As they did so, John glanced at the other three covered vehicles. One was large – a big saloon? One long and low – some sort of flash sports car? The third was smaller. More compact. The Porsche?

Bazza handed John an oily mug. They drifted back over to the yellow car.

"Not married?" Bazza looked at John over the rim of his coffee cup.

"Thinking about it."

Bazza nodded knowingly. "Pity. That you're taken, I mean... Though I can see why. Fella with your looks." He gestured towards the car. "Because what I'm selling you here – this beauty – can only be described as a 'total minge magnet'. Last three times I had it out? Rub of the brush every time... Colour helps, too."

"Yeah." John sipped his coffee. "Docs all in order?"

Bazza looked at him. "Told you about the nun?" The tone was still friendly – but with some sort of underlying inflection.

"So the paperwork's all here?"

"Well, after flattening her moggie, she – the nun – wasn't really up to signing stuff."

"So who actually owns the car?" asked John.

"*Owns* it?... Nobody *actually* owns it... It's just for sale."

John threw out his arm. "Rat! Ran behind those tyres."

Bazza snatched up a short crowbar and ran towards the heap of wheels and tyres at the end of the workshop. He began beating them, shouting, "You bastard! You fucking bastard!"

John eased up the sheeting on the smaller car with his toe. The Porsche.

Bazza came back. "Too fucking clever by half. They say you're never more than a hundred yards from a rat..."

John said, "So, yeah. The price!"

"John! I like you! Way you came across on the phone..."

"Bazza. I just came in off the road!"

"Course you did. I must be catching what old Cruncher's got... So! Look! I'll let you have it for what

314

you're carrying! Four ton – no! Fuck it! How about three-fifty; throw in a set of tyres and sort the seat belt?"

"An MOT?"

"Sure. A year? Two years? You want three? Bazza can do that!"

John tilted his head to one side. "Let me have a think. Get back to you." He left the shed.

Bazza followed him. "Look, mate! Three hundred brick, it's yours!"

John walked round the back of the main garage to the front yard. Crust was standing just out of reach of Cruncher. John nodded almost imperceptibly. Crust began to move towards them.

Bazza caught it. "You fucking bastard." He grabbed John by the coat. "You scabby fucking snitch!"

Crust joined them. "All right, Bazza?" he asked.

"Who the fuck are you? I mean, I smell the crackling, but let me tell you, everything here's straight."

"Bazza. You couldn't lie straight in bed."

"And how come you know my name?"

"A minute of your time," said Crust. "Needn't come to any more than that." He nodded to John. "I'll be in touch."

"Like me to wait, Inspector?" John attempted an official voice. Then, catching Crust's eye, began to walk towards the *Express*.

When he was halfway to it Bazza shouted, "Seize, Cruncher!... Fetch, boy!"

Mr. Cruncher lurched unsteadily to his feet. Began to bark and run in sweeps to the extent of the chain, straining towards John and the car. John climbed in and started the engine. Cruncher stood between the gates, barking. John sat, irresolute. Put his head out of the window. Looked towards Crust. Crust said something quietly to Bazza, who shouted and whistled. Cruncher flopped back into his oil puddle.

John began to move off. Through the open window he heard Bazza shouting, "Rats! Never more than a hundred yards away! Fucking wanker!"

John made the turn out of the gate. In the mirror – Mr. Cruncher, Bazza and Crust, all staring balefully in his direction.

SEQUENCE 101

FRIDAY, 12th MARCH, 1982. 12.30
INT / DAY CONTAINER OFFICE

The manager and the planner looked down onto the berth. Seeing and hearing the wind rising. Loose papers and cardboard chasing themselves in circles. Lighter pieces of dunnage blowing round the berth and into the dock. Even the great spider cranes swaying. Only the ship monolithically still.

The planner pointed at the activity surrounding Raite's two containers – above which swung a crane grab. A group of four dockers stood watching. One of their number now gesturing to the crane driver, far above in his cab, to lower the grab. Raite standing by, moving from one foot to the other.

"Think she'll sail?" asked the planner.

"If money means anything" said the manager.

"Which it doesn't," said the planner. "Unless you have none!" He laughed.

The manager pointed back to Raite's containers. Raite had halted proceedings and was struggling with a padlock on one of the locking bars. Evidently intending to go back inside yet again.

"Wouldn't be a show without Punch," said the planner.

"Unless the intention is to give one," said the manager.

SEQUENCE 102

FRIDAY, 12th MARCH, 1982. 14.00
INT / DAY TEACHING HOSPITAL

"Anything new?" asked Chris, rubbing her thumb and forefinger together.

"Busy! Busy! Busy!" John gave a wolfish smile while eyeing up the large bunch of ribboned flowers on Chris's bedside locker. *Who the fuck had bought her them?* "See, Raite got rid of the Porsche to this fella, Bazza… So Crust and myself went across to Birkenhead this morning. Track it down."

"Finally taken you under his wing?"

"More up in his talons…"

"Why's Crust want it? Surely he can't believe Raite left the money in it?"

John shrugged. "Maybe thought there's a secret compartment somewhere?"

Chris grinned tiredly. "Thought the only secret compartments in Porsches were the seats?"

"Expert on Porsches now, eh, Chris?" He picked up the flowers. Inspected them for a card. Nothing. Flourished them in front of her. "Nice! Though mean a week's wages to most fellas."

Chris stared at him.

"Yeah, well… So Crust sent me in Ucca – undercover – to this Bazza's garage as if looking for a car to replace the *Express*…"

"That be possible?"

John laughed. Shook his head.

"And Bazza?" asked Chris.

"Weirdo. Case is full of them."

Chris nodded.

"So I flashed Crust's cash. Open sesame! Sez-a-me!"

Chris smiled.

"Crust hung round outside. Naturally, not too close to the action. Gave him the nod. Came in. Felt Bazza's collar. I left him to it. Told him it was more important I came back to see you."

"How did he take that?"

John shrugged. "Besides, I've broke the case anyway. It's in the containers."

Chris touched her hair near the cut. Looked puzzled.

"See, Chris, no tales out of school, but Raite's got these two containers. Low-class antiques waiting down at the terminal for shipment to America."

"When?"

"Today. Friday. Sailing eleven tonight… Painting's defo in one of them."

"Hold on, John! Painting?"

Fuck! That's done it! Just carry it through! "See, what I thought was – How could someone like Raite get a mill across the Atlantic, what with everyone looking for both it and him?"

Chris shook her head.

"OK. Put it another way. What's Raite's interests?"

"Sexual assault? Rape?"

"Yeah. And we're all dead sorry. And should never happened… But actually, I'm being serious, Chris!"

She stared at him. Then said, "OK… So what *are* Raite's interests?"

"Paintings, Chris!… Chris! I've heard the fella talk! Knows more than *Whistler's Mother*. Money's now a painting he'll smuggle into America in one of his containers of junk! Maybe disguised as something else… 'Nother painting?"

"One of Aryn's?"

"Chris. I know you're concussed, but it's Arian."

"What does Crust think? This idea?"

"Crust's a copper. Doomed by lack of imagination… But I let him in on it. Thought I owed it to him."

"And Curly? He's been let in on it?"

John stared at the clipboard over her bed. Name. Sex. Religion.

A bell, signalling the end of visiting, rang from the nurses' station. The family at the next bed stood as one, ritually shuffling and moving chairs.

"John?"

"Yeah?"

"You're going, aren't you? On the ship?"

He paused for a moment. "Got to, Chris."

"John, if it is a painting, do you think Raite will be far away? Or Crust?"

John shrugged.

"And if it is there. And somehow you get hold of it…"

"Yeah?"

"What will you do with it? That sort of money?"

"Get it back to Liverpool. Get it off the ship. Use some of it to take you to Paris, maybe? Home of art itself?"

"Seriously, John?! What will… even *could*… you do with it?"

"Possession is nine-tenths of the law."

Chris nodded tiredly as the bell rang again. "You've done really well, John." She stretched towards the water carafe and glass on the table.

John filled a glass and handed it to her. Replaced the carafe.

Chris said, "How's your dad?"

"Snarl! Snarl! Snarl!" said John. "Everything and everybody. Me most of all!" Began to zip up his anorak.

Chris asked, "How will you get on board?"

"Mick's sorted me on that."

"Militant Mick's involved?!"

"Don't worry. Being kept at arm's length."

She stared at him. "How long will it take? To the States?"

"Five days. Fellas often stow away; slip off the other end."

"John… Raite's really clever. I can't see he hasn't thought of all this. How to move and keep control of the painting."

"Yeah. Well… I've been thinking too."

Chris stared into space for a time. "Where will you be on the ship?"

John coughed knowingly. "Containers and cargo go two places. On top – the main deck. And also what's known as the 'Ro-Ro' deck: roll on; roll off. Sort of car ferry idea. Get in from a ramp at the rear of the ship. Pay a bit more to have your containers there. But big as a factory floor, and always chocka with gear."

"And Curly?" asked Chris.

"Yeah… Curly!" John waggled his head from side to side as if in deep thought.

"John. I don't want him to go."

Finally! A break! "Then he won't!" He patted her hand.

"Just… He's young. Whole life in front of him. And being Mum's only boy…"

"Chris, leave it to me." He patted her hand again. Took hold of it.

She gently withdrew. Then pointed to the ward sister severely scanning remaining visitors.

"Yeah." John nodded complacently. "And don't you worry. I'll sort Curly. Just for you!"

She smiled gratefully.

"Chris. Just before I shoot off, I was wondering. Maybe a word about us?"

A young nurse arrived at the end of the bed. "Sister says could you go?"

John glared at her.

The nurse shrugged and moved away.

Chris stared right ahead.

The sister walked quickly to the centre of the ward. Stared at John and Chris. Clapped her hands loudly.

John, face set, said, "Chris?"

Chris continued to stare straight ahead.

"Yeah. Well… That's the way you feel," said John, "'Spose I could always give the nod to Mrs Raite."

Chris looked back at him.

"Not saying she's been coming on or anything. But… Well… Maybe she just sees… smells… success in the wind."

Suddenly the sister, hands on hips, was standing at the end of the bed.

"Yeah. Well. Ship to catch and that." John lifted the topmost of Chris's pillows to plump it. Underneath was an envelope containing a get-well card of some sort; and a photograph tucked beneath the flap. Four greyhounds side by side in what looked like a cobbled yard. Behind, an old brick building with a clock tower, a weathervane shaped like a racehorse on top. John dropped the photo on the bed. Strode away, tugging at his anorak.

Chris closed her eyes and lay back on the pillows.

The ward sister vanished as silently as she had arrived.

Chris opened her eyes again and stared at the ceiling, then at the empty bed opposite. Mrs Bird had died suddenly during the previous night.

John hadn't even asked

SEQUENCE 103

Captain Barratt looked up from his armchair at Harry. "We ready for sea, Harry?"

"Hatches battened. Tanks sounded. Foc's'le drunk!"

Barratt smiled. "Those were the days!" Topped up his rum. "Like one?"

"Not really wise, sir… Weather that's being forecast for tonight."

"Stabilisers. Variable-pitch propellers. What could go wrong?"

Both laughed.

"You wanted to see me, sir?" asked Harry.

Barratt took a sip. "I heard – little bird – you slipped ashore for a couple of hours yesterday?"

Thanks, Roger! "Hospitalised friend, sir. Bad accident. Roger – Mr Drummond – coasting second – assured me he had it all in hand. I should, of course, have asked permission. But I came along and saw your door on the hook. Heard voices. Reckoned it was last-minute stuff with the shoreside crowd… No more than an hour and I really did need to see her."

On the word 'her', Harry and Barratt looked at each other.

"Harry! A chief officer leaving the ship without letting the captain know?!"

"Yes, sir…"

Barratt pointed at the second armchair.

Harry sat.

"I assume that means you're leaving us altogether?" said Barratt.

"This trip'll be my last, I think, sir."

Barratt topped up his drink. "Marriage?"

"If she'll have me…"

"Known her long?"

"I'm not sure that matters."

There was a pause.

"Told your folks?" asked Barratt casually.

"I feel my mother has an inclination of what's happening."

"Anything in mind for afterwards?" Barratt made a sweep with one of his arms. A gesture that encompassed the ship. All other ships. The dock. All other docks. The port. All other ports. All other seas, seaways, and oceans…

"Actually, Captain, I hope to save greyhounds."

Barratt smiled a very carefully calculated smile. Adopted a very carefully modulated tone of voice. "The last seagoing member of the great Rose Line of Liverpool… Finally going to the dogs."

.

SEQUENCE 104

FRIDAY, 12th MARCH, 1982. 21.00
INT / NIGHT RO-RO DECK, *OCEAN SEASPRAY*

Raite stood on the Ro-Ro deck among the sounds of machinery; fans; and metal and wooden boxes being pushed into position by forklift trucks. Of tractors and cars being secured. Of this, and that, and general mayhem.

Holding his clipboard, he moved across to an access shaft built into the ship's outside bulkhead – leading up to the main deck / containers. Opened its door. The steel rungs stretching away upwards. He would wait until they began to close the stern access at about ten, then slip up the access shaft onto the main deck, along to the gangway, off the ship and out of the dock. Use Chris's keys he'd stolen, he'd pick up the *Magdalen* from John's office. Then onto the midnight Irish Ferry. Anyone asking questions later would be told that he'd last been seen wandering the Ro-Ro deck with his clipboard, testing the locks on his containers. He knew half the crew expected him to stow away; the other half for him to vanish overboard.

No one would think of the ferry terminal just down along the Dock Road.

SEQUENCE 105

FRIDAY, 12th MARCH 1982. 21.40
INT / NIGHT BAYONETS

John, dressed as Mick had recommended, sat with his father at the domino table in The Bayonets. "Chris just doesn't want him to go, Dad. Him being the only boy. His ma's really anxious."

Mr O'Rourke drank. "What about what Curly wants?"

John stared into his pint. "Dad, after what Chris's been through, shouldn't we respect her wishes?"

Mick arrived at the table with a sheaf of smudged pamphlets. "'Women's rights'? You know, all the time I was married to that fucking cow I never once hit her with a closed fist!" He put a leaflet in the middle of the table. 'Revolutionising Trotsky's Permanent Revolution'… "NELLI, this Sunday. All Welcome! Come and renew your faith!" Moved on.

Mr O'Rourke threw the leaflet on the floor. "Where were we?"

John sucked his upper lip. "Chris being really upset and not wanting Curly to go."

"Not as upset as Curly'll be, you back-heel him on this!" Mr O'Rourke stood and pointed at John's glass. "Lager?" He took up John's glass and moved to the bar. "Mild and lager, Mick."

Mick took two glasses. Put them under the taps. The door opened. John tensed. A regular entered carrying a brown cardboard box he placed on the counter. Mick lifted the lid and peeped in. Took a roll of notes from his pocket. Peeled off a few. Gave them to the regular. The box went under the counter. Mick began topping off the pints.

The regular opened the door to leave – crossing paths with Curly.

Curly nodded at John. Walked to the bar. "Add a pint of bitter, there, would you, Mick?" Punched John lightly on the shoulder. Winked. Went to the domino table. Sat and began talking to Mr O'Rourke.

John brought the drinks to the table. Everyone settled in.

Curly rubbed his hands; eyes bright and quick. "Right," he said to John. "What time we going?"

John seized his glass. Took a deep swallow.

"How's Chris?" asked Mr O'Rourke.

"Whingeing away like her old self. Hopes to get out tomorrow." Curly turned to John. "Said you and her'd had a good chat about me not going tonight? Nice move, partner!"

John took a breath. "Yeah, we talked... And yeah – bottom line is, she's really worried about you going on the *Seaspray*. And, Curl, I totally see what she means..."

"What's that?" asked Curly.

"Well... That run-in she had with Raite prob'ly made her realise how... well... *fragile* life is..."

Mr O'Rourke coughed loudly. Mick, listening avidly from behind the bar, blew a loud raspberry.

"... How anything can happen right out the blue" continued John doggedly. "Like with her." He drew breath. "'Sides. Someone's needed here; keep an eye on things..."

"Here?" said Curly. "All the action's going to be on that ship."

"Good point, Curl!" said Mr O'Rourke.

"Seconded! Passed on a show of hands!" shouted Mick throwing off a double brandy. Washing it down with a swig of Topsail Schooner.

"No," said John. "We need someone here."

"Why?" asked Curly.

John looked up into his eyes. "Because I say so!"

There was a long silence. Curly sat very still, as if thinking something out. His face white. Mr O'Rourke stared down at the table. Mick gazed across with pursed lips.

"Why?" said Curly again.

John stared back, unable to say anything.

Without sign or warning, Curly jumped to his feet and was out of the door.

John's father looked at him. "You've done it now!"

"Dad. Chris asked me to stop him going."

"You never intended to take him! Chris maybe knew that; tried to give you both a way out." Mr O'Rourke opened his *Albion*. Began to turn the pages.

John stood. Zipped up his anorak. "Right. I'm off!"

His father didn't look up.

Fuck him! But what if something happened on the ship and he didn't make it back? If this was the last time he'd see his father? "Dad!" he said. "Dad!… Dad!"

His father stood slowly. John put his arm round his slumped shoulders and squeezed. Mick gave a wolf whistle.

John pulled open the door of The Bayonets. Gave a sly grin.

Sorted!

SEQUENCE 106

FRIDAY, 12th MARCH, 1982. 13.45
INT / DAY BUYER'S GALLERY, LAS VEGAS

The Buyer stood about three-quarters of the way down his underground office/gallery, staring at the polished dark green brickwork of the wall in front of him. Works on either side had been moved to create a hanging space. Above this had been fitted a spotlight.

The Buyer swayed gently back and forwards on his feet, staring at the blank expanse of wall.

SEQUENCE 107

FRIDAY, 12ᵗʰ MARCH, 1982. 21.55
INT / NIGHT HOTEL ROOM.

Bogger laid out the cards once more. "Still nothing from O'Rourke geezer, eh, Liz?"

Mrs Raite opened the minibar. Unscrewed a gin. Drank from the bottle. "I've a sense something's happening…"

"Maybe a home visit?" Bogger turned over a card. "Got an address?"

"Carey Street rather than Connaught Square."

"That a 'no'?"

"That first day… There was a woman cleaner… Definite interest there."

"Don't help, Liz… No address or anything."

"Liverpool Drum Academy. Floor below O'Rourke's office. Slightly open door."

"One of them nosy fuckers, eh? Got to be worth five minutes of my time."

The phone rang.

Mrs Raite picked up the receiver. Said, "Could you repeat that?" Then, "Who is this? What sort of painting? What ship? *Ocean Seaspray*… Eleven o'clock?… Where's that? Wait! Wait!" She slammed down the receiver and turned to Bogger. "Another Hansel and Gretel."

"I'll fucking Hansel-and-Gretel them."

"Bogger! The money's now a painting inside some container full of dodgy antiques Ronnie's shipping tonight at eleven for New York!"

"The desk geezer again?"

"No; put right through. Maybe that policeman, Crust…"

"Why's he telling us?"

Mrs Raite glanced at her watch. "We need to get going."

"Where?"

"This ship. Get my money. *Get* Ronnie!"

"*Our* money."

"We need to move!"

"Liz! You want; I do! But a copper? A ship? Who knows about ships?!"

"I do." She pointed at the clock.

Bogger caught her by the arm. "How, Liz? How d'you know about ships?"

"Modelling." She saw his face stiffen. "Years ago, Bogg. Long before *us*." She patted his arm. "Bread-and-butter agency work for a cruise line centred around bikinis. *Bikinis in the Bahamas*; *Bikinis in Bali*…"

"You're fucking joking."

"… *Bikinis in Bergen*… fur-trimmed, of course."

"These cruises. How many? Fucking sailors… Girl in every port, yeah?!"

"Bogg! It was work. And so are ships. Non-stop work. The sailors? Mainly they're real sweeties. Innocents." Mrs Raite reached inside Bogger's bathrobe and tugged his penis. "Messing with ropes and lifebelts all day… Far too busy to be bothered with film crews and models…"

Bogger glared at her.

"Look, Bogg. Order a taxi while I'm changing. Afterwards, come into the bedroom. I'll give you a show; faithful Bogger's reward." Mrs Raite turned towards the bedroom, then stopped. "No. We'll use the car instead." She slipped out of her robe. "But come into the bedroom anyway."

Bogger moved towards her.

SEQUENCE 108

FRIDAY, 12th MARCH, 1982. 22.00
INT / NIGHT TAXI
EXT / NIGHT CONTAINER BERTH

John sat on the long back seat of the taxi which was covered in plastic sheeting. A strong smell of Dettol. All the windows open. Colder inside than out.

"Yeah, sorry about the sheeting," said the driver. "And them disinfectant fumes. Drunken fucker I picked up vomited all over the back seat, and now just waiting for it to dry." The cabbie was wearing an eyepatch over his right eye; a wad of cotton wool stuffed underneath. He lit a cigarette. Spat out of the window. "Yeah. Heard the *Seaspray*'s going tonight, so you're obviously a bit pissed off. But 'another day, another dollar', then back with your pay-off, yeah?"

The taxi accelerated to run the red light at Balliol Road; passing the Enterprise Centre on the right.

"Just passed Balliol Road," said the cabbie. "One time I had this Woolly in the back. Boss type. Picked him up at the Adelphi Hotel. Going the container terminal, same as yourself – some big meeting. Sort of cunt never done a real day's work in his life. Funny thing, though. For all his airs and fucking graces, couldn't even pronounce it properly. '*Bail-ee-ol* Road,' he calls it." The cabbie gobbed out of the open window once more. "Who'd be a fucking cabbie? Wish I was bunked up in some nice warm cabin tonight rather than driving round in this pissing cold rain trying to turn an honest penny."

"There yourself, were you?" asked John.

"Wasn't everyone? Couple of trips, the banana boats – Elders & Fyffes. Didn't suit me. All fucking water! No fucking Scotch!"

"Mind if I close the windows?" asked John.

"Rather you didn't, boss… That puke of his stinks. Even with the disinfectant. Not only that. But when I stopped to throw the bastard out he's fucking skint! Had to take his watch." The driver lifted his left hand off the wheel and waggled it to show two watches on his wrist.

John pulled his anorak round him as the wind whistled through the interior of the taxi. He fingered the junior hacksaw in his pocket.

"Yeah," continued the cabbie. "Know there's not much in the way of company – women – once you sail. 'Cept on those Swedish and Noskie jobs that carry stewardesses who all go like rabbits I hear! But still, get the old duty-free booze and fags to keep you happy, right?" As he turned his head back to try and fix John with his good eye, the cab wandered to the other side of the road and back again.

They reached North Park. The cab swung left and down towards the docks.

"What I'm asking," the cabbie said, "ever get any duty-free gear to sell?"

John made a non-committal, vaguely encouraging, noise.

"I'll give you my details." As the taxi slewed across the road once more, the cabbie handed back over his shoulder a heavily embossed piece of pasteboard. "Not many of us have them; just this mate of mine runs them off when he's not doing dole cards. OK, look! When you get back, ring that number and ask for me. Not none of them other fuckers'd – who'd steal Christ off the Cross at three in the afternoon – come back at night for the two thieves."

Then they were suddenly running along the perimeter fence. A quarter of a mile from the main gate.

John said, "Just here, mate! This is fine."

"Sure?" asked the driver. "I can easy run you onto the dock. It's rough out there. Pissing down."

"Just rather walk the last bit... Sort my head." John began to root through his pockets.

The cabbie nodded. "Yeah. Married myself. That fucking sister of hers! Should never have begun poking her." He gestured towards the berth. "Looks like they're just finishing off." He whistled. "Size of the bastard... Even from here."

"Always bigger and more beautiful at night," said John. "Like barmaids."

The taxi driver laughed. "Where'd you get that one? Not your own, right?"

John handed over the note. "Forget the change."

The driver looked at him and then along the deserted road. Put the note in his pocket. Shrugged. Reminded John to ring. Gave a wave. Pulled away.

John crossed the strip of pavement and onto the dirt track alongside the perimeter fence. Found the white-splashed steel paling and began to count away from the gate. Driving forward against both the elements – and himself – like Leypold's 'Wanderer In The Storm'. At the twenty-second paling he bent and pulled that, and the next, apart. Crouched and wriggled through the gap. Straightened up, keeping his back pressed firmly against the fence.

Turned his head slowly, and gazed towards the ship.

SEQUENCE 109

FRIDAY, 12th MARCH, 1982. 22.10
INT / NIGHT BRIDGE, *OCEAN SEASPRAY*

Wind and rain battered the superstructure of the *Seaspray*. Captain Barratt rotated his head in tiny circles as he stared out across the quays, conscious of the malevolent eyes of Wally Jinks fixed on him from the shadows in the wing of the bridge. Barratt's lips moved silently once or twice. Refusing to acknowledge Jinks, and without turning, Barratt inclined himself backwards. "Harry?" he called. Then, impatiently, "Mr Rose!"

Carrying two cups of coffee, Harry emerged from the subdued lighting of the chartroom. "Sorry, sir. Catching up with the sailing second. Good news about his wife… the baby."

"Indeed it is."

"He mentioned you told him that you want him up for'ard if we sail?"

"I think, given conditions, you might be more use here on the bridge... I don't think either of us knows what deck containers might do in extreme conditions."

"It's just I've never heard of a mate – chief officer – not being up for'ard to take out a ship. Not under normal circumstances..."

Barratt gestured outside the windows. "You call this normal?"

They stared at each other.

Eventually Harry said, "Very well, sir." He looked through the bridge window. "Anyway. At least the cargo's squared away."

"Cargo?!" said Barratt with a short laugh.

" '...Ship's booms stretched far above the windy street,
And figureheads gazed down on passers-by –
Old sea-gods, dragons, women with cold faces.
The draymen cried, and flicked their cracking whips...
And wagon-wheels clanked on cobblestones...
Ship's bells were struck at morning, noon, and night,
And ship's dogs barked, and dust blew up the street...
Ashore the fire brick stood in yellow stacks,
With barrels of cement, and cannery tin,
And railroad steel, and chalk, and coal and coke,
And here and there a cargo of pianos.
Great piles of lumber and of high-stacked wheat...
For far-off ports that lie beyond Cape Horn.
The air was redolent with scent of tar,

And ropes, and paint, and barrels full of tallow…
The scent of paint, of oxide and red lead,
Commingled with the cold green water scent.
Great hawsers creaked, and mooring-cables clanked,
And flags danced merrily upon the wind.
…'

"That's Bill Adams '*Frisco*'" said Barratt. "… And *that's* a cargo."

SEQUENCE 110

FRIDAY, 12th MARCH, 1982. 22.20
INT / NIGHT MERCEDES SEVEN STARS CAR PARK

In the car park of The Seven Stars, the Mercedes drew quietly to a stop. Bogger and Mrs Raite watched the constant in-and-out flow from the pub across the road to the dock and back again. Suddenly Mrs Raite put her hand on Bogger's arm. Crossing the dual carriageway, fighting the wind and rain, came Roger Drummond wearing a white boiler suit under his gold-braided uniform jacket. Carrying a clipboard.

"Three cheers for Chertsey!" murmured Mrs Raite.

They watched Roger halt before the door of The Seven Stars. Smooth his hair. Fight for breath.

"Why him?" asked Bogger.

"More bunting than ballast," said Mrs Raite. "Right, Bogg. Out you get."

SEQUENCE 111

John moved away from the fence towards some empty
containers. Threaded his way through them until he
stood in the shadow of the one nearest the stern of the
ship. He stared at the lowered ramp leading to the bright-
yellow-and-red-painted steel interior of the Ro-Ro deck.
A blood-and-fat gaping wound. All the action seemed
concentrated on lashing the final containers into place on
the upper decks. Just a few people left around the stern.
Collecting slats and pieces of packing. Repositioning
wooden cases. All seemingly dressed as he was. Mick had
advised how to behave. 'Keep your head down but stroll
onboard as if you owned the fucking joint. Won't be many
round the back end – unlike Westminster – by time you
get there. And once you're on – a thousand places to hide.
You won't believe what it's like'.

Suddenly, both the quay and the stern were free of
people. John took a deep breath and moved off from the
shadows into the glare of the cargo-loading daylight lights.
Careful to look down towards the stones of the dock;
glancing up at the ship from time to time. Then the huge
stern loomed before him, dwarfing everything except the
spider cranes – now looking skeletally insufficient against
the mass of the vessel.

Then he was at the bottom of the ramp. Suddenly, a
man began walking down carrying a length of hardboard.

As they passed each other, the man said, "Fucking weather!"

John caught his eye and winked. "I'll say."

They crossed. John walked onto the Ro-Ro deck. He'd made it.

He spotted three large wooden crates and slipped behind them, sinking down on his haunches. Gradually he became aware of machinery and noise. Diesel generators. Extractor fans. Shouts. Bangs. The amount of equipment and cargo within view was enormous. It was unbelievable that one ship's hold could contain all this. Lorries, cars, tractors, timber, combine harvesters, boxes, containers of various sizes. Mick was right. A thousand places, a thousand corners, a thousand shadows...

And Raite? Was he here? If so, where? And his two containers? They'd be ticketed, Mick had said. John fingered the hacksaw in his pocket. From his other pocket drew out his 'comfort blanket' – Brick's *They Called Her 'Tequila'*. He stared at the cover. Brick had been sent 'South of the Border' to the Hot Tamales Cantina to meet Tequila. The cover showed her slumped in a chair wearing a sombrero whose hatband consisted of silver dollar pieces. From under it peeped a mass of lustrous black hair. Tequila had a nuclear-radiation tan and a skimpy off-the-shoulder cotton print blouse featuring green lizards. From one corner of her mouth drooped a cigarillo. A blood-red orchid was fixed to a bare shoulder with a large safety-pin. In front of her a bottle of tequila and a large balloon brandy glass in which two scorpions were entwined in a fight to the death.

Things suddenly seemed eerily quiet. John began casting frightened glances around. Was Raite actually on board? Was Crust?… At least he didn't have to worry about Mrs Raite and Bogger.

There came a chorus of yells and shouts and the sound of machinery. The shouts faded. Suddenly there were grating noises, then a thudded clang. The stern door had closed.

John shrank into a space between two packing cases. In desperation, opened *They Called Her 'Tequila'*. His eye fell on a sentence. Brick was speaking. 'Remember, hombre! Everything is a weapon. Even the dirt in your trouser-cuffs. Providing it's the right sort of dirt!'

What a man!

SEQUENCE 112

FRIDAY, 12th MARCH, 1982. 22.40
INT / NIGHT SEVEN STARS

Bogger held open the door of The Seven Stars. Mrs Raite, wearing her fur coat, passed through and picked a table. Every male eye swung towards her, then Bogger, then back to their own business. Bogger ordered drinks. Paid the barman without speaking. Took the drinks across to the table.

Roger stood at the bar, intent on his pint and his clipboard. Jotting down occasional notes about everything in general – nothing in particular.

Mrs Raite drank half her gin. Accepted a cigarette off Bogger. Watched as Roger finished his first pint, immediately holding up his empty glass. As he drank half of his second pint, she rose, walked to the bar and took up a position behind and slightly to one side of him. Opened her fur coat. Underneath she was wearing a red basque. "George, isn't it?" she purred, dropping her voice.

Roger turned, immediately fixing on her breasts. "No… No… Er… 'Fraid not… Actually, it's Roger."

"I could have sworn… Four? Five years ago? The *Antigua Melody*? Only one drink together, I know, but felt we hit it off so well. But both being so busy; me modelling shots for the brochure – *Bikinis in the Bahamas*…"

"As I say, 'fraid not. Though I wish I could say it was…"

"Well, sorry. But you're all so handsome in uniform." She rubbed her fingers lightly up and down the braid on his sleeve. "Second mate?"

Roger nodded.

"Boiler suit?"

"Checking tank seams." Roger waved his clipboard.

"Ah." Mrs Raite leaned forward to peer at it. "So we don't actually know each other?"

"No, but… well… what's… well… someone like you doing here? A container terminal?… Looking… well… very attractive, I must say…"

"Bit of spying, actually."

"Spying?!" Roger shot a quick glance towards the door.

"That *Bikinis in the Bahamas* thing? Went so well British industry are thinking of something along the same lines to promote container ships." Mrs Raite adjusted her basque with one finger. "I'm here for a preliminary look… With my photographer, over there…"

Roger shot a quick look to where Bogger sat with murder in his face. Turned back immediately to Mrs Raite. "Well. Yes. I can see how something like that might raise our profile... Not as bad as we're made out to be – 'workhouses on the water' – and all that! Though not really sure how I could help, especially since we're supposedly sailing at eleven. And – though blowing great guns – I've a feeling she'll go eventually... but certainly not at eleven."

"The people promoting things," Mrs Raite stroked Roger's braid, "felt... well... it's essential to find the right kind of ship. Then identify an officer to possibly use on the shoot itself, *interacting* with us girls. There'll be about six of us!..."

Roger swallowed the second half of his pint. Waved his empty glass in the air.

"But that means," Mrs Raite looking simultaneously bright /enquiring/confused "that myself and the photographer really need to get on board. Quick look round in order to put in a recommendation..." She leaned forward. Took up Roger's fresh pint and had a sip. Rested her breast against his arm for a moment. Looked up into his face. "So might we, Roger? Be able to get a quick look round?"

"Well... Like I said. Supposedly sailing at eleven, but won't go till after midnight this weather... If at all. Still, rather late for any shore personnel get on board now."

"Of course. And, as I recall, we'd need a pass... How would we get that?"

"Well," Roger gave a small laugh, "even second mates have *some* authority..."

"Come and meet Bogger, my photo man... 'Man'," she repeated mockingly. She lifted her left hand. "You've noticed the ring?"

"Well..."

"Bogger and myself!" She leaned in. "Marriage of convenience."

"Ah." Roger's brow creased with this new information.

Mrs Raite pressed a finger against his lips, took his hand and led him to the table. She sat Roger facing Bogger. Caught Bogger's eye; slanted her own towards the toilets. "Bogger, dearest," she began, "this is Roger. Second mate! An important man! I've told him about the brochure. How British container ships can conquer the world with the right modelling shots."

"*Bikinis in the Bilges*?" offered Roger.

"Roger might just be able to get us aboard – quick look round; what situations might be possible... But, Bogger dear, that doesn't mean you can talk all night about light meters and *exposure*... Nor take too many shots of me... Well, maybe one or two in Roger's cabin, but nothing *too* risqué..."

Bogger stared at her. Pursed his lips. Stared at Roger.

Mrs Raite gestured more urgently with her eyes towards the toilets.

Bogger suddenly stood.

Roger jumped.

Bogger bared his teeth. Leaned forward. "Just off shake the snake."

Mrs Raite waited until the door to the toilets closed. "My apologies, Roger. Bogger can be rather crude. 'Overcompensation', I think they call it..."

"It?" queried Roger.

"His, well, *condition*…"

"Nothing serious, I hope?" asked Roger bemusedly.

Mrs Raite silently mouthed, 'Impotent' and took a sip of her drink.

Roger's eyes widened as he mouthed back, 'Impotent?'

Mrs Raite sighed, nodded and held out a cigarette for Roger to light. 'Likes to watch,' she mouthed.

Bogger returned and sat down. Drank some lager. "Where you from?" he asked Roger.

"Ah, Bristol. Well, just outside…"

"Know the East End?"

"Of Bristol?"

"Don't be a cunt!"

Roger stared at Mrs Raite.

Mrs Raite mouthed, 'Overcompensation.'

"Fucking places. Bristol… Scouseville-on-the-Dole… Smoke's the only place, eh, Liz?"

"Bogger, dear," said Mrs Raite, "I hope you don't mind. But I've been telling Roger about some of your little perversions…"

Bogger stared at her.

"Even so, he's still invited us aboard." Mrs Raite stroked Roger's sleeve. "A look round. Some 'socialising'…" She drained her gin. "Shall we go?"

SEQUENCE 113

As they waited for the pilot, Barratt asked casually, "That coasting second, Mr. Drummond. Get away safely once the sailing second joined?"

Harry caught Wally Jinks' eye and laid two fingers across the sleeve of his uniform, signifying the two bars that designated the rank of second mate.

Jinks shrugged. Shook his head.

Barratt gestured off the bridge. "No. Not too much sleep tonight." His head swivelled; he rubbed his eyes. "Containers. Too big, really, anywhere but the Pacific."

"Maybe to us, sir," said Harry. "But for the next generation? Imagine the captain of Cunard's *Savannah* being asked to bring the *Caronia* into Liverpool."

Barratt muttered something. Sipped his coffee. "That shore job? Dog thing?"

Harry chose a light-hearted approach. "Well. Moving through the water, sir, but only at 'dead slow ahead'. Still…"

"You'll be missed, Harry," broke in Barratt. "Just not getting the quality these days. Youngsters can hardly climb the companionway stairs with their pointed shoes. Niagara Falls haircuts. Guitars across their shoulders like crossbows. As for knots and general seamanship?… Ha!" With this loud interjection, Barratt moved quickly across the bridge to look at something on the starboard side of the foredeck.

Someone should say something. But who? And who would believe it? Harry had seen Barratt with the office crowd. The pen-pushers who swarmed-on the end of each voyage for their free drinks and cigarettes. Then it was Barratt the raconteur / Gully-Gully Man. Pouring trebles. Quoting Conrad: Masefield: Marryat... But now, just prior to sailing, these sorts of conditions...

Barratt came back to near the wheel, his head moving in a slow parabola. "So did you ever get to see the chap who owns the place? Wasn't there some problem there?"

Harry made a non-committal noise.

Barratt nodded. "I don't usually offer advice. That which is sought? Usually wrong. That which is unsought? Evidently impertinent! But in your case... Anyway. What was he like? This bloke who owns the property? Reasonable? Sympathetic to your predicament?" He gave a little jump upwards.

"Well, sir. I got to see *him*. Whether or not he saw me is another matter."

"Drunk?"

"Lying on the ground covered in blood."

"Second thoughts, Harry. Maybe better stay at sea."

The phone connecting the engine room rang. Harry moved across and lifted the handset. Listened. "Hang on, I'll ask." Holding the phone, he called across. "Captain! Engine Room wants to know if we're still going tonight?"

"Depends what the pilot tells us," said Barratt. "And if so, probably close to midnight. But we'll go to standby anyway, once the pilot boards... And has that coasting second Drummond actually left?!" He walked off the bridge.

Harry said into the mouthpiece, "Hello? Anyone there?"

A voice replied, "This is the Fourth Engineer speaking to you in English."

Harry sighed. The 'Black Gang'. All probably half-pissed. But who'd work 'down below' otherwise? "Hello! Mate here, Fourth... Look, could you tell the Second we're not sure about going. But will be going to standby, anyway, once the pilot's on... OK?"

"'Dear Mother, sell the pig and fly me home'," said the voice from below. Answering itself in a shaky falsetto: "'Dear son, the pig died last week! Steam on!'"

Harry walked to the wing of the bridge where Jinks was standing. "Wally? Mr Drummond? The coasting second? Has he left the ship?"

Wally's eyes rolled towards the lights of The Seven Stars, far away through the rain, the wind and the dual carriageway.

Harry shook his head. "Look, Wally. Nip down the accommodation, see if he's in his cabin. If his gear's gone, then you and Scouse go to the gangway head and bring it home once the pilot boards. Then back up here. OK?"

Wally nodded. "Mr Mate." Strolled off the bridge.

Harry walked back to the main windows and looked out once more over the dock. But all he saw was Chris in her hospital bed, quiet, contained and golden... Muttered to himself the old steamship rhyme:-

Ev'ry turn of the screw
Brings me closer to you!
Ev'ry turn of the screw
Brings me closer to you!...

Three more weeks...

SEQUENCE 114

FRIDAY, 12th MARCH, 1982. 23.00
INT / NIGHT RO-RO DECK. EXT / NIGHT
STARBOARD ALLEYWAY / GANGWAY

Raite now stood just inside the door of one of the access shafts leading onto the starboard alleyway. His watch showed eleven but the gangway was still down. One man standing on duty. Obviously the ship was not going at eleven. But still, he had to get back to the B&B – collect the painting – then the Irish Ferry for the midnight sailing.

They'd be waiting for him at the gate. Search him. Let him go. Thinking the money was in the containers somewhere. At New York his containers would be impounded; stripped down like a Sickert iron bedstead. By then he'd be travelling anonymously up and down the West Coast of Ireland. His big canvas haversack; wooden easel threaded through its straps. The artist's field kit box. The painting would be in the middle of the sheets of cartridge paper and various drawings. Then the Continent. Marseilles. South America. Mexico. Across the border to the Buyer. He'd out-thought them. Fucking peasants! Not even Bruegel or Bosch peasants. Home Counties / East End / Scouse peasants. The Scouse Peasant School of Painting!… What an awful fucking thought!

He needed to move. He climbed over the access shaft combing onto the main deck. The man at the gangway has been joined by a second. A bulky two-way radio lying on the ship's rail.

Raite strolled towards them clutching his clipboard/papers.

The seamen looked at him.

"Final concerns with my containers," said Raite, waving his sheaf of papers. Then, staring out over the rainswept quay, "Rather you than me."

"Rather the Seven Stars than any of us," said Wally Jinks.

The other QM, Scouse MacGuinness, looked over the rail. Whistled. Pointed. "Look who's back, Wal?... Plus visitors!"

"Visitors? We're about to sail!" Wally stared over and down onto the quay. "See why he's brought 'em, though. Her, anyway."

Raite stepped forward and looked over the rail.

Below was a uniformed jacketed sailor in a white boiler suit. Liz linking his arm. Bogger one step behind, glaring from side to side, up and down. As if by some sort of malign telepathy, Bogger's eyes suddenly shot upward, locking on to Raite's. Bogger's hands came up in an involuntary clutching movement.

"Aye, well," said Wally, still staring over the gangway, "perhaps you'd like to go down first? 'Fore they start up."

He turned to assess Raite's reaction.

No one was there.

SEQUENCE 115

Roger ushered Mrs Raite and Bogger into his cabin. On the drop-down lid of his desk, the usual full ashtrays / empty bottles / blank postcards. Plus a heavy, fourteen-inch Stillson wrench.

Bogger picked up the Stillson. Hefted it as Roger invited Mrs Raite to sit on the daybed.

"Drink?" Roger asked.

"G&T, please, Rog!" said Mrs Raite, bending forward to rub her instep.

Roger eased out a gin bottle from down the side of his bunk mattress. Took a tonic from his fridge. Washed out a toothglass. Handed the drink to Mrs Raite. Turned towards Bogger.

Bogger waggled the Stillson in his direction in an enquiring manner.

"Removing cover nuts on the deep tanks," explained Roger. "Should have gone back to Chippy. But…" Held up the bottle. "Gin for you too… er… Bogger?"

"Scotch," said Bogger. "Who the fuck's 'Chippy'? Coming here, is he? Get this back?" He swung the Stillson casually.

"Ship's carpenter. No. Too busy on deck. Getting ready for sea."

"Aren't you working too, Rog?" throated Mrs Raite.

"I'll be leaving when you do. My relief – the sailing second mate – has arrived, so I'm 'NWV' – 'Not Wanted

349

on Voyage'. Ha-ha! But, like I said, weather like this, we'll certainly be delayed. So time for a drink or two; a very quick tour, though not much of one, I'm afraid. No bridge – Ro-Ro deck. All on standby there now… Then we'll leave together; maybe even… well… go on somewhere?" Roger poured himself a large gin and tonic. A large Scotch for Bogger from another bottle he produced from down the side of his bunk.

"Oh, Rog!" purred Mrs Raite. "No bridge?! You know, filming *Bikinis in Bali* I remember one warm moonlit night the chief officer allowing me to steer for a short time. Of course, I had little idea of what I was doing, but I remember him standing behind me, holding my hands on the spokes of the wheel as he pressed himself into me…"

Bogger struck the end of Roger's desk with the head of the Stillson.

Roger laughed nervously. "Sorry, but old Barratt hates non-essential personnel on the bridge at the best of times…"

"And I was so hoping to meet him. Your captain. Experience once more that wonderful hospitality I remember so well…"

"Tell you what," said Roger. "I'll talk to the office about being your liaison officer. Get myself some new duds, haircut, etc." He turned to look at himself in the mirror. "Old Barratt! You know, they say he was a bit of an 'extreme clipper' himself at one time, far as the ladies went… Ha-ha!… Moth in his canvas now, I'm afraid." He twirled one finger alongside his head. "Still. One or two good yarns about the old days."

"So all the cargo's aboard, is it, Rog? Ready to go?"

"Belts, braces and screw-jacks being tightened as we speak."

"So many containers." Mrs Raite leaned forward once more to rub her instep.

"Plus those on the Ro-Ro deck."

"Ones containing valuables?"

"Antiques. Classic cars and such. But mainly boxed agricultural machinery and the like; large wooden crates…"

"Full of what?" asked Bogger.

"Oh, stuff your average shoreside Johnny puts in large wooden crates. Anything and everything. Imagine a giant gizmo warehouse full of giant gizmos."

"So the sort of romantic place stowaways would hide?" asked Mrs Raite.

"Hide an army on the Ro-Ro deck."

Mrs Raite casually adjusted her basque. "Rog. What if there were an emergency on the Ro-Ro deck? How would you get down there?"

"Access shafts in every alleyway. One just to the right as you go out my cabin. Oval steel door with dogs. Steel ladder leading down to the Ro-Ro deck…"

"Dogs?!" said Bogger.

Roger stared at him. Smiled. Came across. Patted him on the shoulder. "No, no, Bogg! 'Dogs' are sort of steel clamps used to lock access doors without keys or any waste of time. Efficiency first, last and middle, these things."

Mrs Raite leaned forward. Placed her gin on the floor. "No. Not at all like the cruise ships. Cocktails under the awnings. Great yellow moon. Soft calypso music. Handsome young officers in dress whites."

Bogger stood very still. He and Mrs Raite stared at each other.

"Rog?" Mrs Raite husked down her voice even more. "Could you... well... possibly kneel and massage my toes?"

"Massage your toes?!" squeaked Roger.

"Climbing that steep gangway of yours in my high heels..." She bent low to ease off a shoe. Held it up for Roger's inspection.

He took it from her. As he did, she took him by the shoulders and forced him to his knees, facing her.

Roger, thumb near his chest, began to violently gesture backwards with it.

"Bogger?" said Mrs Raite. "I told you in the pub. Just your everyday voyeur. He'll be delighted to see you give me a massage... And not just my toes..."

Roger, now red-faced, turned to Bogger standing behind him. "Er... Help yourself to another, er, Bogger. Or a beer. One or two in the fridge. Couple of cases in the wardrobe..."

Bogger grinned and opened the wardrobe. Eyed up the space inside. Tapped the Stillson in the palm of one hand.

"Rog!" Mrs Raite turned Roger's head back towards her. She leaned forward to take off her other shoe; the red basque with its black lace trimming pushing up her breasts further than ever.

Roger gave a silly grin and raised his face to hers. Bogger moved forward, Stillson raised...

SEQUENCE 116

As if catapulted from a maritime trampoline, the Pilot bounced onto the bridge at a run. Followed a moment later by Wally Jinks.

Barratt immediately walked across and held out his hand.

The Pilot shook it, then whipped off his hat and brushed some water from it. The pilot had a very small bald head at one end of his body, and an equally small pair of feet, in highly polished black leather shoes, at the other. In between, he was round and solid. The head and feet pivots between which turned a globe of the maritime world in a Mersey River pilot's uniform.

Barratt cleared his throat. "Pilot. My chief officer, Harry Rose."

The Pilot nodded pleasantly. "We've met before."

"Harry," said Barratt, "is the gangway in? Did that coasting second mate leave the ship?"

Harry turned to Jinks. "Quartermaster?"

"No, Mr Mate. The gangway is not taken in!"

Barratt laughed wordlessly and shook his head.

"And," said Jinks, "I'll tell you why! I'm at the head of the gangway with Scouse MacGuinness waiting on the pilot when not only does the coasting second mate *not* leave the ship, but he actually comes aboard with *two guests*!"

"Guests?!" gasped Barratt. "We're on the point of going to sea!"

The Pilot went to the bridge windows and stared out blankly across the container tops.

"Chief Officer," said Barratt, "have the second quartermaster report to the bridge."

Harry picked up the two-way radio set, pressed the call button and waited until Scouse MacGuinness's voice said, "Who's that now?"

"Chief officer. Please report to the bridge, Quartermaster."

"What about this gangway, Mr Mate?"

"Immediately, please," said Harry, and rang off.

Barratt raised a finger as if to speak. Walked to the opposite wing of the bridge. Looked down into the dock. Rotated his head once or twice. Walked back to stand near the wheel and Helmsman. The Pilot was now standing staring at the radar screen, head bowed in thought.

Quartermaster MacGuinness bustled onto the bridge, wheezing and puffing.

Harry took the lead. "Quartermaster. Have the coasting second and his guests left yet?"

Scouse shook his head slowly. "A difficult one, Mr Mate. See, they hadn't left by the time I headed up here, but they might have done since…"

Barratt screwed up his eyes. "These guests, quartermaster?… Were they, would you say, seafaring types?"

In the shadows of the wing, Wally Jinks made a noise between clearing his throat and laughing.

"Well, Captain," said MacGuinness, "the male one – male guest, that is. Well… I can only say I was once with someone like him on this tanker I was on in the 'Perishing

Gulf'. Who eventually had to be tied-up in a shower curtain by the daywork crowd. 'Advanced Severe DTs exacerbated by both heatstroke *and* frostbite' – through him finally collapsing in the freezer meat room – as the old man scribed in the logbook. Eventually had to put the bunk chains on him 'till we got home…"

Barratt shook his head, then asked, "And Mr Drummond's other guest?"

"A woman, Captain," said Scouse MacGuinness confidently.

"A woman?" gasped Barratt.

From the shadows, Jinks said, "A type us poor sailors know only too well."

Barratt threw out a quivering arm towards him.

"Wally," said Harry, "perhaps you could go down and look in the coasting second's cabin? If they're still there they *must* leave the ship immediately!"

Jinks nodded. Lit a cigarette. Scratched his rear. Strolled off the bridge.

Barratt addressed MacGuinness. "Quartermaster, bring the gangway home."

"But, Captain. What if they've not gone? If they're still on the piss?… Beg pardon… Still having a farewell bevvy in the coasting second mate's cabin?"

Barratt looked at Harry.

Harry said, "QM Jinks is checking that now. Consult him. If he can't get an answer from the coasting second's cabin I think we can assume they got off while you've been up here."

"Hmm…" said Scouse MacGuinness. Left the bridge, shaking his head.

Barratt turned to the pilot. "To quote Tolstoy, 'All happy families are alike; each unhappy family is unhappy in its own way'. Yes?... And conditions are...?"

The Pilot fanned his face with his uniform cap. In spite of the freezing conditions outside, he was sweating heavily. "Port Radar are saying, although worsening at the moment, they're expecting it to clear. Regarding tugs. I've got two and can get you a third. So up to you whether you go or not."

The captain looked off the bridge towards the dark river, then back at the Pilot. "Possibly another report from the lock?"

The Pilot nodded and went to the VHF transmitter. It crackled into life as he raised the lock. "Hello!... Pilot, *Ocean Seaspray*. Conditions at lock, please?"

The tinny disembodied voice came back immediately. "Hello, *Ocean Seaspray*. Wind westerly five to six, gusting to seven... over."

The Pilot nodded. "Thanks, lock... over." He turned to Captain Barratt. "And that's just at the lock!... Though I hear the Irish Ferry's looking to sail midnight."

Barratt smiled. "Irish Ferry? I don't really think that involves anyone here."

The Pilot said, "Leave it another hour?... See if it improves?"

The Pilot and Harry stared impassively at Barratt, assessing him. The decision he would make. The lives and livelihoods of the sailors waiting on his word of command. A huge, valuable ship with a fortune in cargo, waiting on his command. The owners and their profits waiting on his command. The tugs. A whole industry – a small, busy village; all its businesses and people waiting to spring into life or stand down. All on his command.

Barratt went to the bridge windows; looked in the direction of the Mersey, then across to the immediate surroundings on the berth. The rain whipping the stones of the dock until they glistened. The howling gusts of wind. The ship itself now moving perceptibly on its ropes under the onslaught. "Tide's going... Water's running away," he said over his shoulder. He turned, baring his teeth slightly. "We'll chance it. Get that other tug up, would you, Pilot?" He turned to Harry. "Mr Rose! Tell the engine room we're going!"

Barratt then knelt. Harry wondered if he was about to pray. Instead, he rubbed his fingers across the matting.

"Static electricity," he said. Stood up again.

The Pilot raised an eyebrow in Harry's direction. Harry raised one back.

The Pilot shrugged and strode across towards the VHF. "Going for'ard then, Harry?" he said over his shoulder.

"Mr Rose is staying here. Sailing second mate will be for'ard tonight," announced Barratt.

"The mate's station is up for'ard, Captain," the pilot said.

"This second mate is fully certificated. Extra master's ticket, same as all of us here. Sailed mate on other vessels. And conditions are such tonight that I want Mr Rose here with me. Possibly on the engine-room telegraph/phone."

The captain and the pilot looked at each other. Harry drew breath. The Pilot could object, question this decision; even write a report. He might do that anyway. The sailing second certainly held all the tickets. Had sailed as a mate – on nothing as big as the *Seaspray*. But was as equipped as Harry to oversee what was necessary in the bows of a ship going to sea. Though maybe not this sea. If the Pilot made it an issue? Well, there were all those hundreds of thousands of pounds being held up. There would be questions. Serious questions. Who had *actually* prevented the *Seaspray* going to sea? Who had *actually* cut into profits? Overloaded and over-insured ships figured in every aspect of Liverpool's history – with the families of those drowned too poor and uneducated to ever gain any sort of hearing or recompense… But that was then…

Harry watched the Pilot calculating all the possible future combinations of trouble. For himself. For Barratt. For the ship. Harry wasn't really interested. He thought once again of Chris as he'd seen her in John's office, then in hospital. Her seemingly genuine interest in greyhounds. In him! She could alter his life, and only for the better.

He noticed that the Pilot had apparently accepted Barratt's decision and moved towards his station.

Harry shrugged, then went off the bridge for more coffee.

SEQUENCE 117

FRIDAY, 12th MARCH, 1982. 23.59
INT / NIGHT RO-RO DECK, *OCEAN SEASPRAY*

At first, it hadn't been too bad. The initial movements of the ship had frightened John. But the various non-too-violent stops, goes, and bumps as it manoeuvred out of the locks soon convinced him he had natural Liverpool sea legs. Then came Liverpool Bay and open sea, when cargo-shifting, rolling, crashing, banging, and hanging on for his life presented him a truer picture. Then, miraculously, a slight lull. This was the spherical Pilot leaving the ship. Rolling along the alleyway. Bouncing onto the ship's Jacob's ladder. Ricocheting off one of its bottom rungs into the pilot boat. All the time thinking about Barratt / the possible fate of the *Ocean Seaspray* / his own career.

Once the pilot was away, Barratt took the ship to dead slow ahead, then slow ahead.

John was now very frightened; confined in a creaking, groaning hell of straining metal that seemed to rock, roll, shudder and corkscrew simultaneously. While all the time surrounded by precariously balanced cases and containers and strange implements that threatened to crush him at any moment.

He cast his eyes wildly upwards to see Mrs Raite and Bogger emerge from what looked like some sort of hatch halfway up the wall of the ship onto a horizontal laddered walkway. And then move off hesitantly around it and out of sight. John realised no one had any real idea where they were and how to deal with it. He closed his eyes in despair.

When he reopened them he was looking at Crust. Relief shot through him.

Crust said "Hear about that docker they called 'the Lazy Detective'? Always asleep on a case!"

"They're here," said John. "Bogger; Mrs Raite…"

"Raite, too," said Crust. "But so am I. Deus ex machina; the god from the machine."

John shook his head.

"Classical drama," said Crust. "A crane or other device to enable the appearance of a god – hero – to unravel and resolve the plot."

"Has he got the painting?" asked John. Then, feeling the ship begin to surge, he shouted instinctively, "Hold on!"

The first big sea-roll. Everything on the Ro-Ro deck straining and groaning. Something broke loose deeper in the hold and crashed into something else. The ship shuddered. Jarred. Stabilised. Began to come upright.

Crust and John held on to stanchions.

Crust pulled back his railwayman's coat. He was wearing a shoulder holster.

John yelped. "I thought the police didn't carry guns?!"

"Police've always carried guns" Crust told him. "We just don't MGM it over here."

The ship suddenly screwed, slipped, pitched and fell. Landed with a crash. More roaring and grinding and cargo breaking loose. As the ship was supposed to be on the surface of the sea, John couldn't understand where it could have fallen from – or to.

Crust looked up into the blazing deckhead lights. "Those bastards up there!" he said.

"Who?" asked John.

"Jason and his Argonauts. Who else?!"

SEQUENCE 118

Out of the night, black, white-capped waves creamed back from the bows of the ship, passed down its sides, and raced away to stern. From starboard, great seas, like caped ogres, strode towards, then past the ship. The sea seemed almost plasmic. Neither gas, nor liquid, nor solid, but, like lightning, expanding in all directions.

On the *Seaspray*'s bridge, the only assurance of safety was the constant reverberation from the engine room, expanding up through the fabric of the ship into the bridge floor, giving a sense that the ship was under control, under way, and holding its own.

Barratt stood at the side of the Helmsman; Harry next to him.

"Well, Harry," said Barratt, "we got her out all right."

"Bad, though, Captain…"

"Long as her nose is in it. We don't get caught side-on… Start throwing containers."

"Captain," said Harry, pointing for'ard.

A giant sea climbed over the bow like a huge, black-cloaked, hooded figure. Curling forward, it swept down the deck like an express train, the ship plunging into and under it, as if seeing this as its only means of escape. Harry tensed. The ship, having steadied again, suddenly felt different.

The Helmsman said urgently, "Captain! We're losing way!"

"Engines've stopped," said Harry.

The engine-room phone rang. Harry sprang across and put the speaker to his ear. "Yes… Right, Sec… Right! Soon as you can." He put down the phone and moved across to join the captain looking out over the sea. "Second engineer. Governor's jammed!"

The captain nodded. "Imagine," he said. "A wooden ship. These conditions. All hands out on deck, trying to work sail. No lights!"

Harry smiled encouragingly. "Captain! What do you want? The ship's without power, turning broadside on…"

Barratt pointed off the bridge. A sea swept in from nowhere, striking the ship like a punch to the head. The force threw him and Harry together into a corner. As they struggled to free themselves, Barratt quoted into Harry's ear:-

" '… *The first I remembers, I woke the next morn*
On a three-skysail-yarder bound South round
Cape Horn,
With a suit of old oilskins, and two pairs of socks,
And a fire in my head, and a dose of the pox'."

Barratt's breath was hot; and strong with rum.

SEQUENCE 119

SATURDAY, 13th MARCH, 1982. 00.30
INT / NIGHT ROCKER'S LAIR, DRUM ACADEMY

Charlie, Big Ned, and a music producer named Dagon were sitting smoking dope and drinking.

Dagon wore a tall white top hat, impenetrable sunglasses, and a black poncho with 'DISCATEERE EXTRORDINAIRE' embroidered on it in gold.

Charlie had a new scuffed brown leather airman's jacket with a yellowish fur collar and 'BORN TO LOSE', in large brass studs, set into its back.

Charlie sparked-up. Took a hit. Handed it to Big Ned. Big Ned filled his lungs. Closed his eyes. Handed it on to Dagon. Dagon, with closed mouth, stuck the joint up one nostril. Stopped the other with a finger. Breathed in.

"See," Charlie addressed Big Ned, "Dagon here knows this fella knows this other fella's cousin's got this studio we could cut our first single – LP. Course, Dagon's got to have a drink out of it. Though you don't need to worry about putting *your* hand in your pocket. That's *my* job now."

Charlie took a contract from his inside pocket. Smoothed it out. Took the spliff from Dagon. Handed it to Big Ned. Ned filled his lungs. Closed his eyes. Put his head back.

Charlie offered a pen. "See. You both sign, Dagon gets a bit of any 'futures' for his trouble. We get access to a fully equipped studio, engineers, local radio playtime through 'favours-in', start-up gigs through 'favours owed'… After which, we all should do OK." He proffered the pen. "On you, Big Ned!… But there isn't a group in the 'Pool wouldn't bite your hand off – sell you their sister's knickers – chance of a deal like this."

Without moving his head or opening his eyes, Big Ned held out his hand.

SEQUENCE 120

On the Ro-Ro deck, John and Crust were now lying in a heap alongside the tyres of a very large tractor fastened down with shackles. John attempted to rise to his feet, only to find one of Crust's hands bearing down on his shoulder; the other pointing.

John followed Crust's finger. A lorry door had swung open. Raite, with difficulty, eased himself out. He was holding a gun. He swung himself around to feel the cab steps. Lowered himself carefully to the deck. Looked around quickly; then ducked round the side of the vehicle.

Crust's finger now jabbed upwards. Mrs Raite and Bogger Bone were edging back along the raised crew walkway about thirty feet above the deck.

The ship began to heel.

Crust and John clutched at the tractor fastenings. .

Above, Bogger put an arm round Mrs Raite and pressed her against the side of the ship, holding on to a metal handgrip with one hand to support them.

The ship rolled. The cargo shifted ominously, but not with the same sense of imminent disaster. The ship slowly came upright again.

As it stabilised, Bogger and Mrs Raite crept onwards.

Like the villain in an old pantomime, Raite reappeared from around the lorry and raised his gun in the direction of Bogger and Mrs Raite. Crust levelled his own weapon.

John heard himself shout. What, he didn't know. A primal, instinctive expression of warning.

Somehow his voice must have carried, or Raite caught the vibrations. Whatever, Raite immediately swung in their direction. John felt himself pushed to one side like a feather; simultaneously hearing two gunshots, the sound of ricochet, then silence.

More shots then silence.

John climbed shakily back to his feet, to find himself face to face with Crust. John had a terrifying premonition that Crust was calculating whether or not to kill him. *Can I get away with it? Blame it on Raite?... But his father?... That gang from the church?... How much fuss can they kick up?*

The sums mustn't have worked out. In a contained voice, Crust said, "Think Raite'll shout any warnings 'fore shooting you?"

The ship gave a half-roll and stagger. This time a packing case came crashing from somewhere and thudded into another case alongside them; splintering-off a section.

"We've got to get out" said John staring round wildly. This stuff will turn us to jelly... Look. I didn't mean to shout; it just happened. Can't we take them prisoner or something?"

" 'Who's 'we'?... The justice system needs less to do. Not more!"

John looked at the walkway. It was empty.

"Went into one of the access doors" said Crust. "Heading for the upper decks." Crust gestured with his head and set off towards the ship's hull towards a bottom access door – moving with confidence.

John realised that Crust must have seen the ship's plans. So while none of them really knew where they were, Crust probably knew where he wasn't better than anyone else. Sort of Brick thing.

Crust turned, grabbed John's arm. Pulled him behind a smaller container.

Raite appeared looking from side to side. His gun swinging in a slow arc.

"Bogger got a gun?" asked John.

"Never carries. Feels he doesn't have to... Obviously never heard the old saying. 'God made man: Sam Colt made them equal'."

Raite moved to the shaft door situated under the one used by Mrs Raite and Bogger. Opened it. Listened. Stuck his head in, gun pointing upward. Crust moved into space. Spread his legs trying to sway with the ship. Steadied his gun hand with the other. As he fired, the *Seaspray* gave a sort of grumbling lurch. Even so, Raite reacted, half-falling through the access door, then vanishing within.

"Chipped the paintwork," said Crust, "'stead of his brain."

John looked at him. "What now?"

"Maybe he's just inside, few steps up the ladder, waiting for one of us to poke our head in. After which, he'll head up for Bogger and Liz..."

"Who'll be where?"

"Container tops. Where's left?" Abruptly. "Come on!"

They moved towards the access door. From outside John saw a circular tube stretching upwards, and the bottom rungs of a steel ladder. From inside came the whine of an extractor fan, and a sour, oily machinery smell. Crust waited, looking coldly at John. John blinked, moved forward, then quickly stepped inside, looking upwards for the bullet. The ladder was clear. Crust edged inside and stared up as well. The ship began to roll and they automatically grasped each other's shoulders; tensing their backs against the walls of the access hatch, their faces a few inches apart.

Crust winked. " 'Not tonight, Josephine'." He fixed his bulging, pale, green-yellow eyes on John. "See, when all the criminologists, psychologists, sexologists and codologists have had their say, published their papers and pumped-out enough shit to fill the Atlantic, they're still not up for Bogger. Right?"

John nodded.

"Nor're you! Right?"

John didn't speak.

"But I am! Me and my kind! Right?!"

"Yeah."

"Yes," said Crust. "But you stepped forward and looked up that shaft. And that means something, to me *and* my kind. Not very much – far from it – but something."

SEQUENCE 121

SATURDAY, 13th MARCH, 1982. 01.00
INT / NIGHT BRIDGE, *OCEAN SEASPRAY*

As if brushed with oil, the sea and waves gradually began to abate. The clouds blew away. A full moon appeared.

Barratt became calmer. Standing at the back of the bridge, sipping a coffee.

A general air of relaxation. Though all anticipating the rogue waves that accompany the end of every storm.

The engine-room phone rang. Harry picked up. Listened briefly. "Thanks, Sec." Put down the receiver.

"What say the Black Gang, Harry? Our lads in the stokehold?"

Harry attempted to match Barratt's light-hearted mood. "Second says another five minutes – they'll go to 'Dead Slow Ahead'... Just cooling another case of beer under the condenser."

Captain Barratt beamed. "*Excellento!*" Then, "The wonder was that we didn't throw a container; those right up for'ard must have taken a fair hammering. How's it look out there, Harry? Everything secure?"

Harry walked for'ard and gazed casually out over the containers. His body stiffened. He turned his head to one side, then turned back and looked again.

" *Flying Dutchman*?" asked Barratt.

The full moon made it almost as bright as day. There couldn't really be any mistake. Even so, Harry reached for the night glasses. Took a further long look. Drew a tired breath. "Captain?... This crew?... You recall anyone joining with shoulder-length dark hair and a fur coat?"

Barratt's shoulders sagged. "These days, who can say?"

Wally Jinks emerged from the shadows, followed by Scouse MacGuinness. They, too, looked through the bridge windows. "Yeah," said Jinks. "It's that Judy from the bottom of the gangway... Wonder what she had to do to get that coat?"

"Nothing she could tell her old girl about," said Scouse. "But you're right, Jinksy. It's them… There's that hard-looking bastard."

They watched as Mrs Raite and Bogger swayed about, balancing themselves on the containers. Wondering what to do next.

Raite now appeared from the access carrying a gun.

"There!" said MacGuinness. "That other fella who was waiting to go ashore. Saw them. Just vanished."

"No coasting second mate, though," said Jinks.

Barratt's head rotated into his shoulders. His coffee cup tilted and its contents spilled onto the coir matting. "QM Jinks," he said sternly, "I asked you to check the whereabouts of the coasting second, Mr… ah… Drummond!"

"Captain, I banged his door like a Rimrose Road rent man! Checked the smoke room. Checked the mess room… *Nada*."

"Get the purser immediately. Have him open up the coasting second's cabin. Let me know what you find."

"Captain," said Jinks. Winked at Scouse MacGuinness. The pair sauntered off the bridge.

Barratt walked slowly to the bridge windows and looked out. "My God," he whispered. "My God!"

SEQUENCE 122

On the container tops there were no cups of coffee. No bridge window-combings to cling-to. If you went off the container-tops, you were only going one way. As well, they represented one of the higher points on the ship. And the higher the point on the ship, the greater the angle of arc through which it rolls. On the container tops, you didn't need shoes so much as octopus suckers.

Raite was pointing a gun at Bogger, who was standing about ten feet in from the edge of the containers, Mrs Raite hovering on the periphery. Raite moved forward, gesturing with the gun. Bogger shifted a few inches backwards.

"Bastard!" yelled Mrs Raite.

Raite turned and fired a shot towards her. She jumped and moved back towards the access hatch.

The storm's penultimate rogue wave struck. The ship shuddered sideways; and lifted up as moved by a giant steam shovel. Three containers broke free from near the bow and were cast into the sea. The ship lurched back violently.

Raite staggered and dropped to his knees, as did Mrs Raite.

Bogger kept his balance and immediately moved forwards at a shuffling run, reached Raite and kicked him in the head. Raite dropped the gun.

Bogger snatched up the weapon, now gesturing Raite backwards towards the container's edge.

Mrs Raite stood as if paralysed.

"Right, Ron!" Bogger howled into the wind. "Where's the painting?"

From their access door, Crust and John appeared.

The party was complete.

SEQUENCE 123

SATURDAY, 13th MARCH, 1982. 01.15
INT / NIGHT BRIDGE, *OCEAN SEASPRAY*

"Unbelievable," said Barratt, staring through his binoculars.

Harry cleared his throat. "Don't really know how to tell you this, sir; but I believe I've met one or two of these people before."

"Socially?" asked Barratt.

"Chap investigating my greyhound idea. Name of O'Rourke. He's the smaller one at the access hatch."

"The one without the gun?"

"Yes."

"The North Atlantic," said Barratt reflectively. "The only ocean with its own load mark – WNA: Winter North Atlantic!… Harry, what *are* they doing below? Give the chief a ring, would you?"

Harry gave a small cough. "Sir, the people on the containers, shouldn't we… well… try to…?"

"Try to what?!" Barratt's head described a slow circle. "The sea holds all answers, Harry. The sea and the Great Universal Spirit… No. I don't usually talk like this. But nights – full moon – ship broken down – madmen and a woman in a fur coat on the container tops… Well, somehow…" He gripped Harry's arm. In a voice racked with profound yearning, said, "Why me, Harry? Why me?"

Harry, staring through the bridge windows, pointed. "Captain. Why any of us?"

SEQUENCE 124

SATURDAY, 13th MARCH, 1982 01.20
INT / NIGHT MOBILE HOME, LAKE DISTRICT

In an overgrown wilderness in the Lake District, 'Arry and his bikers were relaxing in their double-width, extra-long, mobile home – their 'Van'. Furnished in the manner in which they had left the flat in Moorfields; plus a large, low, circular table right out of Charlie's Rocker's Lair. Around this table four of the bikers, all wasted, sat rolling-up snorting and drinking.

In the kitchen section, separated by a 'breakfast bar', two topless blondes were preparing food.

The walls of the 'van were covered with examples of 'Arry's art. Plus a large framed poster of Hitler sitting with one arm round Eva Braun – the other round their German shepherd, Blondi. All three staring straight ahead in varying states of paranoia. In front of the poster a group of sandalwood-scented tea-lights burned.

At the far end of the mobile home a naked blonde sprawled on a couch posing for 'Arry who was violently applying paint to a sheet of hardboard.

'Arry drained his glass. Walked to the central table. "'Nother two weeks, supplies'll be running again… Then those fuckers stole our crib… Get my art back." He shook his empty glass. Pointed towards a cider bottle.

One of the bikers stood and made a grasp at it. Too drunk to stand, he crashed forward onto the table.

SEQUENCE 125

SATURDAY, 13th MARCH, 1982. 1.21
EXT / NIGHT CONTAINER TOPS, *OCEAN SEASPRAY*

John and Crust stood near the access door, holding on. Their world reduced to ice-cold wind and spray. The ship wallowing in a strained, but lazy, fashion. They looked across the playing- field formed by the tops of the containers. On the sea edge of an outmost container stood Raite. On the inboard edge of the same container, holding the gun, Bogger; his back to Crust and John.

Crust tapped John on the arm and they began to shuffle slowly forwards. As they did so, Bogger raised the gun and Raite staggered slightly and fell on one knee. Bogger pointed the gun again and seemed to be shouting something, making some demand of Raite. Mrs Raite was edging back towards the access hatch.

Then Bogger was standing over Raite, hitting him on the head with the gun. Raite staggered to his feet and backed up to the very edge of the container. Faced Bogger; Bogger again waving the gun.

John glanced seawards.

SEQUENCE 126

"Captain," asked Harry, "what's he saying? What's he asking him? Captain, your lip-reading?... What's he saying?"

Barratt threw up a hand to command silence. Cleared his throat theatrically. Adjusted the focus on the binoculars and stared across the containers at Raite's bloodied face. "He's saying... He's saying..."

"*Port!*" cried Harry.

Rising out of the sea, like the side of a cathedral roof, was the last great rogue wave of the storm. Harry watched as Crust moved forward, grabbed Mrs Raite and began dragging her back to the access hatch. John stood half-inside the hatch, on the ladder, pulling them in as the wave crashed against the side of the ship. Ronnie and Bogger simply vanished; plucked overboard by the sea, as were a number of containers. The wave rushed across the remaining containers like an express train and through the access hatch, washing John, Crust and Mrs Raite down onto one of the rest platforms.

The ship seemed to give a gigantic heave and sigh.

The engine-room telegraph rang 'Dead Slow Ahead'.

"Don't answer that!" commanded Barratt. "Ring double stop on the telegraphs. Tell them men overboard. Prepare to lower boats."

"Lifebelts?" asked Harry.

The captain shook his head. "Well swept past now... Time for lifebelts was immediately they went." He looked at Harry with sad eyes. "Though an act of mercy *not* to throw them!… *'Euphrosyne is lost',*" he quoted, "*'and Seafarer gone with all hands / And Flying Cloud lies on the seaweed 'midst the scattered bones'.*…" He stared at the floor. "I read them. His lips. Before they went…"

"Captain?" said Harry. "What was it? What did he say?"

The two men stared at each other.

"Captain! What did he say?"

"He realised he was being summoned by the Great Master of Waters and acknowledged that Master's presence. And simply said what he saw as the wave came to take him – *Celestial Vision!*'"

"*Celestial Vision*?" said Harry. "Where've I heard that?"

There was a small cough. Wally Jinks and Scouse MacGuinness were back on the bridge.

"Captain," said Jinks in an unusually serious voice, "about that coasting second mate…"

SEQUENCE 127

FRIDAY, 26th MARCH, 1982. 14. 30
INT / DAY FLOUR STREET

"You just don't realise the power of water," said John.

"You do if you drink in The Bayonets," said his father.

"I had my hands locked solid round the rungs of this ladder inside the access shaft, head down so I could breathe when the sea came in. But when it did, it opened my fingers easy as a baby's and threw me down the hatch, screaming and choking. Luckily Crust and Mrs Raite got washed down first and cushioned my fall. Even so… !"

"John!" Chris shook her head. "What happened then?"

"Sort of limped on to New York. Put in this sort of spare cabin by myself – meals brought by this steward. Six days or so… Which I needed, anyway, to recover."

"Where was Crust?" asked Chris. "Mrs Raite?"

John shrugged. "Crust? Hobnobbing the captain, I suppose. You've seen what he's like for grabbing the limelight. Mrs Raite? Don't know where they had her. Never saw her again. Probably hoping I'd sort something out for her – but – you know – just couldn't be arsed. She'd had her chance with me." John winked at his father. Pointed to the teapot.

His father picked it up and went to the hot-water geyser.

"Thing is," continued John, "and you've got to listen to this! Crust came to see me just 'fore we got to New York. Said we'd be questioned by the New York cops, but to leave it to him. 'Cop speaketh unto cop' – some shit like that. But the main thing was, we didn't find *the money…*"

"Money?" Mr O'Rourke came back with the teapot. "Not the painting?"

"Crust said there no longer was one. Just a missing mill in notes. He had this gun…"

"Gun?!" said Chris.

"… Messing round with it while telling me no painting ever existed. And that the New York cops would begin tearing the ship apart for the cash and would be glad to see us slip off home. That all of us now had to forget the painting!"

Everyone took a sip of tea.

"But Curly…" said Chris.

"Talk to him, Chris. Crust seriously wants this painting never to've existed."

"So he doesn't think it was in one of Raite's containers?"

"Seems the two quartermasters swore Raite was trying to leave the ship prior to her sailing… Raite'd never have done that – the painting was on board."

Chris rose. Began to put on her anorak.

"Chris, catch Curly tonight if you can," said John. "Thing is, I'm meeting Crust tomorrow night in St Joe's. Sort of a close-of-case discussion. Like to be able to tell him Curly's sorted… And sorry. No invites!"

"There's a god after all!" said Mr O'Rourke.

"How's Curly, anyway?" asked John casually.

Chris looked at him. "As you obviously don't rate him, he's off elsewhere. Charlie's offered him a job in the music business."

"Charlie?!" John laughed. Shook his head.

"Curly feels Charlie's got what it takes," said Chris.

"Yeah! Sort of fella can shit into a swinging egg cup from the top of the Liver Buildings… Met thousands of them!…"

"So've we," said Mr O'Rourke.

"From now on," said Chris, "Curly's helping launch The Nurgs. Stuff like that."

"General dogsbody, then?" John smirked.

"No change from working for you," remarked Mr O'Rourke.

John stood. "OK, look. I'd like the two of you to come the office tomorrow. See the changes I've made since I got back."

Chris zipped up her coat. "John, I'm not sure…"

"Chris, you put in so much early on. Went through so much for the firm…"

"Three unpaid days in hospital for a start," said Mr O'Rourke. "Yeah, she does deserve something. How about we all nip up The Bayonets?"

"I really need to go and find Curly," said Chris. "Fill him in on what's happening about the painting. That he's got to keep quiet. You know what he's like for saying more than's good for him."

"Yeah," said John, "I do! Dad, I need to get back the flat; clear up a bit for you and Chris tomorrow."

"Can't even have a pint with me?"

"Just too much on. Though I'll walk up the street with you. If you and Chris come about ten tomorrow morning, I'll spring for a taxi."

"Water peeling his fingers open like a baby," said Mr O'Rourke, following Chris into the hall.

Just before he put out the kitchen light, John opened the fridge. Butter, eggs, an opened tin of beans, cheese, bacon, a bag of tomatoes. Couple of custard tarts.

None of it paid-for by him.

SEQUENCE 128

SATURDAY, 27th MARCH, 1982. 10.00
EXT / DAY MOTORWAY FROM LAKE DISTRICT TO
LIVERPOOL

The five bikes in 'Arry's 'chapter' were on the motorway heading south from the Lakes. The bikers sprawling across their saddles. Pennants snapping like Jack Russells.

'Arry pointed up to an overhead sign signalling Liverpool. As one, they swung onto the slip road.

SEQUENCE 129

SATURDAY, 27th MARCH, 1982. 11.00
INT / DAY LANDING OUTSIDE JOHN'S OFFICE. INT / DAY JOHN'S OFFICE

Mr O'Rourke and Chris stood wedged on the tiny landing, staring at John's newly painted and varnished office door. No more hasp and padlock. Genuine keyhole with a deadlock. Sign redone in gold leaf.

JOHN O'ROURKE
LOCAL AND INTERNATIONAL INVESTIGATIONS

Mr O'Rourke tapped the glass. Turned the handle. Gestured Chris inside.

John was waiting for them, standing on a new fitted carpet. Freshly painted walls and doors. A new door to the bedroom; another to the bathroom. Impressionist prints. Fitted chintzy curtains at the window overlooking Moorfields. Round the walls, heavy-duty black bin bags full of 'Arry's art. The only remainder from the old days was *Celestial Vision*, hanging on the wall opposite the new three-drawer desk and swivel office chair. Smart client chair the other side of the desk.

"Like the new sign?" asked John casually gesturing to the still open door.

Mr O'Rourke tapped 'International investigations'. This your time on the Wirral?"

"New York, Dad. Mid-Atlantic shipping crime" said John closing the door.

Mr O'Rourke pointed at the bin bags.

"Arian's stuff," said John. "Dump it next week."

His father pointed at *Celestial Vision*.

"No. Keeping that… Seems… well… to say so much about me. What I've been through…" John switched on the kettle. "See Curl last night, Chris?"

"Caught him at my mum's. Told him what you said about there never being a painting. Said he wasn't interested, but if you ever need to look for it again, try up your arse." She spoke in a light, friendly voice.

John sighed. Shook his head.

"And you, John?" she continued in the same tone. "Any further thoughts on where it might be?… If it still exists?"

John raised a finger to his mouth. "'Loose lips sink ships'… Couple ideas… Confidential for now."

"Even to your big scuffer mate?" said his father.

"Tried to discuss it with him on the flight back. Ignorant bastard fell asleep on me."

"Could've been worse," said Mr O'Rourke. "Could've stayed awake talking about himself."

John gestured around. "So, Chris. The decor…?"

Chris smiled. "You're the one living here. But except for… " she pointed at *Celestial Vision*, "… the rest should put clients at ease. Get them to trust you."

Mr O'Rourke snorted.

Chris, still smiling, said, "Must've cost a fair bit?"

"They said I was entitled to Mrs Raite's retainer, so I thought… well…"

"Even so…" pressed Chris.

John looked at her. *Fuck!* Had Curly mentioned Raite's money?

"Prints are nice, too," Chris continued. "Choose them yourself?"

"Sort of. Shop where I got the carpet. Manageress talked me into them. Looked as if she wanted to talk me into a bit more…"

Mr O'Rourke laughed out loud.

"Seems they're copies of 'masterpieces'" John told them. "… Though…" John shook his head sadly. "And… well… don't spread this around; but Crust mentioned there could be a bit of a reward…"

"Reward?" said Chris.

"Don't know who from…"

His father said, "I'd find out, I were you. 'Case you end up having to roll up your trouser leg and put your hand up through your arse and out of your mouth to take it. And make sure Curly gets his fair share… What you give me and Chris will be up to you."

John looked towards his father. "You know, Dad. Still be nice knowing what happened to the painting."

His father stared back. "Pity you didn't keep any of the old masterpieces." Pointed at the bin bags.

John looked at him carefully. Went over and sat in his new swivel chair. Chris went to join Mr O'Rourke at the window. Both looked at John, waiting…

John rubbed his chin. "I did. A final going-over 'fore I bagged them... Just the crap they already are."

Chris moved and stood next to one of the French impressionist prints. John felt she could easily be in it. Though it was Brick's *Tramps Take Taming* came to mind. A blonde sprawled on the floor, supporting herself on bent arms. Her blouse in shreds. Red, bloody weals, across her back. A hand in the foreground holding a coiled bullwhip... Maybe one more try?... She couldn't really fuck him off in front of his father.

He stretch-yawned. "You know, Dad. Thought I might have a few days off."

"What from?"

"Mentioned to Chris in the hospital about a weekend in Paris."

"Paris?!" Mr O'Rourke stared at Chris.

"I was delirious," she said.

"Even suggested that she..."

"... By 'she' he means 'Chris'," said Chris.

"... Might join me. See the sights. Convalescence"

"John!"

He looked across quickly. Something in her voice.

"Just after you went, Harry came to see me in hospital."

"Who told him he could do that?!"

"Are you drunk?" asked his father.

"Telling me his plans... A greyhound sanctuary..."

"Yeah. Heard them... Enterprise Allowance people laughed him out the office!"

"That's changed. His mother's definitely going in a home. They've a lot of land..."

"Yeah. They would have."

"… A stable block already fitted out for animals."

John smiled contemptuously and shook his head.

"Plus he can cash in his Merch pension."

'Merch pension'. What the fuck was this? John tried to keep his voice level. "And how're you involved?"

"Go across and help. Sort of glorified kennelmaid. See how it goes. My own room… John, I've had enough. I think I saw Billy – my ex – back on the road… I can't go through any of that again."

"Chris. I mean, *dogs*! Dumb animals!"

"Lots of women turn to animals once they've tried men!"

In the silence that followed, John registered what sounded like a group of motorcycles outside. Shouts that carried up and through the window. Chris turned and looked at Mr O'Rourke. Mr O'Rourke moved across to look down.

John joined him. A distinct feeling of unease. "Bikers," he said.

"Five," said his father. "More chains than Marley's ghost… Looking up here."

John felt a weight beginning to press on his shoulders. Chris moved to the sink and sipped her coffee in what seemed to John some sort of anticipation. His father backed towards one of the walls.

Heavy footsteps pounded up each flight of stairs. The Traitor's Stair creaked loudly five times, and shortly afterwards the office door was thrown open with such violence that its brass knob gouged a hole in John's new paintwork.

Two leather-clad figures moved into the room; the three others remaining in the doorway. The largest of the two had a recently shaven head and an eye tattooed on his forehead. He came across and looked John up and down. Closed his eyes for a couple of seconds to allow John to see the eyes tattooed on his eyelids. Opened them again. *Arian and Co! Fucking hell!* The second biker – a head of thick, matted yellow hair that hung below his shoulders – moved up to join Arian. Filthy leather jackets. Rips, zips, drips. Badges of skulls, battleaxes, guns, Iron Crosses.

John put out a firm hand. "Gentlemen! How can I help?"

They stared at him. Arian pointed at the door. "Who's O'Rourke?"

John put a hand in the air, as if asking to be excused from class. "For my sins." He took out his wallet. "Want a card?"

Arian said, "Fucking magician, are you?"

Yellowhair laughed in a peculiar, mechanical, staccato manner.

"Fucking laugh!" said Arian "Skeleton having a wank on a tin roof."

"Take it easy on the language, lads," said Mr O'Rourke.

Yellowhair looked around. "Old place doesn't look the same now, 'Arry."

John recalled what it had taken to arrest the bikers that first day and get them into the police van. He clapped his hands lightly and smiled. "So, boys! How can I help?!"

"The paintings…" said 'Arry.

"Paintings?"

Yellowhair said, "'Arry wants his paintings." He pointed to *Celestial Vision*. "And the rest!"

John nodded and smiled. Gestured towards the bin bags. "See, lads. Just cracked a big case. Drugs money. Heavy mob from London. Shoot-out at sea... Came back; got the office done. Had your paintings on show as they're obviously the goods... But had to bag them while the decorating was going on. Be re-hanging them Monday. So, you're the artist, then?" He smiled at 'Arry.

"Paints under the moniker of 'Aryan'," said Yellowhair. "Us being true Englishmen and patriots."

"Not Arian the well-known saint?" asked Chris.

'Arry turned to the three bikers by the door. Gestured towards the bin bags. They moved across and began opening the bags and extracting the art. One that had been bent in two to get it into the bag. One with a hole through it. A squashed milk carton. Some covered with the remnants of takeaway curries. Some crushed beer cans.

Chris said, "Impress me here, John, you can take me to Paris any time."

John smiled a sickly smile.

'Arry saw it. In one bound he was over, grabbed John by the lapels and held him face to face. John thought of Raite being held by Bogger in the same position outside the bungalow in West Heartwood. Then he was conscious of an indefinable heavy bodily shock, and was somehow lying on the floor without knowing how he got there. He began to raise himself on one elbow. Blood dripped down his face onto the new carpet.

Suddenly Charlie Um-Pah-Bah was there, carrying a six-pack. He gave a quick, dismissive look at John – now half-sitting holding a handkerchief to his nose. "Not again!" he said... "You all right, Chris?"

Chris nodded.

John's father stepped in front of 'Arry. "You've made your point, pal."

Charlie split the ciders and offered one to 'Arry. "Good to see you again, lads!" he said. "Been thinking about you... Hoping you were all OK."

'Arry hesitated, then accepted the cider. Charlie quickly handed out one each to the other bikers, saving the last for himself. He raised the can. "Cheers, boys!"

All raised and drank. Chris came across and helped John to his feet.

"What's happening?" asked Charlie, looking round at the new decor. His eyes swung past *Celestial Vision*, then returned to it.

'Arry nodded towards John. "This fucker. Going to dump my art! All bent and twisted."

"That's him!" said Charlie.

The bikers laughed. Some of the violence went out of the air.

"Well..." said John.

"Shut up!" said Mr O'Rourke.

"Obviously," said 'Arry, "I got to have redress; compo..."

"Well..." began John.

"... What 'Arry's saying," said Yellowhair, "is he," he pointed at John, "has got to pay damages and that. For the artworks."

"So how much you got?" asked 'Arry, draining his can and throwing it at the new lamp on John's desk.

"Actually," said John, "fitting out this place... Well... I'm more or less skint."

'Arry fixed John with his eyes. Gestured towards Mr O'Rourke. "He your old man?"

"She your girlfriend?" asked Yellowhair. The incipient violence came back again.

Charlie suddenly pointed at *Celestial Vision*. "It shouldn't be here!"

"Too right, mate," said Yellowhair. "Should be in some fucking art gallery!"

"Yeah!"

"Too right!"

"Fucking cream, man. Cream!" From the other bikers.

"What you saying, Skins?" asked 'Arry of Charlie.

"There was this arty psycho perv worked-over Chris there. I walked in on it. Cut him with a can opener. He ran past me, using that painting as a shield. I got wasted that night; next morning found I'd made a note of his name. Think he musta come back later that night; hung it up again. Why?"

'Arry nodded to Yellowhair, who went across, lifted down *Celestial Vision* and brought it over to 'Arry, who hefted it. Hefted it again. Looked at the back of the frame. Made a slashing motion towards Yellowhair. Yellowhair produced a flick knife and handed it to 'Arry, who pried the backing board away from the frame. Squinted inside. Turned the knife and made the gap wider. Squinted inside once more. Looked at Yellowhair. Stuck the painting under his arm.

"OK," he said to the room. "Here's what's happening. We're leaving and we've never been. Anything comes out about any of this, we're back to find you. No matter where, we'll fucking find you and fuck you up. Fuck you up good!" In the profound silence that followed he turned to John, gesturing towards the bin bags and their spilled contents. "I'm leaving these in your charge. Get them sorted and framed up. *Comprende*, fuck-features?!"

John nodded.

'Arry nodded to Yellowhair and the others. At the door, he turned back. "Only thing any of you fuckers got going for you is you're white!" He extended his right arm. "*Seig Heil!*"

The sound of five pairs of boots clumping down the stairs. One of them stamped hard on the Traitor's Stair. Stamped on it twice more. Laughter. Further clumpings which gradually faded. Chris went to the window. Bikes firing up. Pulling away.

"*He's the only guy I want to know / He's a rebel but I love him so...*" croaked Charlie.

John pressed his handkerchief to his nose. Feeling was returning and it was starting to hurt like a bastard. *And look at the new fucking carpet! Ruined!* He pressed harder to stem the bleeding and his rage.

Mr O'Rourke said, "Saved the day again, Charlie."

Charlie said, "Heard the goose-steps up the stairs. Listened a bit. Shot down for some booze; keep them happy... Chris being here and that."

John went to the sink and squeezed out his sodden handkerchief. Charlie saving the day again. Charlie taking Curly into his music business. Chris looking at Charlie with big eyes for helping her wonderful brother. For saving her from the bikers. Fuck him. Charlie was OK in his place, but his place wasn't here. *Maybe slip him a few bob? Promise to take him for a pint sometime?*

"So what was inside that frame?" asked Charlie. "Anyone any ideas?"

Sick smiles all round.

John, still holding the handkerchief in place, managed to take out his wallet and remove a tenner. He walked over to Charlie. "Appreciate your help, Charlie," he said through the handkerchief while holding out the note. "Let's catch up in a bit, shall we?"

In the silence, Charlie looked at him with a bright smile. "That's OK, John. Got my giro yester."

"Take it!" John held out the note. "Covered in blood. But this *is* Liverpool, right?"

"It used to be," said his father.

John folded the note and pushed it into Charlie's top pocket. Charlie's smile grew wider. He took out the note and stared at it. The air was electric.

Chris suddenly came over and took the note from Charlie. "Let's just use it later; go for a drink when we've finished cleaning up. How about we give you a knock on the way down, Charlie?"

Charlie nodded. "That'll do me!" He gave a casual wave and left the room.

"So Raite *did* come back," said John. "Put the painting inside *Celestial Vision*; one behind the other!"

"John!" said his father.

Chris took his arm. "John, even money can't blind you to 'Arry and his bikers."

"But," said John, "can't we...?"

His father looked at him. "Will you never learn?! This is one town you look for trouble – you're going to find it."

"He's right, John," said Chris. "Let's call it a day. Go the pub."

John looked at them. *A painting worth a mint...*

His father, following John's thoughts, said, "You won't be able to spend it if you're dead. That bunch will *kill* you! Can't you understand anything?!"

John finally nodded. Moved to the door. Stood back to allow Chris to leave. Gestured for his father to go next. "Maybe give Charlie that shout, eh, Dad? While I lock up. Yeah, I think we owe him a drink. Saving Chris from Raite that day."

"Yeah," said his father. "Really lucky she was saved by Charlie from Raite…"

John stared at him.

"… Because it meant she was here this afternoon to save you from Charlie." His father began to limp slowly down the stairs.

John's anger swelled like a poisoned abscess. *So close! A million. And so close!* He forced himself to breathe deeply. Turned and surveyed the office. His mood shifted. All his! No Mrs Raite. No Curly. No Bogger. No hassle. Just John O'Rourke, international private eye, of Moorfields. He ran his hand over the gold sign. And how quickly it had come. Hardly a month. Showed he really had what it took to survive *and* break through.

He closed the office door and turned the key. The lock clicked smoothly. He started down the stairs. Began to whistle.

SEQUENCE 130

SATURDAY, 27th MARCH, 1982. 20.40
EXT /NIGHT FLOUR STREET.

Mr O'Rourke and John stood at the top of Flour Street.

Mr O'Rourke said, "What time you meeting Crust?"

"St Joe's at nine… Tie off a few loose ends."

"Why there? And why Saturday night? Everyone about?"

John shrugged. "He's his own man."

"And making you the same," said Mr O'Rourke.

"What's that mean?!"

His father shrugged. "Right. I'm along The Bayonets. An hour or so. Be back at the house sometime after ten. I'll open a can of mild for you."

"Never know; I might decide to stay on in St Joe's."

His father touched his arm. "I wouldn't if I were you, son. Not tonight." With a farewell wave, he began limping to The Bayonets.

SEQUENCE 131

SATURDAY, 27th MARCH, 1982. 21.00
EXT / NIGHT ST JOE'S CHURCH CLUB. INT/NIGHT
ST. JOE'S.

Approaching St Joe's, John slowed for a moment. Did he really want to do this. But that 'citizen's reward'. Chance to impress Crust…

Inside the portico, old Fitzy sat as usual at the green baize trestle table with the cash box on top. Back bent like an 'S' hook. Some old book Irish history. Glass of Scotch. Maybe lend him one of Brick's. *Blondes Bruise Easy?* Give him more to think about in bed than the Black and Tans.

"All right, Fitz?"

Fitz didn't look up. Fairly regular when he was pissed…

As he stood there, John heard a crashing of guitar chords and drums. *Fucking hell! Not The Nurgs again!* He walked past Fitzy's table and through the swing doors. The Nurgs were onstage, setting up, messing around and arguing. The drummer seemed to be missing. Another Saturday night. Tables mostly occupied. The bar again crowded with small, tight groups of men. Father Malachy in the middle, dispensing wisdom and accepting drinks. A small group standing towards the stage steps contained Curly and Charlie. Charlie wearing what looked like some sort of painted cloak.

At the very end of the bar, nearest the stage, Crust stood alone, drinking a pint. In front of him, on the counter, a newspaper. A pen in his hand.

John stood still, waiting to be acknowledged by one of the regulars. No one looked at him directly. All the same, conversation levels had shifted when he entered. OK. He could handle this.

He took a breath. Moved across the dance floor. Began edging along the bar. As he passed Curly's group, he stopped and said, "OK, Curl? Charlie? Fancy a bevvy?"

As if he were a ghost, the conversation never faltered. Laughter continued.

Eventually, because it could end in real trouble, he moved on to where Crust stood. Crust manoeuvred John so that John stood staring down the bar, his back to the stage. Crust shouted for two pints of bitter. John unzipped his anorak. Glanced at what he could see of Crust's paper. Open at a crossword. One of those posh ones. Loads of squares. About half completed. Mr OU Big Brain.

The beer arrived and Crust paid. John put up a thumb by way of greeting to the barman.

The barman said, "Aye" blankly. Moved down to the other end of the bar.

Crust looked at John. "Long day?" he asked sympathetically. Filled in another clue.

John nodded. Took a mouthful of beer.

Crust raised his own glass. "Cheers!" he said.

John, embarrassed at not having waited, took a second hasty mouthful and responded, "Cheers."

"What happened to the nose? Blow too hard?" Crust took a white sealed envelope out of an inside pocket. Held it up for a second. Put it down on the bar. Tapped it with his pen. "Here. Take your dad the pictures."

People were watching. Should he push the envelope back to Crust with one finger like Brick in *Money Talks Tough*; let the lads know he was still one of them? But if he did and lost Crust, would the lads be waiting outside the dole office to take him out on the piss? Would they fuck! The envelope was a message. He was nothing special. No more talented than anyone else. *Well, that's the way it's done. Give the chances to the ones who are nothing special; who'll then do anything to keep them. "Miss! Miss! Please pick me, Miss!" "That's a nice plate of shit you've handed me, boss. Just give me a second*

to get it down…" The old saying: 'It's not what you know –
it's who you know.' Even more important – 'And how you
know them.' Well, he now knew Crust in a way that should
guarantee steady work, with Crust never more than a phone
call away. And no matter what anyone thought, he'd been
there on the *Seaspray.* Had gone up against it with the best of
them. Maybe he should let people know.

"On top of those containers" he said loudly to Crust,
"During that storm! Another world from last time we
were here. 'Member it…?"

'Blanket on the Ground' began then abruptly stopped

"I remember that" said Crust

"Yeah. Nothing like a bit the old 'Country and
Western'" said John

"Those with nothing more to gain consoling those
with nothing left to lose."

Here we go.

" Even so" continued Crust "Watching your dad and
Chris. Other couples. How happy they seemed. Got me
thinking…"

"Oh?"… John drank some of his pint.

"About music and mathematics. How music is
mathematics. Whole notes, half-notes, quarters, eighths,
sixteenths… even thirty-seconds, sixty-fourths…"

Was any of it worth having to listen to this shit?

"…So if music is mathematics, so must be dancing.
Again, how happy your dad and Chris seemed. So if
music and dancing make people happy, and music
and dancing are mathematics, then, syllogistically,
mathematics, music and dancing all make people
happy!"

"Some of the worst fights I've ever seen," John told Crust, "happened out on that dance floor!"

'Blanket on the Ground' crackled into life once more.

Couples began to drift onto the floor.

Crust pointed behind John's head.

John turned. Big Ned was at the front of the stage, waving to someone down the bar as the other members of the group trailed equipment and insults. Still no sign of the drummer.

Then John was elbowed hard against the bar as Charlie hustled past dressed in what looked like a wizard's outfit. Some sort of long cape-cum-coat with astrological markings; a pointy hat with some weird shit painted on it. He mimed masturbating himself in John's direction before climbing up onto the stage.

"What happened to the old drummer?" John asked.

"A few rimshots too many," said Crust.

John drained his pint.

Crust shouted for another two. Pointed again behind John. John turned once more to the stage. Charlie began inserting himself into the mound of drums and cymbals. Big Ned took up the microphone. Held up one hand for silence. The noise levels immediately rose. The band began to argue; the microphones live. A blueprint for the next thirty years.

"Man, what is all this shit?!"

"Only hit I'm interested in 's the one in my pocket!"

"Where's my fucking ale?!"

"'Bridge over Troubled Water'!" shouted a voice from the audience.

"'Bridge over Troubled Water'?" sneered Big Ned. "You serious, pal?! Yeah, sure we'll do it... At your funeral!" He grasped the mic. "OK! OK! OK! Folks! – 'I Rang Up Dr Frankenstein' followed by 'When the Mogadons go to Meltdown'. But! Before that. One to celebrate signing to our new label, Rancid Records, and to show our contempt for the music industry's *insane* desire for money and self-publicity…"

Boos from the audience

"… Our support for working-class socialist solidarity. Yeah. I know you've heard them all say that. Then they get their Rolls-Royces and mansions and next thing they're down on their knees!… Rock 'n' rollers!… On their *knees!*… In front of an even bigger knobhead than themselves being hit on the head with a sword… You couldn't make it up!"

"You couldn't make you up, pal!" shouted a voice.

"Bastard!" shouted someone else.

"Yeah" continued Ned. "A new manager, too. A great name from the original Liverpool scene… One and only Charlie Um-Pah-Bah!"

"Never heard of him!" A voice from the floor.

"What Catholic saint's he named after?!" shouted someone else.

"Looks a right dickhead!" Someone else.

"So. In celebration. The 'golden oldie' that made Charlie's name. Yeah! You know you know it! You know you love it! You know you'll *have* to dance to it!"

At the opening chords of 'The Swiss Maid' John turned back to Crust. He was gone. Two fresh pints remained on the bar. Paper open at the crossword.

John blinked. Suddenly felt very alone. Let down. He had been about to ask the inspector to meet him next week for a drink. Become pals. Establish a relationship, and now... *OK! First thing: shift this free ale!* John took a couple of hefty swallows of the first pint. Glanced at the crossword while he considered what to do next. Total rubbish. All jumbled letters. Not one recognisable word... And that music/mathematics shit! You had to wonder about Crust's mental state.

John turned to the stage.

From inside the drum mountain, Charlie screamed, "*Um-pah-bah! Um-pah-bah! Um-pah-bah! Um-pah-bah! Um-pah-bah! Um-pah-bah-bah!*"

John drained the first pint. Drank half of the second. Took stock. Not a bad night. Three free pints. Crust's envelope. Still had Raite's envelope and the cash from Mrs Raite. Still drawing the forty quid a week off the Enterprise Allowance people. But was all the stress worth it? He drained the second pint. Time to go. There was violence in the air. And once the compass needle stopped swinging it would point at him. But no one had had enough yet.

He turned for the door. As he passed Curly's group, someone said, "Fucking copper's nark!"

Another voice, slowly and clearly, enunciated, "Cunt."

John reached the entrance door and pushed it open. Fitzy totally ignored him.

Thank fuck for that!

SEQUENCE 132

Mr O'Rourke sat in the kitchen with a can of mild and the *Albion* open in front of him. He glanced at the clock… He hadn't stayed long in The Bayonets. Listening to a load of Mick's shit, he'd drunk too much, too fast. Besides, he'd suspected John wouldn't be that late…

He heard the key go in the front door and bent over his paper. John entered the kitchen and sat opposite him.

Mr O'Rourke opened another can. Poured his son a glass of beer. Looked across. "Both back a bit early," he began conversationally. "How'd it go?"

"Saw Crust." John unzipped his anorak. "Think they call it a 'debriefing'."

His father smiled.

"Wasn't that much happening so decided come back; see you."

"Look in at The Bayonets?"

John took a sip of beer. "Couldn't be arsed."

"Maybe just as well…"

John waited.

"Mick was asking about you. Why you haven't been in since you got back off your 'cruise'. That he's got 'business' with you… Not mixed-up with the Danton of the double brandies, are you?"

John shook his head in despair.

"Pissed as a rat," continued Mr O'Rourke. "Doused in that aftershave he wears. Going on about the queers, women, 'limp-wristos', the revolution... Leans over the bar. Grabs me. Tells me he's 'modifying his stance' as regards the 'class struggle'. And what did I think?"

"And what did you?" asked John.

"That his only class struggle is same as yours. How to struggle out of his own class."

John stared into his glass. Could his father be suffering from that 'dementia' he kept reading about in the papers?

"... Slobbers all over me and says he's joining the Labour Party. That he'll be buying a suit. Did I want to go with him and see it fitted?" Mr O'Rourke took out his false teeth. Swished them in his beer to clean them.

"And?" asked John.

"I said if he was buying a politician's suit to make sure it was cut the same way as all the others get theirs done. Plenty room in the arse so they can tuck their tails in." His father took a swig from his glass. "Really stank of that aftershave. And wearing this tie with a coloured pattern. A tie with a *coloured* pattern! In The Bayonets!"

John saw his chance. "Dad. Ever hear any talk about why Mick and his missus separated?"

Mr O'Rourke became perfectly still. Looked at John. "I'd leave that alone."

"Just saying. Sort of whisper I heard; that Mick's missus caught him in one of her dresses..."

"John!" his father said. "Forget it!"

"But all that queer stuff he comes out with... The aftershave and that. Maybe, you think?... Maybe that he himself...?"

His father held up a hand. "You won't remember the Multreens – before your time. The old fella died. Docker. Then just the son and the mother. And… well… rumours… about what was happening there… in that house. The son and the mother. One day, a group of fellas off the road get hold of him – the son – took him down Back Reading Street -"

"'Reedy Bakkie'," said John.

" – And put him in hospital for three months. After which, he and his mother – like Mick's wife – vanished. But while it was happening – down Reedy Backkie – those fellas didn't say why they were putting him in intensive care. And he didn't ask. OK?!"

What sort of answer was that? What did it even *mean*? *Yeah. Probably that dementia…*

"So what about your policeman mate?" asked Mr O'Rourke.

"So-so," said John. "Main thing is, I think he likes me… And you," he added, wanting to give his father a boost.

"I don't give a shit whether he likes me or not." Mr O'Rourke looked genuinely outraged. "I don't like him!"

John swallowed. "He's essential… at the moment."

His father smiled. Drank some beer. "Fancy a hand of crib?"

"Itchy feet, Dad. Thought I'd drop into town; stay at the office tonight."

"OK," said his father. "See anything of Chris or Curly at St Joe's?"

"Curly was there. Didn't see Chris… Maybe having a quiet night in."

"Maybe looking for a bit of peace. Someone with a steady job; future… Not sure that's you."

"No?" said John with a provoking grin.

"Chris has got a lot of friends round here," said Mr O'Rourke.

"Seems everyone has… Except me."

Mr O'Rourke opened a further can of mild. Poured some into both their glasses. "As for Curly, there are people think you worked a fast one on him."

"Now listen, Dad…" John began.

His father gave a look that stopped him. "That you worked a fast one on him, for whatever reasons. And I'm sure you've got good ones…"

John opened his mouth once more to protest.

Mr O'Rourke held up his hand. "You're moving on. You've moved out. You're doing something you want. Good!… And you might make it. As your father, I hope you do. But you've no right involving people who can't follow you. Morally, that is. Who won't say what they're expected to; won't keep quiet when they're supposed to…"

They stared at each other.

John's father nodded at him. "Now finish your beer, and decide what you want to do. Go into town. Or let's take our cans into the front room. Watch the telly."

Another con job. Another invitation to cosy up. Gradually buy himself back in. Keep his mouth shut when he was supposed to – the very thing his father was claiming people like Chris and Curly and the Micks of this world wouldn't do. John smiled. His father watched him steadily.

John stood. Finished his beer. Stretched. "No. Gonna drift into town." He nodded at his father, who nodded back.

John left the kitchen and walked out to the hall. Opened the front door and stared out. He'd take Crust's money with him. Leave the other upstairs in the slit in his mattress. Safe enough. No one would burgle his dad's. Nothing worth having.

Opposite, there was a builder's skip. Someone gutting a room. John took off his anorak. Rolled it. Walked across and threw it in the skip. Walked back to the house, and down the hall. Took down a new car coat he'd bought. Put it on.

Standing on the step, he quietly pulled shut the front door. Began to walk up the street.

SEQUENCE 133

SATURDAY, 27th MARCH, 1982. 22.35
EXT / NIGHT STANLEY ROAD. INT / NIGHT TAXI

From the top of Flour Street, John looked along Stanley Road. The run-down shops and streets that contained his childhood. Fountains Road opposite. Leading up to Goodison Park. Maybe once the cash became regular he'd apply for a season ticket.

He looked up. Sky clear and clean. Where was the *Ocean Seaspray*? *Who fucking cares?* He flagged down a taxi. It slowed, the driver simultaneously giving him a thumbs up and pointing at the back seat. Dropping someone off – then would come back for John. Big deal.

John hitched his coat round himself. Yeah. Drift into the office and have a cold beer. That small Chinese restaurant just round the corner near the Café des Artistes.

Always a few girls there – even late at night. Never know your luck. And what was wrong with paying for it till you got yourself sorted properly? Chris wasn't on; not for him. She'd seen what she could get. What could be out there. Beginning with Harry and his dog parlour. Harry would soon really learn about real storms… Life in a kennel.

John yawned. He was tired. Tired of it all. Even Brick. Look at his latest – *Firm, Ripe and Ready*. The cover showed a pair of gnarled brown hands with cracked and dirty nails reaching out to grasp what looked like two overripe melons stuffed inside what might be a sack. But the book itself! A Californian fruit farm! Workers' rights and pesticides! In the early books, pesticides would have been only a variation on homicides; Brick shooting every pest in sight. *Brick! Of all people! Be joining Greenpeace the next one! But I won't be buying it.*

The taxi pulled up alongside him. In some sort of sync with the diesel engine's *knock-knock-knock*, the refrain from 'The Swiss Maid' began once more in John's head. *Um-pah-bah! Um-pah-bah! Um-pah-bah! Um-pah-bah! Um-pah-bah! Um-pah-bah-bah!* Con artist Charlie. Another prize loser.

Realising the driver was staring at him, John opened the door and climbed in. The driver lit a cigarette and waited for instructions.

First the office. Stash Crust's envelope. Quick beer from his new mini fridge and take it from there. "Moorfields," John said shortly. "Via the Dock Road."

The taxi driver, who'd been on for ten hours, nodded tiredly but flicked a glance in the mirror at John's tone of voice.

The cab threaded its way down to Commercial Road, turned left, cruised along to Athol Street, turned right over the canal bridge, and down onto the Dock Road. It turned left and began to move towards the Pier Head and city centre. What John was beginning to think of as 'home'. The Dock Road was deserted. The great black Dock Wall, on the right, broken only by the gate openings. The Dock Road itself stretching endlessly away towards the distant, floodlit Liver Buildings. Passing the entrance to one of the docks, John glanced through. A few dim lights. The berths empty. Nothing. And the next. And the next.

The driver said neutrally, "They're all gone, mate – the ships. You're twenty years too late."

John felt warm, confident, knowledgeable. "They'll be back," he observed with his new, abrupt assurance.

The driver, who had been awaiting his chance, caught John's eye in the mirror. "Not while you've a hole in your arse, pal! Not while you've a hole in your arse!"

SEQUENCE 134

MONDAY, 29th MARCH, 1982. 11.00
INT / DAY CRUST'S FLAT

"Then it's lost?" asked the Voice.

"I wouldn't say that." Crust swivelled from side to side in his captain's chair. Face tight.

"Then where is it?"

Crust doodled a ship in the frame of a painting.

"Hidden somewhere on the ship, maybe?" He swivelled right round. "Although…"

"Yes?"

"I've this feeling it never made it to the ship."

"Then where?"

"Only person can tell us that is Raite. And he's dead."

"That's what he thinks," said the Voice. "No. He'll have left something somewhere. Somewhere he's been…"

"Cowshitshire? The Porsche? O'Rourke's office where he worked over the girl?"

"Meaning…?"

"If he's hidden it in some barn – dog hole – we'll never find it. The Porsche? No. While according to Busking Bill he was carrying nothing when O'Rourke and his mate brought him back to the Moorfields flat after Bogger did him over. But again, Bill did lose him time to time… Still, we might have lost the painting but we did get two major crims dead."

"Plus that poor bastard sailor," said the Voice.

"Yeah," said Crust. "No one saw that coming. Yeah…"

"Plus the lovely Liz back in the nut school."

"Not our problem."

"For the moment," said the Voice. Then asked, "Fancy a holiday?"

"Well…"

"… Somewhere off the beaten track," suggested the Voice. "Lie low for a bit. Drink steadily but slowly. Let it all drift over you… Through your consciousness… What does – doesn't – ring quite true."

"I've tried that."

"Maybe not hard enough. Not the way I taught you. You *do* remember you're talking to the man who taught you all you know?"

Crust doodled a transistor radio. Eventually said, "What I remember most about the man who 'taught me all I know' is him taking me, early on, to that electric supply warehouse got broken into. Inviting me – strongly – to put that transistor radio under my cape."

There was a pause. "You know, Crusty," said the Voice, "and you *do* know! There's never been any question about you. None at all. The people that count – the lads – well… the lads know, come what may, if the little grey mice in their little grey suits took you upstairs you'd give them fuck all! Absolutely fuck all!"

"But?" said Crust.

"But," agreed the Voice, "with people like you it's sometimes felt – I don't know why – that some insurance is needed… Just in case."

"Of what?" asked Crust.

"Beyond me," said the Voice. "But with all that philosophy and books and music and stuff, I thought you might know yourself." After a pause, he asked, "That radio – what happened to it?"

"After we split up I took it down the river. Threw it in."

"Maybe for the best," said the Voice. "Just BBC tosspots crying into their taxpayer-funded champagne – 'police brutality' this; 'police corruption' that. Yeah, you acted wisely there… Even *very* wisely."

"Well," said Crust, "if nothing else, it's nice to have been on the receiving end of such individual and sympathetic consideration."

"You know," said the Voice thoughtfully, "there must be a fortune in rusty transistors at the bottom of that river waiting for some enterprising scrap man."

SEQUENCE 135

EPILOGUE

FRIDAY, 9th APRIL, 1982. 21.50
EXT / NIGHT GROUNDS SCOTTISH HIGHLANDS
HOTEL
INT / NIGHT HOTEL RECEPTION

Crust parked up. Checked the mirrors. Climbed out stiffly. Stretched. Howling winds. Lashing rain. Bare sere trees and bushes. He gazed around, murmuring…

"In a summer season – when soft was the sun,
I clothed myself in a cloak – as I shepherd were…
And went into this wide world – Its wonders to… Its wonders to…'
What?"

He looked round once more. Highlands of Scotland, the back end of winter. Knowing no one. No-one knowing him. Perfect.

As he began walking towards the main entrance of the hotel, a sudden gust made him stagger. He walked slowly up the wide stone steps to the hotel doors. Caught his reflection in their glass. A full-length Ulster instead of his railwayman's coat. Even more like Rodin's *Balzac*. Smiled his secret smile.

He pushed open the door and moved into reception. Dining room and bar to the right. Broad, thickly carpeted stairs to the left. Reception desk dead ahead. Glowing wood and polished brass. Couple of big, discoloured, heavily varnished oils hanging high on the wall behind the desk. *Still Life with Pint of Heavy and Smoking Haggis. Portrait of a Crofter: Tied Cottages in Background.* Old hotels at the heads of lochs. Victorian/Edwardian watering holes. Understated opulence. A way of life gone with the Purdeys? Private performances of *Parsifal*? The whisky buried under the peat for ten years? Not this Christmas. Below the surface, same twats still owned everything.

Crust gave his name and details to the young, softly spoken, Highland Receptionist. The Receptionist turned to the key rack behind him. On the counter was an open textbook. It seemed to be about silent film. The Receptionist handed Crust a large, solid brass key. Crust took it. Began to fill in the arrival form.

As he did so, he and the Receptionist exchanged pleasantries. Holidays out of season? – Far quieter and more satisfying. Colours in the heather – so varied this time of year. Recent sightings of the Loch Ness monster – did it really exist? An impending on-off/off-on transfer in Scottish football.

"'*Will ye go, lassie, go?*'" intoned Crust.

They both laughed.

A louder burst of laughter came from a group of men who had exited the dining room and were now making their way across the foyer. Crust glanced at them through the mirror at the back of reception. Well dressed against the weather. Well oiled. Well up for anything. One of them – the Cavalier – put his hand on the Companion's shoulder. Then all five – still laughing – moved out into the night. Late-night drinking somewhere. Not Crust's business. But – as always – the professional reacted.

"Bit late for a jaunt?"

"Fishing party up from London," explained the Receptionist. "Few pubs in the surrounding villages have begun late-night ceilidh/folk sessions help meet the winter bills. Want me to get you a taxi?"

"Too tired, thanks," said Crust. "Early start. Get some walking in. Let's hope they have some luck. The fishing."

"I'm sure they will."

Crust nodded and raised his key in a goodnight gesture.

"But as to your walking…" the Receptionist said. "… Aye, well. As to that. Maybe you'll need check the weather. Coming on really bad, supposedly." He glanced at the clock. "Aye. Just ten. Might be something on local radio…"

The Receptionist began twiddling the dial of a polished wooden radio that stood on a shelf at the back of reception. The cross cracklings of channels; then, to a lush but jagged accompaniment, the same old voices bayed:

"Just another night
Trying to turn a bob!
Things go on like this.
Have – to – get – a – a – job!"

Crust stared at the Receptionist.

"Latest and greatest from Liverpool," said the Receptionist. "The Nurgs." Then, in a good imitation, "*You ain't heard nothing yet, folks!*"

"On the contrary," said Crust. "Now I've heard everything… That bar of yours still open?"